The Portable Richard Harding Davis

Richard Harding Davis

Edited by

Thomas Saunders

Publishers

Glendower Media

Whitmore Lake, Michigan

Toronto, Ontario

For information address

**Glendower Media P O Box 661 Whitmore Lake,
Michigan 48189**

TJS/RHD

GDM 0212131008321-P

ISBN 9780914303077

EBOOK ISBN 978-0-914303-09-1

www.glendowermedia.com

DEDICATION

This work is for all of the millions who came to America for the better life, the freedom, the opportunity, the peace in worship and in their lives that has defined America to the world. It is for those who view America as not the enemy, but rather one possible haven for themselves and their families. Hope, charity and tolerance may be a fiction, yet we all believe that it could happen if ideals are coupled with the quest for achievement.

No one believes these old fashioned ideas anymore.

But we want to…

CONTENTS

ACKNOWLEDGMENTS

Without teachers there is no learning to love books and the written word. There are no adventures, no heart stopping moments of suspense, no dawning light as you see the real explanation, no thrill of finding something new that you never suspected before.

This is for my teachers who are legion, the loved and respected of the past and the astounding teachers still to come. In all sizes and kinds, teachers are the most valuable natural resource we have.

The Man Who Was Richard Harding Davis

In theses days of constant celebrity, instant fame and honors for little or no reason, it is hard, if not impossible, to imagine a time when there were virtually no celebrities. Famous people in those times after the Civil War tended to be Presidents, world leaders, great generals and soldiers. Some actors or singers were well known but that tended to be a local phenomenon. There was no such thing as national celebrity and international celebrity was almost unknown.

Almost....but not quite. Some few people, by their daring deeds or incredible work were heard of across the land. But they were very few and they worked for years to become known.

That began to change in the Edwardian age with the rise of popular magazines, newspapers and clubs devoted to most any kind of civic endeavor you could name. Music clubs, writing clubs, lectures on all matter of subjects and a great gathering of literary clubs; in schools, libraries and churches. As these factors began to fall into place the time was ripe for a kind of hero from the people to come forth.

Richard Harding Davis was the son of a poplar woman writer, Rebecca Harding Davis, and the editor of the Philadelphia Public Leger, Lemuel Clarke Davis. After prep school he attended Lehigh University and Johns Hopkins University. He was asked to leave both institutions, due to lack of study and too much social activity, among which was his involvement in starting Lehigh's first football team.

He began his professional career at the Philadelphia Record thru his father's influence but ended up at the New York Sun, where his flamboyant style and choice of topics won him notoriety. It was the dawn of the "Yellow Journalism" and Davis's articles on Slums, Abortions, suicide and executions enlarged his fame that originated in his heart breaking and hard hitting coverage of the Johnstown Flood. He was a witness and reported on the first electric chair execution in 1890 of William Kemmler.

He then began to cover wars and travel over seas, watching everything and seeing the best and the damnedest of the Americans and the other Colonials in those situations.

He covered the Boer War and the Spanish American War. He was on a US Navy ship at the bombardment of Matanzas, Cuba. His reporting led the Navy to remove all reporters from Navy ships in time of war. Undaunted, he went ashore and found his friend Theodore Roosevelt of the Rough Riders fame in their maneuvers. He joined the group, and was made an honorary member by Roosevelt himself, and became the first embedded reporter in a war zone. His stories and descriptions of the valor and actions of the Rough Riders are largely responsible for the world wide fame attached to the troop.

His travels took him to Africa, South America, the Caribbean and Europe. But his newspaper writings were only the beginning. He reworked his war tales into a series of widely popular books aimed straight at the heart of the growing American popular conscience. He was telling tales of what the ideal American could do, and did do as Americans shouldered their responsibility in the world. Manifest Destiny was not an empty slogan to Davis. He wrote about the ideal that he believed Americans could become. He went into the foreign and the familiar to see how Americans would react when faced with adversity, either personal or public. He grew a vision of American Greatness, and used examples of Rich Men, doing the right thing. Of the every day man, uneducated and unpracticed, rising about the petty to save the day. He wrote of women and men sacrificing and achieving dreams, often at cost to themselves. His heroes were always on the side of right and you can bet that if a villain showed up in his story, he would be vanquished in the best American Knight manner.

He wrote about Boy Scouts, spies, Long Shore men, Millionaires and Wall Street men. Of reporters, and scoundrels; of knights and corporate men who all needed to be taught a lesson.

But his favorite subject was members of The 400.

In the late 1890's New York considered itself the center of the universe. It had the wealth, the business, and the culture to make such a claim. But it also had "The 400" ,members of society as named by Mrs. Vanderbilt and members of High Society, as to who was "Somebody" in Social Circles that were worth knowing. Richard Harding Davis saw this elitist type listing and yet he liked some of those young men. Many of them were living on their father's money and doing nothing. But some were becoming well versed in important knowledge like engineering, architecture, building and writing. These were the tales that Davis wrote. And stories of the underground nice guy Courtland Van Bibber. Van Bibber was rich and principled, unlike so many of "The 400" that the public read about in the "Yellow Press." Davis used Van Bibber to expand the tales of American Exceptionalism, as he saw it.

These stories are chosen from Richard Harding Davis' many writings as an introduction to this most fascinating of characters. Richard Harding David wrote in a style that is admittedly old fashioned, admittedly fantastic and melodramatic. This is the America he saw. This is the America that people cheered when he cam to town for one of his famous lectures. (So famous in fact, hat when he came to Harvard University in 1909, the school shut down for the day, because the professors wanted to see Davis as much as the students did.)

He was a man for a different time, a different sensibility and a different, not so cynical and hard- hearted time. The need for achievement before fame will most likely never return to favor when anyone can be famous for almost nothing. But as these stories will show, there is something to be said for achievement.

Thomas Saunders

Ann Arbor, Michigan

2013

Her First Appearance

It was at the end of the first act of the first night of "The Sultana," and every member of the Lester Comic Opera Company, from Lester himself down to the wardrobe woman's son, who would have had to work if his mother lost her place, was sick with anxiety.

There is perhaps only one other place as feverish as it is behind the scenes on the first night of a comic opera, and that is a newspaper office on the last night of a Presidential campaign, when the returns are being flashed on the canvas outside, and the mob is howling, and the editor-in-chief is expecting to go to the Court of St. James if the election comes his way, and the office-boy is betting his wages that it won't.

Such nights as these try men's souls; but Van Bibber passed the stage-door man with as calmly polite a nod as though the piece had been running a hundred nights, and the manager was thinking up souvenirs for the one hundred and fiftieth, and the prima donna had, as usual, begun to hint for a new set of costumes. The stage-door keeper hesitated and was lost, and Van Bibber stepped into the unsuppressed excitement of the place with a pleased sniff at the familiar smell of paint and burning gas, and the dusty odor that came from the scene-lofts above.

For a moment he hesitated in the cross-lights and confusion about him, failing to recognize in their new costumes his old acquaintances of the company; but he saw Kripps, the stage-manager, in the centre of the stage, perspiring and in his shirt-sleeves as always, wildly waving an arm to some one in the flies, and beckoning with the other to the gasman in the front entrance. The stage hands were striking the scene for the first act, and fighting with the set for the second, and dragging out a canvas floor of tessellated marble, and running a throne and a practical pair of steps over it, and aiming the high quaking walls of a palace and abuse at whoever came in their way.

"Now then, Van Bibber," shouted Kripps, with a wild glance of recognition, as the white-and-black figure came towards him, "you know you're the only man in New York who gets behind here to-night. But you can't stay. Lower it, lower it, can't you?" This to the man in the flies. "Any other night goes, but not this night. I can't have it. I—Where is the backing for the centre entrance? Didn't I tell you men——"

Van Bibber dodged two stage hands that were steering a scene at him, stepped over the carpet as it unrolled, and brushed through a group of anxious, whispering chorus people into the quiet of the star's dressing-room.

The star saw him in the long mirror before which he sat, while his dresser tugged at his boots, and threw up his hands desperately.

"Well," he cried, in mock resignation, "are we in it or are we not? Are they in their seats still or have they fled?"

"How are you, John?" said Van Bibber to the dresser. Then he dropped into a big arm-chair in the corner, and got up again with a protesting sigh to light his cigar between the wires around the gas-burner. "Oh, it's going very well. I wouldn't have come around if it wasn't. If the rest of it is as good as the first act, you needn't worry."

Van Bibber's unchallenged freedom behind the scenes had been a source of much comment and perplexity to the members of the Lester Comic Opera Company. He had made his first appearance there during one hot night of the long run of the previous summer, and had continued to be an almost nightly visitor for several weeks. At first it was supposed that he was backing the piece, that he was the "Angel," as those weak and wealthy individuals are called who allow themselves to be led into supplying the finances for theatrical experiments. But as he never peered through the curtain-hole to count the house, nor made frequent trips to the front of it to look at the box sheet, but was, on the contrary, just as undisturbed on a rainy night as on those when the "standing room only" sign blocked the front entrance, this supposition was discarded as untenable. Nor did he show the least interest in the prima donna, or in any of the other pretty women of the company; he did not know them, nor did he make any effort to know them, and it was not until they inquired concerning him outside of the theatre that they learned what a figure in the social life of the city he really was. He spent most of his time in Lester's dressing-room smoking, listening to the reminiscences of Lester's dresser when Lester was on the stage; and this seclusion and his clerical attire of evening dress led the second comedian to call him Lester's father confessor, and to suggest that he came to the theatre only to take the star to task for his sins. And in this the second comedian was unknowingly not so very far wrong. Lester, the comedian, and young Van Bibber had known each other at the university, when Lester's voice and gift of mimicry had made him the leader in the college theatricals; and later, when he had gone upon the stage, and had been cut off by his family even after he had become famous, or on account of it, Van Bibber had gone to visit him, and had found him as simple and sincere and boyish as he had been in the days of his Hasty-Pudding successes. And Lester, for his part, had found Van Bibber as likable as did every one else, and welcomed his quiet voice and youthful knowledge of the world as a grateful relief to the boisterous camaraderie of his professional acquaintances. And he allowed Van Bibber to scold him, and to remind him of what he owed to himself, and to touch, even whether it hurt or not, upon his better side. And in time he admitted to finding his friend's occasional comments on stage matters of value as coming from the point of view of those who look on at the game; and even Kripps, the veteran, regarded him with respect after he had told him that he could turn a set of purple costumes black by throwing a red light on them. To the company, after he came to know them, he was gravely polite, and, to those who knew him if they had overheard, amusingly commonplace in his conversation. He understood them better than they did themselves, and made no mistakes. The women smiled on him, but the men were suspicious and shy of him until they saw that he was quite as shy of the women; and then they made him a confidant, and told him all their woes and troubles, and exhibited all their little jealousies and ambitions, in the innocent hope that he would repeat what they said to Lester. They were simple, unconventional, light-hearted folk, and Van Bibber found them vastly more entertaining and preferable to the silence of the deserted club, where the matting was down, and from whence the regular habitués had departed to the other side or to Newport. He liked the swing of the light, bright music as it came to him through the open door of the dressing-room, and the glimpse he got of the chorus people crowding and pushing for a quick charge up the iron stairway, and the feverish smell of oxygen in the air, and the picturesque disorder of Lester's wardrobe, and the wigs and swords, and the mysterious articles of make-up, all mixed together on a tray with half-finished cigars and autograph books and newspaper notices.

And he often wished he was clever enough to be an artist with the talent to paint the unconsciously graceful groups in the sharply divided light and shadow of the wings as he saw them. The brilliantly colored, fantastically clothed girls leaning against the bare brick wall of the theatre, or whispering together in circles, with their arms close about one another, or reading apart and solitary, or working at some piece of fancy-work as soberly as though they were in a rocking-chair in their own flat, and not leaning against a scene brace, with the glare of the stage and the applause of the house just behind them. He liked to watch them coquetting with the big fireman detailed from the precinct engine-house, and clinging desperately to the curtain wire, or with one of the chorus men on the stairs, or teasing the phlegmatic scene-shifters as they tried to catch a minute's sleep on a pile of canvas. He even forgave the prima donnas' smiling at him from the stage, as he stood watching her from the wings, and smiled back at her with polite cynicism, as though he did not know and she did not know that her smiles were not for him, but to disturb some more interested one in the front row. And so, in time, the company became so well accustomed to him that he moved in and about as unnoticed as the stage-manager himself, who prowled around hissing "hush" on principle, even though he was the only person who could fairly be said to be making a noise.

The second act was on, and Lester came off the stage and ran to the dressing-room and beckoned violently. "Come here," he said; "you ought to see this; the children are doing their turn. You want to hear them. They're great!"

Van Bibber put his cigar into a tumbler and stepped out into the wings. They were crowded on both sides of the stage with the members of the company; the girls were tiptoeing, with their hands on the shoulders of the men, and making futile little leaps into the air to get a better view, and others were resting on one knee that those behind might see over their shoulders. There were over a dozen children before the footlights, with the prima donna in the centre. She was singing the verses of a song, and they were following her movements, and joining in the chorus with high piping voices. They seemed entirely too much at home and too self-conscious: to please Van Bibber; but there was one exception. The one exception was the smallest of them, a very, very little girl, with long auburn hair and black eyes; such a very little girl that every one in the house looked at her first, and then looked at no one else. She was apparently as unconcerned to all about her, excepting the pretty prima donna, as though she were by a piano at home practicing a singing lesson. She seemed to think it was some new sort of a game. When the prima donna raised her arms, the child raised hers; when the prima donna courtesies, she stumbled into one, and straightened herself just in time to get the curls out of her eyes, and to see that the prima donna was laughing at her, and to smile cheerfully back as if to say, "WE are doing our best anyway, aren't we?" She had big, gentle eyes and two wonderful dimples, and in the excitement of the dancing and the singing her eyes laughed and flashed, and the dimples deepened and disappeared and reappeared again. She was as happy and innocent looking as though it was nine in the morning and she was playing school at a kindergarten. From all over the house the women were murmuring their delight, and the men were laughing and pulling their mustaches and nudging each other to "look at the littlest one."

The girls in the wings were rapturous in their enthusiasm, and were calling her absurdly extravagant titles of endearment, and making so much noise that Kripps stopped grinning at her from the entrance, and looked back over his shoulder as he looked when he threatened fines and calls for early rehearsal. And when she had finished finally, and the prima donna and the children ran off together, there was a roar from the house that went to Lester's head like wine, and seemed to leap clear across the footlights and drag the children back again.

"That settles it!" cried Lester, in a suppressed roar of triumph. "I knew that child would catch them."

There were four encores, and then the children and Elise Broughten, the pretty prima donna, came off jubilant and happy, with the Littlest Girl's arms full of flowers, which the management had with kindly forethought prepared for the prima donna, but which that delightful young person and the delighted leader of the orchestra had passed over to the little girl.

"Well," gasped Miss Broughten, as she came up to Van Bibber laughing, and with one hand on her side and breathing very quickly, "will you kindly tell me who is the leading woman now? Am I the prima donna, or am I not? I wasn't in it, was I?"

"You were not," said Van Bibber.

He turned from the pretty prima donna and hunted up the wardrobe woman, and told her he wanted to meet the Littlest Girl. And the wardrobe woman, who was fluttering wildly about and as delighted as though they were all her own children, told him to come into the property-room, where the children were, and which had been changed into a dressing-room that they might be by themselves. The six little girls were in six different states of dishabille, but they were too little to mind that, and Van Bibber was too polite to observe it.

"This is the little girl, sir," said the wardrobe woman, excitedly, proud at being the means of bringing together two such prominent people. "Her name is Madeline. Speak to the gentleman, Madeline; he wants to tell you what a great big hit youse made."

The little girl was seated on one of the cushions of a double throne so high from the ground that the young woman who was pulling off the child's silk stockings and putting woolen ones on in their place did so without stooping. The young woman looked at Van Bibber and nodded somewhat doubtfully and ungraciously, and Van Bibber turned to the little girl in preference. The young woman's face was one of a type that was too familiar to be pleasant.

"Do you rule alone?"

He took the Littlest Girl's small hand in his and shook it solemnly, and said, "I am very glad to know you. Can I sit up here beside you, or do you rule alone?"

"Yes, ma'am—yes, sir," answered the little girl.

Van Bibber put his hands on the arms of the throne and vaulted up beside the girl, and pulled out the flower in his button-hole and gave it to her.

"Now," prompted the wardrobe woman, "what do you say to the gentleman?"

"Thank you, sir," stammered the little girl.

"She is not much used to gentlemen's society," explained the woman who was pulling on the stockings.

"I see," said Van Bibber. He did not know exactly what to say next. And yet he wanted to talk to the child very much, so much more than he generally wanted to talk to most young women, who showed no hesitation in talking to him. With them he had no difficulty whatsoever. There was a doll lying on the top of a chest near them, and he picked this up and surveyed it critically. "Is this your doll?" he asked.

"No," said Madeline, pointing to one of the children, who was much taller than herself; "it's 'at 'ittle durl's. My doll he's dead."

"Dear me!" said Van Bibber. He made a mental note to get a live one in the morning, and then he said: "That's very sad. But dead dolls do come to life."

The little girl looked up at him, and surveyed him intently and critically, and then smiled, with the dimples showing, as much as to say that she understood him and approved of him entirely. Van Bibber answered this sign language by taking Madeline's hand in his and asking her how she liked being a great actress, and how soon she would begin to storm because THAT photographer hadn't sent the proofs. The young woman understood this, and deigned to smile at it, but Madeline yawned a very polite and sleepy yawn, and closed her eyes. Van Bibber moved up closer, and she leaned over until her bare shoulder touched his arm, and while the woman buttoned on her absurdly small shoes, she let her curly head fall on his elbow and rest there. Any number of people had shown confidence in Van Bibber— not in that form exactly, but in the same spirit—and though he was used to being trusted, he felt a sharp thrill of pleasure at the touch of the child's head on his arm, and in the warm clasp of her fingers around his. And he was conscious of a keen sense of pity and sorrow for her rising in him, which he crushed by thinking that it was entirely wasted, and that the child was probably perfectly and ignorantly happy.

"Look at that, now," said the wardrobe woman, catching sight of the child's closed eyelids; "just look at the rest of the little dears, all that excited they can't stand still to get their hats on, and she just as unconcerned as you please, and after making the hit of the piece, too."

"She's not used to it, you see," said the young woman, knowingly; "she don't know what it means. It's just that much play to her."

This last was said with a questioning glance at Van Bibber, in whom she still feared to find the disguised agent of a Children's Aid Society. Van Bibber only nodded in reply, and did not answer her, because he found he could not very well, for he was looking a long way ahead at what the future was to bring to the confiding little being at his side, and thinking of the evil knowledge and temptations that would mar the beauty of her quaintly sweet face, and its strange mark of gentleness and refinement. Outside he could hear his friend Lester shouting the refrain of his new topical song, and the laughter and the hand-clapping came in through the wings and open door, broken but tumultuous.

"Does she come of professional people?" Van Bibber asked, dropping into the vernacular. He spoke softly, not so much that he might not disturb the child, but that she might not understand what he said.

"Yes," the woman answered, shortly, and bent her head to smooth out the child's stage dress across her knees.

Van Bibber touched the little girl's head with his hand and found that she was asleep, and so let his hand rest there, with the curls between his fingers. "Are—are you her mother?" he asked, with a slight inclination of his head. He felt quite confident she was not; at least, he hoped not.

The woman shook her head. "No," she said.

"Who is her mother?"

The woman looked at the sleeping child and then up at him almost defiantly. "Ida Clare was her mother," she said.

Van Bibber's protecting hand left the child as suddenly as though something had burned it, and he drew back so quickly that her head slipped from his arm, and she awoke and raised her eyes and looked up at him questioningly. He looked back at her with a glance of the strangest concern and of the deepest pity. Then he stooped and drew her towards him very tenderly, put her head back in the corner of his arm, and watched her in silence while she smiled drowsily and went to sleep again.

"And who takes care of her now?" he asked.

The woman straightened herself and seemed relieved. She saw that the stranger had recognized the child's pedigree and knew her story, and that he was not going to comment on it. "I do," she said. "After the divorce Ida came to me," she said, speaking more freely. "I used to be in her company when she was doing 'Aladdin,' and then when I left the stage and started to keep an actors' boarding-house, she came to me. She lived on with us a year, until she died, and she made me the guardian of the child. I train children for the stage, you know, me and my sister, Ada Dyer; you've heard of her, I guess. The courts pay us for her keep, but it isn't much, and I'm expecting to get what I spent on her from what she makes on the stage. Two of them other children are my pupils; but they can't touch Madie. She is a better dancer an' singer than any of them. If it hadn't been for the Society keeping her back, she would have been on the stage two years ago. She's great, she is. She'll be just as good as her mother was." Van Bibber gave a little start, and winced visibly, but turned it off into a cough. "And her father," he said hesitatingly, "does he—"

"Her father," said the woman, tossing back her head, "he looks after himself, he does. We don't ask no favors of HIM. She'll get along without him or his folks, thank you. Call him a gentleman? Nice gentleman he is!" Then she stopped abruptly. "I guess, though, you know him," she added. "Perhaps he's a friend of yourn?"

"I just know him," said Van Bibber, wearily.

He sat with the child asleep beside him while the woman turned to the others and dressed them for the third act. She explained that Madie would not appear in the last act, only the two larger girls, so she let her sleep, with the cape of Van Bibber's cloak around her.

Van Bibber sat there for several long minutes thinking, and then looked up quickly, and dropped his eyes again as quickly, and said, with an effort to speak quietly and unconcernedly: "If the little girl is not on in this act, would you mind if I took her home? I have a cab at the stage door, and she's so sleepy it seems a pity to keep her up. The sister you spoke of or some one could put her to bed."

"Yes," the woman said, doubtfully, "Ada's home. Yes, you can take her around, if you want to."

She gave him the address, and he sprang down to the floor, and gathered the child up in his arms and stepped out on the stage. The prima donna had the centre of it to herself at that moment, and all the rest of the company were waiting to go on; but when they saw the little girl in Van Bibber's arms they made a rush at her, and the girls leaned over and kissed her with a great show of rapture and with many gasps of delight.

"Don't," said Van Bibber, he could not tell just why. "Don't."

"Why not?" asked one of the girls, looking up at him sharply.

"She was asleep; you've wakened her," he said, gently.

But he knew that was not the reason. He stepped into the cab at the stage entrance, and put the child carefully down in one corner. Then he looked back over his shoulder to see that there was no one near enough to hear him, and said to the driver, "To the Berkeley Flats, on Fifth Avenue." He picked the child up gently in his arms as the carriage started, and sat looking out thoughtfully and anxiously as they flashed past the lighted shop-windows on Broadway. He was far from certain of this errand, and nervous with doubt, but he reassured himself that he was acting on impulse, and that his impulses were so often good. The hall-boy at the Berkeley said, yes, Mr. Caruthers was in, and Van Bibber gave a quick sigh of relief. He took this as an omen that his impulse was a good one. The young English servant who opened the hall door to Mr. Caruthers's apartment suppressed his surprise with an effort, and watched Van Bibber with alarm as he laid the child on the divan in the hall, and pulled a covert coat from the rack to throw over her.

"Just say Mr. Van Bibber would like to see him," he said, "and you need not speak of the little girl having come with me."

She was still sleeping, and Van Bibber turned down the light in the hall, and stood looking down at her gravely while the servant went to speak to his master.

"Will you come this way, please, sir?" he said.

"You had better stay out here," said Van Bibber, "and come and tell me if she wakes."

Mr. Caruthers was standing by the mantel over the empty fireplace, wrapped in a long, loose dressing-gown which he was tying around him as Van Bibber entered. He was partly undressed, and had been just on the point of getting into bed. Mr. Caruthers was a tall, handsome man, with dark reddish hair, turning below the temples into gray; his mustache was quite white, and his eyes and face showed the signs of either dissipation or of great trouble, or of both. But even in the formless dressing-gown he had the look and the confident bearing of a gentleman, or, at least, of the man of the world. The room was very rich-looking, and was filled with the medley of a man's choice of good paintings and fine china and papered with irregular rows of original drawings and signed etchings. The windows were open, and the lights were turned very low, so that Van Bibber could see the many gas lamps and the dark roofs of Broadway and the Avenue where they crossed a few blocks off, and the bunches of light on the Madison Square Garden, and to the lights on the boats of the East River. From below in the streets came the rattle of hurrying omnibuses and the rush of the hansom cabs. If Mr. Caruthers was surprised at this late visit, he hid it, and came forward to receive his caller as if his presence were expected.

"Excuse my costume, will you?" he said. "I turned in rather early to-night, it was so hot." He pointed to a decanter and some soda bottles on the table and a bowl of ice, and asked, "Will you have some of this?" And while he opened one of the bottles, he watched Van Bibber's face as though he were curious to have him explain the object of his visit. "No, I think not, thank you," said the younger man. He touched his forehead with his handkerchief nervously. "Yes, it is hot," he said.

Mr. Caruthers filled a glass with ice and brandy and soda, and walked back to his place by the mantel, on which he rested his arm, while he clinked the ice in the glass and looked down into it.

"I was at the first night of 'The Sultana' this evening," said Van Bibber, slowly and uncertainly.

"Oh, yes," assented the elder man, politely, and tasting his drink. "Lester's new piece. Was it any good?"

"I don't know," said Van Bibber. "Yes, I think it was. I didn't see it from the front. There were a lot of children in it—little ones;

they danced and sang, and made a great hit. One of them had never been on the stage before. It was her first appearance."

He was turning one of the glasses around between his fingers as he spoke. He stopped, and poured out some of the soda, and drank it down in a gulp, and then continued turning the empty glass between the tips of his fingers.

"It seems to me," he said, "that it is a great pity." He looked up interrogatively at the other, but Mr. Caruthers met his glance without any returning show of interest. "I say," repeated Van Bibber—"I say it seems a pity that a child like that should be allowed to go on in that business. A grown woman can go into it with her eyes open, or a girl who has had decent training can too. But it's different with a child. She has no choice in the matter; they don't ask her permission; and she isn't old enough to know what it means; and she gets used to it and fond of it before she grows to know what the danger is. And then it's too late. It seemed to me that if there was any one who had a right to stop it, it would be a very good thing to let that person know about her—about this child, I mean; the one who made the hit—before it was too late. It seems to me a responsibility I wouldn't care to take myself. I wouldn't care to think that I had the chance to stop it, and had let the chance go by. You know what the life is, and what the temptation a woman—" Van Bibber stopped with a gasp of concern, and added, hurriedly, "I mean we all know—every man knows."

Mr. Caruthers was looking at him with his lips pressed closely together, and his eyebrows drawn into the shape of the letter V. He leaned forward, and looked at Van Bibber intently.

"What is all this about?" he asked. "Did you come here, Mr. Van Bibber, simply to tell me this? What have you to do with it? What have I to do with it? Why did you come?"

"Because of the child."

"What child?"

"Your child," said Van Bibber.

Young Van Bibber was quite prepared for an outbreak of some sort, and mentally braced himself to receive it. He rapidly assured himself that this man had every reason to be angry, and that he, if he meant to accomplish anything, had every reason to be considerate and patient. So he faced Mr. Caruthers with shoulders squared, as though it were a physical shock he had to stand against, and in consequence he was quite unprepared for what followed. For Mr. Caruthers raised his face without a trace of feeling in it, and, with his eyes still fixed on the glass in his hand, set it carefully down on the mantel beside him, and girded himself about with the rope of his robe. When he spoke, it was in a tone of quiet politeness.

"Mr. Van Bibber," he began, "you are a very brave young man. You have dared to say to me what those who are my best friends— what even my own family—would not care to say. They are afraid it might hurt me, I suppose. They have some absurd regard for my feelings; they hesitate to touch upon a subject which in no way concerns them, and which they know must be very painful to me. But you have the courage of your convictions; you have no compunctions about tearing open old wounds; and you come here, unasked and uninvited, to let me know what you think of my conduct, to let me understand that it does not agree with your own ideas of what I ought to do, and to tell me how I, who am old enough to be your father, should behave. You have rushed in where angels fear to tread, Mr. Van Bibber, to show me the error of my ways. I suppose I ought to thank you for it; but I have always said that it is not the wicked people who are to be feared in this world, or who do the most harm. We know them; we can prepare for them, and checkmate them. It is the well-meaning fool who makes all the trouble. For no one knows him until he discloses himself, and the mischief is done before he can be stopped. I think, if you will allow me to say so, that you have demonstrated my theory pretty thoroughly, and have done about as much needless harm for one evening as you can possibly wish. And so, if you will excuse me," he continued, sternly, and moving from his place, "I will ask to say good-night, and will request of you that you grow older and wiser and much more considerate before you come to see me again."

Van Bibber had flushed at Mr. Caruthers's first words, and had then grown somewhat pale, and straightened himself visibly. He did not move when the elder man had finished, but cleared his throat, and then spoke with some little difficulty. "It is very easy to call a man a fool," he said, slowly, "but it is much harder to be called a fool and not to throw the other man out of the window. But that, you see, would not do any good, and I have something to say to you first. I am quite clear in my own mind as to my position, and I am not going to allow anything you have said or can say to annoy me much until I am through. There will be time enough to resent it then. I am quite well aware that I did an unconventional thing in coming here—a bold thing or a foolish thing, as you choose—but the situation is pretty bad, and I did as I would have wished to be done by if I had had a child going to the devil and didn't know it. I should have been glad to learn of it even from a stranger. However," he said, smiling grimly, and pulling his cape about him, "there are other kindly disposed people in the world besides fathers. There is an aunt, perhaps, or an uncle or two; and sometimes, even to-day, there is the chance Samaritan."

Van Bibber picked up his high hat from the table, looked into it critically, and settled it on his head. "Good-night," he said, and walked slowly towards the door. He had his hand on the knob, when Mr. Caruthers raised his head.

"Wait just one minute, please, Mr. Van Bibber?" asked Mr. Caruthers.

Van Bibber stopped with a prompt obedience which would have led one to conclude that he might have put on his hat only to precipitate matters.

"Before you go," said Mr. Caruthers, grudgingly, "I want to say—I want you to understand my position."

"Oh, that's all right," said Van Bibber, lightly, opening the door.

"No, it is not all right. One moment, please. I do not intend that you shall go away from here with the idea that you have tried to do me a service, and that I have been unable to appreciate it, and that you are a much-abused and much-misunderstood young man. Since you have done me the honor to make my affairs your business, I would prefer that you should understand them fully. I do not care to have you discuss my conduct at clubs and afternoon teas with young women until you—"

Van Bibber drew in his breath sharply, with a peculiar whistling sound, and opened and shut his hands. "Oh, I wouldn't say that if I were you," he said, simply.

"I beg your pardon," the older man said, quickly. "That was a mistake. I was wrong. I beg your pardon. But you have tried me very sorely. You have intruded upon a private trouble that you ought to know must be very painful to me. But I believe you meant well. I know you to be a gentleman, and I am willing to think you acted on impulse, and that you will see to-morrow what a mistake you have made. It is not a thing I talk about; I do not speak of it to my friends, and they are far too considerate to speak of it to me. But you have put me on the defensive. You have made me out more or less of a brute, and I don't intend to be so far misunderstood. There are two sides to every story, and there is something to be said about this, even for me."

He walked back to his place beside the mantel, and put his shoulders against it, and faced Van Bibber, with his fingers twisted in the cord around his waist.

"When I married," said Mr. Caruthers, "I did so against the wishes of my people and the advice of all my friends. You know all about that. God help us! Who doesn't?" he added, bitterly. "It was very rich, rare reading for you and for every one else who saw the daily papers, and we gave them all they wanted of it. I took her out of that life and married her because I believed she was as good a woman as any of those who had never had to work for their living, and I was bound that my friends and your friends should recognize her and respect her as my wife had a right to be respected; and I took her abroad that I might give all you sensitive, fine people a chance to get used to the idea of being polite to a woman who had once been a burlesque actress. It began over there in Paris. What I went through then no one knows; but when I came back—and I would never have come back if she had not made me—it was my friends I had to consider, and not her. It was in the blood; it was in the life she had led, and in the life men like you and me had taught her to live. And it had to come out."

The muscles of Mr. Caruthers's face were moving, and beyond his control; but Van Bibber did not see this, for he was looking intently out of the window, over the roofs of the city.

"She had every chance when she married me that a woman ever had," continued the older man. "It only depended on herself. I didn't try to make a housewife of her or a drudge. She had all the healthy excitement and all the money she wanted, and she had a home here ready for her whenever she was tired of travelling about and wished to settle down. And I was—and a husband that loved her as—she had everything—everything that a man's whole thought and love and money could bring to her. And you know what she did."

He looked at Van Bibber, but Van Bibber's eyes were still turned towards the open window and the night.

"And after the divorce—and she was free to go where she pleased, and to live as she pleased and with whom she pleased, without bringing disgrace on a husband who honestly loved her—I swore to my God that I would never see her nor her child again. And I never saw her again, not even when she died. I loved the mother, and she deceived me and disgraced me and broke my heart, and I only wish she had killed me; and I was beginning to love her child, and I vowed she should not live to trick me too. I had suffered as no man I know had suffered; in a way a boy like you cannot understand, and that no one can understand who has not gone to hell and been forced to live after it. And was I to go through that again? Was I to love and care for and worship this child, and have her grow up with all her mother's vanity and animal nature, and have her turn on me some day and show me that what is bred in the bone must tell, and that I was a fool again—a pitiful fond fool? I could not trust her. I can never trust any woman or child again, and least of all that woman's child. She is as dead to me as though she were buried with her mother, and it is nothing to me what she is or what her life is. I know in time what it will be. She has begun earlier than I had supposed, that is all; but she is nothing to me." The man stopped and turned his back to Van Bibber, and hid his head in his hands, with his elbows on the mantelpiece. "I care too much," he said. "I cannot let it mean anything to me; when I do care, it means so much more to me than to other men. They may pretend to laugh and to forget and to outgrow it, but it is not so with me. It means too much." He took a quick stride towards one of the arm-chairs, and threw himself into it. "Why, man," he cried, "I loved that child's mother to the day of her death. I loved that woman then, and, God help me! I love that woman still."

He covered his face with his hands, and sat leaning forward and breathing heavily as he rocked himself to and fro. Van Bibber still stood looking gravely out at the lights that picketed the black surface of the city. He was to all appearances as unmoved by the outburst of feeling into which the older man had been surprised as though it had been something in a play. There was an unbroken silence for a moment, and then it was Van Bibber who was the first to speak.

"I came here, as you say, on impulse," he said; "but I am glad I came, for I have your decisive answer now about the little girl. I have been thinking," he continued, slowly, "since you have been speaking, and before, when I first saw her dancing in front of the footlights, when I did not know who she was, that I could give up a horse or two, if necessary, and support this child instead. Children are worth more than horses, and a man who saves a soul, as it says"—he flushed slightly, and looked up with a hesitating, deprecatory smile— "somewhere, wipes out a multitude of sins. And it may be I'd like to try and get rid of some of mine. I know just where to send her; I know the very place. It's down in Evergreen Bay, on Long Island. They are tenants of mine there, and very nice farm sort of people, who will be very good to her. They wouldn't know anything about her, and she'd forget what little she knows of this present life very soon, and grow up with the other children to be one of them; and then, when she gets older and becomes a young lady, she could go to some school—but that's a bit too far ahead to plan for the present;

but that's what I am going to do, though," said the young man, confidently, and as though speaking to himself. "That theatrical boarding-house person could be bought off easily enough," he went on, quickly, "and Lester won't mind letting her go if I ask it,—and—and that's what I'll do. As you say, it's a good deal of an experiment, but I think I'll run the risk."

He walked quickly to the door and disappeared in the hall, and then came back, kicking the door open as he returned, and holding the child in his arms.

"This is she," he said, quietly. He did not look at or notice the father, but stood, with the child asleep in the bend of his left arm, gazing down at her. "This is she," he repeated; "this is your child."

There was something cold and satisfied in Van Bibber's tone and manner, as though he were congratulating himself upon the engaging of a new groom; something that placed the father entirely outside of it. He might have been a disinterested looker-on.

"She will need to be fed a bit," Van Bibber ran on, cheerfully. "They did not treat her very well, I fancy. She is thin and peaked and tired-looking." He drew up the loose sleeve of her jacket, and showed the bare forearm to the light. He put his thumb and little finger about it, and closed them on it gently. "It is very thin," he said. "And under her eyes, if it were not for the paint," he went on, mercilessly, "you could see how deep the lines are. This red spot on her cheek," he said, gravely, "is where Mary Vane kissed her to-night, and this is where Alma Stantley kissed her, and that Lee girl. You have heard of them, perhaps. They will never kiss her again. She is going to grow up a sweet, fine, beautiful woman—are you not?" he said, gently drawing the child higher up on his shoulder, until her face touched his, and still keeping his eyes from the face of the older man. "She does not look like her mother," he said; "she has her father's auburn hair and straight nose and finer-cut lips and chin. She looks very much like her father. It seems a pity," he added, abruptly. "She will grow up," he went on, "without knowing him, or who he is—or was, if he should die. She will never speak with him, or see him, or take his hand. She may pass him some day on the street and will not know him, and he will not know her, but she will grow to be very fond and to be very grateful to the simple, kindhearted old people who will have cared for her when she was a little girl."

The child in his arms stirred, shivered slightly, and awoke. The two men watched her breathlessly, with silent intentness. She raised her head and stared around the unfamiliar room doubtfully, then turned to where her father stood, looking at him a moment, and passed him by; and then, looking up into Van Bibber's face, recognized him, and gave a gentle, sleepy smile, and, with a sigh of content and confidence, drew her arm up closer around his neck, and let her head fall back upon his breast.

The father sprang to his feet with a quick, jealous gasp of pain. "Give her to me!" he said, fiercely, under his breath, snatching her out of Van Bibber's arms. "She is mine; give her to me!"

Van Bibber closed the door gently behind him, and went jumping down the winding stairs of the Berkeley three steps at a time.

And an hour later, when the English servant came to his master's door, he found him still awake and sitting in the dark by the open window, holding something in his arms and looking out over the sleeping city.

"James," he said, "you can make up a place for me here on the lounge. Miss Caruthers, my daughter, will sleep in my room to-night."

GALLEGHER
A Newspaper Story

We had had so many office-boys before Gallegher came among us that they had begun to lose the characteristics of individuals, and became merged in a composite photograph of small boys, to whom we applied the generic title of "Here, you"; or "You, boy."

We had had sleepy boys, and lazy boys, and bright, "smart" boys, who became so familiar on so short an acquaintance that we were forced to part with them to save our own self-respect.

They generally graduated into district-messenger boys, and occasionally returned to us in blue coats with nickel-plated buttons, and patronized us.

But Gallegher was something different from anything we had experienced before. Gallegher was short and broad in build, with a solid, muscular broadness, and not a fat and dumpy shortness. He wore perpetually on his face a happy and knowing smile, as if you and the world in general did not impress him as seriously as you thought you were, and his eyes, which were very black and very bright, snapped intelligently at you like those of a little black-and-tan terrier.

All Gallegher knew had been learnt on the streets; not a very good school in itself, but one that turns out very knowing scholars. And Gallegher had attended both morning and evening sessions. He could not tell you who the Pilgrim Fathers were, nor could he name the thirteen original States, but he knew all the officers of the twenty-second police district by name, and he could distinguish the clang of a fire-engine's gong from that of a patrol-wagon or an ambulance fully two blocks distant. It was Gallegher who rang the alarm when the Woolwich Mills caught fire, while the officer on the beat was asleep, and it was Gallegher who led the "Black Diamonds" against the "Wharf Rats," when they used to stone each other to their hearts' content on the coal-wharves of Richmond.

I am afraid, now that I see these facts written down, that Gallegher was not a reputable character; but he was so very young and so very old for his years that we all liked him very much nevertheless. He lived in the extreme northern part of Philadelphia, where the cotton-and woolen-mills run down to the river, and how he ever got home after leaving the *Press* building at two in the morning, was one of the mysteries of the office. Sometimes he caught a night car, and sometimes he walked all the way, arriving at the little house, where his mother and himself lived alone, at four in the morning. Occasionally he was given a ride on an early milk-cart, or on one of the newspaper delivery wagons, with its high piles of papers still damp and sticky from the press. He knew several drivers of "night hawks"—those cabs that prowl the streets at night looking for belated passengers—and when it was a very cold morning he would not go home at all, but would crawl into one of these cabs and sleep, curled up on the cushions, until daylight.

Besides being quick and cheerful, Gallegher possessed a power of amusing the *Press's* young men to a degree seldom attained by the ordinary mortal. His clog-dancing on the city editor's desk, when that gentleman was up-stairs fighting for two more columns of space, was always a source of innocent joy to us, and his imitations of the comedians of the variety halls delighted even the dramatic critic, from whom the comedians themselves failed to force a smile.

But Gallegher's chief characteristic was his love for that element of news generically classed as "crime." Not that he ever did anything criminal himself. On the contrary, his was rather the work of the criminal specialist, and his morbid interest in the doings of all queer characters, his knowledge of their methods, their present whereabouts, and their past deeds of transgression often rendered him a valuable ally to our police reporter, whose daily feuilletons were the only portion of the paper Gallegher deigned to read.

In Gallegher the detective element was abnormally developed. He had shown this on several occasions, and to excellent purpose.

Once the paper had sent him into a Home for Destitute Orphans which was believed to be grievously mismanaged, and Gallegher, while playing the part of a destitute orphan, kept his eyes open to what was going on around him so faithfully that the story he told of the treatment meted out to the real orphans was sufficient to rescue the unhappy little wretches from the individual who had them in charge, and to have the individual himself sent to jail.

Gallegher's knowledge of the aliases, terms of imprisonment, and various misdoings of the leading criminals in Philadelphia was almost as thorough as that of the chief of police himself, and he could tell to an hour when "Dutchy Mack" was to be let out of prison, and could identify at a glance "Dick Oxford, confidence man," as "Gentleman Dan, petty thief."

There were, at this time, only two pieces of news in any of the papers. The least important of the two was the big fight between the Champion of the United States and the Would-be Champion, arranged to take place near Philadelphia; the second was the Burbank murder, which was filling space in newspapers all over the world, from New York to Bombay.

Richard F. Burrbank was one of the most prominent of New York's railroad lawyers; he was also, as a matter of course, an owner of much railroad stock, and a very wealthy man. He had been spoken of as a political possibility for many high offices, and, as the counsel for a great railroad, was known even further than the great railroad itself had stretched its system.

At six o'clock one morning he was found by his butler lying at the foot of the hall stairs with two pistol wounds above his heart. He was quite dead. His safe, to which only he and his secretary had the keys, was found open, and $200,000 in bonds, stocks, and money, which had been placed there only the night before, was found missing. The secretary was missing also. His name was Stephen S. Hade, and his name and his description had been telegraphed and cabled to all parts of the world. There was enough circumstantial evidence to show, beyond any question or possibility of mistake, that he was the murderer.

It made an enormous amount of talk, and unhappy individuals were being arrested all over the country, and sent on to New York for identification. Three had been arrested at Liverpool and one man just as he landed at Sydney, Australia. But so far the murderer had escaped.

We were all talking about it one night, as everybody else was all over the country, in the local room, and the city editor said it was worth a fortune to any one who chanced to run across Hade and succeeded in handing him over to the police. Some of us thought Hade had taken passage from some one of the smaller seaports, and others were of the opinion that he had buried himself in some cheap lodging-house in New York, or in one of the smaller towns in New Jersey.

"I shouldn't be surprised to meet him out walking, right here in Philadelphia," said one of the staff. "He'll be disguised, of course, but you could always tell him by the absence of the trigger finger on his right hand. It's missing, you know; shot off when he was a boy."

"You want to look for a man dressed like a tough," said the city editor; "for as this fellow is to all appearances a gentleman, he will try to look as little like a gentleman as possible."

"No, he won't," said Gallegher, with that calm impertinence that made him dear to us. "He'll dress just like a gentleman. Toughs don't wear gloves, and you see he's got to wear 'em. The first thing he thought of after doing for Burrbank was of that gone finger, and how he was to hide it. He stuffed the finger of that glove with cotton so's to make it look like a whole finger, and the first time he takes off that glove they've got him—see, and he knows it. So what youse want to do is to look for a man with gloves on. I've been a-doing it for two weeks now, and I can tell you its hard work, for everybody wears gloves this kind of weather. But if you look long enough you'll find him. And when you think it's him, go up to him and hold out your hand in a friendly way, like a bunco-steerer, and shake his hand; and if you feel that his forefinger ain't real flesh, but just wadded cotton, then grip to it with your right and grab his throat with your left, and holler for help."

There was an appreciative pause.

"I see, gentlemen," said the city editor, dryly, "that Gallegher's reasoning has impressed you; and I also see that before the week is out all of my young men will be under bonds for assaulting innocent pedestrians whose only offence is that they wear gloves in midwinter."

It was about a week after this that Detective Hefflefinger, of Inspector Byrnes's staff, came over to Philadelphia after a burglar, of whose whereabouts he had been misinformed by telegraph. He brought the warrant, requisition, and other necessary papers with him, but the burglar had flown. One of our reporters had worked on a New York paper, and knew Hefflefinger, and the detective came to the office to see if he could help him in his so far unsuccessful search.

He gave Gallegher his card, and after Gallegher had read it, and had discovered who the visitor was, he became so demoralized that he was absolutely useless.

"One of Byrnes's men" was a much more awe-inspiring individual to Gallegher than a member of the Cabinet. He accordingly seized his hat and overcoat, and leaving his duties to be looked after by others, hastened out after the object of his admiration, who found his suggestions and knowledge of the city so valuable, and his company so entertaining, that they became very intimate, and spent the rest of the day together.

In the meanwhile the managing editor had instructed his subordinates to inform Gallegher, when he condescended to return, that his services were no longer needed. Gallegher had played truant once too often. Unconscious of this, he remained with his new friend until late the same evening, and started the next afternoon toward the *Press* office.

As I have said, Gallegher lived in the most distant part of the city, not many minutes' walk from the Kensington railroad station, where trains ran into the suburbs and on to New York.

It was in front of this station that a smoothly shaven, well-dressed man brushed past Gallegher and hurried up the steps to the ticket office.

He held a walking-stick in his right hand, and Gallegher, who now patiently scrutinized the hands of every one who wore gloves, saw that while three fingers of the man's hand were closed around the cane, the fourth stood out in almost a straight line with his palm.

Gallegher stopped with a gasp and with a trembling all over his little body and his brain asked with a throb if it could be possible. But possibilities and probabilities were to be discovered later. Now was the time for action.

He was after the man in a moment, hanging at his heels and his eyes moist with excitement. He heard the man ask for a ticket to Torresdale, a little station just outside of Philadelphia, and when he was out of hearing, but not out of sight, purchased one for the same place.

The stranger went into the smoking-car, and seated himself at one end toward the door. Gallegher took his place at the opposite end.

He was trembling all over, and suffered from a slight feeling of nausea. He guessed it came from fright, not of any bodily harm that might come to him, but at the probability of failure in his adventure and of its most momentous possibilities.

The stranger pulled his coat collar up around his ears, hiding the lower portion of his face, but not concealing the resemblance in his troubled eyes and close-shut lips to the likenesses of the murderer Hade.

They reached Torresdale in half an hour, and the stranger, alighting quickly, struck off at a rapid pace down the country road leading to the station.

Gallegher gave him a hundred yards' start, and then followed slowly after. The road ran between fields and past a few frame-houses set far from the road in kitchen gardens.

Once or twice the man looked back over his shoulder, but he saw only a dreary length of road with a small boy splashing through the slush in the midst of it and stopping every now and again to throw snowballs at belated sparrows.

After a ten minutes' walk the stranger turned into a side road which led to only one place, the Eagle Inn, an old roadside hostelry known now as the headquarters for pothunters from the Philadelphia game market and the battle-ground of many a cock-fight.

Gallegher knew the place well. He and his young companions had often stopped there when out chestnutting on holidays in the autumn.

The son of the man who kept it had often accompanied them on their excursions, and though the boys of the city streets considered him a dumb lout, they respected him somewhat owing to his inside knowledge of dog and cock-fights.

The stranger entered the inn at a side door, and Gallegher, reaching it a few minutes later, let him go for the time being, and set about finding his occasional playmate, young Keppler.

Keppler's offspring was found in the wood-shed.

"'Tain't hard to guess what brings you out here," said the tavern-keeper's son, with a grin; "it's the fight."

"What fight?" asked Gallegher, unguardedly.

"What fight? Why, *the* fight," returned his companion, with the slow contempt of superior knowledge? "It's to come off here to-night. You knew that as well as me; anyway your sportin' editor knows it. He got the tip last night, but that won't help you any. You needn't think there's any chance of your getting a peep at it. Why, tickets is two hundred and fifty apiece!"

"Whew!" whistled Gallegher, "where's it to be?"

"In the barn," whispered Keppler. "I helped 'em fix the ropes this morning, I did."

"Gosh, but you're in luck," exclaimed Gallegher, with flattering envy.
"Couldn't I jest get a peep at it?"

"Maybe," said the gratified Keppler. "There's a winder with a wooden shutter at the back of the barn. You can get in by it, if you have some one to boost you up to the sill."

"Sa-a-y," drawled Gallegher, as if something had but just that moment reminded him. "Who's that gent who come down the road just a bit ahead of me—him with the cape-coat! Has he got anything to do with the fight?"

"Him?" repeated Keppler in tones of sincere disgust. "No-oh, he ain't no sport. He's queer, Dad thinks. He come here one day last week about ten in the morning, said his doctor told him to go out 'en the country for his health. He's stuck up and citified, and wears gloves, and takes his meals private in his room, and all that sort of ruck. They was saying in the saloon last night that they thought he was hiding from something, and Dad, just to try him, asks him last night if he was coming to see the fight. He looked sort of scared, and said he didn't want to see no fight. And then Dad says, 'I guess you mean you don't want no fighters to see you.' Dad didn't mean no harm by it, just passed it as a joke; but Mr. Carleton, as he calls himself, got white as a ghost an' says, 'I'll go to the fight willing enough,' and begins to laugh and joke. And this morning he went right into the bar-room, where all the sports were setting, and said he was going into town to see some friends; and as he starts off he laughs an' says, 'This don't look as if I was afraid of seeing people, does it?' but Dad says it was just bluff that made him do it, and Dad thinks that if he hadn't said what he did, this Mr. Carleton wouldn't have left his room at all."

Gallegher had got all he wanted, and much more than he had hoped for—so much more that his walk back to the station was in the nature of a triumphal march.

He had twenty minutes to wait for the next train, and it seemed an
hour. While waiting he sent a telegram to Hefflefinger at his hotel. It read: "Your man is near the Torresdale station, on Pennsylvania Railroad; take cab, and meet me at station. Wait until I come. GALLEGHER."

With the exception of one at midnight, no other train stopped at Torresdale that evening, hence the direction to take a cab.

The train to the city seemed to Gallegher to drag itself by inches. It stopped and backed at purposeless intervals, waited for an express to precede it, and dallied at stations, and when, at last, it reached the terminus, Gallegher was out before it had stopped and was in the cab and off on his way to the home of the sporting editor.

The sporting editor was at dinner and came out in the hall to see him, with his napkin in his hand. Gallegher explained breathlessly that he had located the murderer for whom the police of two continents were looking, and that he believed, in order to quiet the suspicions of the people with whom he was hiding, that he would be present at the fight that night.

The sporting editor led Gallegher into his library and shut the door.
"Now," he said, "go over all that again."

Gallegher went over it again in detail, and added how he had sent for Hefflefinger to make the arrest in order that it might be kept from the knowledge of the local police and from the Philadelphia reporters.

"What I want Hefflefinger to do is to arrest Hade with the warrant he has for the burglar," explained Gallegher; "and to take him on to New York on the owl train that passes Torresdale at one. It don't get to Jersey City until four o'clock, one hour after the morning papers go to press. Of course, we must fix Hefflefinger so's he'll keep quiet and not tell who his prisoner really is."

The sporting editor reached his hand out to pat Gallegher on the head, but changed his mind and shook hands with him instead.

"My boy," he said, "you are an infant phenomenon. If I can pull the rest of this thing off to-night it will mean the $5,000 reward and fame galore for you and the paper. Now, I'm going to write a note to the managing editor, and you can take it around to him and tell him what you've done and what I am going to do, and he'll take you back on the paper and raise your salary. Perhaps you didn't know you've been discharged?"

"Do you think you ain't a-going to take me with you?" demanded Gallegher.

"Why, certainly not. Why should I? It all lies with the detective and myself now. You've done your share, and done it well. If the man's caught, the reward's yours. But you'd only be in the way now. You'd better go to the office and make your peace with the chief."

"If the paper can get along without me, I can get along without the old paper," said Gallegher, hotly. "And if I ain't a-going with you,

you ain't neither, for I know where Hefflefinger is to be, and you don't, and I won't tell you."

"Oh, very well, very well," replied the sporting editor, weakly capitulating. "I'll send the note by a messenger; only mind, if you lose your place, don't blame me."

Gallegher wondered how this man could value a week's salary against the excitement of seeing a noted criminal run down, and of getting the news to the paper, and to that one paper alone.

From that moment the sporting editor sank in Gallegher's estimation.

Mr. Dwyer sat down at his desk and scribbled off the following note:

"I have received reliable information that Hade, the Burrbank murderer, will be present at the fight to-night. We have arranged it so that he will be arrested quietly and in such a manner that the fact may be kept from all other papers. I need not point out to you that this will be the most important piece of news in the country to- morrow.

"Yours, etc., MICHAEL E. DWYER."

The sporting editor stepped into the waiting cab, while Gallegher whispered the directions to the driver. He was told to go first to a district-messenger office, and from there up to the Ridge Avenue Road, out Broad Street, and on to the old Eagle Inn, near Torresdale. It was a miserable night. The rain and snow were falling together, and freezing as they fell. The sporting editor got out to send his message to the *Press* office, and then lighting a cigar, and turning up the collar of his great-coat, curled up in the corner of the cab.

"Wake me when we get there, Gallegher," he said. He knew he had a long ride, and much rapid work before him, and he was preparing for the strain.

To Gallegher the idea of going to sleep seemed almost criminal. From the dark corner of the cab his eyes shone with excitement, and with the awful joy of anticipation. He glanced every now and then to where the sporting editor's cigar shone in the darkness, and watched it as it gradually burnt more dimly and went out. The lights in the shop windows threw a broad glare across the ice on the pavements, and the lights from the lamp-posts tossed the distorted shadow of the cab, and the horse, and the motionless driver, sometimes before and sometimes behind them.

After half an hour Gallegher slipped down to the bottom of the cab and dragged out a lap-robe, in which he wrapped himself. It was growing colder, and the damp, keen wind swept in through the cracks until the window-frames and woodwork were cold to the touch.

An hour passed, and the cab was still moving more slowly over the rough surface of partly paved streets, and by single rows of new houses standing at different angles to each other in fields covered with ash-heaps and brick-kilns. Here and there the gaudy lights of a drug-store, and the forerunner of suburban civilization, shone from the end of a new block of houses, and the rubber cape of an occasional policeman showed in the light of the lamp-post that he hugged for comfort.

Then even the houses disappeared, and the cab dragged its way between truck farms, with desolate-looking glass-covered beds, and pools of water, half-caked with ice, and bare trees, and interminable fences.

Once or twice the cab stopped altogether, and Gallegher could hear the driver swearing to himself, or at the horse, or the roads. At last they drew up before the station at Torresdale. It was quite deserted, and only a single light cut a swath in the darkness and showed a portion of the platform, the ties, and the rails glistening in the rain. They walked twice past the light before a figure stepped out of the shadow and greeted them cautiously.

"I am Mr. Dwyer, of the *Press*," said the sporting editor, briskly. "You've heard of me, perhaps. Well, there shouldn't be any difficulty in our making a deal, should there? This boy here has found Hade, and we have reason to believe he will be among the spectators at the fight to-night. We want you to arrest him quietly, and as secretly as possible. You can do it with your papers and your badge easily enough. We want you to pretend that you believe he is this burglar you came over after. If you will do this, and take him away without any one so much as suspecting who he really is, and on the train that passes here at 1.20 for New York, we will give you $500 out of the $5,000 reward. If, however, one other paper, either in New York or Philadelphia, or anywhere else, knows of the arrest, you won't get a cent. Now, what do you say?"

The detective had a great deal to say. He wasn't at all sure the man Gallegher suspected was Hade; he feared he might get himself into trouble by making a false arrest, and if it should be the man, he was afraid the local police would interfere.

"We've no time to argue or debate this matter," said Dwyer, warmly. "We agree to point Hade out to you in the crowd. After the fight is over you arrest him as we have directed, and you get the money and the credit of the arrest. If you don't like this, I will arrest the man myself, and have him driven to town, with a pistol for a warrant."

Hefflefinger considered in silence and then agreed unconditionally. "As you say, Mr. Dwyer," he returned. "I've heard of you for a thoroughbred sport. I know you'll do what you say you'll do; and as for me I'll do what you say and just as you say, and it's a very pretty piece of work as it stands."

They all stepped back into the cab, and then it was that they were met by a fresh difficulty, how to get the detective into the barn where the fight was to take place, for neither of the two men had $250 to pay for his admittance.

But this was overcome when Gallegher remembered the window of which young Keppler had told him.

In the event of Hade's losing courage and not daring to show himself in the crowd around the ring, it was agreed that Dwyer should come to the barn and warn Hefflefinger; but if he should come, Dwyer was merely to keep near him and to signify by a prearranged gesture which one of the crowd he was.

They drew up before a great black shadow of a house, dark, forbidding, and apparently deserted. But at the sound of the wheels on the gravel the door opened, letting out a stream of warm, cheerful light, and a man's voice said, "Put out those lights. Don't youse know no better than that?" This was Keppler, and he welcomed Mr. Dwyer with effusive courtesy.

The two men showed in the stream of light, and the door closed on them, leaving the house as it was at first, black and silent, save for the dripping of the rain and snow from the eaves.

The detective and Gallegher put out the cab's lamps and led the horse toward a long, low shed in the rear of the yard, which they now noticed was almost filled with teams of many different makes, from the Hobson's choice of a livery stable to the brougham of the man about town.

"No," said Gallegher, as the cabman stopped to hitch the horse beside the others, "we want it nearest that lower gate. When we newspaper men leave this place we'll leave it in a hurry, and the man who is nearest town is likely to get there first. You won't be a-following of no hearse when you make your return trip."

Gallegher tied the horse to the very gate-post itself, leaving the gate open and allowing a clear road and a flying start for the prospective race to Newspaper Row.

The driver disappeared under the shelter of the porch, and Gallegher and the detective moved off cautiously to the rear of the barn. "This must be the window," said Hefflefinger, pointing to a broad wooden shutter some feet from the ground.

"Just you give me a boost once, and I'll get that open in a jiffy," said Gallegher.

The detective placed his hands on his knees, and Gallegher stood upon his shoulders, and with the blade of his knife lifted the wooden button that fastened the window on the inside, and pulled the shutter open.

Then he put one leg inside over the sill, and leaning down helped to draw his fellow-conspirator up to a level with the window. "I feel just like I was burglarizing a house," chuckled Gallegher, as he dropped noiselessly to the floor below and refastened the shutter. The barn was a large one, with a row of stalls on either side in which horses and cows were dozing. There was a haymow over each row of stalls, and at one end of the barn a number of fence-rails had been thrown across from one mow to the other. These rails were covered with hay.

In the middle of the floor was the ring. It was not really a ring, but a square, with wooden posts at its four corners through which ran a heavy rope. The space enclosed by the rope was covered with sawdust.

Gallegher could not resist stepping into the ring, and after stamping the sawdust once or twice, as if to assure himself that he was really there, began dancing around it and indulging in such a remarkable series of fistic maneuvers with an imaginary adversary that the unimaginative detective precipitately backed into a corner of the barn.

"Now, then," said Gallegher, having apparently vanquished his foe, "you come with me." His companion followed quickly as Gallegher climbed to one of the hay-mows, and crawling carefully out on the fence-rail, stretched himself at full length, face downward. In this position, by moving the straw a little, he could look down, without being himself seen, upon the heads of whosoever stood below. "This is better'n a private box, ain't it?" said Gallegher.

The boy from the newspaper office and the detective lay there in silence, biting at straws and tossing anxiously on their comfortable bed.

It seemed fully two hours before they came. Gallegher had listened without breathing, and with every muscle on a strain, at least a dozen times, when some movement in the yard had led him to believe that they were at the door. And he had numerous doubts and fears. Sometimes it was that the police had learnt of the fight, and had raided Keppler's in his absence, and again it was that the fight had been postponed, or, worst of all, that it would be put off until so late that Mr. Dwyer could not get back in time for the last edition of the paper. Their coming, when at last they came, was heralded by an advance-guard of two sporting men, who stationed themselves at either side of the big door.

"Hurry up, now, gents," one of the men said with a shiver, "don't keep this door open no longer'n is needful."

It was not a very large crowd, but it was wonderfully well selected. It ran, in the majority of its component parts, to heavy white coats with pearl buttons. The white coats were shouldered by long blue coats with astrakhan fur trimmings, the wearers of which preserved a cliqueness not remarkable when one considers that they believed every one else present to be either a crook or a prize-fighter.

There were well-fed, well-groomed club-men and brokers in the crowd, a politician or two, a popular comedian with his manager, amateur boxers from the athletic clubs, and quiet, close-mouthed sporting men from every city in the country. Their names if printed in the papers would have been as familiar as the types of the papers themselves.

And among these men, whose only thought was of the brutal sport to come, was Hade, with Dwyer standing at ease at his shoulder,—Hade, white, and visibly in deep anxiety, hiding his pale face beneath a cloth travelling-cap, and with his chin muffled in a woolen scarf. He had dared to come because he feared his danger from the already suspicious Keppler was less than if he stayed away.

And so he was there, hovering restlessly on the border of the crowd, feeling his danger and sick with fear.

When Hefflefinger first saw him he started up on his hands and elbows and made a movement forward as if he would leap down then and there and carry off his prisoner single-handed.

"Lie down," growled Gallegher; "an officer of any sort wouldn't live three minutes in that crowd."

The detective drew back slowly and buried himself again in the straw, but never once through the long fight which followed did his eyes leave the person of the murderer. The newspaper men took their places in the foremost row close around the ring, and kept looking at their watches and begging the master of ceremonies to "shake it up, do."

There was a great deal of betting, and all of the men handled the great roll of bills they wagered with a flippant recklessness which could only be accounted for in Gallegher's mind by temporary mental derangement. Some one pulled a box out into the ring and the master of ceremonies mounted it, and pointed out in forcible language that as they were almost all already under bonds to keep the peace, it behooved all to curb their excitement and to maintain a severe silence, unless they wanted to bring the police upon them and have themselves "sent down" for a year or two.

Then two very disreputable-looking persons tossed their respective principals' high hats into the ring, and the crowd, recognizing in this relic of the days when brave knights threw down their gauntlets in the lists as only a sign that the fight was about to begin, cheered tumultuously.

This was followed by a sudden surging forward, and a mutter of admiration much more flattering than the cheers had been, when the principals followed their hats, and slipping out of their great-coats, stood forth in all the physical beauty of the perfect brute.

Their pink skin was as soft and healthy looking as a baby's, and glowed in the lights of the lanterns like tinted ivory, and underneath this silken covering the great biceps and muscles moved in and out and looked like the coils of a snake around the branch of a tree.

Gentleman and blackguard shouldered each other for a nearer view; the coachmen, whose metal buttons were unpleasantly suggestive of police, put their hands, in the excitement of the moment, on the shoulders of their masters; the perspiration stood out in great drops on the foreheads of the backers, and the newspaper men bit somewhat nervously at the ends of their pencils.

And in the stalls the cows munched contentedly at their cuds and gazed with gentle curiosity at their two fellow-brutes, who stood waiting the signal to fall upon, and kill each other if need be, for the delectation of their brothers.

"Take your places," commanded the master of ceremonies.

In the moment in which the two men faced each other the crowd became so still that, save for the beating of the rain upon the shingled roof and the stamping of a horse in one of the stalls, the place was as silent as a church.

"Time," shouted the master of ceremonies.

The two men sprang into a posture of defense, which was lost as quickly as it was taken, one great arm shot out like a piston-rod; there was the sound of bare fists beating on naked flesh; there was an exultant indrawn gasp of savage pleasure and relief from the crowd, and the great fight had begun.

How the fortunes of war rose and fell, and changed and rechanged that night, is an old story to those who listen to such stories; and those who do not will be glad to be spared the telling of it. It was, they say, one of the bitterest fights between two men that this country has ever known.

But all that is of interest here is that after an hour of this desperate brutal business the champion ceased to be the favorite; the man whom he had taunted and bullied, and for whom the public had but little sympathy, was proving himself a likely winner, and under his cruel blows, as sharp and clean as those from a cutlass, his opponent was rapidly giving way.

The men about the ropes were past all control now; they drowned Keppler's petitions for silence with oaths and in inarticulate shouts of anger, as if the blows had fallen upon them, and in mad rejoicings. They swept from one end of the ring to the other, with every muscle leaping in unison with those of the man they favored, and when a New York correspondent muttered over his shoulder that this would be the biggest sporting surprise since the Heenan-Sayers fight, Mr. Dwyer nodded his head sympathetically in assent.

In the excitement and tumult it is doubtful if any heard the three quickly repeated blows that fell heavily from the outside upon the big doors of the barn. If they did, it was already too late to mend matters, for the door fell, torn from its hinges, and as it fell a captain of police sprang into the light from out of the storm, with his lieutenants and their men crowding close at his shoulder.

In the panic and stampede that followed, several of the men stood as helplessly immovable as though they had seen a ghost; others made a mad rush into the arms of the officers and were beaten back against the ropes of the ring; others dived headlong into the stalls, among the horses and cattle, and still others shoved the rolls of money they held into the hands of the police and begged like children to be allowed to escape.

The instant the door fell and the raid was declared Hefflefinger slipped over the cross rails on which he had been lying, hung for an instant by his hands, and then dropped into the centre of the fighting mob on the floor. He was out of it in an instant with the agility of a pickpocket, was across the room and at Hade's throat like a dog. The murderer, for the moment, was the calmer man of the two.

"Here," he panted, "hands off, now. There's no need for all this violence. There's no great harm in looking at a fight, is there? There's a hundred-dollar bill in my right hand; take it and let me slip out of this. No one is looking. Here."

But the detective only held him the closer.

"I want you for burglary," he whispered under his breath. "You've got to come with me now, and quick. The less fuss you make the better for both of us. If you don't know who I am, you can feel my badge under my coat there. I've got the authority. It's all regular, and when we're out of this d—d row I'll show you the papers."

He took one hand from Hade's throat and pulled a pair of handcuffs from his pocket.

"It's a mistake. This is an outrage," gasped the murderer, white and trembling, but dreadfully alive and desperate for his liberty. "Let me go, I tell you! Take your hands off of me! Do I look like a burglar, you fool?"

"I know who you look like," whispered the detective, with his face close to the face of his prisoner. "Now, will you go easy as a burglar, or shall I tell these men who you are and what I *do* want you for? Shall I call out your real name or not? Shall I tell them? Quick, speak up; shall I?"

There was something so exultant—something so unnecessarily savage in the officer's face that the man he held saw that the detective knew him for what he really was, and the hands that had held his throat slipped down around his shoulders, or he would have fallen. The man's eyes opened and closed again, and he swayed weakly backward and forward, and choked as if his throat were dry and burning. Even to such a hardened connoisseur in crime as Gallegher, who stood closely by, drinking it in, there was something so abject in the man's terror that he regarded him with what was almost a touch of pity.

"For God's sake," Hade begged, "let me go. Come with me to my room and I'll give you half the money. I'll divide with you fairly. We can both get away. There's a fortune for both of us there. We both can get away. You'll be rich for life. Do you understand—for life!"

But the detective, to his credit, only shut his lips the tighter.

"That's enough," he whispered, in return. "That's more than I expected. You've sentenced yourself already. Come!"

Two officers in uniform barred their exit at the door, but Hefflefinger smiled easily and showed his badge.

"One of Byrnes's men," he said, in explanation; "came over expressly to take this chap. He's a burglar; 'Arlie' Lane, *alias* Carleton. I've shown the papers to the captain. It's all regular. I'm just going to get his traps at the hotel and walk him over to the station. I guess we'll push right on to New York to-night."

The officers nodded and smiled their admiration for the representative of what is, perhaps, the best detective force in the world, and let him pass.

Then Hefflefinger turned and spoke to Gallegher, who still stood as watchful as a dog at his side. "I'm going to his room to get the bonds and stuff," he whispered; "then I'll march him to the station and take that train. I've done my share; don't forget yours!"

"Oh, you'll get your money right enough," said Gallegher. "And, sa-ay," he added, with the appreciative nod of an expert, "do you know, you did it rather well."

Mr. Dwyer had been writing while the raid was settling down, as he had been writing while waiting for the fight to begin. Now he walked over to where the other correspondents stood in angry conclave.

The newspaper men had informed the officers who hemmed them in that they represented the principal papers of the country, and were expostulating vigorously with the captain, who had planned the raid, and who declared they were under arrest.

"Don't be an ass, Scott," said Mr. Dwyer, who was too excited to be polite or politic. "You know our being here isn't a matter of choice. We came here on business, as you did, and you've no right to hold us."

"If we don't get our stuff on the wire at once," protested a New York man, "we'll be too late for to-morrow's paper, and——"

Captain Scott said he did not care a profanely small amount for to-morrow's paper, and that all he knew was that to the station-house the newspaper men would go. There they would have a hearing, and if the magistrate chose to let them off, that was the magistrate's business, but that his duty was to take them into custody.

"But then it will be too late, don't you understand?" shouted Mr. Dwyer. "You've got to let us go *now*, at once."

"I can't do it, Mr. Dwyer," said the captain, "and that's all there is to it. Why, haven't I just sent the president of the Junior Republican Club to the patrol-wagon, the man that put this coat on me, and do you think I can let you fellows go after that? You were all put under bonds to keep the peace not three days ago, and here you're at it—fighting like badgers. It's worth my place to let one of you off."

What Mr. Dwyer said next was so uncomplimentary to the gallant Captain Scott that that overwrought individual seized the sporting editor by the shoulder, and shoved him into the hands of two of his men.

This was more than the distinguished Mr. Dwyer could brook, and he excitedly raised his hand in resistance. But before he had time to do anything foolish his wrist was gripped by one strong, little hand, and he was conscious that another was picking the pocket of his great-coat.

He slapped his hands to his sides, and looking down, saw Gallegher standing close behind him and holding him by the wrist. Mr. Dwyer had forgotten the boy's existence, and would have spoken sharply if something in Gallegher's innocent eyes had not stopped him.

Gallegher's hand was still in that pocket, in which Mr. Dwyer had shoved his note-book filled with what he had written of Gallegher's work and Hade's final capture, and with a running descriptive account of the fight. With his eyes fixed on Mr. Dwyer, Gallegher drew it out, and with a quick movement shoved it inside his waistcoat. Mr. Dwyer gave a nod of comprehension. Then glancing at his two guardsmen, and finding that they were still interested in the wordy battle of the correspondents with their chief, and had seen nothing, he stooped and whispered to Gallegher: "The forms are locked at twenty minutes to three. If you don't get there by that time it will be of no use, but if you're on time you'll beat the town—and the country too."

Gallegher's eyes flashed significantly, and nodding his head to show he understood, started boldly on a run toward the door. But the officers who guarded it brought him to an abrupt halt, and, much to Mr. Dwyer's astonishment drew from him what was apparently a torrent of tears.

"Let me go to me father. I want me father," the boy shrieked, hysterically. "They've 'rested father. Oh, daddy, daddy. They're a-goin' to take you to prison."

"Who is your father, sonny?" asked one of the guardians of the gate.

"Keppler's me father," sobbed Gallegher. "They're a-goin' to lock him up, and I'll never see him no more."

"Oh, yes, you will," said the officer, good-naturedly; "he's there in that first patrol-wagon. You can run over and say good night to him, and then you'd better get to bed. This ain't no place for kids of your age."

"Thank you, sir," sniffed Gallegher, tearfully, as the two officers raised their clubs, and let him pass out into the darkness.

The yard outside was in a tumult, horses were stamping, and plunging, and backing the carriages into one another; lights were flashing from every window of what had been apparently an uninhabited house, and the voices of the prisoners were still raised in angry expostulation.

Three police patrol-wagons were moving about the yard, filled with unwilling passengers, who sat or stood, packed together like sheep, and with no protection from the sleet and rain.

Gallegher stole off into a dark corner, and watched the scene until his eyesight became familiar with the position of the land.

Then with his eyes fixed fearfully on the swinging light of a lantern with which an officer was searching among the carriages, he groped his way between horses' hoofs and behind the wheels of carriages to the cab which he had himself placed at the furthermost gate. It was still there, and the horse, as he had left it, with its head turned toward the city. Gallegher opened the big gate noiselessly, and worked nervously at the hitching strap. The knot was covered with a thin coating of ice, and it was several minutes before he could loosen it. But his teeth finally pulled it apart, and with the reins in his hands he sprang upon the wheel. And as he stood so, a shock of fear ran down his back like an electric current, his breath left him, and he stood immovable, gazing with wide eyes into the darkness.

The officer with the lantern had suddenly loomed up from behind a carriage not fifty feet distant, and was standing perfectly still, with his lantern held over his head, peering so directly toward Gallegher that the boy felt that he must see him. Gallegher stood with one foot on the hub of the wheel and with the other on the box waiting to spring. It seemed a minute before either of them moved, and then the officer took a step forward, and demanded sternly, "Who is that? What are you doing there?"

There was no time for parley then. Gallegher felt that he had been taken in the act, and that his only chance lay in open flight. He leaped up on the box, pulling out the whip as he did so, and with a quick sweep lashed the horse across the head and back. The animal sprang forward with a snort, narrowly clearing the gate-post, and plunged off into the darkness.

"Stop!" cried the officer.

So many of Gallegher's acquaintances among the 'longshoremen and mill hands had been challenged in so much the same manner that Gallegher knew what would probably follow if the challenge was disregarded. So he slipped from his seat to the footboard below, and ducked his head.

The three reports of a pistol, which rang out briskly from behind him, proved that his early training had given him a valuable fund of useful miscellaneous knowledge.

"Don't you be scared," he said, reassuringly, to the horse; "he's firing in the air."

The pistol-shots were answered by the impatient clangor of a patrol- wagon's gong, and glancing over his shoulder Gallegher saw its red and green lanterns tossing from side to side and looking in the darkness like the side-lights of a yacht plunging forward in a storm.

"I hadn't bargained to race you against no patrol-wagons," said Gallegher to his animal; "but if they want a race, we'll give them a tough tussle for it, won't we?"

Philadelphia, lying four miles to the south, sent up a faint yellow glow to the sky. It seemed very far away, and Gallegher's braggadocio grew cold within him at the loneliness of his adventure and the thought of the long ride before him.

It was still bitterly cold.

The rain and sleet beat through his clothes, and struck his skin with a sharp chilling touch that set him trembling.

Even the thought of the over-weighted patrol-wagon probably sticking in the mud some safe distance in the rear, failed to cheer him, and the excitement that had so far made him callous to the cold died out and left him weaker and nervous. But his horse was chilled with the long standing, and now leaped eagerly forward, only too willing to warm the half-frozen blood in its veins.

"You're a good beast," said Gallegher, plaintively. "You've got more nerve than me. Don't you go back on me now. Mr. Dwyer says we've got to beat the town." Gallegher had no idea what time it was as he rode through the night, but he knew he would be able to find out from a big clock over a manufactory at a point nearly three-quarters of the distance from Keppler's to the goal.

He was still in the open country and driving recklessly, for he knew the best part of his ride must be made outside the city limits.

He raced between desolate-looking corn-fields with bare stalks and patches of muddy earth rising above the thin covering of snow, truck farms and brick-yards fell behind him on either side. It was very lonely work, and once or twice the dogs ran yelping to the gates and barked after him.

Part of his way lay parallel with the railroad tracks, and he drove for some time beside long lines of freight and coal cars as they stood resting for the night. The fantastic Queen Anne suburban stations were dark and deserted, but in one or two of the block-towers he could see the operators writing at their desks, and the sight in some way comforted him.

Once he thought of stopping to get out the blanket in which he had wrapped himself on the first trip, but he feared to spare the time, and drove on with his teeth chattering and his shoulders shaking with the cold.

He welcomed the first solitary row of darkened houses with a faint cheer of recognition. The scattered lamp-posts lightened his spirits, and even the badly paved streets rang under the beats of his horse's feet like music. Great mills and manufactories, with only a night- watchman's light in the lowest of their many stories, began to take the place of the gloomy farm-houses and gaunt trees that had startled him with their grotesque shapes. He had been driving nearly an hour, he calculated, and in that time the rain had changed to a wet snow, that fell heavily and clung to whatever it touched. He passed block after block of trim workmen's houses, as still and silent as the sleepers within them, and at last he turned the horse's head into Broad Street, the city's great thoroughfare, that stretches from its one end to the other and cuts it evenly in two.

He was driving noiselessly over the snow and slush in the street; with his thoughts bent only on the clock-face he wished so much to see, when a hoarse voice challenged him from the sidewalk. "Hey, you, stop there, hold up!" said the voice.

Gallegher turned his head, and though he saw that the voice came from under a policeman's helmet, his only answer was to hit his horse sharply over the head with his whip and to urge it into a gallop.

This, on his part, was followed by a sharp, shrill whistle from the policeman. Another whistle answered it from a street-corner one block ahead of him. "Whoa," said Gallegher, pulling on the reins. "There's one too many of them," he added, in apologetic explanation. The horse stopped, and stood, breathing heavily, with great clouds of steam rising from its flanks.

"Why in hell didn't you stop when I told you to?" demanded the voice, now close at the cab's side.

"I didn't hear you," returned Gallegher, sweetly. "But I heard you whistle, and I heard your partner whistle, and I thought maybe it was me you wanted to speak to, so I just stopped."

"You heard me well enough. Why aren't your lights lit?" demanded the voice.

"Should I have 'em lit?" asked Gallegher, bending over and regarding them with sudden interest.

"You know you should, and if you don't, you've no right to be driving that cab. I don't believe you're the regular driver, anyway. Where'd you get it?"

"It ain't my cab, of course," said Gallegher, with an easy laugh. "It's Luke McGovern's. He left it outside Cronin's while he went in to get a drink, and he took too much, and me father told me to drive it round to the stable for him. I'm Cronin's son. McGovern ain't in no condition to drive. You can see yourself how he's been misusing the horse. He puts it up at Bachman's livery stable, and I was just going around there now."

Gallegher's knowledge of the local celebrities of the district confused the zealous officer of the peace. He surveyed the boy with a steady stare that would have distressed a less skilful liar, but Gallegher only shrugged his shoulders slightly, as if from the cold, and waited with apparent indifference to what the officer would say next.

In reality his heart was beating heavily against his side, and he felt that if he was kept on a strain much longer he would give way and break down. A second snow-covered form emerged suddenly from the shadow of the houses.

"What is it, Reeder?" it asked.

"Oh, nothing much," replied the first officer.

"This kid hadn't any lamps lit, so I called to him to stop and he didn't do it, so I whistled to you. It's all right, though. He's just taking it round to Bachman's. Go ahead," he added, sulkily.

"Get up!" chirped Gallegher. "Good night," he added, over his shoulder.

Gallegher gave a hysterical little gasp of relief as he trotted away from the two policemen, and poured bitter maledictions on their heads for two meddling fools as he went.

"They might as well kill a man as scare him to death," he said, with an attempt to get back to his customary flippancy. But the effort was somewhat pitiful, and he felt guiltily conscious that a salt, warm tear was creeping slowly down his face, and that a lump that would not keep down was rising in his throat.

"'Tain't no fair thing for the whole police force to keep worrying at a little boy like me," he said, in shame-faced apology. "I'm not doing nothing wrong, and I'm half froze to death, and yet they keep a- nagging at me."

It was so cold that when the boy stamped his feet against the footboard to keep them warm, sharp pains shot up through his body, and when he beat his arms about his shoulders, as he had seen real cabmen do, the blood in his finger-tips tingled so acutely that he cried aloud with the pain.

He had often been up that late before, but he had never felt so sleepy. It was as if some one was pressing a sponge heavy with chloroform near his face, and he could not fight off the drowsiness that lay hold of him.

He saw, dimly hanging above his head, a round disc of light that seemed like a great moon, and which he finally guessed to be the clock-face for which he had been on the look-out. He had passed it before he realized this; but the fact stirred him into wakefulness again, and when his cab's wheels slipped around the City Hall corner, he remembered to look up at the other big clock-face that keeps awake over the railroad station and measures out the night.

He gave a gasp of consternation when he saw that it was half-past two and that there was but ten minutes left to him. This, and the many electric lights and the sight of the familiar pile of buildings, startled him into a semi-consciousness of where he was and how great was the necessity for haste.

He rose in his seat and called on the horse, and urged it into a reckless gallop over the slippery asphalt. He considered nothing else but speed, and looking neither to the left nor right dashed off down Broad Street into Chestnut, where his course lay straight away to the office, now only seven blocks distant.

Gallegher never knew how it began, but he was suddenly assaulted by shouts on either side, his horse was thrown back on its haunches, and he found two men in cabmen's livery hanging at its head, and patting its sides, and calling it by name. And the other cabmen who have their stand at the corner were swarming about the carriage, all of them talking and swearing at once, and gesticulating wildly with their whips.

They said they knew the cab was McGovern's, and they wanted to know where he was, and why he wasn't on it; they wanted to know where Gallegher had stolen it, and why he had been such a fool as to drive it into the arms of its owner's friends; they said that it was about time that a cab-driver could get off his box to take a drink without having his cab run away with, and some of them called loudly for a policeman to take the young thief in charge.

Gallegher felt as if he had been suddenly dragged into consciousness out of a bad dream, and stood for a second like a half-awakened somnambulist.

They had stopped the cab under an electric light, and its glare shone coldly down upon the trampled snow and the faces of the men around him.

Gallegher bent forward, and lashed savagely at the horse with his whip.

"Let me go," he shouted, as he tugged impotently at the reins. "Let me go, I tell you. I haven't stole no cab, and you've got no right to stop me. I only want to take it to the *Press* office," he begged. "They'll send it back to you all right. They'll pay you for the trip. I'm not running away with it. The driver's got the collar—he's 'rested—and I'm only a-going to the *Press* office. Do you hear me?" he cried, his voice rising and breaking in a shriek of passion and disappointment. "I tell you to let go those reins. Let me go, or I'll kill you. Do you hear me? I'll kill you." And leaning forward, the boy struck savagely with his long whip at the faces of the men about the horse's head.

Some one in the crowd reached up and caught him by the ankles, and with a quick jerk pulled him off the box, and threw him on to the street. But he was up on his knees in a moment, and caught at the man's hand.

"Don't let them stop me, mister," he cried, "please let me go. I didn't steal the cab, sir. S'help me, I didn't. I'm telling you the truth. Take me to the *Press* office, and they'll prove it to you. They'll pay you anything you ask 'em. It's only such a little ways now, and I've come so far, sir. Please don't let them stop me," he sobbed, clasping the man about the knees. "For Heaven's sake, mister, let me go!"

The managing editor of the *Press* took up the India-rubber speaking-tube at his side, and answered, "Not yet" to an inquiry the night editor had already put to him five times within the last twenty minutes.

Then he snapped the metal top of the tube impatiently, and went up-stairs. As he passed the door of the local room, he noticed that the reporters had not gone home, but were sitting about on the tables and chairs, waiting. They looked up inquiringly as he passed, and the city editor asked, "Any news yet?" and the managing editor shook his head.

The compositors were standing idle in the composing-room, and their foreman was talking with the night editor.

"Well," said that gentleman, tentatively.

"Well," returned the managing editor, "I don't think we can wait; do you?"

"It's a half-hour after time now," said the night editor, "and we'll miss the suburban trains if we hold the paper back any longer. We can't afford to wait for a purely hypothetical story. The chances are all against the fight's having taken place or this Hade's having been arrested."

"But if we're beaten on it—" suggested the chief. "But I don't think that is possible. If there were any story to print, Dwyer would have had it here before now."

The managing editor looked steadily down at the floor.

"Very well," he said, slowly, "we won't wait any longer. Go ahead," he added, turning to the foreman with a sigh of reluctance. The foreman whirled himself about, and began to give his orders; but the two editors still looked at each other doubtfully.

As they stood so, there came a sudden shout and the sound of people running to and fro in the reportorial rooms below. There was the tramp of many footsteps on the stairs, and above the confusion they heard the voice of the city editor telling some one to "run to Madden's and get some brandy, quick."

No one in the composing-room said anything; but those compositors who had started to go home began slipping off their overcoats, and every one stood with his eyes fixed on the door.

It was kicked open from the outside, and in the doorway stood a cab-driver and the city editor, supporting between them a pitiful little figure of a boy, wet and miserable, and with the snow melting on his clothes and running in little pools to the floor. "Why, it's Gallegher," said the night editor, in a tone of the keenest disappointment.

Gallegher shook himself free from his supporters, and took an unsteady step forward, his fingers fumbling stiffly with the buttons of his waistcoat.

"Mr. Dwyer, sir," he began faintly, with his eyes fixed fearfully on the managing editor, "he got arrested—and I couldn't get here no sooner, 'cause they kept a-stopping me, and they took me cab from under me—but—" he pulled the notebook from his breast and held it out with its covers damp and limp from the rain, "but we got Hade, and here's Mr. Dwyer's copy."

And then he asked, with a queer note in his voice, partly of dread and partly of hope, "Am I in time, sir?"

The managing editor took the book, and tossed it to the foreman, who ripped out its leaves and dealt them out to his men as rapidly as a gambler deals out cards.

Then the managing editor stooped and picked Gallegher up in his arms, and, sitting down, began to unlace his wet and muddy shoes.

Gallegher made a faint effort to resist this degradation of the managerial dignity; but his protest was a very feeble one, and his head fell back heavily on the managing editor's shoulder.

To Gallegher the incandescent lights began to whirl about in circles, and to burn in different colors; the faces of the reporters kneeling before him and chafing his hands and feet grew dim and unfamiliar, and the roar and rumble of the great presses in the basement sounded far away, like the murmur of the sea.

And then the place and the circumstances of it came back to him again sharply and with sudden vividness.

Gallegher looked up, with a faint smile, into the managing editor's face. "You won't turn me off for running away, will you?" he whispered.

The managing editor did not answer immediately. His head was bent, and he was thinking, for some reason or other, of a little boy of his own, at home in bed. Then he said, quietly, "Not this time, Gallegher."

Gallegher's head sank back comfortably on the older man's shoulder, and he smiled comprehensively at the faces of the young men crowded around him. "You hadn't ought to," he said, with a touch of his old impudence, "'cause—I beat the town."

AN UNFINISHED STORY

Mrs. Trevelyan, as she took her seat, shot a quick glance down the length of her table and at the arrangement of her guests, and tried to learn if her lord and master approved. But he was listening to something Lady Arbuthnot, who sat on his right, was saying, and, being a man, failed to catch her meaning, and only smiled unconcernedly and cheerfully back at her. But the wife of the Austrian Minister, who was her very dearest friend, saw and appreciated, and gave her a quick little smile over her fan, which said that the table was perfect, the people most interesting, and that she could possess her soul in peace. So Mrs. Trevelyan pulled at the tips of her gloves and smiled upon her guests. Mrs. Trevelyan was not used to questioning her powers, but this dinner had been almost impromptu, and she had been in doubt. It was quite unnecessary, for her dinner carried with it the added virtue of being the last of the season, an encore to all that had gone before—a special number by request on the social programme. It was not one of many others stretching on for weeks, for the summer's change and leisure began on the morrow, and there was nothing hanging over her guests that they must go on to later. They knew that their luggage stood ready locked and strapped at home; they could look before them to the whole summer's pleasure, and they were relaxed and ready to be pleased, and broke simultaneously into a low murmur of talk and laughter. The windows of the dining-room stood open from the floor, and from the tiny garden that surrounded the house, even in the great mass of stucco and brick of encircling London, came the odor of flowers and of fresh turf. A soft summer-night wind moved the candles under their red shades; and gently as though they rose from afar, and not only from across the top of the high wall before the house, came the rumble of the omnibuses passing farther into the suburbs, and the occasional quick rush of a hansom over the smooth asphalt. It was a most delightful choice of people, gathered at short notice and to do honor to no one in particular, but to give each a chance to say good-by before he or she met the yacht at

Southampton or took the club train to Homburg. They all knew each other very well; and if there was a guest of the evening, it was one of the two Americans—either Miss Egerton, the girl who was to marry Lord Arbuthnot, whose mother sat on Trevelyan's right, or young Gordon, the explorer, who has just come out of Africa. Miss Egerton was a most strikingly beautiful girl, with a strong, fine face, and an earnest, interested way when she spoke, which the English found most attractive. In appearance she had been variously likened by Trevelyan, who was painting her portrait, to a druidess, a vestal virgin, and a Greek goddess; and Lady Arbuthnot's friends, who thought to please the girl, assured her that no one would ever suppose her to be an American—their ideas of the American young woman having been gathered from those who pick out tunes with one finger on the pianos in the public parlors of the Métropole. Miss Egerton was said to be intensely interested in her lover's career, and was as ambitious for his success in the House as he was himself. They were both very much in love, and showed it to others as little as people of their class do. The others at the table were General Sir Henry Kent; Phillips, the novelist; the Austrian Minister and his young wife; and Trevelyan, who painted portraits for large sums of money and figure pieces for art; and some simply fashionable smart people who were good listeners, and who were rather disappointed that the American explorer was no more sun-burned than other young men who had stayed at home, and who had gone in for tennis or yachting.

The worst of Gordon was that he made it next to impossible for one to lionize him. He had been back in civilization and London only two weeks, unless Cairo and Shepheard's Hotel are civilization, and he had been asked everywhere, and for the first week had gone everywhere. But whenever his hostess looked for him, to present another and not so recent a lion, he was generally found either humbly carrying an ice to some neglected dowager, or talking big game or international yachting or tailors to a circle of younger sons in the smoking-room, just as though several hundred attractive and distinguished people were not waiting to fling the speeches they had prepared on Africa at him, in the drawing-room above. He had suddenly disappeared during the second week of his stay in London, which was also the last week of the London season, and managers of lecture tours and publishers and lion-hunters, and even friends who cared for him for himself, had failed to find him at his lodgings. Trevelyan, who had known him when he was a travelling correspondent and artist for one of the great weeklies, had found him at the club the night before, and had asked him to his wife's impromptu dinner, from which he had at first begged off, but, on learning who was to be there, had changed his mind and accepted. Mrs. Trevelyan was very glad he had come; she had always spoken of him as a nice boy, and now that he had become famous she liked him none the less, but did not show it before people as much as she had been used to do. She forgot to ask him whether he knew his beautiful compatriot or not; but she took it for granted that they had met, if not at home, at least in London, as they had both been made so much of, and at the same houses.

The dinner was well on its way towards its end, and the women had begun to talk across the table, and to exchange bankers' addresses, and to say "Be sure and look us up in Paris," and "When do you expect to sail from Cowes?" They were enlivened and interested, and the present odors of the food and flowers and wine, and the sense of leisure before them, made it seem almost a pity that such a well-suited gathering should have to separate for even a summer's pleasure.

The Austrian Minister was saying this to his hostess, when Sir Henry Kent, who had been talking across to Phillips, the novelist, leaned back in his place and said, as though to challenge the attention of every one, "I can't agree with you, Phillips. I am sure no one else will."

"Dear me," complained Mrs. Trevelyan, plaintively, "what have you been saying now, Mr. Phillips? He always has such debatable theories," she explained.

"On the contrary, Mrs. Trevelyan," answered the novelist, "it is the other way. It is Sir Henry who is making all the trouble. He is attacking one of the oldest and dearest platitudes I know." He paused for the general to speak, but the older man nodded his head for him to go on. "He has just said that fiction is stranger than truth," continued the novelist. "He says that I—that people who write could never interest people who read if they wrote of things as they really are. They select, he says—they take the critical moment in a man's life and the crises, and want others to believe that that is what happens every day. Which it is not, so the general says. He thinks that life is commonplace and uneventful—that is, uneventful in a picturesque or dramatic way. He admits that women's lives are saved from drowning, but that they are not saved by their lovers, but by a longshoreman with a wife and six children, who accepts five pounds for doing it. That's it, is it not?" he asked.

The general nodded and smiled. "What I said to Phillips was," he explained, "that if things were related just as they happen, they would not be interesting. People do not say the dramatic things they say on the stage or in novels; in real life they are commonplace or sordid—or disappointing. I have seen men die on the battle-field, for instance, and they never cried, 'I die that my country may live,' or 'I have got my promotion at last;' they just stared up at the surgeon and said, 'Have I got to lose that arm?' or 'I am killed, I think.' You see, when men are dying around you, and horses are plunging, and the batteries are firing, one doesn't have time to think up the appropriate remark for the occasion. I don't believe, now, that Pitt's last words were, 'Roll up the map of Europe.' A man who could change the face of a continent would not use his dying breath in making epigrams. It was one of his secretaries or one of the doctors who said that. And the man who was capable of writing home, 'All is lost but honor,' was just the sort of a man who would lose more battles than he would win. No; you, Phillips," said the general, raising his voice as he became more confident and conscious that be held the centre of the stage, "and you, Trevelyan, don't write and paint every-day things as they are. You introduce something for a contrast or for an effect; a red coat in a landscape for the bit of color you want, when in real life the red coat would not be within miles; or you have a band of music playing a popular air in the street when a murder is going on inside the house. You do it because it is effective; but it isn't true. Now Mr. Caithness was telling us the other night at the club, on this very matter—"

"Oh, that's hardly fair," laughed Trevelyan; "you've rehearsed all this before. You've come prepared."

"No, not at all," frowned the general, sweeping on. "He said that before he was raised to the bench, when he practiced criminal law, he had brought word to a man that he was to be reprieved, and to another that he was to die. Now, you know," exclaimed the general, with a shrug, and appealing to the table, "how that would be done on the stage or in a novel, with the prisoner bound ready for execution, and a galloping horse, and a fluttering piece of white paper, and all that. Well, now, Caithness told us that he went into the man's cell and said, 'You have been reprieved, John,' or William, or whatever the fellow's name was. And the man looked at him and said: 'Is that so? That's good—that's good;' and that was all he said. And then, again, he told one man whose life he had tried very hard to save: 'The Home Secretary has refused to intercede for you. I saw him at his house last night at nine o'clock.' And the murderer, instead of saying, 'My God! what will my wife and children do?' looked at him, and repeated, 'At nine o'clock last night!' just as though that were the important part of the message."

"Well, but, general," said Phillips, smiling, "that's dramatic enough as it is, I think. Why—"

"Yes," interrupted the general, quickly and triumphantly. "But that is not what you would have made him say, is it? That's my point."

"There was a man told me once," Lord Arbuthnot began, leisurely—"he was a great chum of mine, and it illustrates what Sir Henry has said, I think—he was engaged to a girl, and he had a misunderstanding or an understanding with her that opened both their eyes, at a dance, and the next afternoon he called, and they talked it over in the drawing-room, with the tea-tray between them, and agreed to end it. On the stage he would have risen and said, 'Well, the comedy is over, the tragedy begins, or the curtain falls;' and she would have gone to the piano and played Chopin sadly while he made his exit. Instead of which he got up to go without saying anything, and as he rose he upset a cup and saucer on the tea-table, and said, 'Oh, I beg your pardon;' and she said, 'It isn't broken;' and he went out. You see," the young man added, smiling, "there were two young people whose hearts were breaking, and yet they talked of teacups, not because they did not feel, but because custom is too strong on us and too much for us. We do not say dramatic things or do theatrical ones. It does not make interesting reading, but it is the truth."

"Exactly," cut in the Austrian Minister, eagerly. "And then there is the prerogative of the author and of the playwright to drop a curtain whenever he wants to, or to put a stop to everything by ending the chapter. That isn't fair. That is an advantage over nature. When some one accuses some one else of doing something dreadful at the play, down comes the curtain quick and keeps things at fever point, or the chapter ends with a lot of stars, and the next page begins with a description of a sunset two weeks later. To be true, we ought to be told what the man who is accused said in the reply, or what happened during those two weeks before the sunset. The author really has no right to choose only the critical moments, and to shut out the commonplace, every-day life by a sort of literary closure. That is, if he claims to tell the truth."

Phillips raised his eyebrows and looked carefully around the table. "Does any one else feel called upon to testify?" he asked.

"It's awful, isn't it, Phillips," laughed Trevelyan, comfortably, "to find that the photographer is the only artist, after all? I feel very guilty."

"You ought to," pronounced the general, gaily. He was very well satisfied with himself at having held his own against these clever people. "And I am sure Mr. Gordon will agree with me, too," he went on, confidently, with a bow towards the younger man. "He has seen more of the world than any of us, and he will tell you, I am sure, that what happens only suggests the story; it is not complete in itself. That it always needs the author's touch, just as the rough diamond—"

"Oh, thanks, thanks, general," laughed Phillips. "My feelings are not hurt as badly as that."

Gordon had been turning the stem of a wineglass slowly between his thumb and his finger while the others were talking, and looking down at it smiling. Now he raised his eyes as though he meant to speak, and then dropped them again. "I am afraid, Sir Henry," he said, "that I don't agree with you at all."

Those who had said nothing felt a certain satisfaction that they had not committed themselves. The Austrian Minister tried to remember what it was he had said, and whether it was too late to retreat, and the general looked blankly at Gordon and said, "Indeed?"

"You shouldn't have called on that last witness, Sir Henry," said Phillips, smiling. "Your case was very good as it was."

"I am quite sure," said Gordon, seriously, "that the story Phillips will never write is a true story, but he will not write it because people would say it is impossible, just as you have all seen sunsets sometimes that you knew would be laughed at if any one tried to paint them. We all know such a story, something in our own lives, or in the lives of our friends. Not ghost stories, or stories of adventure, but of ambitions that come to nothing, of people who were rewarded or punished in this world instead of in the next, and love stories."

Phillips looked at the young man keenly and smiled. "Especially love stories," he said.

Gordon looked back at him as if he did not understand.

"Tell it, Gordon," said Mr. Trevelyan.

"Yes," said Gordon, nodding his head in assent, "I was thinking of a particular story. It is as complete, I think, and as dramatic as any of those we read. It is about a man I met in Africa. It is not a long story," he said, looking around the table tentatively, "but it ends badly."

There was a silence much more appreciated than a polite murmur of invitation would have been, and the simply smart people settled themselves rigidly to catch every word for future use. They realized that this would be a story which had not as yet appeared in the newspapers, and which would not make a part of Gordon's book. Mrs. Trevelyan smiled encouragingly upon her former protégé; she was sure he was going to do himself credit; but the American girl chose this chance, when all the other eyes were turned expectantly towards the explorer, to look at her lover.

"We were on our return march from Lake Tchad to the Mobangi," said Gordon. "We had been travelling over a month, sometimes by water and sometimes through the forest, and we did not expect to see any other white men besides those of our own party for several months to come. In the middle of a jungle late one afternoon I found this man lying at the foot of a tree. He had been cut and beaten and left for dead. It was as much of a surprise to me, you understand, as it would be to you if you were driving through Trafalgar Square in a hansom, and an African lion should spring up on your horses' haunches. We believed we were the only white men that had ever succeeded in getting that far south. Crampel had tried it, and no one knows yet whether he is dead or alive; Doctor Schlemen had been eaten by cannibals, and Major Bethume had turned back two hundred miles farther north; and we could no more account for this man's presence than if he had been dropped from the clouds. Lieutenant Royce, my surgeon, went to work at him, and we halted where we were for the night. In about an hour the man moved and opened his eyes. He looked up at us and said, 'Thank God!'—because we were white, I suppose—and went off into unconsciousness again. When he came to the next time, he asked Royce, in a whisper, how long he had to live. He wasn't the sort of a man you had to lie to about a thing like that, and Royce told him he did not think he could live for more than an hour or two. The man moved his head to show that he understood, and raised his hand to his throat and began pulling at his shirt, but the effort sent him off into a fainting-fit again. I opened his collar for him as gently as I could, and found that his fingers had clinched around a silver necklace that he wore about his neck, and from which there hung a gold locket shaped like a heart."

Gordon raised his eyes slowly from the observation of his finger-tips as they rested on the edge of the table before him to those of the American girl who sat opposite. She had heard his story so far without any show of attention, and had been watching, rather with a touch of fondness in her eyes, the clever, earnest face of Arbuthnot, who was following Gordon's story with polite interest. But now, at Gordon's last words, she turned her eyes to him with a look of awful indignation, which was followed, when she met his calmly polite look of inquiry, by one of fear and almost of entreaty.

"When the man came to," continued Gordon, in the same conventional monotone, "he begged me to take the chain and locket to a girl whom he said I would find either in London or in New York. He gave me the address of her banker. He said: 'Take it off my neck before you bury me; tell her I wore it ever since she gave it to me. That it has been a charm and loadstone to me. That when the locket rose and fell against my breast, it was as if her heart were pressing against mine and answering the beating and throbbing of the blood in my veins.'"

Gordon paused, and returned to the thoughtful scrutiny of his finger-tips.

"The man did not die," he said, raising his head. "Royce brought him back into such form again that in about a week we were able to take him along with us on a litter. But he was very weak, and would lie for hours sleeping when we rested, or mumbling and raving in a fever. We learned from him at odd times that he had been trying to reach Lake Tchad, to do what we had done, without any means of doing it. He had had not more than a couple of dozen porters and a corporal's guard of Senegalese soldiers. He was the only white man in the party, and his men had turned on him, and left him as we found him, carrying off with them his stock of provisions and arms. He had undertaken the expedition on a promise from the French government to make him governor of the territory he opened up if he succeeded, but he had had no official help. If he failed, he got nothing; if he succeeded, he did so at his own expense and by his own endeavors. It was only a wonder he had been able to get as far as he did. He did not seem to feel the failure of his expedition. All that was lost in the happiness of getting back alive to this woman with whom he was in love. He had been three days alone before we found him, and in those three days, while he waited for death, he had thought of nothing but that he would never see her again. He had resigned himself to this, had given up all hope, and our coming seemed like a miracle to him. I have read about men in love, I have seen it on the stage, I have seen it in real life, but I never saw a man so grateful to God and so happy and so insane over a woman as this man was. He raved about her when he was feverish, and he talked and talked to me about her when he was in his senses. The porters could not understand him, and he found me sympathetic, I suppose, or else he did not care, and only wanted to speak of her to some one, and so he told me the story over and over again as I walked beside the litter, or as we sat by the fire at night. She must have been a very remarkable girl. He had met her first the year before, on one of the Italian steamers that ply from New York to Gibraltar. She was travelling with her father, who was an invalid going to Tangier for his health; from Tangier they were to go on up to Nice and Cannes, and in the spring to Paris and on to London for this season just over. The man was going from Gibraltar to Zanzibar, and then on into the Congo. They had met the first night out; they had separated thirteen days later at Gibraltar, and in that time the girl had fallen in love with him, and had promised to marry him if he would let her, for he was very proud. He had to be. He had absolutely nothing to offer her. She is very well known at home. I mean her family is: they have lived in New York from its first days, and they are very rich. The girl had lived a life as different from his as the life of a girl in society must be from that of a vagabond. He had been an engineer, a newspaper correspondent, an officer in a Chinese army, and had built bridges in South America, and led their little revolutions there, and had seen service on the desert in the French army of Algiers. He had no home or nationality even, for he had left America when he was sixteen; he had no family, had saved no money, and was trusting everything to the success of this expedition into Africa to make him known and to give him position. It was the story of Othello and Desdemona over again. His blackness lay from her point of view, or rather would have lain from the point of view of her friends, in the fact that he was as helplessly ineligible a young man as a cowboy. And he really had lived a life of which he had no great reason to be proud. He had existed entirely for excitement, as other men live to drink until they kill themselves by it; nothing he had done had counted for much except his bridges. They are still standing. But the things he had written are lost in the columns of the daily papers. The soldiers he had fought with knew him only as a man who cared more for the fighting than for what the fighting was about, and he had been as ready to write on one side as to fight on the other. He was a rolling stone, and had been a rolling stone from the time he was sixteen and had run away to sea, up to the day he had met this girl, when he was just thirty. Yet you can see how such a man would attract a young, impressionable girl, who had met only those men whose actions are bounded by the courts of law or Wall Street, or the younger set who drive coaches and who live the life of the clubs. She had gone through life as some people go through picture-galleries, with their catalogues marked at the best pictures. She knew nothing of the little fellows whose work was skied, who were trying to be known, who were not of her world, but who toiled and prayed and hoped to be famous. This man came into her life suddenly with his stories of adventure and strange people and strange places, of things done for the love of doing them and not for the reward or reputation, and he bewildered her at first, I suppose, and then fascinated, and then won her. You can imagine how it was, these two walking the deck together during the day, or sitting side by side when the night came on, the ocean stretched before them. The daring of his present undertaking, the absurd glamour that is thrown over those who have gone into that strange country from which some travellers return, and the picturesqueness of his past life. It is no wonder the girl made too much of him. I do not think he knew what was coming. He did not pose before her. I am quite sure, from what I knew of him, that he did not. Indeed, I believed him when he said that he had fought against the more than interest she had begun to show for him. He was the sort of man women care for, but they had not been of this woman's class or calibre. It came to him like a sign from the heavens. It was as if a goddess had stooped to him. He told her when they separated that if he succeeded—if he opened this unknown country, if he was rewarded as they had promised to reward him—he might dare to come to her; and she called him her knight-errant, and gave him her chain and locket to wear, and told him, whether he failed or succeeded it meant nothing to her, and that her life was his while it lasted, and her soul as well.

"I think," Gordon said, stopping abruptly, with an air of careful consideration, "that those were her words as he repeated them to me."

He raised his eyes thoughtfully towards the face of the girl opposite, and then glanced past her, as if he were trying to recall the words the man had used. The fine, beautiful face of the woman was white and drawn around the lips, and she gave a quick, appealing glance at her hostess, as if she would beg to be allowed to go. But Mrs. Trevelyan and her guests were watching Gordon or toying with the things in front of them. The dinner had been served, and not even the soft movements of the servants interrupted the young man's story.

"You can imagine a man," Gordon went on, more lightly, "finding a hansom cab slow when he is riding from the station to see the woman he loves; but imagine this man urging himself and the rest of us to hurry when we were in the heart of Africa, with six months' travel in front of us before we could reach the first limits of civilization. That is what this man did. When he was still on his litter he used to toss and turn, and abuse the bearers and porters and myself because we moved so slowly. When we stopped for the night he would chafe and fret at the delay; and when the morning came he was the first to wake, if he slept at all, and eager to push on. When at last he was able to walk, he worked himself into a fever again, and it was only when Royce warned him that he would kill himself if he kept on that he submitted to be carried, and forced himself to be patient. And all the time the poor devil kept saying how unworthy he was of her, how miserably he had wasted his years, how unfitted he was for the great happiness which had come into his life. I suppose every man says that when he is in love; very properly, too; but the worst of it was, in this man's case, that it was so very true. He was unworthy of her in everything but his love for her. It used to frighten me to see how much he cared. Well, we got out of it at last, and reached Alexandria, and saw white faces once more, and heard women's voices, and the strain and fear of failure were over, and we could breathe again. I was quite ready enough to push on to London, but we had to wait a week for the steamer, and during that time that man made my life miserable. He had done so well, and would have done so much more if he had had my equipment, that I tried to see that he received all the credit due him. But he would have none of the public receptions, and the audience with the khedive, or any of the fuss they made over us. He only wanted to get back to her. He spent the days on the quay watching them load the steamer, and counting the hours until she was to sail; and even at night he would leave the first bed he had slept in for six months, and would come into my room and ask me if I would not sit up and talk with him until daylight. You see, after he had given up all thought of her, and believed himself about to die without seeing her again, it made her all the dearer, I suppose, and made him all the more fearful of losing her again.

"He became very quiet as soon as we were really under way, and Royce and I hardly knew him for the same man. He would sit in silence in his steamer-chair for hours, looking out at the sea and smiling to himself, and sometimes, for he was still very weak and feverish, the tears would come to his eyes and run down his cheeks. 'This is the way we would sit,' he said to me one night, 'with the dark purple sky and the strange Southern stars over our heads, and the rail of the boat rising and sinking below the line of the horizon. And I can hear her voice, and I try to imagine she is still sitting there, as she did the last night out, when I held her hands between mine.'" Gordon paused a moment, and then went on more slowly: "I do not know whether it was that the excitement of the journey overland had kept him up or not, but as we went on he became much weaker and slept more, until Royce became anxious and alarmed about him. But he did not know it himself; he had grown so sure of his recovery then that he did not understand what the weakness meant. He fell off into long spells of sleep or unconsciousness, and woke only to be fed, and would then fall back to sleep again. And in one of these spells of unconsciousness he died. He died within two days of land. He had no home and no country and no family, as I told you, and we buried him at sea. He left nothing behind him, for the very clothes he wore were those we had given him—nothing but the locket and the chain which he had told me to take from his neck when he died."

Gordon's voice had grown very cold and hard. He stopped and ran his fingers down into his pocket and pulled out a little leather bag.

The people at the table watched him in silence as he opened it and took out a dull silver chain with a gold heart hanging from it.

"This is it," he said, gently. He leaned across the table, with his eyes fixed on those of the American girl, and dropped the chain in front of her. "Would you like to see it?" he said.

The rest moved curiously forward to look at the little heap of gold and silver as it lay on the white cloth. But the girl, with her eyes half closed and her lips pressed together, pushed it on with her hand to the man who sat next her, and bowed her head slightly, as though it was an effort for her to move at all. The wife of the Austrian Minister gave a little sigh of relief.

"I should say your story did end badly, Mr. Gordon," she said. "It is terribly sad, and so unnecessarily so."

"I don't know," said Lady Arbuthnot, thoughtfully—"I don't know; it seems to me it was better. As Mr. Gordon says, the man was hardly worthy of her. A man should have something more to offer a woman than love; it is a woman's prerogative to be loved. Any number of men may love her; it is nothing to their credit: they cannot help themselves."

"Well," said General Kent, "if all true stories turn out as badly as that one does, I will take back what I said against those the story-writers tell. I prefer the ones Anstey and Jerome make up. I call it a most unpleasant story."

"But it isn't finished yet," said Gordon, as he leaned over and picked up the chain and locket. "There is still a little more."

"Oh, I beg your pardon!" said the wife of the Austrian Minister, eagerly. "But then," she added, "you can't make it any better. You cannot bring the man back to life."

"No," said Gordon, "but I can make it a little worse."

"Ah, I see," said Phillips, with a story-teller's intuition—"the girl."

"The first day I reached London I went to her banker's and got her address," continued Gordon. "And I wrote, saying I wanted to see her, but before I could get an answer I met her the next afternoon at a garden-party. At least I did not meet her; she was pointed out to me. I saw a very beautiful girl surrounded by a lot of men, and asked who she was, and found out it was the woman I had written to, the owner of the chain and locket; and I was also told that her engagement had just been announced to a young Englishman of family and position, who had known her only a few months, and with whom she was very much in love. So you see," he went on, smiling, "that it was better that he died, believing in her and in her love for him. Mr. Phillips, now, would have let him live to return and find her married; but Nature is kinder than writers of fiction, and quite as dramatic."

Phillips did not reply to this, and the general only shook his head doubtfully and said nothing. So Mrs. Trevelyan looked at Lady Arbuthnot, and the ladies rose and left the room. When the men had left them, a young girl went to the piano, and the other women seated themselves to listen; but Miss Egerton, saying that it was warm, stepped out through one of the high windows on to the little balcony that overhung the garden. It was dark out there and cool, and the rumbling of the encircling city sounded as distant and as far off as the reflection seemed that its million lights threw up to the sky above. The girl leaned her face and bare shoulder against the rough stone wall of the house, and pressed her hands together, with her fingers locking and unlocking and her rings cutting through her gloves. She was trembling slightly, and the blood in her veins was hot and tingling. She heard the voices of the men as they entered the drawing-room, the momentary cessation of the music at the piano, and its renewal, and then a figure blocked the light from the window, and Gordon stepped out of it and stood in front of her with the chain and locket in his hand. He held it towards her, and they faced each other for a moment in silence.

"Will you take it now?" he said.

The girl raised her head, and drew herself up until she stood straight and tall before him. "Have you not punished me enough?" she asked, in a whisper. "Are you not satisfied? Was it brave? Was it manly? Is that what you have learned among your savages—to torture a woman?" She stopped with a quick sob of pain, and pressed her hands against her breast.

Gordon observed her, curiously, with cold consideration. "What of the sufferings of the man to whom you gave this?" he asked. "Why not consider him? What was your bad quarter of an hour at the table, with your friends around you, to the year he suffered danger and physical pain for you—for you, remember?"

The girl hid her face for a moment in her hands, and when she lowered them again her cheeks were wet and her voice was changed and softer. "They told me he was dead," she said. "Then it was denied, and then the French papers told of it again, and with horrible detail, and how it happened."

Gordon took a step nearer her. "And does your love come and go with the editions of the daily papers?" he asked, fiercely. "If they say to-morrow morning that Arbuthnot is false to his principles or his party, that he is a bribe-taker, a man who sells his vote, will you believe them and stop loving him?" He gave a sharp exclamation of disdain. "Or will you wait," he went on, bitterly, "until the Liberal organs have had time to deny it? Is that the love, the life, and the soul you promised the man who—"

There was a soft step on the floor of the drawing-room, and the tall figure of young Arbuthnot appeared in the opening of the window as he looked doubtfully out into the darkness. Gordon took a step back into the light of the window, where he could be seen, and leaned easily against the railing of the balcony. His eyes were turned towards the street, and he noticed over the wall the top of a passing omnibus and the glow of the men's pipes who sat on it.

"Miss Egerton?" asked Arbuthnot, his eyes still blinded by the lights of the room he had left. "Is she here? Oh, is that you?" he said, as he saw the movement of the white dress. "I was sent to look for you," he said. "They were afraid something was wrong." He turned to Gordon, as if in explanation of his lover-like solicitude. "It has been rather a hard week, and it has kept one pretty well on the go all the time, and I thought Miss Egerton looked tired at dinner."

The moment he had spoken, the girl came towards him quickly, and put her arm inside of his, and took his hand.

He looked down at her wonderingly at this show of affection, and then drew her nearer, and said, gently, "You are tired, aren't you? I came to tell you that Lady Arbuthnot is going. She is waiting for you."

It struck Gordon, as they stood there, how handsome they were and how well suited. They took a step towards the window, and then the young nobleman turned and looked out at the pretty garden and up at the sky, where the moon was struggling against the glare of the city.

"It is very pretty and peaceful out here," he said, "is it not? It seems a pity to leave it. Good-night, Gordon, and thank you for your story." He stopped, with one foot on the threshold, and smiled. "And yet, do you know," he said, "I cannot help thinking you were guilty of doing just what you accused Phillips of doing. I somehow thought you helped the true story out a little. Now didn't you? Was it all just as you told it? Or am I wrong?"

"No," Gordon answered; "you are right. I did change it a little, in one particular."

"And what was that, may I ask?" said Arbuthnot.

"The man did not die," Gordon answered.

Arbuthnot gave a quick little sigh of sympathy. "Poor devil!" he said, softly; "poor chap!" He moved his left hand over and touched the hand of the girl, as though to reassure himself of his own good fortune. Then he raised his eyes to Gordon's with a curious, puzzled look in them. "But then," he said, doubtfully, "if he is not dead, how did you come to get the chain?"

The girl's arm within his own moved slightly, and her fingers tightened their hold upon his hand.

"Oh," said Gordon, indifferently, "it did not mean anything to him, you see, when he found he had lost her, and it could not mean anything to her. It is of no value. It means nothing to any one— except, perhaps, to me."

The Bar Sinister

Part I

THE Master was walking most unsteady, his legs tripping each other. After the fifth or sixth round, my legs often go the same way.

But even when the Master's legs bend and twist a bit, you mustn't think he can't reach you. Indeed, that is the time he kicks most frequent. So I kept behind him in the shadow, or ran in the middle of the street. He stopped at many public houses with swinging doors, those doors that are cut so high from the sidewalk that you can look in under them, and see if the Master is inside. At night, when I peep beneath them, the man at the counter will see me first and say, "Here's the Kid, Jerry, come to take you home. Get a move on you." and the Master will stumble out and follow me. It's lucky for us I'm so white, for, no matter how dark the night, he can always see me ahead, just out of reach of his boot. At night the Master certainly does see most amazing. Sometimes he sees two or four of me, and walks in a circle, so that I have to take him by the leg of his trousers and lead him into the right road. One night, when he was very nasty-tempered and I was coaxing him along, two men passed us, and one of them says "Look at that brute!" and the other asks, "Which?" and they both laugh. The Master he cursed them good and proper.

But this night, whenever we stopped at a public house, the Master's pals left it and went on with us to the next. They spoke quite civil to me, and when the Master tried a flying kick, they gives him a shove. "Do you want us to lose our money?" says the pals.

I had had nothing to eat for a day and a night, and just before we set out the Master gives me a wash under the hydrant. Whenever I am locked up until all the slop-pans in our alley are empty, and made to take a bath, and the Master's pals speak civil and feel my ribs, I know something is going to happen. And that night, when every time they see a policeman under a lamp-post, they dodged across the street, and when at the last one of them picked me up and hid me under his jacket, I began to tremble; for I knew what it meant. It meant that I was to fight again for the Master.

I don't fight because I like fighting. I fight because if I didn't the other dog would find my throat, and the Master would lose his stakes, and I would be very sorry for him, and ashamed. Dogs can pass me and I can pass dogs, and I'd never pick a fight with none of them. When I see two dogs standing on their hind legs in the streets, clawing each other's ears, and snapping for each other's windpipes, or howling and swearing and rolling in the mud, I feel sorry they should act so, and pretend not to notice. If he'd let me, I'd like to pass the time of day with every dog I meet. But there's something about me that no nice dog can abide.

When I trot up to nice dogs, nodding and grinning, to make friends, they always tell me to be off.

"Go to the devil!" they bark at me. "Get out!" And when I walk away they shout "Mongrel!" and "Gutterdog!" and sometimes, after my back is turned, they rush me. I could kill most of them with three shakes, breaking the backbone of the little ones and squeezing the throat of the big ones. But what's the good? They are nice dogs; that's why I try to make up to them: and, though it's not for them to say it, I am a street dog, and if I try to push into the company of my betters, I suppose it's their right to teach me my place.

Of course they don't know I'm the best fighting bull-terrier of my weight in Montreal. That's why it wouldn't be fair for me to take notice of what they shout. They don't know that if I once locked my jaws on them I'd carry away whatever I touched. The night I fought Kelly's White Rat, I wouldn't loosen up until the Master made a noose in my leash and strangled me; and, as for that Ottawa dog if the handlers hadn't thrown red pepper down my nose I never would have let go of him. I don't think the handlers treated me quite right that time, but maybe they didn't know the Ottawa dog was dead. I did.

I learned my fighting from my mother when I was very young. We slept in a lumberyard on the river-front, and by day hunted for food along the wharves. When we got it, the other tramp-dogs would try to take it off us, and then it was wonderful to see mother fly at them and drive them away. All I know of fighting I learned from mother, watching her picking the ash-heaps for me when I was too little to fight for myself. No one ever was so good to me as mother. When it snowed and the ice was in the St. Lawrence, she used to hunt alone, and bring me back new bones, and she'd sit and laugh to see me trying to swallow 'em whole. I was just a puppy then; my teeth was falling out. When I was able to fight we kept the whole river-range to ourselves, I had the genuine long "punishing" jaw, so mother said, and there wasn't a man or a dog that dared worry us.

Those were happy days, those were; and we lived well, share and share alike, and when we wanted a bit of fun, we chased the fat old wharf-rats!

My, how they would squeal!

Then the trouble came. It was no trouble to me. I was too young to care then. But mother took it so to heart that she grew ailing, and wouldn't go abroad with me by day. it was the same old scandal that they're always bringing up against me. I was so young then that I didn't know. I couldn't see any difference between mother-and other mothers.

But one day a pack of curs we drove off snarled back some new names at her, and mother dropped her head and ran, just as though they had whipped us. After that she wouldn't go out with me except in the dark, and one day she went away and never came back, and, though I hunted for her in every court and alley and back street of Montreal, I never found her.

One night, a month after mother ran away, I asked Guardian, the old blind mastiff, whose Master is the night watchman on our slip, what it all meant. And he told me.

"Every dog in Montreal knows," he says, "except you; and every Master knows. So I think it's time you knew."

Then he tells me that my father, who had treated mother so bad, was a great and noble gentleman from London. "Your father had twenty two registered ancestors, had your father," old Guardian says, "and in him was the best bull-terrier blood of England, the most ancientest, the most royal; the winning 'blue-ribbon' blood, that breeds champions. He had sleepy pink eyes and thin pink lips, and he was as white all over as his own white teeth, and under his white skin you could see his muscles, hard and smooth, like the links of a steel chain. When your father stood still, and tipped his nose in the air, it was just as though he was saying, 'Oh, yes, you common dogs and men, you may well stare. It must be a rare treat for you colonials to see real English royalty.' He certainly was pleased with hisself, was your father. He looked just as proud and haughty as one of them stone dogs in Victoria Park-them as is cut out of white marble. And you're like him," says the old mastiff-"by that, of course, meaning you're white, same as him. That's the only likeness. But, you see, the trouble is, Kid--well, you see, Kid, the trouble is—you rmother--"

"That will do," I said, for then I understood without his telling me, and I got up and walked away, holding my head and tail high in the air. But I was, oh, so miserable, and I wanted to see mother that very minute ,and tell her that I didn't care.

Mother is what I am, a street-dog; there's no royal blood in mother's veins, nor is she like that father of mine, nor--and that's the worst she's not even like me. For while I, when I'm washed for a fight, am as white as clean snow, she--and this is our trouble--she, my mother, is a black-and-tan.

When mother hid herself from me, I was twelve months old and able to take care of myself, and as, after mother left me, the wharves were never the same, I moved uptown and met the Master. Before he came, lots of other men folks had tried to make up to me, and to whistle me home. But they either tried patting me or coaxing me with a piece of meat; so I didn't take to 'em. But one day the Master pulled me out of a street fight by the hind-legs, and kicked me good.

"You want to fight. do you?" says he. "I'll give you all the fighting you want!" he says, and he kicks me again. So I knew he was my Master, and I followed him home. Since that day I've pulled off many fights for him, and they've brought dogs from all over the province to have a go at me; but up to that night none, under thirty pounds, had ever downed me.

But that night, so soon as they carried me into the ring, I saw the dog was overweight, and that I was no match for him. it was asking too much of a puppy. The Master should have known I couldn't do it. Not that I mean to blame the Master, for when sober, which he sometimes was,--though not, as you might say, his habit,--he was most kind to me, and let me out to find food, if I could get it, and only kicked me when I didn't pick him up at night and lead him home.

But kicks will stiffen the muscles, and starving a dog so as to get him ugly-tempered for a fight may make him nasty, but it's weakening to his insides, and it causes the legs to wobble.

The ring was in a hall back of a public house. There was a red-hot whitewashed stove in one corner, and the ring in the other. I lay in the Master's lap, wrapped in my blanket, and, spite of the stove, shivering awful; but I always shiver before a fight: I can't help gettin' excited.
While the men-folks were a-flashing their money and taking their last drink at the bar, a little Irish groom in gaiters came up to me and give me the back of his hand to smell, and scratched me behind the cars.

"You poor little pup," says he; "you haven't no show," he says. "That brute in the tap-room he'll eat your heart out."

"That's what you think," says the Master, snarling. "I'll lay you a quid the Kid chews him up."

The groom he shook his head, but kept looking at me so sorry-like that I begun to get a bit sad myself. He seemed like he couldn't bear to leave off a-patting of me, and he says, speaking low just like he would to a man-folk, "well, good luck to you, little pup," which I thought so civil of him that I reached up and licked his hand. I don't do that to many men. And the Master he knew I didn't, and took on dreadful.

"What 'ave you got on the back of your hand?" says he, jumping up.

"Soap!' says the groom, quick as a rat. "That's more than you've got on yours. Do you want to smell of it?" and he sticks his fist under the Master's nose. But the pals pushed in between 'em.

"He tried to poison the Kid" shouts the Master.

"Oh, one fight at a time," says the referee. "Get into the ring, Jerry We're waiting." So we went into the ring.

I never could just remember what did happen in that ring. He give me no time to spring. He fell on me like a horse. I couldn't keep my feet against him, and though, as I saw, he could get his hold when he liked, he wanted to chew me over a bit first. I was wondering if they'd be able to pry him off me, when, in the third round, he took his hold; and I begun to drown, just as I did when I fell into the river off the Red C slip. He closed deeper and deeper on my throat, and everything went black and red and bursting; and then, when I was sure I were dead, the handlers pulled him off, and the Master give me a kick that brought me to. But I couldn't move none, or even wink, both eyes being shut with lumps.

"He's a cur!" yells the Master, "a sneaking, cowardly cur! He lost the fight for me," says he, "because he's a ------ cowardly cur." And he kicks me again in the lower ribs, so that I go sliding across the sawdust.

"There's gratitude fer yer," yells the Master. "I've fed that dog, and nussed that dog and housed him like a prince; and now he puts his tail between his legs and sells me out, he does. He's a coward!

I've done with him, I am. I'd sell him for a pipeful of tobacco." He picked me up by the tail, and swung me for the men-folks to see. "Does any gentleman here want to buy a dog," he says, "to make into sausage meat?" he says. "That's all he's good for."

Then I heard the little Irish groom say, "I'll give you ten bob for the dog."

And another voice says, "Ah, don't you do it; the dog's same as dead--mebbe he is dead."

"Ten shillings!" says the Master, and his voice sobers a bit; "make it two pounds and he's yours."

But the pals rushed in again.

"Don't you be a fool, Jerry," they say. "You'll be sorry for this when you're. sober. The Kid's worth a fiver." One of my eyes was not so swelled up as the other, and as I hung by my tail, I opened it, and saw one of the pals take the groom by the shoulder.

"You ought to give 'im five pounds for that dog, mate," he says; "that's no ordinary dog. That dog's got good blood in him, that dog has. Why, his father--that very dog's father--"

I thought he never would go on. He waited like he wanted to be sure the groom was listening.

"That very dog's father," says the pal, "is Regent Royal, son of Champion Regent Monarch, champion bull-terrier of England for four years."

I was sore, and torn, and chewed most awful, but what the pal said sounded so fine that I wanted to wag my tail, only couldn't, owing to my hanging from it.

But the Master calls out: "Yes, his father was Regent Royal; who's saying he wasn't but the pup's a cowardly cur, that's what his pup is.

And why? I'll tell you why: because his mother was a black-and-tan street-dog, that's why!"

I don't see how I got the strength, but, someway I threw myself out of the Master's grip and fell at his feet, and turned over and fastened all my teeth in his ankle, just across the bone.

When I woke, after the pals had kicked me off him, I was in the smoking-car of a railroad-train, lying in the lap of the little groom, and he was rubbing my open wounds with a greasy yellow stuff, exquisite to the smell and most agreeable to lick off.

PART II

"WELL, what's your name--Nolan? Well, Nolan, these references are satisfactory," said the young gentleman my new Master called "Mr. Wyndham, sir" . . . "I'll take you on as second man. You can begin to-day."

My new Master shuffled his feet and put his finger to his forehead. "Thank you. sir," says he. Then he choked like he had swallowed a fish-bone. "I have a little dawg, sir," says he.

"You can't keep him" says "Mr. Wyndham, sir," very short.

"'E's only a puppy, sir," says my new Master; "'e wouldn't go outside the stables, sir."

"It's not that," says "Mr. Wyndham, sir." "I have a large kennel of very fine dogs; they're the best of their breed in America. I don't allow strange dogs on the premises."

The Master shakes his head, and motions me with his cap, and I crept out from behind the door. "I'm sorry, sir," says the Master. "Then I can't take the place. I can't get along without the dawg, sir."

"Mr. Wyndham, sir," looked at me that fierce that I guessed he was going to whip me, so I turned over on my back and begged with my legs and tail.

"Why, you beat him!" says "Mr. Wyndham, sir," very stern.

"No fear!" the Master says, getting very red. "The party I bought him off taught him that. He never learnt that from me!" He picked me up in his arms, and to show "Mr. Wyndham, sir," how well I loved the Master, I bit his chin and hands.

"Mr. Wyndham, sir," turned over the letters the Master had given him.
"Well, these references certainly are very strong," he says. "I guess I'll let the dog stay. Only see you keep him away from the kennels--- or you'll both go."

"Thank you, sir," says the Master, grinning like a cat when she's safe behind the area railing.

"He's not a bad bull-terrier," says "Mr. Wyndham, sir," feeling my head.
"Not that I know much about the smooth-coated breeds. My dogs are St. Bernards." He stopped patting me and held up my nose.
"What's the matter with his ears?" he says. "They're chewed to pieces. Is this a fighting dog?" he asks, quick and rough like.

I could have laughed. If he hadn't been holding my nose, I certainly would have had a good grin at him. Me the best under thirty pounds in the Province of Quebec, and him asking if I was a fighting dog! I ran to the Master and hung down my head modest-like, waiting for him to tell my list of battles, but the Master he coughs in his cap most painful.
"Fightin' dawg, sir!" he cries. "Lor' bless you sir, the Kid don't know the word. E's just a puppy sir, same as you see; a pet dog, so to speak. E's a regular old lady's lap-dog the Kid is."

"Well, you keep him away from my St. Bernards," says "Mr. Wyndham,sir," . . . "or they might make a mouthful of him."

"Yes, sir; that they might," says the Master. But when we gets outside he slaps his knee and laughs inside hisself, and winks at me most sociable.

The Master's new home was in the country, in a province they called Long Island. There was a high stone wall about his home with big iron gates to it, same as Godfrey's brewery; and there was a house with five red roofs; and the stables, where I lived, was cleaner than the aerated bakery shop.

And then there was the kennels; but they was like nothing else in this world that ever I see. For the first days I couldn't sleep of nights for fear some one would catch me lying in such a cleaned-up place, and would chase me out of it; and when I did fall to sleep I'd dream I was back in the old Master's attic, shivering tinder the rusty stove, which never had no coals in it, with the Master flat on his back on the cold floor, with his clothes on. And I'd wake up scared and whimpering, and find myself on the new Master's cot with his hand on the quilt beside me; and I'd see the glow of the big stove, and hear the high-quality horses below-stairs stamping in their straw-lined boxes, and I'd snoop the sweet smell of hay and harness-soap and go to sleep again. The stables was my jail, so the Master said, but I don't ask no better home than that jail.

"Now, Kid," says he, sitting on the top of a bucket upside down, "you've got to understand this. When I whistle it means you're not to go out of this 'ere yard. These stables is your jail. If you leave 'em I'll have to leave 'em too, and over the seas, in the County Mayo, an old mother will 'ave to leave her bit of a cottage. For two pounds I must be sending her every month, or she'll have naught to eat, nor no thatch over 'er head. I can't lose my place, Kid, so see you don't lose it for me. You must keep away from the kennels," says he; "they're not for the likes of you. The kennels are for the quality. I wouldn't take a litter of them woolly dogs for one wag of your tail, Kid, but for all that they are your betters, same as the gentry up in the big house are my betters. I know my place and keep away from the gentry, and you keep away from the champions."

So I never goes out of the stables. All day I just lay in the sun on the stone flags, licking my jaws, and watching the grooms wash down the carriages, and the only care I had was to see they didn't get gay and turn the hose on me. There wasn't even a single rat to plague me. Such stables I never did see.

"Nolan," says the head groom, "some day that dog of yours will give you the slip. You can't keep a street-dog tied up all his life. It's against his natur'." The head groom is a nice old gentleman, but he doesn't know everything. just as though I'd been a street-dog because I liked it! As if I'd rather poke for my vittles in ash-heaps than have 'em handed me in a wash-basin, and would sooner bite and fight than be polite and sociable. If I'd had mother there I couldn't have asked for nothing more. But I'd think of her snooping in the gutters, or freezing of nights under the bridges, or, what's worst of all, running through the hot streets with her tongue down, so wild and crazy for a drink that the people would shout "mad dog" at her and stone her. Water's so good that I don't blame the men folks for locking it up inside their houses: but when the hot days come, I think they might remember that those are the dog days, and leave a little water outside in a trough, like they do for the horses. Then we wouldn't go mad, and the policemen wouldn't shoot us. I had so much of everything I wanted that it made me think a lot of the days when I hadn't nothing, and if I could have given what I had to mother, as she used to share with me, I'd have been the happiest dog in the land. Not that I wasn't happy then, and most grateful to the Master, too, and if I'd only minded him, the trouble wouldn't have come again.

But one day the coachman says that the little lady they called Miss Dorothy had come back from school, and that same morning she runs over to the stables to pat her ponies, and she sees me.

"Oh, what a nice little, white little dog!" said she. "Whose little dog are you?" says she.

"That's my dog, miss," says the Master. "'Is name is Kid." And I ran up to her most polite, and licks her fingers, for I never see so pretty and kind a lady.

"You must come with me and call on my new puppies," says she, picking me up in her arms and starting off with me.

"Oh, but please, miss," cries Nolan, "Mr. Wyndham give orders that the Kid's not to go to the kennels!"

"That'll be all right," says the little lady; "they're my kennels too. And the puppies will like to play with him."

You wouldn't believe me if I was to tell you of the style of them quality-dogs. If I hadn't seen it myself I wouldn't have believed it neither. The Viceroy of Canada don't live no better. There was forty of them, but each one had his own house and a yard--most exclusive--and a cot and a drinking-basin all to hisself. They had servants standing round waiting to feed 'em when they was hungry, and valets to wash em; and they had their hair combed and brushed like the grooms must when they go out on the box. Even the puppies had overcoats with their names on 'em in blue letters, and the name of each of those they called champions was painted up fine over his front door just like it was a public house or a veterinary's. They were the biggest St. Bernards I ever did see. I could have walked under them if they'd have let me. But they were very proud and haughty dogs, and looked only once at me, and then sniffed in the air. The little lady's own dog was an old gentleman bull-dog. He'd come along with us, and when he notices how taken aback I was with all I see, 'e turned quite kind and affable and showed me about.

"Jimmy Jocks," Miss Dorothy called him, but, owing to his weight, he walked most dignified and slow, waddling like a duck, as you might say, and looked much too proud and handsome for such a silly name.

"That's the runway, and that's the trophy house," says he to me, "and that over there is the hospital, where you have to go if you get distemper, and the vet gives you beastly medicine."

"And which of these is your 'ouse, sir?" asks I, wishing to be respectful. But he looked that hurt and haughty. "I don't live in the kennels," says he, most contemptuous. "I am a house-dog. I sleep in

Miss Dorothy's room. And at lunch I'm let in with the family, if the visitors don't mind. They 'most always do, but they're too polite to say so. Besides," says he, smiling most condescending, visitors are always afraid of me. It's because I'm so ugly," says he. "I suppose," says he, screwing up his wrinkles and speaking very slow and impressive, "I suppose I'm the ugliest bulldog in America;" and as he seemed to be so pleased to think hisself so, I said, "Yes, sir; you certainly are the ugliest ever I seen." At which he nodded his head most approving.

"But I couldn't hurt 'em, as you say," he goes on, though I hadn't said nothing like that, being too polite. "I'm too old," he says; "I haven't any teeth. The last time one of those grizzly bears," said he, glaring at the big St. Bernards, "took a hold of me, he nearly was my death," says he. I thought his eyes would pop out of his head, he seemed so wrought up about it. "He rolled me around in the dirt, he did," says Jimmy Jocks "an' I couldn't get up. It was low," says Jimmy Jocks making a face like he had a bad taste in his mouth. "Low, that's what I call it--bad form, you understand, young man, not done in my set-- and--and low." He growled 'way down in his stomach, and puffed hisself out, panting and blowing like he had been on a run.

"I'm not a street fighter," he says, scowling at a St. Bernard marked "Champion." "And when my rheumatism is not troubling me," he says, "I endeavor to be civil to all dogs, so long as they are gentlemen."

"Yes, sir," said I, for even to me he had been most affable.

At this we had come to a little house off by itself, and Jimmy Jocks invites me in. "This is their trophy room," he says, "where they keep their prizes. Mine," he says, rather grandlike, "are on the sideboard." Not knowing what a sideboard might be, I said, "Indeed, sir, that must be very gratifying." But he only wrinkled up his chops as much as to say, "It is my right."

The trophy-room was as wonderful as any public house I ever see.

On the walls was pictures of nothing but beautiful St. Bernard dogs, and rows and rows of blue and red and yellow ribbons; and when I asked Jimmy Jocks why they was so many more of blue than of the others, he laughs and says, "Because these kennels always win." And there was many shining cups on the shelves, which Jimmy Jocks told me were prizes won by the champions.

"Now, sir, might I ask you, sir," says I, "wot is a champion?"

At that he panted and breathed so hard I thought he would bust hisself. "My dear young friend!" says he, "wherever have you been educated? A champion is a--a champion," he says. "He must win nine blue ribbons in the 'open' class. You follow me that is--against all comers. Then he has the title before his name, and they put his photograph in the sporting papers. You know, of course, that I am a champion," says he. 'I am Champion Woodstock Wizard III and the two other Woodstock Wizards, my father and uncle, were both champions."

"But I thought your name was Jimmy Jocks," I said.

He laughs right out at that.

"That's my kennel name, not my registered name," he says. "Why, certainly you know that every dog has two names. Now, for instance, what's your registered name and number?" says he.

"I've got only one name," I says, "Just Kid."

Woodstock Wizard puffs at that and wrinkles up his forehead and pops out his eyes.

"Who are your people?" says he. "Where is your home?"
"At the stable, sir," I said. "My Master is the second groom."

At that Woodstock Wizard III looks at me for quite a bit without winking, and stares all around the room over my head.

"Oh, well," says he at last, "you're a very civil young dog," says he, "and I blame no one for what he can't help." which I thought most fair and liberal. "And I have known many bull-terriers that were champions," says he, "though as a rule they mostly run with fire-engines and to fighting. For me, I wouldn't care to run through the streets after a hose-cart, nor to fight," says he: "but each to his taste."

I could not help thinking that if Woodstock Wizard III tried to follow a fire-engine he would die of apoplexy, and seeing he'd lost his teeth, it was lucky he had no taste for fighting; but, after his being so condescending, I didn't say nothing.

"Anyway," says he, "every smooth-coated dog is better than any hairy old camel like those St. Bernards, and if ever you're hungry down at the stables, young man, come up to the house and I'll give you a

bone. I can't eat them myself, but I bury them around the garden from force of habit and in case a friend should drop in. Ah, I see my mistress coming," he says, "and I bid you good day. I regret," he says, "that our different social position prevents our meeting frequent, for you're a worthy young dog with a proper respect for your betters, and in this country there's precious few of them have that." Then he waddles off, leaving me alone and very sad, for he was the first dog in many days that had spoke to me. But since he showed, seeing that I was a stable-dog, he didn't want my company, I waited for him to get well away. It was not a cheerful place to wait, the trophy-house. The pictures of the champions seemed to scowl at me, and ask what right such as I had even to admire them, and the blue and gold ribbons and the silver cups made me very miserable. I had never won no blue ribbons or silver cups, only stakes for the old Master to spend in the publics; and I hadn't won them for being a beautiful high-quality dog, but just for fighting--which, of course, as Woodstock Wizard Ill says, is low. So I started for the stables, with my head down and my tail between my legs, feeling sorry I had ever left the Master.
But I had more reason to be sorry before I got back to him.

The trophy-house was quite a bit from the kennels, and as I left it I see Miss Dorothy and Woodstock Wizard Ill walking back toward them, and also, that a big St. Bernard, his name was Champion Red

Elfberg, had broke his chain and was running their way. When he reaches old Jimmy Jocks he lets out a roar like a grain-steamer in a fog, and he makes three leaps for him. Old Jimmy Jocks was about a fourth his size; but he plants his feet and curves his back, and his hair goes up around his neck like a collar. But he never had no show at no time, for the grizzly bear, as Jimmy Jocks had called him, lights on old Jimmy's back and tries to break it, and old Jimmy Jocks snaps his gums and claws the grass, panting and groaning awful. But he can't do nothing, and the grizzly bear just rolls him under him, biting and tearing cruel. The odds was all that Woodstock Wizard III was going to be killed; I had fought enough to see that: but not knowing the rules of the game among champions, I didn't like to interfere between two gentlemen who might be settling a private affair, and, as it were, take it as presuming of me. So I stood by, though I was shaking terrible, and holding myself in like I was on a leash. But at that

Woodstock Wizard III, who was underneath, sees me through the dust, and calls very faint, "Help, you!" he says. "Take him in the hind-leg," he says. "He's murdering me," he says. And then the little Miss Dorothy, who was crying, and calling to the kennel-men, catches at the Red Elfberg's hind-legs to pull him off, and the brute, keeping his front pats well in Jimmy's stomach, turns his big head and snaps at her. So that was all I asked for, thank you. I went up under him. It was really nothing. He stood so high that I had only to take off about three feet from him and come in from the side, and my long "punishing jaw," as mother was always talking about, locked on his woolly throat, and my back teeth met. I couldn't shake him, but I shook myself, and every time I shook myself there was thirty pounds of weight tore at his windpipes. I couldn't see nothing for his long hair, but I heard Jimmy Jocks puffing and blowing on one side, and munching the brute's leg with his old gums. Jimmy was an old sport that day, was Jimmy, or Woodstock Wizard III, as I should say. When the Red Elfberg was out and down I had to run, or those kennel-men would have had my life. They chased me right into the stables; and from under the hay I watched the head groom take down a carriage whip and order them to the right about. Luckily Master and the young grooms were out, or that day there'd have been fighting for everybody.

Well, it nearly did for me and the Master. "Mr. Wyndham, sir," comes raging to the stables. I'd half killed his best prize-winner, he says, and had oughter be shot, and he gives the Master his notice. But Miss Dorothy she follows him, and says it was his Red Elfberg what began the fight, and that I'd saved Jimmy's life, and that old Jimmy Jocks was worth more to her than all the St. Bernards in the Swiss mountains-wherever they may be. And that I was her champion, anyway. Then she cried over me most beautiful, and over Jimmy Jocks, too, who was that tied up in bandages he couldn't even waddle. So when he heard that side of it, "Mr. Wyndham, sir," told us that if Nolan put me on a chain we could stay. So it came out all right for everybody but me. I was glad the Master kept his place, but I'd never worn a chain before, and it disheartened me. But that was the least of it. For the quality-dogs couldn't forgive my whipping their champion, and they came to the fence between the kennels and the stables, and laughed through the bars, barking most cruel words at me. I couldn't understand how they found it out, but they knew. After the fight Jimmy Jocks was most condescending to me, and he said the grooms had boasted to the kennel-men that I was a son of Regent Royal, and that when the kennel men asked who was my mother they had had to tell them that too. Perhaps that was the way of it, but, however, the scandal got out, and every one of the quality-dogs knew that I was a street-dog and the son of a black-and-tan.

"These misalliances will occur," said Jimmy Jocks, in his old-fashioned way; "but no well-bred dog," says he, looking most scornful at the St.Bernards, who were howling behind the palings, "would refer to your misfortune before you, certainly not cast it in your face. I myself remember your father's father, when he made his debut at the Crystal Palace. He took four blue ribbons and three specials."

But no sooner than Jimmy would leave me the St. Bernards would take to howling again, insulting mother and insulting me. And when I tore at my chain, they, seeing they were safe, would howl the more. It was never the same after that; the laughs and the jeers cut into my heart, and the chain bore heavy on my spirit. I was so sad that sometimes I wished I was back in the gutter again, where no one was better than me, and some nights I wished I was dead. If it hadn't been for the Master being so kind, and that it would have looked like I was blaming mother, I would have twisted my leash and hanged myself.

About a month after my fight, the word was passed through the kennels that the New York Show was coming, and such goings on as followed I never did see. If each of them had been matched to fight for a thousand pounds and the gate, they couldn't have trained more conscientious. But perhaps that's just my envy. The kennel-men rubbed 'em and scrubbed 'ern, and trims their hair and curls and combs it, and some dogs. they fatted and some they starved. No one talked of nothing but the Show, and the chances "our kennels" had against the other kennels, and if this one of our champions would win over that one, and whether them as hoped to be champions had better show in the "open" or the "limit" class, and whether this dog would beat his own dad, or whether his little puppy sister couldn't beat the two of 'em. Even the grooms had their money up, and day or night you heard nothing but praises of "our" dogs, until I, being so far out of it, couldn't have felt meaner if I had been running the streets with a can to my tail. I knew shows were not for such as me, and so all day I lay stretched at the end of my chain, pretending I was asleep, and only too glad that they had something so important to think of that they could leave me alone.

But one day, before the Show opened, Miss Dorothy came to the stables with "Mr. Wyndham, sir," and seeing me chained up and so miserable, she takes me in her arms.

"You poor little tyke!" says she. "It's cruel to tie him up so; he's eating his heart out, Nolan," she says. "I don't know nothing about bull-terriers," says she, "but I think Kid's got good points," says she, "and you ought to show him. Jimmy Jocks has three legs on the Rensselaer Cup now, and I'm going to show him this time, so that he can get the fourth; and, if you wish, I'll enter your dog too. How would you like that, Kid?" says she. "How would you like to see the most beautiful dogs in the world? Maybe you'd meet a pal or two," says she. "It would cheer you up, wouldn't it, Kid?" says she. But I was so upset I could only wag my tail most violent. "He says it would!" says she, though, being that excited, I hadn't said nothing.

So "Mr. Wyndham, sir," laughs, and takes out a piece of blue paper and sits down at the head groom's table.

"What's the name of the father of your dog, Nolan?" says he. And Nolan says: "The man I got him off told me he was a son of Champion Regent Royal, sir. But it don't seem likely, does it?" says Nolan.

"It does not!" says "Mr. Wyndham, sir," short-like.

"Aren't you sure, Nolan?" says Miss Dorothy.

"No, miss," says the Master.

"Sire unknown," says "Mr. Wyndham, sir," and writes it down.

"Date of birth?" asks "Mr. Wyndham, sir."

"I--I--unknown, sir," says Nolan. And "Mr. Wyndham, sir," writes it down.

"Breeder?" says "Mr. Wyndham, sir."

"Unknown," says Nolan, getting very red around the jaws, and I drops my head and tail. And "Mr. Wyndham, sir," writes that down.

"Mother's name says "Mr. Wyndham, sir."

"She was a-unknown," says the Master. And I licks his hand.

"Dam unknown," says "Mr. Wyndham, sir," and writes it down. Then he takes the paper and reads out loud: "'Sire unknown, dam unknown, breeder unknown, date of birth unknown.' You'd better call him the 'Great Unknown'," says he. "Who's paying his entrance fee?"
"I am," says Miss Dorothy.

Two weeks after we all got on a train for New York, Jimmy Jocks and me following Nolan in the smoking-car, and twenty-two of the St. Bernards in boxes and crates and on chains and leashes. Such a barking and howling I never did hear; and when they sees me going, too, they laughs fit to kill.

"Wot is this-a circus?" says the railroad man.

But I had no heart in it. I hated to go. I knew I was no "show" dog, even though Miss Dorothy and the Master did their best to keep me from sharing them. For before we set out Miss Dorothy brings a man from town who scrubbed and rubbed me, and sandpapered my tail, which hurt most awful, and shaved my ears with the Master's razor, so you could 'most see clear through 'em, and sprinkles me over with pipe clay, till I shines like a Tommy's cross-belts.

"Upon my word!" says Jimmy Jocks when he first sees me. "Wot a swell you are! You're the image of your grand-dad when he made his debut at the Crystal Palace. He took four firsts and three specials." But I knew he was only trying to throw heart into me. They might scrub, and they might rub, and they might pipe-clay, but they couldn't pipe-clay the insides of me, and they was black-and-tan.

Then we came to a garden, which it was not, but the biggest hall in the world. Inside there was lines of benches a few miles long, and on them sat every dog in America. If all the dog-snatchers in Montreal had worked night and day for a year, they couldn't have caught so many dogs. An they was all shouting and barking and howling so vicious that my heart stopped beating. For at first I thought they was all enraged at my presuming to intrude. But after I got in my place they kept at it just the same, barking at every dog as he came in: daring him to fight, and ordering him out, and asking him what breed of dog he thought he was, anyway. Jimmy Jocks was chained just behind me, and he said he never see so fine a show. "That's a hot class you're in, my lad," he says, looking over into my street, where there were thirty bull-terriers. They was all as white as cream, and each so beautiful that if I could have broke my chain I would have run all the way home and hid myself under the horse-trough.

All night long they talked and sang, and passed greetings with old pals, and the homesick puppies howled dismal. Them that couldn't sleep wouldn't let no others sleep, and all the electric lights burned in the roof, and in my eyes. I could hear Jimmy Jocks snoring peaceful, but I could only doze by jerks, and when I dozed I dreamed horrible. All the dogs in the hall seemed coming at me for daring to intrude, with their jaws red and open, and their eyes blazing like the lights in the roof. "You're a street-dog! Get out, you street-dog!" they yells. And as they drives me out, the pipe-clay drops off me, and they laugh and shriek; and when I looks down I see that I have turned into a black-and-tan.

They was most awful dreams, and next morning, when Miss Dorothy comes and gives me water in a pan, I begs and begs her to take me home; but she can't understand. "How well Kid is!" she says. And when I jumps into the Master's arms and pulls to break my chain, he says, "If he knew all as he had against him, miss, he wouldn't be so gay." And from a book they reads out the names of the beautiful highbred terriers which I have got to meet. And I can't make 'em understand that I only want to run away and hide myself where no one will see me.

Then suddenly men comes hurrying down our street and begins to brush the beautiful bull-terriers; and the Master rubs me with a towel so excited that his hands trembles awful, and Miss Dorothy tweaks my ears between her gloves, so that the blood runs to 'em, and they turn pink and stand up straight and sharp.

"Now, then, Nolan," says she, her voice shaking just like his fingers, "keep his head up-and never let the judge lose sight of him." When I hears that my legs breaks under me, for I knows all about judges.

Twice the old Master goes up before the judge for fighting me with other dogs, and the judge promises him if he ever does it again he'll chain him up in jail. I knew he'd find me out. A judge can't be fooled by no pipe-clay. He can see right through you, and he reads your insides.

The judging-ring, which is where the judge holds out, was so like a fighting-pit that when I come in it, and find six other dogs there, I springs into position, so that when they lets us go I can defend myself. But the Master smooths down my hair and whispers, "Hold 'ard, Kid, hold 'ard. This ain't a fight," says he. "Look your prettiest," he whispers. "Please, Kid, look your prettiest;" and he pulls my leash so tight that I can't touch my pats to the sawdust, and my nose goes up in the air. There was millions of people a-watching us from the railings, and three of our kennel-men, too, making fun of the Master and me, and Miss Dorothy with her chin just reaching to the rail, and her eyes so big that I thought she was a-going to cry. It was awful to think that when the judge stood up and exposed me, all those people, and Miss Dorothy, would be there to see me driven from the Show.

The judge he was a fierce-looking man with specs on his nose, and a red beard. When I first come in he didn't see me, owing to my being too quick for him and dodging behind the Master. But when the Master drags me round and I pulls at the sawdust to keep back, the judge looks at us careless-like, and then stops and glares through his specs, and I knew it was all up with me.

"Are there any more?" asks the judge to the gentleman at the gate, but never taking his specs from me.

The man at the gate looks in his book. "Seven in the novice class," says he. "They're all here. You can go ahead," and he shuts the gate.

The judge he doesn't hesitate a moment. He just waves his hand toward the corner of the ring. "Take him away," he says to the Master, "over there, and keep him away;" and he turns and looks most solemn at the six beautiful bullterriers. I don't know how I crawled to that corner. I wanted to scratch under the sawdust and dig myself a grave. The kennel-men they slapped the rail with their hands and laughed at the Master like they would fall over. They pointed at me in the corner, and their sides just shaked. But little Miss Dorothy she presses her lips tight against the rail, and I see tears rolling from her eyes. The Master he hangs his head like he had been whipped. I felt most sorry for him than all. He was so red, and he was letting on not to see the kennel-men, and blinking his eyes. If the judge had ordered me right out it wouldn't have disgraced us so, but it was keeping me there while he was judging the highbred dogs that hurt so hard. With all those people staring, too. And his doing it so quick, without no doubt nor questions. You can't fool the judges. They see inside you.

But he couldn't make up his mind about them high-bred dogs. He scowls at 'em, and he glares at 'em, first with his head on the one side and then on the other. And he feels of 'em, and orders 'em to run about. And Nolan leans against the rails, with his head hung down, and pats me. And Miss Dorothy comes over beside him, but don't say nothing, only wipes her eye with her finger. A man on the other side of the rail he says to the Master, "The judge don't like your dog?"

"No," says the Master.

"Have you ever shown him before?" says the man.

"No," says the Master, "and I'll never show him again. He's my dog," says the Master, "and he suits me! And I don't care what no judges think." And when he says them kind words, I licks his hand most grateful.

The judge had two of the six dogs on a little platform in the middle of the ring, and he had chased the four other dogs into the corners, where they was licking their chops, and letting on they didn't care, same as Nolan was.

The two dogs on the platform was so beautiful that the judge hisself couldn't tell which was the best of 'em, even when he stoops down and holds their heads together. But at last he gives a sigh, and brushes the sawdust off his knees, and goes to the table in the ring, where there was a man keeping score, and heaps and heaps of blue and gold and red and yellow ribbons. And the judge picks up a bunch of 'em and walks to the two gentlemen who was holding the beautiful dogs, and he says to each, "What's his number?" and he hands each gentleman a ribbon. And then he turned sharp and comes straight at the Master.

"What's his number?" says the judge. And Master was so scared that he couldn't make no answer.

But Miss Dorothy claps her hands and cries out like she was laughing, "Three twenty-six," and the judge writes it down and shoves Master the blue ribbon.

I bit the Master, and I jumps and bit Miss Dorothy, and I waggled so hard that the Master couldn't hold me. When I get to the gate Miss

Dorothy snatches me up and kisses me between the ears, right before millions of people, and they both hold me so tight that I didn't know which of them was carrying of me. But one thing I knew, for I listened hard, as it was the judge hisself as said it.

"Did you see that puppy I gave first to?" says the judge to the gentleman at the gate.

"I did. He was a bit out of his class," says the gate gentleman.

"He certainly was!" says the judge, and they both laughed.

But I didn't care. They couldn't hurt me then, not with Nolan holding the blue ribbon and Miss Dorothy hugging my ears, and the kennel-men sneaking away, each looking like he'd been caught with his nose under the lid of the slop can.

We sat down together, and we all three just talked as fast as we could. They was so pleased that I couldn't help feeling proud myself, and I barked and leaped about so gay that all the bull-terriers in our street stretched on their chains and howled at me.

"Just look at him!" says one of those I had beat. "What's he giving hisself airs about?"

"Because he's got one blue ribbon!" says another of 'em. "Why, when I was a puppy I used to eat 'em, and if that judge could ever learn to know a toy from a mastiff, I'd have had this one."

But Jimmy Jocks he leaned over from his bench and says, "Well done, Kid. Didn't I tell you so?" What he 'ad told me was that I might get a "commended," but I didn't remind him.

"Didn't I tell you," says Jimmy Jocks, "that I saw your grandfather make his debut at the Crystal?"

"Yes, sir, you did, sir," says I, for I have no love for the men of my family.

A gentleman with a showing-leash around his neck comes up just then and looks at me very critical. "Nice dog you've got, Miss Wyndham," says he; "would you care to sell him?"

"He's not my dog," says Miss Dorothy, holding me tight. "I wish he were."

"He's not for sale, sir," says the Master, and I was that glad.

"Oh, he's yours, is he?" says the gentleman, looking hard at Nolan. "Well, I'll give you a hundred dollars for him," says he, careless-like.

"Thank you, sir; he's not for sale," says Nolan, but his eyes get very big. The gentleman he walked away; but I watches him, and he talks to a man in a golf-cap, and by and by the man comes along our street, looking at all the dogs, and stops in front of me.

"This your dog?" says he to Nolan. "Pity he's so leggy," says he. "If he had a good tail, and a longer stop, and his ears were set higher, he'd be a good dog. As he is, I'll give you fifty dollars for him."

But, before the Master could speak, Miss Dorothy laughs and says: "You're Mr. Polk's kennel-man, I believe. Well, you tell Mr. Polk from me that the dog's not for sale now any more than he was five minutes ago, and that when he is, he'll have to bid against me for him."

The man looks foolish at that, but he turns to Nolan quick-like. "I'll give you three hundred for him," he says.

"Oh, indeed!" whispers Miss Dorothy, like she was talking to herself. "That's it, is it?" And she turns and looks at me just as though she had never seen me before. Nolan he was a-gaping, too, with his mouth open. But he holds me tight.

"He's not for sale," he growls, like he was frightened; and the man looks black and walks away.

'Why, Nolan!" cries Miss Dorothy, "Mr. Polk knows more about bull-terriers than any amateur in America. What can he mean? Why, Kid is no more than a puppy! Three hundred dollars for a puppy!"

"And he ain't no thoroughbred, neither!" cries the Master. "He's 'Unknown,' ain't he? Kid can't help it, of course, but his mother, miss-"

I dropped my head. I couldn't bear he should tell Miss Dorothy. I couldn't bear she should know I had stolen my blue ribbon.

But the Master never told, for at that a gentleman runs up, calling, "Three twenty-six, three twenty six!" And Miss Dorothy says, "Here he is; what is it?"

"The Winners' class," says the gentleman. "Hurry, please; the judge is waiting for him."

Nolan tries to get me off the chain on to a showing-leash, but he shakes so, he only chokes me. "What is it, miss?" he says. "What is it?"

"The Winners' class," says Miss Dorothy. "The judge wants him with the winners of the other classes--to decide which is the best. It's only a form," says she. "He has the champions against him now."

"Yes," says the gentleman, as he hurries us to the ring. "I'm afraid it's only a form for your dog, but the judge wants all the winners, puppy class even."

We had got to the gate, and the gentleman there was writing down my number.

"Who won the open?" asks Miss Dorothy.

"Oh, who would?" laughs the gentleman. "The old champion, of course. He's won for three years now. There he is. Isn't he wonderful?" says he; and he points to a dog that's standing proud and haughty on the platform in the middle of the ring.

I never see so beautiful a dog-so fine and clean and noble, so white like he had rolled hisself in flour, holding his nose up and his eyes shut, same as though no one was worth looking at. Aside of him we other dogs, even though we had a blue ribbon apiece, seemed like lumps of mud. He was a royal gentleman, a king, he was. His master didn't have to hold his head with no leash. He held it hisself, standing as still as an iron dog on a lawn, like he knew all the people was looking at him. And so they was, and no one around the ring pointed at no other dog but him.

"Oh, what a picture!" cried Miss Dorothy. "He's like a marble figure by a great artist-one who loved dogs. Who is he?" says she, looking in her book. 'I don't keep up with terriers."

"Oh, you know him," says the gentleman. "He is the champion of champions, Regent Royal."

The Master's face went red.

"And this is Regent Royal's son," cries he, and he pulls me quick into the ring, and plants me on the platform next my father.

I trembled so that I near fell. My legs twisted like a leash. But my father he never looked at me. He only smiled the same sleepy smile, and he still kept his eyes half shut, like as no one, no, not even his own son, was worth his lookin' at.

The judge he didn't let me stay beside my father, but, one by one, he placed the other dogs next to him and measured and felt and pulled at them. And each one he put down, but he never put my father down. And then he comes over and picks up me and sets me back on the platform, shoulder to shoulder with the Champion Regent Royal, and goes down on his knees, and looks into our eyes.

The gentleman with my father he laughs, and says to the judge, "Thinking of keeping us here all day, John?" But the judge he doesn't hear him, and goes behind us and runs his hand down my side, and holds back my ears, and takes my jaws between his fingers. The crowd around the ring is very deep now, and nobody says nothing. The gentleman at the score-table, he is leaning forward, with his elbows on his knees and his eyes very wide, and the gentleman at the gate is whispering quick to Miss Dorothy, who has turned white. I stood as stiff as stone. I didn't even breathe. But out of the corner of my eye I could see my father licking his pink chops, and yawning just a little, like he was bored.

The judge he had stopped looking fierce and was looking solemn, Something inside him seemed a-troubling him awful. The more he stares at us now, the more solemn he gets, and when he touches us he does it gentle, like he was patting us. For a long time he kneels in the sawdust, looking at my father and at me, and no one around the ring says nothing to nobody.
Then the judge takes a breath and touches me sudden. "It's his," he says.
But he lays his hand just as quick on my father. "I'm sorry," says he.

The gentleman holding my father cries: "Do you mean to tell me-"

And the judge he answers, "I mean the other is the better dog." He takes my father's head between his hands and looks down at him most sorrowful. "The king is dead," says he. "Long live the king! Goodbye, Regent," he says.

The crowd around the railings clapped their hands, and some laughed scornful, and every one talks fast, and I start for the gate, so dizzy that I can't see my way. But my father pushes in front of me, walking very daintily, and smiling sleepy, same as he had just been waked, with his head high and his eyes shut, looking at nobody.

So that is how I "came by my inheritance," as Miss Dorothy calls it; and just for that, though I couldn't feel where I was any different, the crowd follows me to my bench, and pats me, and coos at me, like I was a baby in a baby carriage. And the handlers have to hold 'em back so that the gentlemen from the papers can make pictures of me, and Nolan walks me up and down so proud, and the men shake their heads and says, "He certainly is the true type, he is!" And the pretty ladies ask Miss Dorothy, who sits beside me letting me lick her gloves to show the crowd what friends we is, "Aren't you afraid he'll bite you?" And Jimmy Jocks calls to me, "Didn't I tell you so? I always knew you were one of us. Blood will out, Kid; blood will out. I saw your grandfather," says he, "make his debut at the Crystal Palace. But he was never the dog you are!"

After that, if I could have asked for it, there was nothing I couldn't get. You might have thought I was a snow-dog, and they was afeard I'd melt. If I wet my pats, Nolan gave me a hot bath and chained me to the stove; if I couldn't eat my food, being stuffed full by the cook,--for I am a house-dog now, and let in to lunch, whether there is visitors or not,--Nolan would run to bring the vet. It was all tommy rot, as Jimmy says, but meant most kind. I couldn't scratch myself comfortable, without Nolan giving me nasty drinks, and rubbing me outside till it burnt awful; and I wasn't let to eat bones f or fear of spoiling my "beautiful" mouth, what mother used to call my "punishing jaw;" and my food was cooked special on a gas-stove; and

Miss Dorothy gives me an overcoat, cut very stylish like the champions', to wear when we goes out carriage-driving.

After the next Show where I takes three blue ribbons, four silver cups, two medals, and brings home forty five dollars for Nolan, they gives me a "registered" name, same as Jimmy's. Miss Dorothy wanted to call me "Regent Heir Apparent;" but I was that glad when Nolan says, "No; Kid don't owe nothing to his father, only to you and hisself. So, if you please, miss, we'll call him Wyndham Kid." And so they did, and you can see it on my overcoat in blue letters, and painted top of my kennel. It was all too hard to understand. For days I just sat and wondered if I was really me, and how it all come about, and why everybody was so kind. But oh, it was so good they was, for if they hadn't been I'd never have got the thing I most wished after. But, because they was kind, and not liking to deny me nothing, they gave it me, and it was more to me than anything in the world.

It came about one day when we was out driving. We was in the cart they calls the dog-cart because it's the one Miss Dorothy keeps to take Jimmy and me for an airing. Nolan was up behind, and me, in my new overcoat, was sitting beside Miss Dorothy. I was admiring the view, and thinking how good it was to have a horse pull you about so that you needn't get yourself splashed and have to be washed, when I hears a dog calling loud for help, and I pricks up my ears and looks over the horse's head. And I sees something that makes me tremble down to my toes. In the road before us three big dogs was chasing a little old lady-dog. She had a string to her tail, where some boys had tied a can, and she was dirty with mud and ashes, and most awful. She was too far done up to get away, and too old to help herself, but she was making a fight for her life, snapping her old gums savage, and dying game. All this I see in a wink, and then the three dogs pinned her down, and I can't stand it no longer, and clears the wheel and lands in the road on my head. It was my stylish overcoat done that, and I cursed it proper, but I gets my pats again quick, and makes a rush for the fighting. Behind me I hear Miss Dorothy cry: "They'll kill that old dog. Wait, take my whip. Beat them off her!

The Kid can take care of himself;" and I hear Nolan fall into the road, and the horse come to a stop. The old lady-dog was down, and the three was eating her vicious; but as I come up, scattering the pebbles, she hears, and thinking it's one more of them, she lifts her head, and my heart breaks open like some one had sunk his teeth in it. For, under the ashes and the dirt and the blood, I can see who it is, and I know that my mother has come back to me.

I gives a yell that throws them three dogs off their legs.

"Mother!" I cries. "I'm the Kid," I cries. "I'm coming to you. Mother, I'm coming!"

And I shoots over her at the throat of the big dog, and the other two they sinks their teeth into that stylish overcoat and tears it off me, and that sets me free, and I lets them have it. I never had so fine a fight as that! What with mother being there to see, and not having been let to mix up in no fights since I become a prizewinner, it just naturally did me good, and it wasn't three shakes before I had 'em yelping. Quick as a wink, mother she jumps into help me, and I just laughed to see her. It was so like old times. And Nolan he made me laugh, too. He was like a hen on a bank, shaking the butt of his whip, but not daring to cut in for fear of hitting me.

"Stop it, Kid," he says, "stop it. Do you want to be all torn up?" says he. "Think of the Boston show," says he. "Think of Chicago. Think of Danbury. Don't you never want to be a champion?"

How was I to think of all them places when I had three dogs to cut up at the same time? But in a minute two of 'em begs for mercy, and mother and me lets 'em run away. The big one he ain't able to run away. Then mother and me we dances and jumps, and barks and laughs, and bites each other and rolls each other in the road. There never was two dogs so happy as we. And Nolan he whistles and calls and begs me to come to him; but I just laugh and play larks with mother.

"Now, you come with me," says I, "to my new home, and never try to run away again." And I shows her our house with the five red roofs, set on the top of the hill. But mother trembles awful, and says: "They'd never let me in such a place. Does the Viceroy live there, Kid?" says she. And I laugh at her. "No; I do," I says. "And if they won't let you live there, too, you and me will go back to the streets together, for we must never be parted no more." So we trots up the hill side by side, with Nolan trying to catch me, and Miss Dorothy laughing at him from the cart.

"The Kid's made friends with the poor old dog," says she. "Maybe he knew her long ago when he ran the streets himself. Put her in here beside me, and see if he doesn't follow."

So when I hears that I tells mother to go with Nolan and sit in the cart; but she says no-that she'd soil the pretty lady's frock; but I tells her to do as I say, and so Nolan lifts her, trembling still, into the cart, and I runs alongside, barking joyful.

When we drives into the stables I takes mother to my kennel, and tells her to go inside it and make herself at home. "Oh, but he won't let me!" says she.

"Who won't let you?" says I, keeping my eye on Nolan, and growling a bit nasty, just to show I was meaning to have my way.

"Why, Wyndham Kid," says she, looking up at the name on my kennel.

"But I'm Wyndham Kid!" says I. "You!" cries mother. "You! Is my little Kid the great Wyndham Kid the dogs all talk about?" And at that, she being very old, and sick, and nervous, as mothers are, just drops down in the straw and weeps bitter.

Well, there ain't much more than that to tell. Miss Dorothy she settled it.

"If the Kid wants the poor old thing in the stables," says she, "let her

110

stay."

"You see," says she, "she's a black-and-tan, and his mother was a black-and-tan, and maybe that's what makes Kid feel so friendly toward her," says she.

"Indeed, for me," says Nolan, "she can have the best there is. I'd never drive out no dog that asks for a crust nor a shelter," he says. "But what will Mr. Wyndham do?"

"He'll do what I say," says Miss Dorothy, "and if I say she's to stay, she will stay, and I say-she's to stay!"

And so mother and Nolan and me found a home. Mother was scared at first--not being used to kind people; but she was so gentle and loving that the grooms got fonder of her than of me, and tried to make me jealous by patting of her and giving her the pick of the vittles. But that was the wrong way to hurt my feelings. That's all, I think. Mother is so happy here that I tell her we ought to call it the Happy Hunting Grounds, because no one hunts you, and there is nothing to hunt; it just all comes to you. And so we live in peace, mother sleeping all day in the sun, or behind the stove in the head groom's office, being fed twice a day regular by Nolan, and all the day by the other grooms most irregular.

And as for me, I go hurrying around the country to the bench shows, winning money and cups for Nolan, and taking the blue ribbons away from father.

VAN BIBBER AT THE RACES

Young Van Bibber had never spent a Fourth of July in the city, as he had always understood it was given over to armies of small boys on that day, who sat on all the curbstones and set off fire-crackers, and that the thermometer always showed ninety degrees in the shade, and cannon boomed and bells rang from daybreak to midnight. He had refused all invitations to join any Fourth-of-July parties at the seashore or on the Sound or at Tuxedo, because he expected his people home from Europe, and had to be in New York to meet them. He was accordingly greatly annoyed when he received a telegram saying they would sail in a boat a week later.

He finished his coffee at the club on the morning of the Fourth about ten o'clock, in absolute solitude, and with no one to expect and nothing to anticipate; so he asked for a morning paper and looked up the amusements offered for the Fourth. There were plenty of excursions with brass bands, and refreshments served on board, baseball matches by the hundred, athletic meetings and picnics by the dozen, but nothing that seemed to exactly please him.

The races sounded attractive, but then he always lost such a lot of money, and the crowd pushed so, and the sun and the excitement made his head ache between the eyes and spoiled his appetite for dinner. He had vowed again and again that he would not go to the races; but as the day wore on and the solitude of the club became oppressive and the silence of the Avenue began to tell on him, he changed his mind, and made his preparations accordingly.

First, he sent out after all the morning papers and read their tips on the probable winners. Very few of them agreed, so he took the horse which most of them seemed to think was best, and determined to back it, no matter what might happen or what new tips he might get later. Then he put two hundred dollars in his pocket-book to bet with, and twenty dollars for expenses, and sent around for his field-glasses.

He was rather late in starting, and he made up his mind on the way to Morris Park that he would be true to the list of winners he had written out, and not make any side bets on any suggestions or inside information given him by others. He vowed a solemn vow on the rail of the boat to plunge on each of the six horses he had selected from the newspaper tips, and on no others. He hoped in this way to win something. He did not care so much to win, but he hated to lose. He always felt so flat and silly after it was over; and when it happened, as it often did, that he had paid several hundred dollars for the afternoon's sport, his sentiments did him credit.

"I shall probably, or rather certainly, be tramped on and shoved," soliloquized Van Bibber.

"I shall smoke more cigars than are good for me, and drink more than I want, owing to the unnatural excitement and heat, and I shall be late for my dinner. And for all this I shall probably pay two hundred dollars. It really seems as if I were a young man of little intellect, and yet thousands of others are going to do exactly the same thing."

The train was very late. One of the men in front said they would probably just be able to get their money up in time for the first race. A horse named Firefly was Van Bibber's choice, and he took one hundred dollars of his two hundred to put up on her. He had it already in his hand when the train reached the track, and he hurried with the rest towards the bookmakers to get his one hundred on as quickly as possible. But while he was crossing the lawn back of the stand, he heard cheers and wild yells that told him they were running the race at that moment.

"Raceland!" "Raceland!" "Raceland by a length!" shouted the crowd.

"Who's second?" a fat man shouted at another fat man.

"Firefly," called back the second, joyously, "and I've got her for a place and I win eight dollars."

"Ah!" said Van Bibber, as he slipped his one hundred dollars back in his pocket, "good thing I got here a bit late."

"What'd you win, Van Bibber?" asked a friend who rushed past him, clutching his tickets as though they were precious stones.

"I win one hundred dollars," answered Van Bibber, calmly, as he walked on up into the boxes. It was delightfully cool up there, and to his satisfaction and surprise he found several people there whom he knew. He went into Her box and accepted some *pâté* sandwiches and iced champagne, and chatted and laughed with Her so industriously, and so much to the exclusion of all else, that the horses were at the starting-post before he was aware of it, and he had to excuse himself hurriedly and run to put up his money on Bugler, the second on his list. He decided that as he had won one hundred dollars on the first race he could afford to plunge on this one, so he counted out fifty more, and putting this with the original one hundred dollars, crowded into the betting-ring and said, "A hundred and fifty on Bugler straight."

"Bugler's just been scratched," said the bookie, leaning over Van Bibber's shoulder for a greasy five-dollar bill.

"Will you play anything else?" he asked, as the young gentleman stood there irresolute.

"No, thank you," said Van Bibber, remembering his vow, and turning hastily away. "Well," he mused, "I'm one hundred and fifty dollars better off than I might have been if Bugler hadn't been scratched and hadn't won. One hundred and fifty dollars added to one hundred makes two hundred and fifty dollars. That puts me 'way ahead of the game. I am fifty dollars better off than when I left New York. I'm playing in great luck." So, on the strength of this, he bought out the man who sells bouquets, and ordered more champagne to be sent up to the box where She was sitting, and they all congratulated him on his winnings, which were suggested by his generous and sudden expenditures.

"You must have a great eye for picking a winner," said one of the older men, grudgingly.

"Y-e-s," said Van Bibber, modestly. "I know a horse when I see it, I think; and," he added to himself, "that's about all."

His horse for the third race was Rover, and the odds were five to one against him. Van Bibber wanted very much to bet on Pirate King instead, but he remembered his vow to keep to the list he had originally prepared, whether he lost or won. This running after strange gods was always a losing business. He took one hundred dollars in five-dollar bills, and went down to the ring and put the hundred up on Rover and returned to the box. The horses had been weighed in and the bugle had sounded, and three of the racers were making their way up the track, when one of them plunged suddenly forward and went down on his knees and then stretched out dead. Van Bibber was confident it was Rover, although he had no idea which the horse was, but he knew his horse would not run. There was a great deal of excitement, and people who did not know the rule, which requires the return of all money if any accident happens to a horse on the race-track between the time of weighing in and arriving at the post, were needlessly alarmed. Van Bibber walked down to the ring and received his money back with a smile.

"I'm just one hundred dollars better off than I was three minutes ago," he said. "I've really had a most remarkable day."

Mayfair was his choice for the fourth race, and she was selling at three to one. Van Bibber determined to put one hundred and seventy-five dollars up on her, for, as he said, he had not lost on any one race yet. The girl in the box was very interesting, though, and Van Bibber found a great deal to say to her. He interrupted himself once to call to one of the messenger-boys who ran with bets, and gave him one hundred and seventy-five dollars to put on Mayfair.

Several other gentlemen gave the boy large sums as well, and Van Bibber continued to talk earnestly with the girl. He raised his head to see Mayfair straggle in a bad second, and shrugged his shoulders. "How much did you lose?" she asked.

"Oh, 'bout two hundred dollars," said Van Bibber; "but it's the first time I've lost to-day, so I'm still ahead." He bent over to continue what he was saying, when a rude commotion and loud talking caused those in the boxes to raise their heads and look around. Several gentlemen were pointing out Van Bibber to one of the Pinkerton detectives, who had a struggling messenger-boy in his grasp.

"These gentlemen say you gave this boy some money, sir," said the detective. "He tried to do a welsh with it, and I caught him just as he was getting over the fence. How much and on what horse, sir?"

Van Bibber showed his memoranda, and the officer handed him over one hundred and seventy-five dollars.

"Now, let me see," said Van Bibber, shutting one eye and calculating intently, "one hundred and seventy-five to three hundred and fifty dollars makes me a winner by five hundred and twenty-five dollars. That's purty good, isn't it? I'll have a great dinner at Delmonico's to-night. You'd better all come back with me!"

But She said he had much better come back with her and her party on top of the coach and take dinner in the cool country instead of the hot, close city, and Van Bibber said he would like to, only he did wish to get his one hundred dollars up on at least one race. But they said "no," they must be off at once, for the ride was a long one, and Van Bibber looked at his list and saw that his choice was Jack Frost, a very likely winner, indeed; but, nevertheless, he walked out to the enclosure with them and mounted the coach beside the girl on the back seat, with only the two coachmen behind to hear what he chose to say.

And just as they finally were all harnessed up and the horn sounded, the crowd yelled, "They're off," and Van Bibber and all of them turned on their high seats to look back.

"Magpie wins," said the whip.

"And Jack Frost's last," said another.

"And I win my one hundred dollars," said Van Bibber. "It's really very curious," he added, turning to the girl. "I started out with two hundred dollars to-day, I spent only twenty-five dollars on flowers, I won six hundred and twenty-five dollars, and I have only one hundred and seventy-five dollars to show for it, and yet I've had a very pleasant Fourth."

A Wasted Day

When its turn came, the private secretary, somewhat apologetically, laid the letter in front of the Wisest Man in Wall Street.

"From Mrs. Austin, probation officer, Court of General Sessions," he explained. "Wants a letter about Spear. He's been convicted of theft. Comes up for sentence Tuesday."

"Spear?" repeated Arnold Thorndike.

"Young fellow, stenographer, used to do your letters last summer going in and out on the train."

The great man nodded. "I remember. What about him?"

The habitual gloom of the private secretary was lightened by a grin.

"Went on the loose; had with him about five hundred dollars belonging to the firm; he's with Isaacs & Sons now, shoe people on Sixth Avenue. Met a woman, and woke up without the money. The next morning he offered to make good, but Isaacs called in a policeman. When they looked into it, they found the boy had been drunk. They tried to withdraw the charge, but he'd been committed. Now, the probation officer is trying to get the judge to suspend sentence. A letter from you, sir, would--"

It was evident the mind of the great man was elsewhere. Young men who, drunk or sober, spent the firm's money on women who disappeared before sunrise did not appeal to him. Another letter submitted that morning had come from his art agent in Europe. In Florence he had discovered the Correggio he had been sent to find. It was undoubtedly genuine, and he asked to be instructed by cable. The price was forty thousand dollars. With one eye closed, and the other keenly regarding the inkstand, Mr. Thorndike decided to pay the price; and with the facility of long practice dismissed the Correggio, and snapped his mind back to the present.

"Spear had a letter from us when he left, didn't he?" he asked. "What he has developed into, SINCE he left us--" he shrugged his shoulders. The secretary withdrew the letter, and slipped another in its place.

"Homer Firth, the landscape man," he chanted, "wants permission to use blue flint on the new road, with turf gutters, and to plant silver firs each side. Says it will run to about five thousand dollars a mile."

"No!" protested the great man firmly, "blue flint makes a country place look like a cemetery. Mine looks too much like a cemetery now. Landscape gardeners!" he exclaimed impatiently. "Their only idea is to insult nature. The place was better the day I bought it, when it was running wild; you could pick flowers all the way to the gates." Pleased that it should have recurred to him, the great man smiled. "Why, Spear," he exclaimed, "always took in a bunch of them for his mother. Don't you remember, we used to see him before breakfast wandering around the grounds picking flowers?" Mr. Thorndike nodded briskly. "I like his taking flowers to his mother."

"He SAID it was to his mother," suggested the secretary gloomily.

"Well, he picked the flowers, anyway," laughed Mr. Thorndike. "He didn't pick our pockets. And he had the run of the house in those days. As far as we know," he dictated, "he was satisfactory. Don't say more than that."

119

The secretary scribbled a mark with his pencil. "And the landscape man?"

"Tell him," commanded Thorndike, "I want a wood road, suitable to a farm; and to let the trees grow where God planted them."

As his car slid downtown on Tuesday morning the mind of Arnold Thorndike was occupied with such details of daily routine as the purchase of a railroad, the Japanese loan, the new wing to his art gallery, and an attack that morning, in his own newspaper, upon his pet trust. But his busy mind was not too occupied to return the salutes of the traffic policemen who cleared the way for him. Or, by some genius of memory, to recall the fact that it was on this morning young Spear was to be sentenced for theft. It was a charming morning. The spring was at full tide, and the air was sweet and clean. Mr. Thorndike considered whimsically that to send a man to jail with the memory of such a morning clinging to him was adding a year to his sentence. He regretted he had not given the probation officer a stronger letter. He remembered the young man now, and favorably. A shy, silent youth, deft in work, and at other times conscious and embarrassed. But that, on the part of a stenographer, in the presence of the Wisest Man in Wall Street, was not unnatural. On occasions, Mr. Thorndike had put even royalty-- frayed, impecunious royalty, on the lookout for a loan--at its ease.

The hood of the car was down, and the taste of the air, warmed by the sun, was grateful. It was at this time, a year before, that young Spear picked the spring flowers to take to his mother. A year from now where would young Spear be?

It was characteristic of the great man to act quickly, so quickly that his friends declared he was a slave to impulse. It was these same impulses, leading so invariably to success, that made his enemies call him the Wisest Man. He leaned forward and touched the chauffeur's shoulder. "Stop at the Court of General Sessions," he commanded. What he proposed to do would take but a few minutes. A word, a personal word from him to the district attorney, or the judge, would be enough. He recalled that a Sunday Special had once calculated that the working time of Arnold Thorndike brought him in two hundred dollars a minute. At that rate, keeping Spear out of prison would cost a thousand dollars.

Out of the sunshine Mr. Thorndike stepped into the gloom of an echoing rotunda, shut in on every side, hung by balconies, lit, many stories overhead, by a dirty skylight. The place was damp, the air acrid with the smell of stale tobacco juice, and foul with the presence of many unwashed humans. A policeman, chewing stolidly, nodded toward an elevator shaft, and other policemen nodded him further on to the office of the district attorney. There Arnold Thorndike breathed more freely. He was again among his own people. He could not help but appreciate the dramatic qualities of the situation; that the richest man in Wall Street should appear in person to plead for a humble and weaker brother. He knew he could not escape recognition, his face was too well known, but, he trusted, for the sake of Spear, the reporters would make no display of his visit. With a deprecatory laugh, he explained why he had come. But the outburst of approbation he had anticipated did not follow.

The district attorney ran his finger briskly down a printed card. "Henry Spear," he exclaimed, "that's your man. Part Three, Judge Fallon. Andrews is in that court." He walked to the door of his private office. "Andrews!" he called.

He introduced an alert, broad-shouldered young man of years of much indiscretion and with a charming and inconsequent manner.

"Mr. Thorndike is interested in Henry Spear, coming up for sentence in Part Three this morning. Wants to speak for him. Take him over with you."

The district attorney shook hands quickly, and retreated to his private office. Mr. Andrews took out a cigarette and, as he crossed the floor, lit it.

"Come with me," he commanded. Somewhat puzzled, slightly annoyed, but enjoying withal the novelty of the environment and the curtness of his reception, Mr. Thorndike followed. He decided that, in his ignorance, he had wasted his own time and that of the prosecuting attorney. He should at once have sent in his card to the judge. As he understood it, Mr. Andrews was now conducting him to that dignitary, and, in a moment, he would be free to return to his own affairs, which were the affairs of two continents. But Mr. Andrews led him to an office, bare and small, and offered him a chair, and handed him a morning newspaper. There were people waiting in the room; strange people, only like those Mr. Thorndike had seen on ferry-boats. They leaned forward toward young Mr. Andrews, fawning, their eyes wide with apprehension.

Mr. Thorndike refused the newspaper. "I thought I was going to see the judge," he suggested.

"Court doesn't open for a few minutes yet," said the assistant district attorney. "Judge is always late, anyway."

Mr. Thorndike suppressed an exclamation. He wanted to protest, but his clear mind showed him that there was nothing against which, with reason, he could protest. He could not complain because these people were not apparently aware of the sacrifice he was making. He had come among them to perform a kindly act. He recognized that he must not stultify it by a show of irritation. He had precipitated himself into a game of which he did not know the rules. That was all. Next time he would know better. Next time he would send a clerk. But he was not without a sense of humor, and the situation as it now was forced upon him struck him as amusing. He laughed good-naturedly and reached for the desk telephone.

"May I use this?" he asked. He spoke to the Wall Street office. He explained he would be a few minutes late. He directed what should be done if the market opened in a certain way. He gave rapid orders on many different matters, asked to have read to him a cablegram he expected from Petersburg, and one from Vienna.

"They answer each other," was his final instruction. "It looks like peace."

Mr. Andrews with genial patience had remained silent. Now he turned upon his visitors. A Levantine, burly, unshaven, and soiled, towered truculently above him. Young Mr. Andrews with his swivel chair tilted back, his hands clasped behind his head, his cigarette hanging from his lips, regarded the man dispassionately.

"You gotta hell of a nerve to come to see me," he commented cheerfully. To Mr. Thorndike, the form of greeting was novel. So greatly did it differ from the procedure of his own office, that he listened with interest.

"Was it you," demanded young Andrews, in a puzzled tone, "or your brother who tried to knife me?" Mr. Thorndike, unaccustomed to cross the pavement to his office unless escorted by bank messengers and plain-clothes men, felt the room growing rapidly smaller; the figure of the truculent Greek loomed to heroic proportions. The hand of the banker went vaguely to his chin, and from there fell to his pearl pin, which he hastily covered.

"Get out!" said young Andrews, "and don't show your face here--"

The door slammed upon the flying Greek. Young Andrews swung his swivel chair so that, over his shoulder, he could see Mr. Thorndike. "I don't like his face," he explained.

A kindly eyed, sad woman with a basket on her knee smiled upon Andrews with the familiarity of an old acquaintance.

"Is that woman going to get a divorce from my son," she asked, "now that he's in trouble?"

"Now that he's in Sing Sing?" corrected Mr. Andrews. "I HOPE so! She deserves it. That son of yours, Mrs. Bernard," he declared emphatically, "is no good!"

The brutality shocked Mr. Thorndike. For the woman he felt a thrill of sympathy, but at once saw that it was superfluous. From the secure and lofty heights of motherhood, Mrs. Bernard smiled down upon the assistant district attorney as upon a naughty child. She did not even deign a protest. She continued merely to smile. The smile reminded Thorndike of the smile on the face of a mother in a painting by Murillo he had lately presented to the chapel in the college he had given to his native town.

"That son of yours," repeated young Andrews, "is a leech. He's robbed you, robbed his wife. Best thing I ever did for YOU was to send him up the river."

The mother smiled upon him beseechingly.

"Could you give me a pass?" she said.

Young Andrews flung up his hands and appealed to Thorndike.

"Isn't that just like a mother?" he protested. "That son of hers has broken her heart, tramped on her, cheated her; hasn't left her a cent; and she comes to me for a pass, so she can kiss him through the bars! And I'll bet she's got a cake for him in that basket!"

The mother laughed happily; she knew now she would get the pass.

"Mothers," explained Mr. Andrews, from the depth of his wisdom, "are all like that; your mother, my mother. If you went to jail, your mother would be just like that."

Mr. Thorndike bowed his head politely. He had never considered going to jail, or whether, if he did, his mother would bring him cake in a basket. Apparently there were many aspects and accidents of life not included in his experience.

Young Andrews sprang to his feet, and, with the force of a hose flushing a gutter, swept his soiled visitors into the hall.

"Come on," he called to the Wisest Man, "the court is open."

In the corridors were many people, and with his eyes on the broad shoulders of the assistant district attorney, Thorndike pushed his way through them. The people who blocked his progress were of the class unknown to him. Their looks were anxious, furtive, miserable. They stood in little groups, listening eagerly to a sharp-faced lawyer, or, in sullen despair, eying each other. At a door a tipstaff laid his hand roughly on the arm of Mr. Thorndike.

"That's all right, Joe," called young Mr. Andrews, "he's with Me." They entered the court and passed down an aisle to a railed enclosure in which were high oak chairs. Again, in his effort to follow, Mr. Thorndike was halted, but the first tipstaff came to his rescue. "All right," he signaled, "he's with Mr. Andrews."

Mr. Andrews pointed to one of the oak chairs. "You sit there," he commanded, "it's reserved for members of the bar, but it's all right. You're with Me."

Distinctly annoyed, slightly bewildered, the banker sank between the arms of a chair. He felt he had lost his individuality. Andrews had become his sponsor. Because of Andrews he was tolerated. Because Andrews had a pull he was permitted to sit as an equal among police-court lawyers. No longer was he Arnold Thorndike. He was merely the man "with Mr. Andrews."

Then even Andrews abandoned him. "The judge'll be here in a minute, now," said the assistant district attorney, and went inside a railed enclosure in front of the judge's bench. There he greeted another assistant district attorney whose years were those of even greater indiscretion than the years of Mr. Andrews. Seated on the rail, with their hands in their pockets and their backs turned to Mr. Thorndike, they laughed and talked together. The subject of their discourse was one Mike Donlin, as he appeared in vaudeville.

To Mr. Thorndike it was evident that young Andrews had entirely forgotten him. He arose, and touched his sleeve. With infinite sarcasm Mr. Thorndike began: "My engagements are not pressing, but--"

A court attendant beat with his palm upon the rail.

"Sit down!" whispered Andrews. "The judge is coming."

Mr. Thorndike sat down.

The court attendant droned loudly words Mr. Thorndike could not distinguish. There was a rustle of silk, and from a door behind him the judge stalked past. He was a young man, the type of the Tammany politician. On his shrewd, alert, Irish-American features was an expression of unnatural gloom. With a smile Mr. Thorndike observed that it was as little suited to the countenance of the young judge as was the robe to his shoulders. Mr. Thorndike was still smiling when young Andrews leaned over the rail.

"Stand up!" he hissed. Mr. Thorndike stood up.

After the court attendant had uttered more unintelligible words, every one sat down; and the financier again moved hurriedly to the rail.

"I would like to speak to him now before he begins," he whispered. "I can't wait."

Mr. Andrews stared in amazement. The banker had not believed the young man could look so serious.

"Speak to him, Now!" exclaimed the district attorney. 'You've got to wait till your man comes up. If you speak to the judge, Now--" The voice of Andrews faded away in horror.

Not knowing in what way he had offended, but convinced that it was only by the grace of Andrews he had escaped a dungeon, Mr. Thorndike retreated to his arm-chair.

The clock on the wall showed him that, already, he had given to young Spear one hour and a quarter. The idea was preposterous. No one better than himself knew what his time was really worth. In half an hour there was a board meeting; later, he was to hold a post mortem on a railroad; at every moment questions were being asked by telegraph, by cable, questions that involved the credit of individuals, of firms, of even the country. And the one man who could answer them was risking untold sums only that he might say a good word for an idle apprentice. Inside the railed enclosure a lawyer was reading a typewritten speech. He assured his honor that he must have more time to prepare his case. It was one of immense importance. The name of a most respectable business house was involved, and a sum of no less than nine hundred dollars. Nine hundred dollars! The contrast struck Mr. Thorndike's sense of humor full in the centre. Unknowingly, he laughed, and found himself as conspicuous as though he had appeared suddenly in his night-clothes. The tipstaffs beat upon the rail, the lawyer he had interrupted uttered an indignant exclamation, Andrews came hurriedly toward him, and the young judge slowly turned his head.

"Those persons," he said, "who cannot respect the dignity of this court will leave it." As he spoke, with his eyes fixed on those of Mr. Thorndike, the latter saw that the young judge had suddenly recognized him. But the fact of his identity did not cause the frown to relax or the rebuke to halt unuttered. In even, icy tones the judge continued: "And it is well they should remember that the law is no respecter of persons and that the dignity of this court will be enforced, no matter who the offender may happen to be."

Andrews slipped into the chair beside Mr. Thorndike, and grinned sympathetically.

"Sorry!" he whispered. "Should have warned you. We won't be long now," he added encouragingly. "As soon as this fellow finishes his argument, the judge'll take up the sentences. Your man seems to have other friends; Isaacs & Sons are here, and the type-writer firm who taught him; but what YOU say will help most. It won't be more than a couple of hours now."

"A couple of hours!" Mr. Thorndike raged inwardly. A couple of hours in this place where he had been publicly humiliated. He smiled, a thin, shark-like smile. Those who made it their business to study his expressions, on seeing it, would have fled. Young Andrews, not being acquainted with the moods of the great man, added cheerfully: "By one o'clock, anyway."

Mr. Thorndike began grimly to pull on his gloves. For all he cared now young Spear could go hang. Andrews nudged his elbow.

"See that old lady in the front row?" he whispered. "That's Mrs. Spear. What did I tell you; mothers are all alike. She's not taken her eyes off you since court opened. She knows you're her one best bet."

Impatiently Mr. Thorndike raised his head. He saw a little, white- haired woman who stared at him. In her eyes was the same look he had seen in the eyes of men who, at times of panic, fled to him, beseeching, entreating, forcing upon him what was left of the wreck of their fortunes, if only he would save their honor.

"And here come the prisoners," Andrews whispered. "See Spear? Third man from the last." A long line, guarded in front and rear, shuffled into the court-room, and, as ordered, ranged themselves against the wall. Among them were old men and young boys, well dressed, clever-looking rascals, collarless tramps, fierce-eyed aliens, smooth-shaven, thin-lipped Broadwayards--and Spear.

Spear, his head hanging, with lips white and cheeks ashen, and his eyes heavy with shame.

Mr. Thorndike had risen, and, in farewell, was holding out his hand to Andrews. He turned, and across the court-room the eyes of the financier and the stenographer met. At the sight of the great man, Spear flushed crimson, and then his look of despair slowly disappeared; and into his eyes there came incredulously hope and gratitude. He turned his head suddenly to the wall.

Mr. Thorndike stood irresolute, and then sank back into his chair.

The first man in the line was already at the railing, and the questions put to him by the judge were being repeated to him by the other assistant district attorney and a court attendant. His muttered answers were in turn repeated to the judge.

"Says he's married, naturalized citizen, Lutheran Church, die-cutter by profession."

The probation officer, her hands filled with papers, bustled forward and whispered.

"Mrs. Austin says," continued the district attorney, "she's looked into this case, and asks to have the man turned over to her. He has a wife and three children; has supported them for five years."

"Is the wife in court?" the judge said.

A thin, washed-out, pretty woman stood up, and clasped her hands in front of her.

"Has this man been a good husband to you, madam?" asked the young judge.

The woman broke into vehement assurances. No man could have been a better husband. Would she take him back? Indeed she would take him back. She held out her hands as though she would physically drag her husband from the pillory.

The judge bowed toward the probation officer, and she beckoned the prisoner to her.

Other men followed, and in the fortune of each Mr. Thorndike found himself, to his surprise, taking a personal interest. It was as good as a play. It reminded him of the Sicilians he had seen in London in their little sordid tragedies. Only these actors were appearing in their proper persons in real dramas of a life he did not know, but which appealed to something that had been long untouched, long in disuse. It was an uncomfortable sensation that left him restless because, as he appreciated, it needed expression, an outlet. He found this, partially, in praising, through Andrews, the young judge who had publicly rebuked him. Mr. Thorndike found him astute, sane; his queries intelligent, his comments just. And this probation officer, she, too, was capable, was she not? Smiling at his interest in what to him was an old story, the younger man nodded.

"I like her looks," whispered the great man. "Like her clear eyes and clean skin. She strikes me as able, full of energy, and yet womanly. These men when they come under her charge," he insisted, eagerly, "need money to start again, don't they?" He spoke anxiously. He believed he had found the clew to his restlessness. It was a desire to help; to be of use to these failures who had fallen and who were being lifted to their feet. Andrews looked at him curiously. "Anything you give her," he answered, "would be well invested."

"If you will tell me her name and address?" whispered the banker. He was much given to charity, but it had been perfunctory, it was extended on the advice of his secretary. In helping here, he felt a genial glow of personal pleasure. It was much more satisfactory than giving an Old Master to his private chapel.

In the rear of the court-room there was a scuffle that caused every one to turn and look. A man, who had tried to force his way past the tipstaffs, was being violently ejected, and, as he disappeared, he waved a paper toward Mr. Thorndike. The banker recognized him as his chief clerk. Andrews rose anxiously. "That man wanted to get to you. I'll see what it is. Maybe it's important."

Mr. Thorndike pulled him back.

"Maybe it is," he said dryly. "But I can't see him now, I'm busy."

Slowly the long line of derelicts, of birds of prey, of sorry, weak failures, passed before the seat of judgment. Mr. Thorndike had moved into a chair nearer to the rail, and from time to time made a note upon the back of an envelope. He had forgotten the time or had chosen to disregard it. So great was his interest that he had forgotten the particular derelict he had come to serve, until Spear stood almost at his elbow.

Thorndike turned eagerly to the judge, and saw that he was listening to a rotund, gray little man with beady, bird-like eyes who, as he talked, bowed and gesticulated. Behind him stood a younger man, a more modern edition of the other. He also bowed and, behind gold eye-glasses, smiled ingratiatingly.

The judge nodded, and leaning forward, for a few moments fixed his eyes upon the prisoner.

"You are a very fortunate young man," he said. He laid his hand upon a pile of letters. "When you were your own worst enemy, your friends came to help you. These letters speak for you; your employers, whom you robbed, have pleaded with me in your favor. It is urged, in your behalf, that at the time you committed the crime of which you are found guilty, you were intoxicated. In the eyes of the law, that is no excuse. Some men can drink and keep their senses. It appears you can not. When you drink you are a menace to yourself-- and, as is shown by this crime, to the community. Therefore, you must not drink. In view of the good character to which your friends have testified, and on the condition that you do not touch liquor, I will not sentence you to jail, but will place you in charge of the probation officer."

The judge leaned back in his chair and beckoned to Mr. Andrews. It was finished. Spear was free, and from different parts of the courtroom people were moving toward the door. Their numbers showed that the friends of the young man had been many. Mr. Thorndike felt a certain twinge of disappointment. Even though the result relieved and pleased him, he wished, in bringing it about, he had had some part.

He begrudged to Isaacs & Sons the credit of having given Spear his liberty. His morning had been wasted. He had neglected his own interests, and in no way assisted those of Spear. He was moving out of the railed enclosure when Andrews called him by name.

"His honor," he said impressively, "wishes to speak to you."

The judge leaned over his desk and shook Mr. Thorndike by the hand. Then he made a speech. The speech was about public-spirited citizens who, to the neglect of their own interests, came to assist the ends of justice, and fellow-creatures in misfortune. He purposely spoke in a loud voice, and every one stopped to listen.

"The law, Mr. Thorndike, is not vindictive," he said. "It wishes only to be just. Nor can it be swayed by wealth or political or social influences. But when there is good in a man, I, personally, want to know it, and when gentlemen like yourself, of your standing in this city, come here to speak a good word for a man, we would stultify the purpose of justice if we did not listen. I thank you for coming, and I wish more of our citizens were as unselfish and public-spirited."

It was all quite absurd and most embarrassing, but inwardly Mr. Thorndike glowed with pleasure. It was a long time since any one had had the audacity to tell him he had done well. From the friends of Spear there was a ripple of applause, which no tipstaff took it upon himself to suppress, and to the accompaniment of this, Mr. Thorndike walked to the corridor. He was pleased with himself and with his fellow-men. He shook hands with Isaacs & Sons, and congratulated them upon their public spirit, and the type-writer firm upon their public spirit. And then he saw Spear standing apart regarding him doubtfully.

Spear did not offer his hand, but Mr. Thorndike took it, and shook it, and said: "I want to meet your mother."

And when Mrs. Spear tried to stop sobbing long enough to tell him how happy she was, and how grateful, he instead told her what a fine son she had, and that he remembered when Spear used to carry flowers to town for her. And she remembered it, too, and thanked him for the flowers. And he told Spear, when Isaacs & Sons went bankrupt, which at the rate they were giving away their money to the Hebrew Hospital would be very soon, Spear must come back to him. And Isaacs & Sons were delighted at the great man's pleasantry, and afterward repeated it many times, calling upon each other to bear witness, and Spear felt as though some one had given him a new backbone, and Andrews, who was guiding Thorndike out of the building, was thinking to himself what a great confidence man had been lost when Thorndike became a banker.

The chief clerk and two bank messengers were waiting by the automobile with written calls for help from the office. They pounced upon the banker and almost lifted him into the car.

"There's still time!" panted the chief clerk.

"There is not!" answered Mr. Thorndike. His tone was rebellious, defiant. It carried all the authority of a spoiled child of fortune. "I've wasted most of this day," he declared, "and I intend to waste the rest of it. Andrews," he called, "jump in, and I'll give you a lunch at Sherry's."

The vigilant protector of the public dashed back into the building.

"Wait till I get my hat!" he called.

As the two truants rolled up the avenue the spring sunshine warmed them, the sense of duties neglected added zest to their holiday, and young Mr. Andrews laughed aloud.

Mr. Thorndike raised his eyebrows inquiringly. "I was wondering," said Andrews, "how much it cost you to keep Spear out of jail?"

"I don't care," said the great man guiltily; "it was worth it."

MY DISREPUTABLE FRIEND, MR. RAEGEN

Rags Raegen was out of his element. The water was his proper element—the water of the East River by preference. And when it came to "running the roofs," as he would have himself expressed it, he was "not in it."

On those other occasions when he had been followed by the police, he had raced them toward the river front and had dived boldly in from the wharf, leaving them staring blankly and in some alarm as to his safety. Indeed, three different men in the precinct, who did not know of young Raegen's aquatic prowess, had returned to the station-house and seriously reported him to the sergeant as lost, and regretted having driven a citizen into the river, where he had been unfortunately drowned. It was even told how, on one occasion, when hotly followed, young Raegen had dived off Wakeman's Slip, at East Thirty-third Street, and had then swum back under water to the landing-steps, while the policeman and a crowd of stevedores stood watching for him to reappear where he had sunk. It is further related that he had then, in a spirit of recklessness, and in the possibility of the policeman's failing to recognize him, pushed his way through the crowd from the rear and plunged in to rescue the supposedly drowned man. And that after two or three futile attempts to find his own corpse, he had climbed up on the dock and told the officer that he had touched the body sticking in the mud. And, as a result of this fiction, the river-police dragged the river-bed around Wakeman's Slip with grappling irons for four hours, while Rags sat on the wharf and directed their movements.

But on this present occasion the police were standing between him and the river, and so cut off his escape in that direction, and as they had seen him strike McGonegal and had seen McGonegal fall, he had to run for it and seek refuge on the roofs. What made it worse was that he was not in his own hunting-grounds, but in McGonegal's, and while any tenement on Cherry Street would have given him shelter, either for love of him or fear of him, these of Thirty-third Street were against him and "all that Cherry Street gang," while "Pike" McGonegal was their darling and their hero. And, if Rags had known it, any tenement on the block was better than Case's, into which he first turned, for Case's was empty and untenanted, save in one or two rooms, and the opportunities for dodging from one to another were in consequence very few. But he could not know this, and so he plunged into the dark hall- way and sprang up the first four flights of stairs, three steps at a jump, with one arm stretched out in front of him, for it was very dark and the turns were short. On the fourth floor he fell headlong over a bucket with a broom sticking in it, and cursed whoever left it there. There was a ladder leading from the sixth floor to the roof, and he ran up this and drew it after him as he fell forward out of the wooden trap that opened on the flat tin roof like a companion-way of a ship. The chimneys would have hidden him, but there was a policeman's helmet coming up from another companion-way, and he saw that the Italians hanging out of the windows of the other tenements were pointing at him and showing him to the officer. So he hung by his hands and dropped back again. It was not much of a fall, but it jarred him, and the race he had already run had nearly taken his breath from him. For Rags did not live a life calculated to fit young men for sudden trials of speed.

He stumbled back down the narrow stairs, and, with a vivid recollection of the bucket he had already fallen upon, felt his way cautiously with his hands and with one foot stuck out in front of him. If he had been in his own bailiwick, he would have rather enjoyed the tense excitement of the chase than otherwise, for there he was at home and knew all the cross-cuts and where to find each broken paling in the roof-fences, and all the traps in the roofs. But here he was running in a maze, and what looked like a safe passage-way might throw him head on into the outstretched arms of the officers.

And while he felt his way his mind was terribly acute to the fact that as yet no door on any of the landings had been thrown open to him, either curiously or hospitably as offering a place of refuge. He did not want to be taken, but in spite of this he was quite cool, and so, when he heard quick, heavy footsteps beating up the stairs, he stopped himself suddenly by placing one hand on the side of the wall and the other on the banister and halted, panting. He could distinguish from below the high voices of women and children and excited men in the street, and as the steps came nearer he heard some one lowering the ladder he had thrown upon the roof to the sixth floor and preparing to descend. "Ah!" snarled Raegen, panting and desperate, "youse think you have me now, sure, don't you?" It rather frightened him to find the house so silent, for, save the footsteps of the officers, descending and ascending upon him, he seemed to be the only living person in all the dark, silent building.

He did not want to fight.

He was under heavy bonds already to keep the peace, and this last had surely been in self-defense, and he felt he could prove it. What he wanted now was to get away, to get back to his own people and to lie hidden in his own cellar or garret, where they would feed and guard him until the trouble was over. And still, like the two ends of a vise, the representatives of the law were closing in upon him. He turned the knob of the door opening to the landing on which he stood, and tried to push it in, but it was locked. Then he stepped quickly to the door on the opposite side and threw his shoulder against it. The door opened, and he stumbled forward sprawling. The room in which he had taken refuge was almost bare, and very dark; but in a little room leading from it he saw a pile of tossed-up bedding on the floor, and he dived at this as though it was water, and crawled far under it until he reached the wall beyond, squirming on his face and stomach, and flattening out his arms and legs. Then he lay motionless, holding back his breath, and listening to the beating of his heart and to the footsteps on the stairs. The footsteps stopped on the landing leading to the outer room, and he could hear the murmur of voices as the two men questioned one another. Then the door was kicked open, and there was a long silence, broken sharply by the click of a revolver.

"Maybe he's in there," said a bass voice. The men stamped across the floor leading into the dark room in which he lay, and halted at the entrance. They did not stand there over a moment before they turned and moved away again; but to Raegen, lying with blood-vessels choked, and with his hand pressed across his mouth, it seemed as if they had been contemplating and enjoying his agony for over an hour. "I was in this place not more than twelve hours ago," said one of them easily. "I come in to take a couple out for fighting. They were yelling 'murder' and 'police,' and breaking things; but they went quiet enough. The man is a stevedore, I guess, and him and his wife used to get drunk regular and carry on up here every night or so. They got thirty days on the Island."

"Who's taking care of the rooms?" asked the bass voice. The first voice said he guessed "no one was," and added: "There ain't much to take care of, that I can see." "That's so," assented the bass voice. "Well," he went on briskly, "he's not here; but he's in the building, sure, for he put back when he seen me coming over the roof. And he didn't pass me, neither, I know that, anyway," protested the bass voice. Then the bass voice said that he must have slipped into the flat below, and added something that Raegen could not hear distinctly, about Schaffer on the roof, and their having him safe enough, as that red-headed cop from the Eighteenth Precinct was watching on the street. They closed the door behind them, and their footsteps clattered down the stairs, leaving the big house silent and apparently deserted. Young Raegen raised his head, and let his breath escape with a great gasp of relief, as when he had been a long time under water, and cautiously rubbed the perspiration out of his eyes and from his forehead. It had been a cruelly hot, close afternoon, and the stifling burial under the heavy bedding, and the excitement, had left him feverishly hot and trembling. It was already growing dark outside, although he could not know that until he lifted the quilts an inch or two and peered up at the dirty window-panes. He was afraid to rise, as yet, and flattened himself out with an impatient sigh, as he gathered the bedding over his head again and held back his breath to listen. There may have been a minute or more of absolute silence in which he lay there, and then his blood froze to ice in his veins, his breath stopped, and he heard, with a quick gasp of terror, the sound of something crawling toward him across the floor of the outer room. The instinct of self-defense moved him first to leap to his feet, and to face and fight it, and then followed as quickly a foolish sense of safety in his hiding-place; and he called upon his greatest strength, and, by his mere brute will alone, forced his forehead down to the bare floor and lay rigid, though his nerves jerked with unknown, unreasoning fear. And still he heard the sound of this living thing coming creeping toward him until the instinctive terror that shook him overcame his will, and he threw the bed-clothes from him with a hoarse cry, and sprang up trembling to his feet, with his back against the wall, and with his arms thrown out in front of him wildly, and with the willingness in them and the power in them to do murder.

The room was very dark, but the windows of the one beyond let in a little stream of light across the floor, and in this light he saw moving toward him on its hands and knees a little baby who smiled and nodded at him with a pleased look of recognition and kindly welcome.

The fear upon Raegen had been so strong and the reaction was so great that he dropped to a sitting posture on the heap of bedding and laughed long and weakly, and still with a feeling in his heart that this apparition was something strangely unreal and menacing.

But the baby seemed well pleased with his laughter, and stopped to throw back its head and smile and coo and laugh gently with him as though the joke was a very good one which they shared in common. Then it struggled solemnly to its feet and came pattering toward him on a run, with both bare arms held out, and with a look of such confidence in him, and welcome in its face, that Raegen stretched out his arms and closed the baby's fingers fearfully and gently in his own.

He had never seen so beautiful a child. There was dirt enough on its hands and face, and its torn dress was soiled with streaks of coal and ashes. The dust of the floor had rubbed into its bare knees, but the face was like no other face that Rags had ever seen. And then it looked at him as though it trusted him, and just as though they had known each other at some time long before, but the eyes of the baby somehow seemed to hurt him so that he had to turn his face away, and when he looked again it was with a strangely new feeling of dissatisfaction with himself and of wishing to ask pardon. They were wonderful eyes, black and rich, and with a deep superiority of knowledge in them, a knowledge that seemed to be above the knowledge of evil; and when the baby smiled at him, the eyes smiled too with confidence and tenderness in them that in some way frightened Rags and made him move uncomfortably. "Did you know that youse scared me so that I was going to kill you?" whispered Rags, apologetically, as he carefully held the baby from him at arm's length. "Did you?" But the baby only smiled at this and reached out its hand and stroked Rag's cheek with its fingers. There was something so wonderfully soft and sweet in this that Rags drew the baby nearer and gave a quick, strange gasp of pleasure as it threw its arms around his neck and brought the face up close to his chin and hugged him tightly. The baby's arms were very soft and plump, and its cheek and tangled hair were warm and moist with perspiration, and the breath that fell on Raegen's face was sweeter than anything he had ever known. He felt wonderfully and for some reason uncomfortably happy, but the silence was oppressive.

"What's your name, little 'un?" said Rags. The baby ran its arms more closely around Raegen's neck and did not speak, unless its cooing in Raegen's ear was an answer. "What did you say your name was?" persisted Raegen, in a whisper. The baby frowned at this and stopped cooing long enough to say: "Marg'ret," mechanically and without apparently associating the name with herself or anything else. "Margaret, eh!" said Raegen, with grave consideration. "It's a very pretty name," he added, politely, for he could not shake off the feeling that he was in the presence of a superior being. "An' what did you say your dad's name was?" asked Raegen, awkwardly. But this was beyond the baby's patience or knowledge, and she waived the question aside with both arms and began to beat a tattoo gently with her two closed fists on Raegen's chin and throat. "You're mighty strong now, ain't you?" mocked the young giant, laughing. "Perhaps you don't know, Missie," he added, gravely, "that your dad and mar are doing time on the Island, and you won't see 'em again for a month." No, the baby did not know this nor care apparently; she seemed content with Rags and with his company. Sometimes she drew away and looked at him long and dubiously, and this cut Rags to the heart, and he felt guilty, and unreasonably anxious until she smiled reassuringly again and ran back into his arms, nestling her face against his and stroking his rough chin wonderingly with her little fingers.

Rags forgot the lateness of the night and the darkness that fell upon the room in the interest of this strange entertainment, which was so much more absorbing, and so much more innocent than any other he had ever known. He almost forgot the fact that he lay in hiding, that he was surrounded by unfriendly neighbors, and that at any moment the representatives of local justice might come in and rudely lead him away. For this reason he dared not make a light, but he moved his position so that the glare from an electric lamp on the street outside might fall across the baby's face, as it lay alternately dozing and awakening, to smile up at him in the bend of his arm. Once it reached inside the collar of his shirt and pulled out the scapular that hung around his neck, and looked at it so long, and with such apparent seriousness, that Rags was confirmed in his fear that this kindly visitor was something more or less of a superhuman agent, and his efforts to make this supposition coincide with the fact that the angel's parents were on Blackwell's Island, proved one of the severest struggles his mind had ever experienced. He had forgotten to feel hungry, and the knowledge that he was acutely so, first came to him with the thought that the baby must obviously be in greatest need of food herself. This pained him greatly, and he laid his burden down upon the bedding, and after slipping off his shoes, tip-toed his way across the room on a foraging expedition after something she could eat. There was a half of a ham-bone, and a half loaf of hard bread in a cupboard, and on the table he found a bottle quite filled with wretched whiskey. That the police had failed to see the baby had not appealed to him in any way, but that they should have allowed this last find to remain unnoticed pleased him intensely, not because it now fell to him, but because they had been cheated of it. It really struck him as so humorous that he stood laughing silently for several minutes, slapping his thigh with every outward exhibition of the keenest mirth. But when he found that the room and cupboard were bare of anything else that might be eaten he sobered suddenly. It was very hot, and though the windows were open, the perspiration stood upon his face, and the foul close air that rose from the court and street below made him gasp and pant for breath. He dipped a wash rag in the water from the spigot in the hall, and filled a cup with it and bathed the baby's face and wrists. She woke and sipped up the water from the cup eagerly, and then looked up at him, as if to ask for something more. Rags soaked the crusty bread in the water, and put it to the baby's lips, but after nibbling at it eagerly she shook her head and looked up at him again with such reproachful pleading in her eyes, that Rags felt her silence more keenly than the worst abuse he had ever received.

It hurt him so, that the pain brought tears to his eyes.

"Deary girl," he cried, "I'd give you anything you could think of if I had it. But I can't get it, see? It ain't that I don't want to—good Lord, little 'un, you don't think that, do you?"

The baby smiled at this, just as though she understood him, and touched his face as if to comfort him, so that Rags felt that same exquisite content again, which moved him so strangely whenever the child caressed him, and which left him soberly wondering. Then the baby crawled up onto his lap and dropped asleep, while Rags sat motionless and fanned her with a folded newspaper, stopping every now and then to pass the damp cloth over her warm face and arms. It was quite late now. Outside he could hear the neighbors laughing and talking on the roofs, and when one group sang hilariously to an accordion, he cursed them under his breath for noisy, drunken fools, and in his anger lest they should disturb the child in his arms, expressed an anxious hope that they would fall off and break their useless necks. It grew silent and much cooler as the night ran out, but Rags still sat immovable, shivering slightly every now and then and cautiously stretching his stiff legs and body. The arm that held the child grew stiff and numb with the light burden, but he took a fierce pleasure in the pain, and became hardened to it, and at last fell into an uneasy slumber from which he awoke to pass his hands gently over the soft yielding body, and to draw it slowly and closer to him. And then, from very weariness, his eyes closed and his head fell back heavily against the wall, and the man and the child in his arms slept peacefully in the dark corner of the deserted tenement.

The sun rose hissing out of the East River, a broad, red disc of
heat. It swept the cross-streets of the city as pitilessly as the search-
light of a man-of-war sweeps the ocean. It blazed brazenly into open
windows, and changed beds into gridirons on which the sleepers
tossed and turned and woke unrefreshed and with throats dry and
parched. Its glare awakened Rags into a startled belief that the place
about him was on fire, and he stared wildly until the child in his arms
brought him back to the knowledge of where he was. He ached in
every joint and limb, and his eyes smarted with the dry heat, but the
baby concerned him most, for she was breathing with hard, long,
irregular gasps, her mouth was open and her absurdly small fists were
clenched, and around her closed eyes were deep blue rings. Rags felt
a cold rush of fear and uncertainties come over him as he stared
about him helplessly for aid. He had seen babies look like this before,
in the tenements; they were like this when the young doctors of the
Health Board climbed to the roofs to see them, and they were like
this, only quiet and still, when the ambulance came clattering up the
narrow streets, and bore them away. Rags carried the baby into the
outer room, where the sun had not yet penetrated, and laid her down
gently on the coverlets; then he let the water in the sink run until it
was fairly cool, and with this bathed the baby's face and hands and
feet, and lifted a cup of the water to her open lips. She woke at this
and smiled again, but very faintly, and when she looked at him he felt
fearfully sure that she did not know him, and that she was looking
through and past him at something he could not see.

He did not know what to do, and he wanted to do so much.
Milk was the only thing he was quite sure babies cared for, but in
want of this he made a mess of bits of the dry ham and crumbs of
bread, moistened with the raw whiskey, and put it to her lips on the
end of a spoon. The baby tasted this, and pushed his hand away, and
then looked up and gave a feeble cry, and seemed to say, as plainly as
a grown woman could have said or written, "It isn't any use, Rags.
You are very good to me, but, indeed, I cannot do it. Don't worry,
please; I don't blame you."

"Great Lord," gasped Rags, with a queer choking in his throat,
"but ain't she got grit." Then he bethought him of the people who he
still believed inhabited the rest of the tenement, and he concluded

that as the day was yet so early they might still be asleep, and that while they slept, he could "lift"—as he mentally described the act—whatever they might have laid away for breakfast. Excited with this hope, he ran noiselessly down the stairs in his bare feet, and tried the doors of the different landings. But each he found open and each room bare and deserted. Then it occurred to him that at this hour he might even risk a sally into the street. He had money with him, and the milk-carts and bakers' wagons must be passing every minute. He ran back to get the money out of his coat, delighted with the chance and chiding himself for not having dared to do it sooner. He stood over the baby a moment before he left the room, and flushed like a girl as he stooped and kissed one of the bare arms. "I'm going out to get you some breakfast," he said. "I won't be gone long, but if I should," he added, as he paused and shrugged his shoulders, "I'll send the sergeant after you from the station-house. If I only wasn't under bonds," he muttered, as he slipped down the stairs. "If it wasn't for that they couldn't give me more'n a month at the most, even knowing all they do of me. It was only a street fight, anyway, and there was some there that must have seen him pull his pistol." He stopped at the top of the first flight of stairs and sat down to wait. He could see below the top of the open front door, the pavement and a part of the street beyond, and when he heard the rattle of an approaching cart he ran on down and then, with an oath, turned and broke up-stairs again. He had seen the ward detectives standing together on the opposite side of the street.

"Wot are they doing out a bed at this hour?" he demanded angrily. "Don't they make trouble enough through the day, without prowling around before decent people are up? I wonder, now, if they're after me." He dropped on his knees when he reached the room where the baby lay, and peered cautiously out of the window at the detectives, who had been joined by two other men, with whom they were talking earnestly. Raegen knew the new-comers for two of McGonegal's friends, and concluded, with a momentary flush of pride and self-importance, that the detectives were forced to be up at this early hour solely on his account. But this was followed by the afterthought that he must have hurt McGonegal seriously, and that he was wanted in consequence very much. This disturbed him most, he was surprised to find, because it precluded his going forth in search of food. "I guess I can't get you that milk I was looking for," he said, jocularly, to the baby, for the excitement elated him. "The sun outside isn't good for me health." The baby settled herself in his arms and slept again, which sobered Rags, for he argued it was a bad sign, and his own ravenous appetite warned him how the child suffered. When he again offered her the mixture he had prepared for her, she took it eagerly, and Rags breathed a sigh of satisfaction. Then he ate some of the bread and ham himself and swallowed half the whiskey, and stretched out beside the child and fanned her while she slept. It was something strangely incomprehensible to Rags that he should feel so keen a satisfaction in doing even this little for her, but he gave up wondering, and forgot everything else in watching the strange beauty of the sleeping baby and in the odd feeling of responsibility and self-respect she had brought to him.

He did not feel it coming on, or he would have fought against it, but the heat of the day and the sleeplessness of the night before, and the fumes of the whiskey on his empty stomach, drew him unconsciously into a dull stupor, so that the paper fan slipped from his hand, and he sank back on the bedding into a heavy sleep. When he awoke it was nearly dusk and past six o'clock, as he knew by the newsboys calling the sporting extras on the street below. He sprang up, cursing himself, and filled with bitter remorse.

"I'm a drunken fool, that's what I am," said Rags, savagely. "I've let her lie here all day in the heat with no one to watch her." Margaret was breathing so softly that he could hardly discern any life at all, and his heart almost stopped with fear. He picked her up and fanned and patted her into wakefulness again and then turned desperately to the window and looked down. There was no one he knew or who knew him as far as he could tell on the street, and he determined recklessly to risk another sortie for food.

"Why, it's been near two days that child's gone without eating," he said, with keen self-reproach, "and here you've let her suffer to save yourself a trip to the Island. You're a hulking big loafer, you are," he ran on, muttering, "and after her coming to you and taking notice of you and putting her face to yours like an angel." He slipped off his shoes and picked his way cautiously down the stairs.

As he reached the top of the first flight a newsboy passed, calling the evening papers, and shouted something which Rags could not distinguish. He wished he could get a copy of the paper. It might tell him, he thought, something about himself. The boy was coming nearer, and Rags stopped and leaned forward to listen.

"Extry! Extry!" shouted the newsboy, running. "Sun, World, and Mail.
Full account of the murder of Pike McGonegal by Ragsey Raegen."

The lights in the street seemed to flash up suddenly and grow dim again, leaving Rags blind and dizzy.

"Stop," he yelled, "stop. Murdered, no, by God, no," he cried, staggering half-way down the stairs; "stop, stop!" But no one heard Rags, and the sound of his own voice halted him. He sank back weak and sick upon the top step of the stairs and beat his hands together upon his head.

"It's a lie, it's a lie," he whispered, thickly. "I struck him in self-defense, s'help me. I struck him in self-defense. He drove me to it. He pulled his gun on me. I done it in self-defense."

And then the whole appearance of the young tough changed, and the terror and horror that had showed on his face turned to one of low sharpness and evil cunning. His lips drew together tightly and he breathed quickly through his nostrils, while his fingers locked and unlocked around his knees. All that he had learned on the streets and wharves and roof-tops, all that pitiable experience and dangerous knowledge that had made him a leader and a hero among the thieves and bullies of the river-front he called to his assistance now. He faced the fact flatly and with the cool consideration of an uninterested counselor. He knew that the history of his life was written on Police Court blotters from the day that he was ten years old, and with pitiless detail; that what friends he had he held more by fear than by affection, and that his enemies, who were many, only wanted just such a chance as this to revenge injuries long suffered and bitterly cherished, and that his only safety lay in secret and instant flight. The ferries were watched, of course; he knew that the depots, too, were covered by the men whose only duty was to watch the coming and to halt the departing criminal. But he knew of one old man who was too wise to ask questions and who would row him over the East River to Astoria, and of another on the west side whose boat was always at the disposal of silent white-faced young men who might come at any hour of the night or morning, and whom he would pilot across to the Jersey shore and keep well away from the lights of the passing ferries and the green lamp of the police boat. And once across, he had only to change his name and write for money to be forwarded to that name, and turn to work until the thing was covered up and forgotten. He rose to his feet in his full strength again, and intensely and agreeably excited with the danger, and possibly fatal termination, of his adventure, and then there fell upon him, with the suddenness of a blow, the remembrance of the little child lying on the dirty bedding in the room above.

"I can't do it," he muttered fiercely; "I can't do it," he cried, as if he argued with some other presence. "There's a rope around me neck, and the chances are all against me; it's every man for himself and no favor." He threw his arms out before him as if to push the thought away from him and ran his fingers through his hair and over his face. All of his old self rose in him and mocked him for a weak fool, and showed him just how great his personal danger was, and so he turned and dashed forward on a run, not only to the street, but as if to escape from the other self that held him back. He was still without his shoes, and in his bare feet, and he stopped as he noticed this and turned to go up stairs for them, and then he pictured to himself the baby lying as he had left her, weakly unconscious and with dark rims around her eyes, and he asked himself excitedly what he would do, if, on his return, she should wake and smile and reach out her hands to him.

"I don't dare go back," he said, breathlessly. "I don't dare do it; killing's too good for the likes of Pike McGonegal, but I'm not fighting babies. An' maybe, if I went back, maybe I wouldn't have the nerve to leave her; I can't do it," he muttered, "I don't dare go back." But still he did not stir, but stood motionless; with one hand trembling on the stair-rail and the other clenched beside him, and so fought it on alone in the silence of the empty building.

The lights in the stores below came out one by one, and the minutes passed into half-hours, and still he stood there with the noise of the streets coming up to him below speaking of escape and of a long life of ill-regulated pleasures, and up above him the baby lay in the darkness and reached out her hands to him in her sleep.

The surly old sergeant of the Twenty-first Precinct station-house had read the evening papers through for the third time and was dozing in the fierce lights of the gas-jet over the high desk when a young man with a white, haggard face came in from the street with a baby in his arms.

"I want to see the woman thet look after the station-house—quick," he said.

The surly old sergeant did not like the peremptory tone of the young man nor his general appearance, for he had no hat, nor coat, and his feet were bare; so he said, with deliberate dignity, that the char-woman was up-stairs lying down, and what did the young man want with her? "This child," said the visitor, in a queer thick voice, "she's sick. The heat's come over her, and she ain't had anything to eat for two days, an' she's starving. Ring the bell for the matron, will yer, and send one of your men around for the house surgeon." The sergeant leaned forward comfortably on his elbows, with his hands under his chin so that the gold lace on his cuffs shone effectively in the gaslight. He believed he had a sense of humor and he chose this unfortunate moment to exhibit it.

"Did you take this for a dispensary, young man?" he asked; "or," he continued, with added facetiousness, "a foundling hospital?"

The young man made a savage spring at the barrier in front of the high desk. "Damn you," he panted, "ring that bell, do you hear me, or I'll pull you off that seat and twist your heart out."

The baby cried at this sudden outburst, and Rags fell back, patting it with his hand and muttering between his closed teeth. The sergeant called to the men of the reserve squad in the reading-room beyond, and to humor this desperate visitor, sounded the gong for the janitress. The reserve squad trooped in leisurely with the playing-cards in their hands and with their pipes in their mouths.

"This man," growled the sergeant, pointing with the end of his cigar to Rags, "is either drunk, or crazy, or a bit of both."

The char-woman came down stairs majestically, in a long, loose wrapper, fanning herself with a palm-leaf fan, but when she saw the child, her majesty dropped from her like a cloak, and she ran toward her and caught the baby up in her arms. "You poor little thing," she murmured, "and, oh, how beautiful!" Then she whirled about on the men of the reserve squad: "You, Conners," she said, "run up to my room and get the milk out of my ice-chest; and Moore, put on your coat and go around and tell the surgeon I want to see him. And one of you crack some ice up fine in a towel. Take it out of the cooler. Quick, now."

Raegen came up to her fearfully. "Is she very sick?" he begged; "she ain't going to die, is she?"

"Of course not," said the woman, promptly, "but she's down with the heat, and she hasn't been properly cared for; the child looks half-starved. Are you her father?" she asked, sharply. But Rags did not speak, for at the moment she had answered his question and had said the baby would not die, he had reached out swiftly, and taken the child out of her arms and held it hard against his breast, as though he had lost her and some one had been just giving her back to him.

His head was bending over hers, and so he did not see Wade and Heffner, the two ward detectives, as they came in from the street, looking hot, and tired, and anxious. They gave a careless glance at the group, and then stopped with a start, and one of them gave a long, low whistle.

"Well," exclaimed Wade, with a gasp of surprise and relief. "So Raegen, you're here, after all, are you? Well, you did give us a chase, you did. Who took you?"

The men of the reserve squad, when they heard the name of the man for whom the whole force had been looking for the past two days, shifted their positions slightly, and looked curiously at Rags, and the woman stopped pouring out the milk from the bottle in her hand, and stared at him in frank astonishment. Raegen threw back his head and shoulders, and ran his eyes coldly over the faces of the semicircle of men around him.

"Who took me?" he began defiantly, with a swagger of braggadocio, and then, as though it were hardly worth while, and as though the presence of the baby lifted him above everything else, he stopped, and raised her until her cheek touched his own. It rested there a moment, while Rag stood silent.

"Who took me?" he repeated, quietly, and without lifting his eyes from the baby's face. "Nobody took me," he said. "I gave myself up."

One morning, three months later, when Raegen had stopped his ice-cart in front of my door, I asked him whether at any time he had ever regretted what he had done.

"Well, sir," he said, with easy superiority, "seeing that I've shook the gang, and that the Society's decided her folks ain't fit to take care of her, we can't help thinking we are better off, see?

"But, as for my ever regretting it, why, even when things was at the worst, when the case was going dead against me, and before that cop, you remember, swore to McGonegal's drawing the pistol, and when I used to sit in the Tombs expecting I'd have to hang for it, well, even then, they used to bring her to see me every day, and when they'd lift her up, and she'd reach out her hands and kiss me through the bars, why—they could have took me out and hung me, and been damned to 'em, for all I'd have cared."

REAL SOLDIERS OF FORTUNE

MAJOR-GENERAL HENRY RONALD DOUGLAS MACIVER

ANY sunny afternoon, on Fifth Avenue, or at night in the _table d'hote_ restaurants of University Place, you may meet the soldier of fortune who of all his brothers in arms now living is the most remarkable. You may have noticed him; a stiffly erect, distinguished-looking man, with gray hair, an imperial of the fashion of Louis Napoleon, fierce blue eyes, and across his forehead a sabre cut.

This is Henry Ronald Douglas MacIver, for some time in India an ensign in the Sepoy mutiny; in Italy, lieutenant under Garibaldi; in Spain, captain under Don Carlos; in our Civil War, major in the Confederate army; in Mexico, lieutenant-colonel under the Emperor Maximilian; colonel under Napoleon III, inspector of cavalry for the Khedive of Egypt, and chief of cavalry and general of brigade of the army of King Milan of Servia. These are only a few of his military titles. In 1884 was published a book giving the story of his life up to that year. It was called "Under Fourteen Flags." If to-day General MacIver were to reprint the book, it would be called "Under Eighteen Flags."

MacIver was born on Christmas Day, 1841, at sea, a league off the shore of Virginia. His mother was Miss Anna Douglas of that State; Ronald MacIver, his father, was a Scot, a Rossshire gentleman, a younger son of the chief of the Clan MacIver. Until he was ten years old young MacIver played in Virginia at the home of his father. Then, in order that he might be educated, he was shipped to Edinburgh to an uncle, General Donald Graham. After five years his uncle obtained for him a commission as ensign in the Honorable East India Company, and at sixteen, when other boys are preparing for college, MacIver was in the Indian Mutiny, fighting, not for a flag, nor a

150

country, but as one fights a wild animal, for his life. He was wounded in the arm, and, with a sword, cut over the head. As a safeguard against the sun the boy had placed inside his helmet a wet towel. This saved him to fight another day, but even with that protection the sword sank through the helmet, the towel, and into the skull. To-day you can see the scar. He was left in the road for dead, and even after his wounds had healed, was six weeks in the hospital.

This tough handling at the very start might have satisfied some men, but in the very next war MacIver was a volunteer and wore the red shirt of Garibaldi. He remained at the front throughout that campaign, and until within a few years there has been no campaign of consequence in which he has not taken part. He served in the Ten Years' War in Cuba, in Brazil, in Argentina, in Crete, in Greece, twice in Spain in Carlist revolutions, in Bosnia, and for four years in our Civil War under Generals Jackson and Stuart around Richmond. In this great war he was four times wounded.

It was after the surrender of the Confederate army, that, with other Southern officers, he served under Maximilian in Mexico; in Egypt, and in France. Whenever in any part of the world there was fighting, or the rumor of fighting, the procedure of the general invariably was the same. He would order himself to instantly depart for the front, and on arriving there would offer to organize a foreign legion. The command of this organization always was given to him. But the foreign legion was merely the entering wedge. He would soon show that he was fitted for a better command than a band of undisciplined volunteers, and would receive a commission in the regular army. In almost every command in which he served that is the manner in which promotion came. Sometimes he saw but little fighting, sometimes he should have died several deaths, each of a nature more unpleasant than the others. For in war the obvious danger of a bullet is but a three hundred to one shot, while in the pack against the combatant the jokers are innumerable. And in the career of the general the unforeseen adventures are the most interesting. A man who in eighteen campaigns has played his part would seem to have earned exemption from any other risks, but often it was outside the battle-field that MacIver encountered the greatest danger. He fought several duels, in two of which he killed his adversary; several attempts were made to assassinate him, and while on his way to Mexico he was captured by hostile Indians. On returning from an expedition in Cuba he was cast adrift in an open boat and for days was without food.

Long before I met General MacIver I had read his book and had heard of him from many men who had met him in many different lands while engaged in as many different undertakings. Several of the older war correspondents knew him intimately; Bennett Burleigh of the _Telegraph_ was his friend, and E. F. Knight of the _Times_ was one of those who volunteered for a filibustering expedition which MacIver organized against New Guinea. The late Colonel Ochiltree of Texas told me tales of MacIver's bravery, when as young men they were fellow officers in the Southern army, and Stephen Bonsal had met him when MacIver was United States Consul at Denia in Spain. When MacIver arrived at this post, the ex-consul refused to vacate the Consulate, and MacIver wished to settle the difficulty with dueling pistols. As Denia is a small place, the inhabitants feared for their safety, and Bonsal, who was our _charge d'affaires_ then, was sent from Madrid to adjust matters. Without bloodshed he got rid of the ex-consul, and later MacIver so endeared himself to the Denians that they begged the State Department to retain him in that place for the remainder of his life.

Before General MacIver was appointed to a high position at the St. Louis Fair, I saw much of him in New York. His room was in a side street in an old-fashioned boarding-house, and overlooked his neighbor's back yard and a typical New York City sumac tree; but when the general talked one forgot he was within a block of the Elevated, and roamed over all the world. On his bed he would spread out wonderful parchments, with strange, heathenish inscriptions, with great seals, with faded ribbons.
These were signed by Sultans, Secretaries of War, Emperors, filibusters.
They were military commissions, titles of nobility, brevets for decorations, instructions and commands from superior officers. Translated the phrases ran: "Imposing special confidence in," "we appoint," or "create," or "declare," or "In recognition of services rendered to our person," or "country," or "cause," or "For bravery on the field of battle we bestow the Cross----"

As must a soldier, the general travels "light," and all his worldly possessions were crowded ready for mobilization into a small compass. He had his sword, his field blanket, his trunk, and the tin dispatch boxes that held his papers. From these, like a conjurer, he would draw souvenirs of all the world. From the embrace of faded letters, he would unfold old photographs, daguerrotypes, and miniatures of fair women and adventurous men: women who now are queens in exile, men who, lifted on waves of absinthe, still, across a _cafe_ table, tell how they will win back a crown.

Once in a written document the general did me the honor to appoint me his literary executor, but as he is young, and as healthy as myself, it never may be my lot to perform such an unwelcome duty. And to-day all one can write of him is what the world can read in "Under Fourteen Flags," and some of the "foot-notes to history" which I have copied from his scrap-book. This scrap-book is a wonderful volume, but owing to "political" and other reasons, for the present, of the many clippings from newspapers it contains there are only a few I am at liberty to print. And from them it is difficult to make a choice. To sketch in a few thousand words a career that had developed under Eighteen Flags is in its very wealth embarrassing.

Here is one story, as told by the scrap-book, of an expedition that failed. That it failed was due to a British Cabinet Minister; for had Lord Derby possessed the imagination of the Soldier of Fortune, his Majesty's dominions might now be the richer by many thousands of square miles and many thousands of black subjects.

On October 29, 1883, the following appeared in the London _Standard_:
"The New Guinea Exploration and Colonization Company is already chartered, and the first expedition expects to leave before Christmas." "The prospectus states settlers intending to join the first party must contribute one hundred pounds toward the company. This subscription will include all expenses for passage money. Six months' provisions will be provided, together with tents and arms for protection. Each subscriber of one hundred pounds is to obtain a certificate entitling him to one thousand acres."

The view of the colonization scheme taken by the _Times_ of London, of the same date, is less complaisant. "The latest commercial sensation is a proposed company for the seizure of New Guinea. Certain adventurous gentlemen are looking out for one hundred others who have money and a taste for buccaneering. When the company has been completed, its share-holders are to place themselves under military regulations, sail in a body for New Guinea, and without asking anybody's leave, seize upon the island and at once, in some unspecified way, proceed to realize large profits. If the idea does not suggest comparisons with the large designs of Sir Francis Drake, it is at least not unworthy of Captain Kidd."

When we remember the manner in which some of the colonies of Great Britain were acquired, the _Times_ seems almost squeamish. In a Melbourne paper, June, 1884, is the following paragraph:

"Toward the latter part of 1883 the Government of Queensland planted the flag of Great Britain on the shores of New Guinea. When the news reached England it created a sensation. The Earl of Derby, Secretary for the Colonies, refused, however, to sanction the annexation of New Guinea, and in so doing acted contrary to the sincere wish of every right-thinking Anglo-Saxon under the Southern Cross.

"While the subsequent correspondence between the Home and Queensland governments was going on, Brigadier-General H. R. MacIver originated and organized the New Guinea Exploration and Colonization Company in London, with a view to establishing settlements on the island. The company, presided over by General Beresford of the British Army, and having an eminently representative and influential board of directors, had a capital of two hundred and fifty thousand pounds, and placed the supreme command of the expedition in the hands of General MacIver.
Notwithstanding the character of the gentlemen composing the board of directors, and the truly peaceful nature of the expedition, his

Lordship informed General MacIver that in the event of the latter's attempting to land on New Guinea, instructions would be sent to the officer in command of her Majesty's fleet in the Western Pacific to fire upon the company's vessel. This meant that the expedition would be dealt with as a filibustering one."

In _Judy_, September 21, 1887, appears:

"We all recollect the treatment received by Brigadier-General MacIver. In the action he took with respect to the annexation of New Guinea. The General, who is a sort of Pizarro, with a dash of D'Artagnan, was treated in a most scurvy manner by Lord Derby. Had MacIver not been thwarted in his enterprise, the whole of New Guinea would now have been under the British flag, and we should not be cheek-by-jowl with the Germans, as we are in too many places."

Society, September 3, 1887, says:

"The New Guinea expedition proved abortive, owing to the blundering shortsightedness of the then Government, for which Lord Derby was chiefly responsible, but what little foothold we possess in New Guinea, is certainly due to General MacIver's gallant effort."

Copy of statement made by J. Rintoul Mitchell, June 2, 1887:

"About the latter end of the year 1883, when I was editor-in-chief of the _Englishman_ in Calcutta, I was told by Captain de Deaux, assistant secretary in the Foreign Office of the Indian Government, that he had received a telegram from Lord Derby to the effect that if General MacIver ventured to land upon the coast of New Guinea it would become the duty of Lord Ripon, Viceroy, to use the naval forces at his command for the purpose of deporting General MacI. Sir Auckland Calvin can certify to this, as it was discussed in the Viceregal Council."

Just after our Civil War MacIver was interested in another expedition which also failed. Its members called themselves the Knights of Arabia, and their object was to colonize an island much nearer to our shores than New Guinea. MacIver, saying that his oath prevented, would never tell me which island this was, but the reader can choose from among Cuba, Haiti, and the Hawaiian group. To have taken Cuba, the "colonizers" would have had to fight not only Spain, but the Cubans themselves, on whose side they were soon fighting in the Ten Years' War; so Cuba may be eliminated. And as the expedition was to sail from the Atlantic side, and not from San Francisco, the island would appear to be the Black Republic. From the records of the times it would seem that the greater number of the Knights of Arabia were veterans of the Confederate army, and there is no question but that they intended to subjugate the blacks of Haiti and form a republic for white men in which slavery would be recognized. As one of the leaders of this filibustering expedition, MacIver was arrested by General Phil Sheridan and for a short time cast into jail.

This chafed the general's spirit, but he argued philosophically that imprisonment for filibustering, while irksome, brought with it no reproach. And, indeed, sometimes the only difference between a filibuster and a government lies in the fact that the government fights the gun-boats of only the enemy while a filibuster must dodge the boats of the enemy and those of his own countrymen. When the United States went to war with Spain there were many men in jail as filibusters, for doing that which at the time the country secretly approved, and later imitated. And because they attempted exactly the same thing for which Dr. Jameson was imprisoned in Holloway Jail, two hundred thousand of his countrymen are now wearing medals.

The by-laws of the Knights of Arabia leave but little doubt as to its object.

By-law No. II reads:

"We, as Knights of Arabia, pledge ourselves to aid, comfort, and protect all Knights of Arabia, especially those who are wounded in obtaining our grand object.

"III--Great care must be taken that no unbeliever or outsider shall gain any insight into the mysteries or secrets of the Order.

"IV--The candidate will have to pay one hundred dollars cash to the Captain of the Company, and the candidate will receive from the Secretary a Knight of Arabia bond for one hundred dollars in gold, with ten per cent interest, payable ninety days after the recognition of (The Republic of----) by the United States, or any government.

"V--All Knights of Arabia will be entitled to one hundred acres of land, location of said land to be drawn for by lottery. The products are coffee, sugar, tobacco, and cotton."

A local correspondent of the New York _Herald_ writes of the arrest of MacIver as follows:

"When MacIver will be tried is at present unknown, as his case has assumed a complicated aspect. He claims British protection as a subject of her British Majesty, and the English Consul has forwarded a statement of his case to Sir Frederick Bruce at Washington, accompanied by a copy of the by-laws. General Sheridan also has forwarded a statement to the Secretary of War, accompanied not only by the by-laws, but very important documents, including letters from Jefferson Davis, Benjamin, the Secretary of State of the Confederate States, and other personages prominent in the Rebellion, showing that MacIver enjoyed the highest confidence of the Confederacy."

As to the last statement, an open letter I found in his scrap-book is an excellent proof. It is as follows: "To officers and members of all camps of United Confederate Veterans: It affords me the greatest pleasure to say that the bearer of this letter, General Henry Ronald MacIver, was an officer of great gallantry in the Confederate Army, serving on the staff at various times of General Stonewall Jackson, J. E. B. Stuart, and E. Kirby Smith, and that his official record is one of which any man may be proud.

"Respectfully, MARCUS J. WRIGHT, "_Agent for the Collection of Confederate Records_.

"War Records office, War Department, Washington, July 8, 1895."

At the close of the war duels between officers of the two armies were not infrequent. In the scrap-book there is the account of one of these affairs sent from Vicksburg to a Northern paper by a correspondent who was an eye-witness of the event. It tells how Major MacIver, accompanied by Major Gillespie, met, just outside of Vicksburg, Captain Tomlin of Vermont, of the United States Artillery Volunteers. The duel was with swords. MacIver ran Tomlin through the body. The correspondent writes:

"The Confederate officer wiped his sword on his handkerchief. In a few seconds Captain Tomlin expired. One of Major MacIver's seconds called to him: 'He is dead; you must go. These gentlemen will look after the body of their friend.' A negro boy brought up the horses, but before mounting MacIver said to Captain Tomlin's seconds: 'My friends are in haste for me to go. Is there anything I can do? I hope you consider that this matter has been settled honorably?'

"There being no reply, the Confederates rode away."

In a newspaper of to-day so matter-of-fact an acceptance of an event so tragic would make strange reading.

From the South MacIver crossed through Texas to join the Royalist army under the Emperor Maximilian. It was while making his way, with other Confederate officers, from Galveston to El Paso, that MacIver was captured by the Indians. He was not ill-treated by them, but for three months was a prisoner, until one night, the Indians having camped near the Rio Grande, he escaped into Mexico. There he offered his sword to the Royalist commander, General Mejia, who placed him on his staff, and showed him some few skirmishes. At Monterey MacIver saw big fighting, and for his share in it received the title of Count, and the order of Guadaloupe. In June, contrary to all rules of civilized war, Maximilian was executed and the empire was at an end. MacIver escaped to the coast, and from Tampico took a sailing vessel to Rio de Janeiro. Two months later he was wearing the uniform of another emperor, Dom Pedro, and, with the rank of lieutenant-colonel, was in command of the Foreign Legion of the armies of Brazil and Argentina, which at that time as allies were fighting against Paraguay.

MacIver soon recruited seven hundred men, but only half of these ever reached the front. In Buenos Ayres cholera broke out and thirty thousand people died, among the number about half the Legion. MacIver was among those who suffered, and before he recovered was six weeks in hospital. During that period, under a junior officer, the Foreign Legion was sent to the front, where it was disbanded.

On his return to Glasgow, MacIver foregathered with an old friend, Bennett Burleigh, whom he had known when Burleigh was a lieutenant in the navy of the Confederate States. Although today known as a distinguished war correspondent, in those days Burleigh was something of a soldier of fortune himself, and was organizing an expedition to assist the Cretan insurgents against the Turks. Between the two men it was arranged that MacIver should precede the expedition to Crete and prepare for its arrival. The Cretans received him gladly, and from the provisional government he received a commission in which he was given "full power to make war on land and sea against the enemies of Crete, and particularly against the Sultan of Turkey and the Turkish forces, and to burn, destroy, or capture any vessel bearing the Turkish flag."

This permission to destroy the Turkish navy single-handed strikes one as more than generous, for the Cretans had no navy, and before one could begin the destruction of a Turkish gun-boat it was first necessary to catch it and tie it to a wharf.

At the close of the Cretan insurrection MacIver crossed to Athens and served against the brigands in Kisissia on the borders of Albania and Thessaly as volunteer aide to Colonel Corroneus, who had been commander-in-chief of the Cretans against the Turks. MacIver spent three months potting at brigands, and for his services in the mountains was recommended for the highest Greek decoration.

From Greece it was only a step to New York, and almost immediately MacIver appears as one of the Goicouria-Christo expedition to Cuba, of which Goicouria was commander-in-chief, and two famous American officers, Brigadier-General Samuel C. Williams was a general and Colonel Wright Schumburg was chief of staff.

In the scrap-book I find "General Order No. 11 of the Liberal Army of the Republic of Cuba, issued at Cedar Keys, October 3, 1869." In it Colonel MacIver is spoken of as in charge of officers not attached to any organized corps of the division. And again:

"General Order No. V, Expeditionary Division, Republic of Cuba, on board _Lilian_," announces that the place to which the expedition is bound has been changed, and that General Wright Schumburg, who now is in command, orders "all officers not otherwise commissioned to join Colonel MacIver's 'Corps of Officers.'"

The _Lilian_ ran out of coal, and to obtain firewood put in at Cedar Keys. For two weeks the patriots cut wood and drilled upon the beach, when they were captured by a British gun-boat and taken to Nassau. There they were set at liberty, but their arms, boat, and stores were confiscated.

In a sailing vessel MacIver finally reached Cuba, and under Goicouria, who had made a successful landing, saw some "help yourself" fighting. Goicouria's force was finally scattered, and MacIver escaped from the Spanish soldiery only by putting to sea in an open boat, in which he endeavored to make Jamaica.

On the third day out he was picked up by a steamer and again landed at Nassau, from which place he returned to New York.
At that time in this city there was a very interesting man named Thaddeus P. Mott, who had been an officer in our army and later had entered the service of Ismail Pasha. By the Khedive he had

been appointed a general of division and had received permission to reorganize the Egyptian army.

His object in coming to New York was to engage officers for that service. He came at an opportune moment. At that time the city was filled with men who, in the Rebellion, on one side or the other, had held command, and many of these, unfitted by four years of soldiering for any other calling, readily accepted the commissions which Mott had authority to offer. New York was not large enough to keep MacIver and Mott long apart, and they soon came to an understanding. The agreement drawn up between them is a curious document. It is written in a neat hand on sheets of foolscap tied together like a Commencement-day address, with blue ribbon. In it MacIver agrees to serve as colonel of cavalry in the service of the Khedive. With a few legal phrases omitted the document reads as follows:

"Agreement entered into this 24th day of March, 1870, between the Government of his Royal Highness and the Khedive of Egypt, represented by General Thaddeus P. Mott of the first part, and H. R. H. MacIver of New York City.

"The party of the second part, being desirous of entering into the service of party of the first part, in the military capacity of a colonel of cavalry, promises to serve and obey party of the first part faithfully and truly in his military capacity during the space of five years from this date; that the party of the second part waives all claims of protection usually afforded to Americans by consular and diplomatic agents of the United States, and expressly obligates himself to be subject to the orders of the party of the first part, and to make, wage, and vigorously prosecute war against any and all the enemies of party of the first part; that the party of the second part will not under any event be governed, controlled by, or submit to, any order, law, mandate, or proclamation issued by the Government of the United States of America, forbidding party of the second part to serve party of the first part to make war according to any of the provisions herein contained, _it being, however, distinctly understood_ that nothing herein contained shall be construed as obligating party of the second part to bear arms or wage war against the United States of America.

"Party of the first part promises to furnish party of the second part with horses, rations, and pay him for his services the same salary now paid to colonels of cavalry in United States army, and will furnish him quarters suitable to his rank in army. Also promises, in the case of illness caused by climate, that said party may resign his office and shall receive his expenses to America and two months' pay; that he receives one-fifth of his regular pay during his active service, together with all expenses of every nature attending such enterprise."

It also stipulates as to what sums shall be paid his family or children in case of his death.

To this MacIver signs this oath:

"In the presence of the ever-living God, I swear that I will in all things honestly, faithfully, and truly keep, observe, and perform the obligations and promises above enumerated, and endeavor to conform to the wishes and desires of the Government of his Royal Highness, the Khedive of Egypt, in all things connected with the furtherance of his prosperity, and the maintenance of his throne."

On arriving at Cairo, MacIver was appointed inspector-general of cavalry, and furnished with a uniform, of which this is a description: "It consisted of a blue tunic with gold spangles, embroidered in gold up the sleeves and front, neat-fitting red trousers, and high patent-leather boots, while the inevitable fez completed the gay costume."

The climate of Cairo did not agree with MacIver, and, in spite of his "gay costume," after six months he left the Egyptian service. His honorable discharge was signed by Stone Bey, who, in the favor of the Khedive, had supplanted General Mott.

It is a curious fact that, in spite of his ill health, immediately after leaving Cairo, MacIver was sufficiently recovered to at once plunge into the Franco-Prussian War. At the battle of Orleans, while on the staff of General Chanzy, he was wounded. In this war his rank was that of a colonel of cavalry of the auxiliary army.

His next venture was in the Carlist uprising of 1873, when he formed a Carlist League, and on several occasions acted as bearer of important messages from the "King," as Don Carlos was called, to the sympathizers with his cause in France and England.

MacIver was promised, if he carried out successfully a certain mission upon which he was sent, and if Don Carlos became king, that he would be made a marquis. As Don Carlos is still a pretender, MacIver is still a general. Although in disposing of his sword MacIver never allowed his personal predilections to weigh with him, he always treated himself to a hearty dislike of the Turks, and we next find him fighting against them in Herzegovina with the Montenegrins. And when the Servians declared war against the same people, MacIver returned to London to organize a cavalry brigade to fight with the Servian army.

Of this brigade and of the rapid rise of MacIver to highest rank and honors in Servia, the scrap-book is most eloquent. The cavalry brigade was to be called the Knights of the Red Cross.

In a letter to the editor of the _Hour_, the general himself speaks of it in the following terms:

"It may be interesting to many of your readers to learn that a select corps of gentlemen is at present in course of organization under the above title with the mission of proceeding to the Levant to take measures in case of emergency for the defense of the Christian population, and more especially of British subjects who are to a great extent unprovided with adequate means of protection from the religious furies of the Mussulmans. The lives of Christian women and children are in hourly peril from fanatical hordes. The Knights will be carefully chosen and kept within strict military control, and will be under command of a practical soldier with large experience of the Eastern countries. Templars and all other crusaders are invited to give aid and sympathy."

Apparently MacIver was not successful in enlisting many Knights, for a war correspondent at the capital of Servia, waiting for the war to begin, writes as follows:

"A Scotch soldier of fortune, Henry MacIver, a colonel by rank, has arrived at Belgrade with a small contingent of military adventurers. Five weeks ago I met him in Fleet Street, London, and had some talk about his 'expedition.' He had received a commission from the Prince of Servia to organize and command an independent cavalry brigade, and he then was busily enrolling his volunteers into a body styled 'The Knights of the Red Cross.' I am afraid some of his bold crusaders have earned more distinction for their attacks on Fleet Street bars than they are likely to earn on Servian battle-fields, but then I must not anticipate history."

Another paper tells that at the end of the first week of his service as a Servian officer, MacIver had enlisted ninety men, but that they were scattered about the town, many without shelter and rations:

"He assembled his men on the Rialto, and in spite of official expostulation, the men were marched up to the Minister's four abreast--and they marched fairly well, making a good show. The War Minister was taken by storm, and at once granted everything. It has raised the English colonel's popularity with his men to fever heat."

This from the _Times_, London:

"Our Belgrade correspondent telegraphs last night:
"'There is here at present a gentleman named MacIver. He came from England to offer himself and his sword to the Servians. The Servian Minister of War gave him a colonel's commission. This morning I saw him drilling about one hundred and fifty remarkably

fine-looking fellows, all clad in a good serviceable cavalry uniform, and he has horses.'"

Later we find that:
"Colonel MacIver's Legion of Cavalry, organizing here, now numbers over two hundred men."

And again:

"Prince Nica, a Roumanian cousin of the Princess Natalie of Servia, has joined Colonel MacIver's cavalry corps."

Later, in the _Court Journal_, October 28, 1876, we read:

"Colonel MacIver, who a few years ago was very well known in military circles in Dublin, now is making his mark with the Servian army. In the war against the Turks, he commands about one thousand Russo-Servian cavalry."

He was next to receive the following honors:

"Colonel MacIver has been appointed commander of the cavalry of the Servian armies on the Morava and Timok, and has received the Cross of the Takovo Order from General Tchemaieff for gallant conduct in the field, and the gold medal for valor."

Later we learn from the _Daily News_:

"Mr. Lewis Farley, Secretary of the 'League in Aid of Christians of Turkey,' has received the following letter, dated Belgrade, October 10, 1876:

"'DEAR SIR: In reference to the embroidered banner so kindly worked by an English lady and forwarded by the League to Colonel MacIver, I have great pleasure in conveying to you the following particulars. On Sunday morning, the flag having been previously consecrated by the archbishop, was conducted by a guard of honor to the palace, and Colonel MacIver, in the presence of Prince Milan and a numerous suite, in the name and on behalf of yourself and the fair donor, delivered it into the hands of the Princess Natalie. The gallant Colonel wore upon this occasion his full uniform as brigade commander and chief of cavalry of the Servian army, and bore upon his breast the 'Gold Cross of Takovo' which he received after the battles of the 28th and 30th of September, in recognition of the heroism and bravery he displayed upon these eventful days. The beauty of the decoration was enhanced by the circumstances of its bestowal, for on the evening of the battle of the 30th, General Tchernaieff approached Colonel MacIver, and, unclasping the cross from his own breast, placed it upon that of the Colonel.

"'(Signed.) HUGH JACKSON,

"'_Member of Council of the League_.'"

In Servia and in the Servian army MacIver reached what as yet is the highest point of his career, and of his life the happiest period.

He was _general de brigade_, which is not what we know as a brigade general, but is one who commands a division, a major-general. He was a great favorite both at the palace and with the people, the pay was good, fighting plentiful, and Belgrade gay and amusing. Of all the places he has visited and the countries he has served, it is of this Balkan kingdom that the general seems to speak most fondly and with the greatest feeling. Of Queen Natalie he was and is a most loyal and chivalric admirer, and was ever ready, when he found any one who did not as greatly respect the lady, to offer him the choice of swords or pistols. Even for Milan he finds an extenuating word.

After Servia the general raised more foreign legions, planned further expeditions; in Central America reorganized the small armies of the small republics, served as United States Consul, and offered his sword to President McKinley for use against Spain. But with Servia the most active portion of the life of the general ceased, and the rest has been a repetition of what went before. At present his time is divided between New York and Virginia, where he has been offered an executive position in the approaching Jamestown Exposition. Both North and South he has many friends, many admirers. But his life is, and, from the nature of his profession, must always be, a lonely one.

While other men remain planted in one spot, gathering about them a home, sons and daughters, an income for old age, MacIver is a rolling stone, a piece of floating sea-weed; as the present King of England called him fondly, "that vagabond soldier."

To a man who has lived in the saddle and upon transports, "neighbor" conveys nothing, and even "comrade" too often means one who is no longer living.

With the exception of the United States, of which he now is a naturalized citizen, the general has fought for nearly every country in the world, but if any of those for which he lost his health and blood, and for which he risked his life, remembers him, it makes no sign. And the general is too proud to ask to be remembered. To-day there is no more interesting figure than this man who in years is still young enough to lead an army corps, and who, for forty years, has been selling his sword and risking his life for presidents, pretenders, charlatans, and emperors.

He finds some mighty changes: Cuba, which he fought to free, is free; men of the South, with whom for four years he fought shoulder to shoulder, are now wearing the blue; the empire of Mexico, for which he fought, is a republic; the empire of France, for which he fought, is a republic; the empire of Brazil, for which he fought is a republic; the dynasty in Servia, to which he owes his greatest honors, has been wiped out by murder. From none of the eighteen countries he has served has he a pension, berth, or billet, and at sixty he finds himself at home in every land, but with a home in none.

Still he has his sword, his blanket, and in the event of war, to obtain a commission he has only to open his tin boxes and show the commissions already won. Indeed, any day, in a new uniform, and under the Nineteenth Flag, the general may again be winning fresh victories and honors.

And so, this brief sketch of him is left unfinished. We will mark it--_To be continued_.

General MacIver

AN EXPERIMENT IN ECONOMY

Of course, Van Bibber lost all the money he saved at the races on the Fourth of July. He went to the track the next day, and he saw the whole sum melt away, and in his vexation tried to "get back," with the usual result. He plunged desperately, and when he had reached his rooms and run over his losses, he found he was a financial wreck, and that he, as his sporting friends expressed it, "would have to smoke a pipe" for several years to come, instead of indulging in Regalias. He could not conceive how he had come to make such a fool of himself, and he wondered if he would have enough confidence to spend a dollar on luxuries again.

It was awful to contemplate the amount he had lost. He felt as if it were sinful extravagance to even pay his car-fare up-town, and he contemplated giving his landlord the rent with keen distress. It almost hurt him to part with five cents to the conductor, and as he looked at the hansoms dashing by with lucky winners inside he groaned audibly.

"I've got to economize," he soliloquized. "No use talking; must economize. I'll begin to-morrow morning and keep it up for a month. Then I'll be on my feet again. Then I can stop economizing, and enjoy myself. But no more races; never, never again."

He was delighted with this idea of economizing. He liked the idea of self-punishment that it involved, and as he had never denied himself anything in his life, the novelty of the idea charmed him. He rolled over to sleep, feeling very much happier in his mind than he had been before his determination was taken, and quite eager to begin on the morrow. He arose very early, about ten o'clock, and recalled his idea of economy for a month, as a saving clause to his having lost a month's spending money.

He was in the habit of taking his coffee and rolls and a parsley omelette, at Delmonico's every morning. He decided that he would start out on his road of economy by omitting the omelette and ordering only a pot of coffee. By some rare intuition he guessed that there were places up-town where things were cheaper than at his usual haunt, only he did not know where they were. He stumbled into a restaurant on a side street finally, and ordered a cup of coffee and some rolls.

The waiter seemed to think that was a very poor sort of breakfast, and suggested some nice chops or a bit of steak or "ham and eggs, sah," all of which made Van Bibber shudder. The waiter finally concluded that Van Bibber was poor and couldn't afford any more, which, as it happened to be more or less true, worried that young gentleman; so much so, indeed, that when the waiter brought him a check for fifteen cents, Van Bibber handed him a half-dollar and told him to "keep the change."

The satisfaction he felt in this wore off very soon when he appreciated that, while he had economized in his breakfast, his vanity had been very extravagantly pampered, and he felt how absurd it was when he remembered he would not have spent more if he had gone to Delmonico's in the first place. He wanted one of those large black Regalias very much, but they cost entirely too much. He went carefully through his pockets to see if he had one with him, but he had not, and he determined to get a pipe. Pipes are always cheap.

"What sort of a pipe, sir?" said the man behind the counter.

"A cheap pipe," said Van Bibber.

"But what sort?" persisted the man.

Van Bibber thought a brier pipe, with an amber mouth-piece and a silver band, would about suit his fancy. The man had just such a pipe, with trade-marks on the brier and hall-marks and "Sterling" on the silver band. It lay in a very pretty silk box, and there was another mouth-piece you could screw in, and a cleaner and top piece with which to press the tobacco down. It was most complete, and only five dollars. "Isn't that a good deal for a pipe?" asked Van Bibber. The man said, being entirely unprejudiced, that he thought not. It was cheaper, he said, to get a good thing at the start. It lasted longer. And cheap pipes bite your tongue. This seemed to Van Bibber most excellent reasoning. Some Oxford-Cambridge mixture attracted Van Bibber on account of its name. This cost one dollar more. As he left the shop he saw a lot of pipes, brier and corn-cob and Sallie Michaels, in the window marked, "Any of these for a quarter." This made him feel badly, and he was conscious he was not making a success of his economy. He started back to the club, but it was so hot that he thought he would faint before he got there; so he called a hansom, on the principle that it was cheaper to ride and keep well than to walk and have a sunstroke.

He saw some people that he knew going by in a cab with a pile of trunks on the top of it, and that reminded him that they had asked him to come down and see them off when the steamer left that afternoon. So he waved his hand when they passed, and bowed to them, and cried, "See you later," before he counted the consequences. He did not wish to arrive empty-handed, so he stopped in at a florist's and got a big basket of flowers and another of fruit, and piled them into the hansom.

When be came to pay the driver he found the trip from Thirty-fifth Street to the foot of Liberty was two dollars and a half, and the fruit and flowers came to twenty-two dollars. He was greatly distressed over this, and could not see how it had happened. He rode back in the elevated for five cents and felt much better. Then some men just back from a yachting trip joined him at the club and ordered a great many things to drink, and of course he had to do the same, and seven dollars were added to his economy fund. He argued that this did not matter, because he signed a check for it, and that he would not have to pay for it until the end of the month, when the necessity of economizing would be over.

Still, his conscience did not seem convinced, and he grew very desperate. He felt he was not doing it at all properly, and he determined that he would spend next to nothing on his dinner. He remembered with a shudder the place he had taken the tramp to dinner, and he vowed that before he would economize as rigidly as that he would starve; but he had heard of the *table d'hôte* places on Sixth Avenue, so he went there and wandered along the street until he found one that looked clean and nice. He began with a heavy soup, shoved a rich, fat, fried fish over his plate, and followed it with a queer *entrée* of spaghetti with a tomato dressing that satisfied his hunger and killed his appetite as if with the blow of a lead pipe. But he went through with the rest of it, for he felt it was the truest economy to get his money's worth, and the limp salad in bad oil and the ice-cream of sour milk made him feel that eating was a positive pain rather than a pleasure; and in this state of mind and body, drugged and disgusted, he lighted his pipe and walked slowly towards the club along Twenty-sixth Street.

He looked in at the *café* at Delmonico's with envy and disgust, and, going disheartened on, passed the dining-room windows that were wide open and showed the heavy white linen, the silver, and the women coolly dressed and everybody happy.

And then there was a wild waving of arms inside, and white hands beckoning him, and he saw with mingled feelings of regret that the whole party of the Fourth of July were inside and motioning to him. They made room for him, and the captain's daughter helped him to olives, and the chaperon told how they had come into town for the day, and had been telegraphing for him and Edgar and Fred and "dear Bill," and the rest said they were so glad to see him because they knew he could appreciate a good dinner if any one could.

But Van Bibber only groaned, and the awful memories of the lead-like spaghetti and the bad oil and the queer cheese made him shudder, and turned things before him into a Tantalus feast of rare cruelty. There were Little Neck clams, delicious cold consommé, and white fish, and French chops with a dressing of truffles, and Roman punch and woodcock to follow, and crisp lettuce and toasted crackers-and-cheese, with a most remarkable combination of fruits and ices; and Van Bibber could eat nothing, and sat unhappily looking at his plate and shaking his head when the waiter urged him gently. "Economy!" he said, with disgusted solemnity. "It's all tommy rot. It wouldn't have cost me a cent to have eaten this dinner, and yet

I've paid half a dollar to make myself ill so that I can't. If you know how to economize, it may be all right; but if you don't understand it, you must leave it alone. It's dangerous. I'll economize no more."

And he accordingly broke his vow by taking the whole party up to see the lady who would not be photographed in tights, and put them in a box where they were gagged by the comedian, and where the soubrette smiled on them and all went well.

"SOMEWHERE IN FRANCE"

Marie Gessler, known as Marie Chaumontel, Jeanne d'Avrechy, the Countess d'Aurillac, was German. Her father, who served through the Franco-Prussian War, was a German spy. It was from her mother she learned to speak French sufficiently well to satisfy even an Academician and, among Parisians, to pass as one. Both her parents were dead. Before they departed, knowing they could leave their daughter nothing save their debts, they had had her trained as a nurse. But when they were gone, Marie in the Berlin hospitals played politics, intrigued, indiscriminately misused the appealing, violet eyes. There was a scandal; several scandals. At the age of twenty-five she was dismissed from the Municipal Hospital, and as now—save for the violet eyes—she was without resources, as a *compagnon de voyage* with a German doctor she travelled to Monte Carlo. There she abandoned the doctor for Henri Ravignac, a captain in the French Aviation Corps, who, when his leave ended, escorted her to Paris.

The duties of Captain Ravignac kept him in barracks near the aviation field, but Marie he established in his apartments on the Boulevard Haussmann. One day he brought from the barracks a roll of blue-prints, and as he was locking them in a drawer, said: "The Germans would pay through the nose for those!" The remark was indiscreet, but then Marie had told him she was French, and any one would have believed her.

The next morning the same spirit of adventure that had exiled her from the Berlin hospitals carried her with the blue-prints to the German embassy. There, greatly shocked, they first wrote down her name and address, and then, indignant at her proposition, ordered her out. But the day following a strange young German who was not at all indignant, but, on the contrary, quite charming, called upon Marie. For the blue-prints he offered her a very large sum, and that same hour with them and Marie departed for Berlin. Marie did not need the money. Nor did the argument that she was serving her country greatly impress her. It was rather that she loved intrigue. And so she became a spy.

Henri Ravignac, the man she had robbed of the blue-prints, was tried by court martial. The charge was treason, but Charles Ravignac, his younger brother, promised to prove that the guilty one was the girl, and to that end obtained leave of absence and spent much time and money. At the trial he was able to show the record of Marie in Berlin and Monte Carlo; that she was the daughter of a German secret agent; that on the afternoon the prints disappeared Marie, with an agent of the German embassy, had left Paris for Berlin. In consequence of this the charge of selling military secrets was altered to one of "gross neglect," and Henri Ravignac was sentenced to two years in the military prison at Tours. But he was of an ancient and noble family, and when they came to take him from his cell in the Cherche-Midi, he was dead. Charles, his brother, disappeared. It was said he also had killed himself; that he had been appointed a military attaché in South America; that to revenge his brother he had entered the secret service; but whatever became of him no one knew. All that was certain was that, thanks to the act of Marie Gessler, on the rolls of the French army the ancient and noble name of Ravignac no longer appeared.

In her chosen profession Marie Gessler found nothing discreditable. Of herself her opinion was not high, and her opinion of men was lower. For her smiles she had watched several sacrifice honor, duty, loyalty; and she held them and their kind in contempt. To lie, to cajole, to rob men of secrets they thought important, and of secrets the importance of which they did not even guess, was to her merely an intricate and exciting game.

She played it very well. So well that in the service her advance was rapid. On important missions she was sent to Russia, through the Balkans; even to the United States. There, with credentials as an army nurse, she inspected our military hospitals and unobtrusively asked many innocent questions.

When she begged to be allowed to work in her beloved Paris, "they" told her when war came "they" intended to plant her inside that city, and that, until then, the less Paris knew of her the better.

But just before the great war broke, to report on which way Italy might jump, she was sent to Rome, and it was not until September she was recalled. The telegram informed her that her Aunt Elizabeth was ill, and that at once she must return to Berlin. This, she learned from the code book wrapped under the cover of her thermos bottle, meant that she was to report to the general commanding the German forces at Soissons.

From Italy she passed through Switzerland, and, after leaving Basle, on military trains was rushed north to Luxemburg, and then west to Laon. She was accompanied by her companion, Bertha, an elderly and respectable, even distinguished-looking female. In the secret service her number was 528. Their passes from the war office described them as nurses of the German Red Cross. Only the Intelligence Department knew their real mission. With her also, as her chauffeur, was a young Italian soldier of fortune, Paul Anfossi. He had served in the Belgian Congo, in the French Foreign Legion in Algiers, and spoke all the European languages. In Rome, where as a wireless operator he was serving a commercial company, in selling Marie copies of messages he had memorized, Marie had found him useful, and when war came she obtained for him, from the Wilhelmstrasse, the number 292. From Laon, in one of the automobiles of the General Staff, the three spies were driven first to Soissons, and then along the road to Meaux and Paris, to the village of Neufchelles. They arrived at midnight, and in a château of one of the champagne princes, found the colonel commanding the Intelligence Bureau. He accepted their credentials, destroyed them, and replaced them with a *laisser-passer* signed by the mayor of Laon. That dignitary, the colonel explained, to citizens of Laon fleeing to Paris and the coast had issued many passes. But as now between Laon and Paris there were three German armies, the refugees had been turned back and their passes confiscated.

"From among them," said the officer, "we have selected one for you. It is issued to the wife of Count d'Aurillac, a captain of reserves, and her aunt, Madame Benet. It asks for those ladies and their chauffeur, Briand, a safe-conduct through the French military lines. If it gets you into Paris you will destroy it and assume another name. The Count d'Aurillac is now with his regiment in that city. If he learned of the presence there of his wife, he would seek her, and that would not be good for you. So, if you reach Paris, you will become a Belgian refugee. You are highborn and rich. Your château has been destroyed. But you have money. You will give liberally to the Red Cross. You will volunteer to nurse in the hospitals. With your sad story of ill treatment by us, with your high birth, and your knowledge of nursing, which you acquired, of course, only as an amateur, you should not find it difficult to join the Ladies of France, or the American Ambulance. What you learn from the wounded English and French officers and the French doctors you will send us through the usual channels."

"When do I start?" asked the woman.

"For a few days," explained the officer, "you remain in this château. You will keep us informed of what is going forward after we withdraw."

"Withdraw?" It was more of an exclamation than a question. Marie was too well trained to ask questions.

"We are taking up a new position," said the officer, "on the Aisne."

The woman, incredulous, stared.

"And we do not enter Paris?"

"*You* do," returned the officer. "That is all that concerns you. We will join you later—in the spring. Meanwhile, for the winter we entrench ourselves along the Aisne. In a chimney of this château we have set up a wireless outfit. We are leaving it intact. The chauffeur Briand—who, you must explain to the French, you brought with you from Laon, and who has been long in your service—will transmit whatever you discover. We wish especially to know of any movement toward our left. If they attack in front from Soissons, we are prepared; but of any attempt to cross the Oise and take us in flank, you must warn us."

The officer rose and hung upon himself his field-glasses, map-cases, and side-arms.

"We leave you now," he said. "When the French arrive you will tell them your reason for halting at this château was that the owner, Monsieur Iverney, and his family are friends of your husband. You found us here, and we detained you. And so long as you can use the wireless, make excuses to remain. If they offer to send you on to Paris, tell them your aunt is too ill to travel."

"But they will find the wireless," said the woman. "They are sure to use the towers for observation, and they will find it."

"In that case," said the officer, "you will suggest to them that we fled in such haste we had no time to dismantle it. Of course, you had no knowledge that it existed, or, as a loyal French woman, you would have at once told them." To emphasize his next words the officer pointed at her: "Under no circumstances," he continued, "must you be suspected. If they should take Briand in the act, should they have even the least doubt concerning him, you must repudiate him entirely. If necessary, to keep your own skirts clear, it would be your duty yourself to denounce him as a spy."

"Your first orders," said the woman, "were to tell them Briand had been long in my service; that I brought him from my home in Laon."

"He might be in your service for years," returned the colonel, "and you not know he was a German agent."

"If to save myself I inform upon him," said Marie, "of course you know you will lose him."

The officer shrugged his shoulders. "A wireless operator," he retorted, "we can replace. But for you, and for the service you are to render in Paris, we have no substitute. *You* must not be found out. You are invaluable."

The spy inclined her head. "I thank you," she said.

The officer sputtered indignantly.

"It is not a compliment," he exclaimed; "it is an order. You must not be found out!"

Withdrawn some two hundred yards from the Paris road, the château stood upon a wooded hill. Except directly in front, trees of great height surrounded it. The tips of their branches brushed the windows; interlacing, they continued until they overhung the wall of the estate. Where it ran with the road the wall gave way to a lofty gate and iron fence, through which those passing could see a stretch of noble turf, as wide as a polo-field, borders of flowers disappearing under the shadows of the trees; and the château itself, with its terrace, its many windows, its high-pitched, sloping roof, broken by towers and turrets.

Through the remainder of the night there came from the road to those in the château the roar and rumbling of the army in retreat. It moved without panic, disorder, or haste, but unceasingly. Not for an instant was there a breathing-spell. And when the sun rose, the three spies—the two women and the chauffeur—who in the great château were now alone, could see as well as hear the gray column of steel rolling past below them.

The spies knew that the gray column had reached Claye, had stood within fifteen miles of Paris, and then upon Paris had turned its back. They knew also that the reverberations from the direction of Meaux, that each moment grew more loud and savage, were the French "seventy-fives" whipping the gray column forward. Of what they felt the Germans did not speak. In silence they looked at each other, and in the eyes of Marie was bitterness and resolve.

179

Toward noon Marie met Anfossi in the great drawing-room that stretched the length of the terrace and from the windows of which, through the park gates, they could see the Paris road.

"This, that is passing now," said Marie, "is the last of our rear-guard. Go to your tower," she ordered, "and send word that except for stragglers and the wounded our column has just passed through Neufchelles, and that any moment we expect the French." She raised her hand impressively. "From now," she warned, "we speak French, we think French, we *are* French!"

Anfossi, or Briand, as now he called himself, addressed her in that language. His tone was bitter. "Pardon my lese-majesty," he said, "but this chief of your Intelligence Department is a *dummer Mensch*. He is throwing away a valuable life."

Marie exclaimed in dismay. She placed her hand upon his arm, and the violet eyes filled with concern.

"Not yours!" she protested.

"Absolutely!" returned the Italian. "I can send nothing by this knapsack wireless that they will not learn from others; from airmen, Uhlans, the peasants in the fields. And certainly I will be caught. Dead I am dead, but alive and in Paris the opportunities are unending. From the French Legion Etranger I have my honorable discharge. I am an expert wireless operator and in their Signal Corps I can easily find a place. Imagine me, then, on the Eiffel Tower. From the air I snatch news from all of France, from the Channel, the North Sea. You and I could work together, as in Rome. But here, between the lines, with a pass from a village *sous préfet*, it is ridiculous. I am not afraid to die. But to die because some one else is stupid, that is hard."

Marie clasped his hand in both of hers.

"You must not speak of death," she cried; "you know I must carry out my orders, that I must force you to take this risk. And you know that thought of harm to you tortures me!"

Quickly the young man disengaged his hand. The woman exclaimed with anger.

"Why do you doubt me?" she cried.

Briand protested vehemently.

"I do not doubt you."

"My affection, then?" In a whisper that carried with it the feeling of a caress Marie added softly: "My love?"

The young man protested miserably. "You make it very hard, mademoiselle," he cried. "You are my superior officer, I am your servant. Who am I that I should share with others—"

The woman interrupted eagerly.

"Ah, you are jealous!" she cried. "Is that why you are so cruel? But when I *tell* you I love you, and only you, can you not *feel* it is the truth?"

The young man frowned unhappily.

"My duty, mademoiselle!" he stammered.

With an exclamation of anger Marie left him. As the door slammed behind her, the young man drew a deep breath. On his face was the expression of ineffable relief.

In the hall Marie met her elderly companion, Bertha, now her aunt, Madame Benet.

"I heard you quarrelling," Bertha protested. "It is most indiscreet. It is not in the part of the Countess d'Aurillac that she makes love to her chauffeur."

Marie laughed noiselessly and drew her farther down the hall. "He is imbecile!" she exclaimed. "He will kill me with his solemn face and his conceit. I make love to him—yes—that he may work the more willingly. But he will have none of it. He is jealous of the others."

Madame Benet frowned.

"He resents the others," she corrected. "I do not blame him. He is a gentleman!"

"And the others," demanded Marie; "were they not of the most noble families of Rome?"

"I am old and I am ugly," said Bertha, "but to me Anfossi is always as considerate as he is to you who are so beautiful."

"An Italian gentleman," returned Marie, "does not serve in Belgian Congo unless it is the choice of that or the marble quarries."

"I do not know what his past may be," sighed Madame Benet, "nor do I ask. He is only a number, as you and I are only numbers. And I beg you to let us work in harmony. At such a time your love-affairs threaten our safety. You must wait."

Marie laughed insolently. "With the Du Barry," she protested, "I can boast that I wait for no man."

"No," replied the older woman; "you pursue him!"

Marie would have answered sharply, but on the instant her interest was diverted. For one week, by day and night, she had lived in a world peopled only by German soldiers. Beside her in the railroad carriage, on the station platforms, at the windows of the trains that passed the one in which she rode, at the grade crossings, on the bridges, in the roads that paralleled the tracks, choking the streets of the villages and spread over the fields of grain, she had seen only the gray-green uniforms. Even her professional eye no longer distinguished regiment from regiment, dragoon from grenadier, Uhlan from Hussar or Landsturm. Stripes, insignia, numerals, badges of rank, had lost their meaning. Those who wore them no longer were individuals. They were not even human. During the three last days the automobile, like a motor-boat fighting the tide, had crept through a gray-green river of men, stained, as though from the banks, by mud and yellow clay. And for hours, while the car was blocked, and in fury the engine raced and purred, the gray-green river had rolled past her, slowly but as inevitably as lava down the slope of a volcano, bearing on its surface faces with staring eyes, thousands and thousands of eyes, some fierce and bloodshot, others filled with weariness, homesickness, pain. At night she still saw them: the white faces under the sweat and dust, the eyes dumb, inarticulate, asking the answer. She had been suffocated by German soldiers, by the mass of them, engulfed and smothered; she had stifled in a land inhabited only by gray-green ghosts.

And suddenly, as though a miracle had been wrought, she saw upon the lawn, riding toward her, a man in scarlet, blue, and silver. One man riding alone.

Approaching with confidence, but alert; his reins fallen, his hands nursing his carbine, his eyes searched the shadows of the trees, the empty windows, even the sun-swept sky. His was the new face at the door, the new step on the floor. And the spy knew had she beheld an army corps it would have been no more significant, no more menacing, than the solitary *chasseur à cheval* scouting in advance of the enemy.

"We are saved!" exclaimed Marie, with irony. "Go quickly," she commanded, "to the bedroom on the second floor that opens upon the staircase, so that you can see all who pass. You are too ill to travel. They must find you in bed."

"And you?" said Bertha.

"I," cried Marie rapturously, "hasten to welcome our preserver!"

The preserver was a peasant lad. Under the white dust his cheeks were burned a brown-red, his eyes, honest and blue, through much staring at the skies and at horizon lines, were puckered and encircled with tiny wrinkles. Responsibility had made him older than his years, and in speech brief. With the beautiful lady who with tears of joy ran to greet him, and who in an ecstasy of happiness pressed her cheek against the nose of his horse, he was unimpressed. He returned to her papers and gravely echoed her answers to his questions. "This château," he repeated, "was occupied by their General Staff; they have left no wounded here; you saw the last of them pass a half-hour since." He gathered up his reins.

Marie shrieked in alarm. "You will not leave us?" she cried.

For the first time the young man permitted himself to smile. "Others arrive soon," he said.

He touched his shako, wheeled his horse in the direction from which he had come, and a minute later Marie heard the hoofs echoing through the empty village.

When they came, the others were more sympathetic. Even in times of war a beautiful woman is still a beautiful woman. And the staff officers who moved into the quarters so lately occupied by the enemy found in the presence of the Countess d'Aurillac nothing to distress them. In the absence of her dear friend, Madame Iverney, the châtelaine of the château, she acted as their hostess. Her chauffeur showed the company cooks the way to the kitchen, the larder, and the charcoal-box. She, herself, in the hands of General Andre placed the keys of the famous wine-cellar, and to the surgeon, that the wounded might be freshly bandaged, entrusted those of the linen-closet. After the indignities she had suffered while "detained" by *les Boches*, her delight and relief at again finding herself under the protection of her own people would have touched a heart of stone. And the hearts of the staff were not of stone. It was with regret they gave the countess permission to continue on her way. At this she exclaimed with gratitude. She assured them, were her aunt able to travel, she would immediately depart.

"In Paris she will be more comfortable than here," said the kind surgeon. He was a reservist, and in times of peace a fashionable physician and as much at his ease in a boudoir as in a field hospital. "Perhaps if I saw Madame Benet?"

At the suggestion the countess was overjoyed. But they found Madame Benet in a state of complete collapse. The conduct of the Germans had brought about a nervous breakdown.

"Though the bridges are destroyed at Meaux," urged the surgeon, "even with a detour, you can be in Paris in four hours. I think it is worth the effort."

But the mere thought of the journey threw Madame Benet into hysterics. She asked only to rest, she begged for an opiate to make her sleep. She begged also that they would leave the door open, so that when she dreamed she was still in the hands of the Germans, and woke in terror, the sound of the dear French voices and the sight of the beloved French uniforms might reassure her. She played her part well. Concerning her Marie felt not the least anxiety. But toward Briand, the chauffeur, the new arrivals were less easily satisfied.

The general sent his adjutant for the countess. When the adjutant had closed the door General Andre began abruptly:

"The chauffeur Briand," he asked, "you know him; you can vouch for him?"

"But, certainly!" protested Marie. "He is an Italian."

As though with sudden enlightenment, Marie laughed. It was as if now in the suspicion of the officer she saw a certain reasonableness. "Briand was so long in the Foreign Legion in Algiers," she explained, "where my husband found him, that we have come to think of him as French. As much French as ourselves, I assure you."

The general and his adjutant were regarding each other questioningly.

"Perhaps I should tell the countess," began the general, "that we have learned—"

The signal from the adjutant was so slight, so swift, that Marie barely intercepted it.

The lips of the general shut together like the leaves of a book. To show the interview was at an end, he reached for a pen.

"I thank you," he said.

"Of course," prompted the adjutant, "Madame d'Aurillac understands the man must not know we inquired concerning him."

General Andre frowned at Marie.

"Certainly not!" he commanded. "The honest fellow must not know that even for a moment he was doubted."

Marie raised the violet eyes reprovingly.

"I trust," she said with reproach, "I too well understand the feelings of a French soldier to let him know his loyalty is questioned."

With a murmur of appreciation the officers bowed and with a gesture of gracious pardon Marie left them.

Outside in the hall, with none but orderlies to observe, like a cloak the graciousness fell from her. She was drawn two ways. In her work Anfossi was valuable. But Anfossi suspected was less than of no value; he became a menace, a death-warrant.

General Andre had said, "We have learned—" and the adjutant had halted him. What had he learned? To know that, Marie would have given much. Still, one important fact comforted her. Anfossi alone was suspected. Had there been concerning herself the slightest doubt, they certainly would not have allowed her to guess her companion was under surveillance; they would not have asked one who was herself suspected to vouch for the innocence of a fellow conspirator. Marie found the course to follow difficult. With Anfossi under suspicion his usefulness was for the moment at an end; and to accept the chance offered her to continue on to Paris seemed most wise. On the other hand, if, concerning Anfossi, she had succeeded in allaying their doubts, the results most to be desired could be attained only by remaining where they were.

Their position inside the lines was of the greatest strategic value. The rooms of the servants were under the roof, and that Briand should sleep in one of them was natural. That to reach or leave his room he should constantly be ascending or descending the stairs also was natural. The field-wireless outfit, or, as he had disdainfully described it, the "knapsack" wireless, was situated not in the bedroom he had selected for himself, but in one adjoining. At other times this was occupied by the maid of Madame Iverney. To summon her maid Madame Iverney, from her apartment on the second floor, had but to press a button. And it was in the apartment of Madame Iverney, and on the bed of that lady, that Madame Benet now reclined. When through the open door she saw an officer or soldier mount the stairs, she pressed the button that rang a bell in the room of the maid. In this way, long before whoever was ascending the stairs could reach the top floor, warning of his approach came to Anfossi. It gave him time to replace the dust-board over the fireplace in which the wireless was concealed and to escape into his own bedroom. The arrangement was ideal. And already information picked up in the halls below by Marie had been conveyed to Anfossi to relay in a French cipher to the German General Staff at Rheims.

Marie made an alert and charming hostess. To all who saw her it was evident that her mind was intent only upon the comfort of her guests. Throughout the day many came and went, but each she made welcome; to each as he departed she called "*bonne chance.*" Efficient, tireless, tactful, she was everywhere: in the dining-room, in the kitchen, in the bedrooms, for the wounded finding mattresses to spread in the gorgeous salons of the champagne prince; for the soldier-chauffeurs carrying wine into the courtyard, where the automobiles panted and growled, and the arriving and departing shrieked for right of way. At all times an alluring person, now the one woman in a tumult of men, her smart frock covered by an apron, her head and arms bare, undismayed by the sight of the wounded or by the distant rumble of the guns, the Countess d'Aurillac was an inspiring and beautiful picture. The eyes of the officers, young and old, informed her of that fact, one of which already she was well aware. By the morning of the next day she was accepted as the owner of the château. And though continually she reminded the staff she was present only as the friend of her schoolmate, Madame Iverney, they deferred to her as to a hostess. Many of them she already saluted by name, and to those who with messages were constantly motoring to and from the front at Soissons she was particularly kind. Overnight the legend of her charm, of her devotion to the soldiers of all ranks, had spread from Soissons to Meaux, and from Meaux to Paris. It was noon of that day when from the window of the second story Marie saw an armored automobile sweep into the courtyard. It was driven by an officer, young and appallingly good-looking, and, as was obvious by the way he spun his car, one who held in contempt both the law of gravity and death. That he was some one of importance seemed evident. Before he could alight the adjutant had raced to meet him. With her eye for detail Marie observed that the young officer, instead of imparting information, received it. He must, she guessed, have just arrived from Paris, and his brother officer either was telling him the news or giving him his orders. Whichever it might be, in what was told him the new arrival was greatly interested. One instant in indignation his gauntleted fist beat upon the steering-wheel, the next he smiled with pleasure. To interpret this pantomime was difficult; and, the better to inform herself, Marie descended the stairs.

As she reached the lower hall the two officers entered. To the spy the man last to arrive was always the one of greatest importance; and Marie assured herself that through her friend, the adjutant, to meet with this one would prove easy.

But the chauffeur commander of the armored car made it most difficult. At sight of Marie, much to her alarm, as though greeting a dear friend, he snatched his kepi from his head and sprang toward her.

"The major," he cried, "told me you were here, that you are Madame d'Aurillac." His eyes spoke his admiration. In delight he beamed upon her. "I might have known it!" he murmured. With the

confidence of one who is sure he brings good news, he laughed happily. "And I," he cried, "am 'Pierrot'!"

Who the devil "Pierrot" might be the spy could not guess. She knew only that she wished by a German shell "Pierrot" and his car had been blown to tiny fragments. Was it a trap, she asked herself, or was the handsome youth really some one the Countess d'Aurillac should know. But, as from his introducing himself it was evident he could not know that lady very well, Marie took courage and smiled.

"*Which* 'Pierrot'?" she parried.

"Pierre Thierry!" cried the youth.

To the relief of Marie he turned upon the adjutant and to him explained who Pierre Thierry might be.

"Paul d'Aurillac," he said, "is my dearest friend. When he married this charming lady I was stationed in Algiers, and but for the war I might never have met her."

To Marie, with his hand on his heart in a most charming manner, he bowed. His admiration he made no effort to conceal.

"And so," he said, "I know why there is war!"

The adjutant smiled indulgently, and departed on his duties, leaving them alone. The handsome eyes of Captain Thierry were raised to the violet eyes of Marie. They appraised her boldly and as boldly expressed their approval.

In burlesque the young man exclaimed indignantly: "Paul deceived me!" he cried. "He told me he had married the most beautiful woman in Laon. He has married the most beautiful woman in France!"

To Marie this was not impertinence, but gallantry.

This was a language she understood, and this was the type of man, because he was the least difficult to manage, she held most in contempt.

"But about you, Paul did not deceive me," she retorted. In apparent confusion her eyes refused to meet his. "He told me 'Pierrot' was a most dangerous man!"

She continued hurriedly. With wifely solicitude she asked concerning Paul. She explained that for a week she had been a prisoner in the château, and, since the mobilization, of her husband save that he was with his regiment in Paris she had heard nothing. Captain Thierry was able to give her later news. Only the day previous, on the boulevards, he had met Count d'Aurillac. He was at the Grand Hôtel, and as Thierry was at once motoring back to Paris he would give Paul news of their meeting. He hoped he might tell him that soon his wife also would be in Paris. Marie explained that only the illness of her aunt prevented her from that same day joining her husband. Her manner became serious.

"And what other news have you?" she asked. "Here on the firing-line we know less of what is going forward than you in Paris."

So Pierre Thierry told her all he knew. They were preparing dispatches he was at once to carry back to the General Staff, and, for the moment, his time was his own. How could he better employ it than in talking of the war with a patriotic and charming French woman?

In consequence Marie acquired a mass of facts, gossip, and guesses. From these she mentally selected such information as, to her employers across the Aisne, would be of vital interest.

And to rid herself of Thierry and on the fourth floor seek Anfossi was now her only wish. But, in attempting this, by the return of the adjutant she was delayed. To Thierry the adjutant gave a sealed envelope.

"Thirty-one, Boulevard des Invalides," he said. With a smile he turned to Marie. "And you will accompany him!"

"I!" exclaimed Marie. She was sick with sudden terror.

But the tolerant smile of the adjutant reassured her.

"The count, your husband," he explained, "has learned of your detention here by the enemy, and he has besieged the General Staff to have you convoyed safely to Paris." The adjutant glanced at a field telegram he held open in his hand. "He asks," he continued, "that you be permitted to return in the car of his friend, Captain Thierry, and that on arriving you join him at the Grand Hôtel."

Thierry exclaimed with delight.

"But how charming!" he cried. "To-night you must both dine with me at La Rue's." He saluted his superior officer. "Some petrol, sir," he said. "And I am ready." To Marie he added: "The car will be at the steps in five minutes." He turned and left them.

The thoughts of Marie, snatching at an excuse for delay, raced madly. The danger of meeting the Count d'Aurillac, her supposed husband, did not alarm her. The Grand Hôtel has many exits, and, even before they reached it, for leaving the car she could invent an excuse that the gallant Thierry would not suspect. But what now concerned her was how, before she was whisked away to Paris, she could convey to Anfossi the information she had gathered from Thierry. First, of a woman overcome with delight at being reunited with her husband she gave an excellent imitation; then she exclaimed in distress: "But my aunt, Madame Benet!" she cried. "I cannot leave her!"

"The Sisters of St. Francis," said the adjutant, "arrive within an hour to nurse the wounded. They will care also for your aunt."

Marie concealed her chagrin. "Then I will at once prepare to go," she said.

The adjutant handed her a slip of paper. "Your *laisser-passer* to Paris," he said. "You leave in five minutes, madame!"

As temporary hostess of the château Marie was free to visit any part of it, and as she passed her door a signal from Madame Benet told her that Anfossi was on the fourth floor, that he was at work, and that the coast was clear. Softly, in the felt slippers she always wore, as she explained, in order not to disturb the wounded, she mounted the staircase. In her hand she carried the housekeeper's keys, and as an excuse it was her plan to return with an armful of linen for the arriving Sisters. But Marie never reached the top of the stairs. When her eyes rose to the level of the fourth floor she came to a sudden halt. At what she saw terror gripped her, bound her hand and foot, and turned her blood to ice.

At her post for an instant Madame Benet had slept, and an officer of the staff, led by curiosity, chance, or suspicion, had, unobserved and unannounced, mounted to the fourth floor. When Marie saw him he was in front of the room that held the wireless. His back was toward her, but she saw that he was holding the door to the room ajar, that his eye was pressed to the opening, and that through it he had pushed the muzzle of his automatic. What would be the fate of Anfossi Marie knew. Nor did she for an instant consider it. Her thoughts were of her own safety; that she might live. Not that she might still serve the Wilhelmstrasse, the Kaiser, or the Fatherland; but that she might live. In a moment Anfossi would be denounced, the château would ring with the alarm, and, though she knew Anfossi would not betray her, by others she might be accused. To avert suspicion from herself she saw only one way open. She must be the first to denounce Anfossi.

Like a deer she leaped down the marble stairs and, in a panic she had no need to assume, burst into the presence of the staff.

"Gentlemen!" she gasped, "my servant—the chauffeur—Briand is a spy! There is a German wireless in the château. He is using it! I have seen him." With exclamations, the officers rose to their feet. General Andre alone remained seated. General Andre was a veteran of many Colonial wars: Cochin-China, Algiers, Morocco. The great war, when it came, found him on duty in the Intelligence Department. His aquiline nose, bristling white eyebrows, and flashing, restless eyes gave him his nickname of *l'Aigle*.

In amazement, the flashing eyes were now turned upon Marie. He glared at her as though he thought she suddenly had flown mad.

"A German wireless!" he protested. "It is impossible!"

"I was on the fourth floor," panted Marie, "collecting linen for the Sisters. In the room next to the linen closet I heard a strange buzzing sound. I opened the door softly. I saw Briand with his back to me seated by an instrument. There were receivers clamped to his ears! My God! The disgrace. The disgrace to my husband and to me, who vouched for him to you!" Apparently in an agony of remorse, the fingers of the woman laced and interlaced. "I cannot forgive myself!"

The officers moved toward the door, but General Andre halted them. Still in a tone of incredulity, he demanded: "When did you see this?"

Marie knew the question was coming, knew she must explain how she saw Briand, and yet did not see the staff officer who, with his prisoner, might now at any instant appear. She must make it plain she had discovered the spy and left the upper part of the house before the officer had visited it. When that was she could not know, but the chance was that he had preceded her by only a few minutes.

"When did you see this?" repeated the general.

"But just now," cried Marie; "not ten minutes since."

"Why did you not come to me at once?"

"I was afraid," replied Marie. "If I moved I was afraid he might hear me, and he, knowing I would expose him, would kill me—and so *escape you!*" There was an eager whisper of approval. For silence, General Andre slapped his hand upon the table.

"Then," continued Marie, "I understood with the receivers on his ears he could not have heard me open the door, nor could he hear me leave, and I ran to my aunt. The thought that we had harbored such an animal sickened me, and I was weak enough to feel faint. But only for an instant. Then I came here." She moved swiftly to the door. "Let me show you the room," she begged; "you can take him in the act." Her eyes, wild with the excitement of the chase, swept the circle. "Will you come?" she begged.

Unconscious of the crisis he interrupted, the orderly on duty opened the door.

"Captain Thierry's compliments," he recited mechanically, "and is he to delay longer for Madame d'Aurillac?"

With a sharp gesture General Andre waved Marie toward the door. Without rising, he inclined his head. "Adieu, madame," he said. "We act at once upon your information. I thank you!"

As she crossed from the hall to the terrace, the ears of the spy were assaulted by a sudden tumult of voices. They were raised in threats and curses. Looking back, she saw Anfossi descending the stairs. His hands were held above his head; behind him, with his automatic, the staff officer she had surprised on the fourth floor was driving him forward. Above the clenched fists of the soldiers that ran to meet him, the eyes of Anfossi were turned toward her. His face was expressionless. His eyes neither accused nor reproached. And with the joy of one who has looked upon and then escaped the guillotine, Marie ran down the steps to the waiting automobile. With a pretty cry of pleasure she leaped into the seat beside Thierry. Gayly she threw out her arms. "To Paris!" she commanded. The handsome eyes of Thierry, eloquent with admiration, looked back into hers. He stooped, threw in the clutch, and the great gray car, with the machine gun and its crew of privates guarding the rear, plunged through the park.

"To Paris!" echoed Thierry.

In the order in which Marie had last seen them, Anfossi and the staff officer entered the room of General Andre, and upon the soldiers in the hall the door was shut. The face of the staff officer was grave, but his voice could not conceal his elation.

"My general," he reported, "I found this man in the act of giving information to the enemy. There is a wireless—"

General Andre rose slowly. He looked neither at the officer nor at his prisoner. With frowning eyes he stared down at the maps upon his table.

"I know," he interrupted. "Some one has already told me." He paused, and then, as though recalling his manners, but still without raising his eyes, he added: "You have done well, sir."

In silence the officers of the staff stood motionless. With surprise they noted that, as yet, neither in anger nor curiosity had General Andre glanced at the prisoner. But of the presence of the general the spy was most acutely conscious. He stood erect, his arms still raised, but his body strained forward, and on the averted eyes of the general his own were fixed.

In an agony of supplication they asked a question.

At last, as though against his wish, toward the spy the general turned his head, and their eyes met. And still General Andre was silent. Then the arms of the spy, like those of a runner who has finished his race and breasts the tape exhausted, fell to his sides. In a voice low and vibrant he spoke his question.

"It has been so long, sir," he pleaded. "May I not come home?"

General Andre turned to the astonished group surrounding him. His voice was hushed like that of one who speaks across an open grave.

"Gentlemen," he began, "my children," he added. "A German spy, a woman, involved in a scandal your brother in arms, Henri Ravignac. His honor, he thought, was concerned, and without honor he refused to live. To prove him guiltless his younger brother Charles asked leave to seek out the woman who had betrayed Henri, and by us was detailed on secret service. He gave up home, family, friends. He lived in exile, in poverty, at all times in danger of a swift and ignoble death. In the War Office we know him as one who has given to his country services she cannot hope to reward. For she cannot return to him the years he has lost. She cannot return to him his brother. But she can and will clear the name of Henri Ravignac, and upon his brother Charles bestow promotion and honors."

The general turned and embraced the spy. "My children," he said, "welcome your brother. He has come home."

Before the car had reached the fortifications, Marie Gessler had arranged her plan of escape. She had departed from the château without even a hand-bag, and she would say that before the shops closed she must make purchases.

Le Printemps lay in their way, and she asked that, when they reached it, for a moment she might alight. Captain Thierry readily gave permission.

From the department store it would be most easy to disappear, and in anticipation Marie smiled covertly. Nor was the picture of Captain Thierry impatiently waiting outside unamusing.

But before Le Printemps was approached, the car turned sharply down a narrow street. On one side, along its entire length, ran a high gray wall, grim and forbidding. In it was a green gate studded with iron bolts. Before this the automobile drew suddenly to a halt.

The crew of the armored car tumbled off the rear seat, and one of them beat upon the green gate. Marie felt a hand of ice clutch at her throat. But she controlled herself.

"And what is this?" she cried gayly.

At her side Captain Thierry was smiling down at her, but his smile was hateful.

"It is the prison of St. Lazare," he said. "It is not becoming," he added sternly, "that the name of the Countess d'Aurillac should be made common as the Paris road!"

Fighting for her life, Marie thrust herself against him; her arm that throughout the journey had rested on the back of the driving-seat caressed his shoulders; her lips and the violet eyes were close to his.

"Why should you care?" she whispered fiercely. "You have *me!* Let the Count d'Aurillac look after the honor of his wife himself."

The charming Thierry laughed at her mockingly.

"He means to," he said. "I *am* the Count d'Aurillac!"

The Messengers

When Ainsley first moved to Lone Lake Farm all of his friends asked him the same question. They wanted to know, if the farmer who sold it to him had abandoned it as worthless, how one of the idle rich, who could not distinguish a plough from a harrow, hoped to make it pay? His answer was that he had not purchased the farm as a means of getting richer by honest toil, but as a retreat from the world and as a test of true friendship. He argued that the people he knew accepted his hospitality at Sherry's because, in any event, they themselves would be dining within a taxicab fare of the same place. But if to see him they travelled all the way to Lone Lake Farm, he might feel assured that they were friends indeed.

Lone Lake Farm was spread over many acres of rocky ravine and forest, at a point where Connecticut approaches New York, and between it and the nearest railroad station stretched six miles of an execrable wood road. In this wilderness, directly upon the lonely lake, and at a spot equally distant from each of his boundary lines, Ainsley built himself a red brick house. Here, in solitude, he exiled himself; ostensibly to become a gentleman farmer; in reality to wait until Polly Kirkland had made up her mind to marry him.

Lone Lake, which gave the farm its name, was a pond hardly larger than a city block. It was fed by hidden springs, and fringed about with reeds and cat-tails, stunted willows and shivering birch. From its surface jutted points of the same rock that had made farming unremunerative, and to these miniature promontories and islands Ainsley, in keeping with a fancied resemblance, gave such names as the Needles, St. Helena, and the Isle of Pines. From the edge of the pond that was farther from the house rose a high hill, heavily wooded. At its base, oak and chestnut trees spread their branches over the water, and when the air was still were so clearly reflected in the pond that the leaves seemed to float upon the surface. To the smiling expanse of the farm the lake was what the eye is to the human countenance. The oaks were its eyebrows, the fringe of reeds its lashes, and, in changing mood, it flashed with happiness or brooded in somber melancholy. For Ainsley it held a deep attraction. Through the summer evenings, as the sun set, he would sit on the brick terrace and watch the fish leaping, and listen to the venerable bull-frogs croaking false alarms of rain. Indeed, after he met Polly Kirkland, staring moodily at the lake became his favorite form of exercise. With a number of other men, Ainsley was very much in love with Miss Kirkland, and unprejudiced friends thought that if she were to choose any of her devotees, Ainsley should be that one. Ainsley heartily agreed in this opinion, but in persuading Miss Kirkland to share it he had not been successful. This was partly his own fault; for when he dared to compare what she meant to him with what he had to offer her he became a mass of sodden humility. Could he have known how much Polly Kirkland envied and admired his depth of feeling, entirely apart from the fact that she herself inspired that feeling, how greatly she wished to care for him in the way he cared for her, life, even alone in the silences of Lone Lake, would have been a beautiful and blessed thing. But he was so sure she was the most charming and most wonderful girl in all the world, and he an unworthy and despicable being, that when the lady demurred, he faltered, and his pleading, at least to his own ears, carried no conviction.

"When one thinks of being married," said Polly Kirkland gently, "it isn't a question of the man you can live with, but the man you can't live without. And I am sorry, but I've not found that man."

"I suppose," returned Ainsley gloomily, "that my not being able to live without you doesn't affect the question in the least?"

"You HAVE lived without me," Miss Kirkland pointed out reproachfully, "for thirty years."

"Lived!" almost shouted Ainsley. "Do you call THAT living? What was I before I met you? I was an ignorant beast of the field. I knew as much about living as one of the cows on my farm. I could sleep twelve hours at a stretch, or, if I was in New York, I NEVER slept. I was a Day and Night Bank of health and happiness, a great, big, useless puppy. And now I can't sleep, can't eat, can't think--

except of you. I dream about you all night, think about you all day, go through the woods calling your name, cutting your initials in tree trunks, doing all the fool things a man does when he's in love, and I am the most miserable man in the world--and the happiest!"

He finally succeeded in making Miss Kirkland so miserable also that she decided to run away. Friends had planned to spend the early spring on the Nile and were eager that she should accompany them. To her the separation seemed to offer an excellent method of discovering whether or not Ainsley was the man she could not "live without."

Ainsley saw in it only an act of torture, devised with devilish cruelty.

"What will happen to me," he announced firmly, "is that I will plain DIE! As long as I can see you, as long as I have the chance to try and make you understand that no one can possibly love you as I do, and as long as I know I am worrying you to death, and no one else is, I still hope. I've no right to hope, still I do. And that one little chance keeps me alive. But Egypt! If you escape to Egypt, what hold will I have on you? You might as well be in the moon. Can you imagine me writing love-letters to a woman in the moon? Can I send American Beauty roses to the ruins of Karnak? Here I can telephone you; not that I ever have anything to say that you want to hear, but because I want to listen to your voice, and to have you ask, 'Oh! Is that *You*?' as though you were glad it WAS me. But Egypt! Can I call up Egypt on the long-distance? If you leave me now, you'll leave me forever, for I'll drown myself in Lone Lake."

The day she sailed away he went to the steamer, and, separating her from her friends and family, drew her to the side of the ship farther from the wharf, and which for the moment, was deserted. Directly below a pile-driver, with rattling of chains and shrieks from her donkey-engine, was smashing great logs; on the deck above, the ship's band was braying forth fictitious gayety, and from every side they were assailed by the raucous whistles of ferry-boats. The surroundings were not conducive to sentiment, but for the first time Polly Kirkland seemed a little uncertain, a little frightened; almost on the verge of tears, almost persuaded to surrender. For the first time she laid her hand on Ainsley's arm, and the shock sent the blood to his heart and held him breathless. When the girl looked at him there was something in her eyes that neither he nor any other man had ever seen there.

"The last thing I tell you," she said, "the thing I want you to remember, is this, that, though I do not care--I *want* to care."

Ainsley caught at her hand and, to the delight of the crew of a passing tug-boat, kissed it rapturously. His face was radiant. The fact of parting from her had caused him real suffering, had marked his face with hard lines. Now, hope and happiness smoothed them away and his eyes shone with his love for her. He was trembling, laughing, jubilant.

"And if you should!" he begged. "How soon will I know? You will cable," he commanded. "You will cable 'Come,' and the same hour I'll start toward you. I'll go home now," he cried, "and pack!"

The girl drew away. Already she regretted the admission she had made. In fairness and in kindness to him she tried to regain the position she had abandoned.

"But a change like that," she pleaded, "might not come for years, may never come!" To recover herself, to make the words she had uttered seem less serious, she spoke quickly and lightly.

"And how could I *CABLE* such a thing!" she protested. "It would be far too sacred, too precious. You should be able to FEEL that the change has come."

"I suppose I should," assent Ainsley, doubtfully; "but it's a long way across two oceans. It would be safer if you'd promise to use the cable. Just one word: 'Come.'"

The girl shook her head and frowned.

"If you can't feel that the woman you love loves you, even across the world, you cannot love her very deeply."

"I don't have to answer that!" said Ainsley.

"I will send you a sign," continued the girl, hastily; "a secret wireless message. It shall be a test. If you love me you will read it at once. You will know the instant you see it that it comes from me. No one else will be able to read it; but if you love me, you will know that I love you.

Whether she spoke in metaphor or in fact, whether she was "playing for time," or whether in her heart she already intended to soon reward him with a message of glad tidings, Ainsley could not decide. And even as he begged her to enlighten him the last whistle blew, and a determined officer ordered him to the ship's side.

"Just as in everything that is beautiful," he whispered eagerly, "I always see something of you, so now in everything wonderful I will read your message. But," he persisted, "how shall I be *sure*?"

The last bag of mail had shot into the hold; the most reluctant of the visitors were being hustled down the last remaining gangplank. Ainsley's state was desperate.

"Will it be in symbol, or in cipher?" he demanded. "Must I read it in the sky, or will you hide it in a letter, or--where? Help me! Give me just a hint!"

The girl shook her head.

"You will read it--in your heart," she said.

From the end of the wharf Ainsley watched the funnels of the ship disappear in the haze of the lower bay. His heart was sore and heavy, but in it there was still room for righteous indignation. "Read it in my heart!" he protested. "How the devil can I read it in my heart? I want to read it *Printed* in a cablegram."

Because he had always understood that young men in love found solace for their misery in solitude and in communion with nature, he at once drove his car to Lone Lake. But his misery was quite genuine, and the emptiness of the brick house only served to increase his loneliness. He had built the house for her, though she had never visited it, and was associated with it only through the somewhat indefinite medium of the telephone box. But in New York they had been much together. And Ainsley quickly decided that in revisiting those places where he had been happy in her company he would derive from the recollection some melancholy consolation. He accordingly raced back through the night to the city; nor did he halt until he was at the door of her house. She had left it only that morning, and though it was locked in darkness, it still spoke of her. At least it seemed to bring her nearer to him than when he was listening to the frogs in the lake, and crushing his way through the pines.

He was not hungry, but he went to a restaurant where, when he was host, she had often been the honored guest, and he pretended they were at supper together and without a chaperon. Either the illusion or the supper cheered him, for he was encouraged to go on to his club. There in the library, with the aid of an atlas, he worked out where, after thirteen hours of moving at the rate of twenty-two knots an hour, she should be at that moment. Having determined that fact to his own satisfaction, he sent a wireless after the ship. It read: "It is now midnight and you are in latitude 40 degrees north, longitude 68 degrees west, and I have grown old and gray waiting for the sign."

The next morning, and for many days after, he was surprised to find that the city went on as though she still were in it. With unfeeling regularity the sun rose out of the East River. On Broadway electric-light signs flashed, street-cars pursued each other, taxicabs bumped and skidded, women, and even men, dared to look happy, and had apparently taken some thought to their attire. They did not respect even his widower hood. They smiled upon him, and asked him jocularly about the farm and his "crops," and what he was doing in New York. He pitied them, for obviously they were ignorant of the fact that in New York there were art galleries, shops, restaurants of great interest, owing to the fact that Polly Kirkland had visited them. They did not know that on upper Fifth Avenue were houses of which she had deigned to approve, or which she had destroyed with ridicule, and that to walk that avenue and halt before each of these houses was an inestimable privilege.

Each day, with pathetic vigilance, Ainsley examined his heart for the promised sign. But so far from telling him that the change he longed for had taken place, his heart grew heavier, and as weeks went by and no sign appeared, what little confidence he had once enjoyed passed with them.

But before hope entirely died, several false alarms had thrilled him with happiness. One was a cablegram from Gibraltar in which the only words that were intelligible were "congratulate" and "engagement." This lifted him into an ecstasy of joy and excitement, until, on having the cable company repeat the message, he learned it was a request from Miss Kirkland to congratulate two mutual friends who had just announced their engagement, and of whose address she was uncertain. He had hardly recovered from this disappointment than he was again thrown into a tumult by the receipt of a mysterious package from the custom-house containing an intaglio ring. The ring came from Italy, and her ship had touched at Genoa. The fact that it was addressed in an unknown handwriting did not disconcert him, for he argued that to make the test more difficult she might disguise the handwriting. He at once carried the intaglio to an expert at the Metropolitan Museum, and when he was told that it represented Cupid feeding a fire upon an altar, he reserved a stateroom on the first steamer bound for the Mediterranean. But before his ship sailed, a letter, also from Italy, from his aunt Maria, who was spending the winter in Rome, informed him that the ring was a Christmas gift from her. In his rage he unjustly condemned Aunt Maria as a meddling old busybody, and gave her ring to the cook.

After two months of pilgrimages to places sacred to the memory of Polly Kirkland, Ainsley found that feeding his love on post-mortems was poor fare, and, in surrender, determined to evacuate New York. Since her departure he had received from Miss Kirkland several letters, but they contained no hint of a change in her affections, and search them as he might, he could find no cipher or hidden message. They were merely frank, friendly notes of travel; at first filled with gossip of the steamer, and later telling of excursions around Cairo. If they held any touch of feeling they seemed to show that she was sorry for him, and as she could not regard him in any way more calculated to increase his discouragement, he, in utter hopelessness, retreated to the solitude of the farm. In New York he left behind him two trunks filled with such garments as a man would need on board a steamer and in the early spring in Egypt. They had been packed and in readiness since the day she sailed away, when she had told him of the possible sign. But there had been no sign. Nor did he longer believe in one. So in the baggage-room of a hotel the trunks were abandoned, accumulating layers of dust and charges for storage.

At the farm the snow still lay in the crevices of the rocks and beneath the branches of the evergreens, but under the wet, dead leaves little flowers had begun to show their faces. The "backbone of the winter was broken" and spring was in the air. But as Ainsley was certain that his heart also was broken, the signs of spring did not console him. At each week-end he filled the house with people, but they found him gloomy and he found them dull. He liked better the solitude of the midweek days. Then for hours he would tramp through the woods, pretending she was at his side, pretending he was helping her across the streams swollen with winter rains and melted snow. On these excursions he cut down trees that hid a view he thought she would have liked, he cut paths over which she might have walked. Or he sat idly in a flat- bottomed scow in the lake and made pretence of fishing. The loneliness of the lake and the isolation of the boat suited his humor. He did not find it true that misery loves company. At least to human beings he preferred his companions of Lone Lake--the beaver building his home among the reeds, the kingfisher, the blue heron, the wild fowl that in their flight north rested for an hour or a day upon the peaceful waters. He looked upon them as his guests, and when they spread their wings and left him again alone he felt he had been hardly used.

It was while he was sunk in this state of melancholy, and some months after Miss Kirkland had sailed to Egypt, that hope returned.

205

For a week-end he had invited Holden and Lowell, two former classmates, and Nelson Mortimer and his bride. They were all old friends of their host and well acquainted with the cause of his discouragement. So they did not ask to be entertained, but, disregarding him, amused themselves after their own fashion. It was late Friday afternoon. The members of the house-party had just returned from a tramp through the woods and had joined Ainsley on the terrace, where he stood watching the last rays of the sun leave the lake in darkness. All through the day there had been sharp splashes of rain with the clouds dull and forbidding, but now the sun was sinking in a sky of crimson, and for the morrow a faint moon held out a promise of fair weather.

Elsie Mortimer gave a sudden exclamation, and pointed to the east. "Look!" she said.

The men turned and followed the direction of her hand. In the fading light, against a background of somber clouds that the sun could not reach, they saw, moving slowly toward them and descending as they moved, six great white birds. When they were above the tops of the trees that edged the lake, the birds halted and hovered uncertainly, their wings lifting and falling, their bodies slanting and sweeping slowly, in short circles.

The suddenness of their approach, their presence so far inland, something unfamiliar and foreign in the way they had winged their progress, for a moment held the group upon the terrace silent.

"They are gulls from the Sound," said Lowell.

"They are too large for gulls," returned Mortimer. "They might be wild geese, but," he answered himself, in a puzzled voice, "it is too late; and wild geese follow a leader."

As though they feared the birds might hear them and take alarm, the men, unconsciously, had spoken in low tones.

"They move as though they were very tired," whispered Elsie Mortimer.

"I think," said Ainsley, "they have lost their way."

But even as he spoke, the birds, as though they had reached their goal, spread their wings to the full length and sank to the shallow water at the farthest margin of the lake.

As they fell the sun struck full upon them, turning their great pinions into flashing white and silver.

"Oh!" cried the girl, "but they are beautiful!"

Between the house and the lake there was a ridge of rock higher than the head of a man, and to this Ainsley and his guests ran for cover. On hands and knees, like hunters stalking game, they scrambled up the face of the rock and peered cautiously into the pond. Below them, less than one hundred yards away, on a tiny promontory, the six white birds stood motionless. They showed no sign of fear. They could not but know that beyond the lonely circle of the pond were the haunts of men. From the farm came the tinkle of a cow-bell, the bark of a dog, and in the valley, six miles distant, rose faintly upon the stillness of the sunset hour the rumble of a passing train. But if these sounds carried, the birds gave no heed. In each drooping head and dragging wing, in the forward stoop of each white body, weighing heavily on the slim, black legs, was written utter weariness, abject fatigue. To each even to lower his bill and sip from the cool waters was a supreme effort. And in their exhaustion so complete was something humanly helpless and pathetic.

To Ainsley the mysterious visitors made a direct appeal. He felt as though they had thrown themselves upon his hospitality. That they showed such confidence that the sanctuary would be kept sacred touched him. And while his friends spoke eagerly, he remained silent, watching the drooping, ghost-like figures, his eyes filled with pity.

"I have seen birds like those in Florida," Mortimer was whispering, "but they were not migratory birds."

"And I've seen white cranes in the Adirondacks," said Lowell, "but never six at one time."

"They're like no bird I ever saw out of a zoo," declared Elsie Mortimer. "Maybe they ARE from the Zoo? Maybe they escaped from the Bronx?"

"The Bronx is too near," objected Lowell. "These birds have come a great distance. They move as though they had been flying for many days."

As though the absurdity of his own thought amused him, Mortimer laughed softly.

"I'll tell you what they DO look like," he said. "They look like that bird you see on the Nile, the sacred Ibis, they--"

Something between a gasp and a cry startled him into silence. He found his host staring wildly, his lips parted, his eyes open wide.

"Where?" demanded Ainsley. "Where did you say?" His voice was so hoarse, so strange, that they all turned and looked.

"On the Nile," repeated Mortimer. "All over Egypt. Why?"

Ainsley made no answer. Unclasping his hold, he suddenly slid down the face of the rock, and with a bump lit on his hands and knees. With one bound he had cleared a flower-bed. In two more he had mounted the steps to the terrace, and in another instant had disappeared into the house.

"What happened to him?" demanded Elsie Mortimer.

"He's gone to get a gun!" exclaimed Mortimer. "But he mustn't! How can he think of shooting them?" he cried indignantly. "I'll put a stop to that!"

In the hall he found Ainsley surrounded by a group of startled servants.

"You get that car at the door in five minutes!" he was shouting, "and *You* telephone the hotel to have my trunks out of the cellar and on board the Kron Prinz Albert by midnight. Then you telephone Hoboken that I want a cabin, and if they haven't got a cabin I want the captain's. And tell them anyway I'm coming on board to-night, and I'm going with them if I have to sleep on deck. And *You*," he cried, turning to Mortimer, "take a shotgun and guard that lake, and if anybody tries to molest those birds--shoot him! They've come from Egypt! From Polly Kirkland! She sent them! They're a sign!"

"Are you going mad?" cried Mortimer.

"No!" roared Ainsley. "I'm going to Egypt, and I'm going *Now!*"

Polly Kirkland and her friends were travelling slowly up the Nile, and had reached Luxor. A few hundred yards below the village their dahabiyeh was moored to the bank, and, on the deck, Miss Kirkland was watching a scarlet sun sink behind two palm-trees. By the grace of that special Providence that cares for drunken men, citizens of the United States, and lovers, her friends were on shore, and she was alone. For this she was grateful, for her thoughts were of a melancholy and tender nature and she had no wish for any companion save one. In consequence, when a steam-launch, approaching at full speed with the rattle of a quick-firing gun, broke upon her meditations, she was distinctly annoyed.

But when, with much ringing of bells and shouting of orders, the steam-launch rammed the paint off her dahabiyeh, and a young man flung himself over the rail and ran toward her, her annoyance passed, and with a sigh she sank into his outstretched, eager arms.

Half an hour later Ainsley laughed proudly and happily.

"Well!" he exclaimed, "you can never say I kept *You* waiting. I didn't lose much time, did I? Ten minutes after I got your C. Q. D. signal I was going down the Boston Post Road at seventy miles an hour."

"My what?" said the girl.

"The sign!" explained Ainsley. "The sign you were to send me to tell me"--he bent over her hands and added gently--"that you cared for me."

"Oh, I remember," laughed Polly Kirkland. "I was to send you a sign, wasn't I? You were to 'read it in your heart'," she quoted.

"And I did," returned Ainsley complacently. "There were several false alarms, and I'd almost lost hope, but when the messengers came I knew them."

With puzzled eyes the girl frowned and raised her head.

"Messengers?" she repeated. "I sent no message. Of course," she went on, "when I said you would 'read it in your heart' I meant that if you *really* loved me you would not wait for a sign, but you would just *Come*!" She sighed proudly and contentedly. "And you came. You understood that, didn't you?" she asked anxiously.

For an instant Ainsley stared blankly, and then to hide his guilty countenance drew her toward him and kissed her.

"Of course," he stammered--"of course I understood. That was why I came. I just couldn't stand it any longer."

Breathing heavily at the thought of the blunder he had so narrowly avoided, Ainsley turned his head toward the great red disk that was disappearing into the sands of the desert. He was so long silent that the girl lifted her eyes, and found that already he had forgotten her presence and, transfixed, was staring at the sky. On his face were bewilderment and wonder and a touch of awe. The girl followed the direction of his eyes, and in the swiftly gathering darkness saw coming slowly toward them, and descending as they came, six great white birds.

They moved with the last effort of complete exhaustion. In the drooping head and dragging wings of each was written utter weariness, abject fatigue. For a moment they hovered over the dahabiyeh and above the two young lovers, and then, like tired travelers who had reached their journey's end, they spread their wings and sank to the muddy waters of the Nile and into the enveloping night.

"Some day," said Ainsley, "I have a confession to make to you."

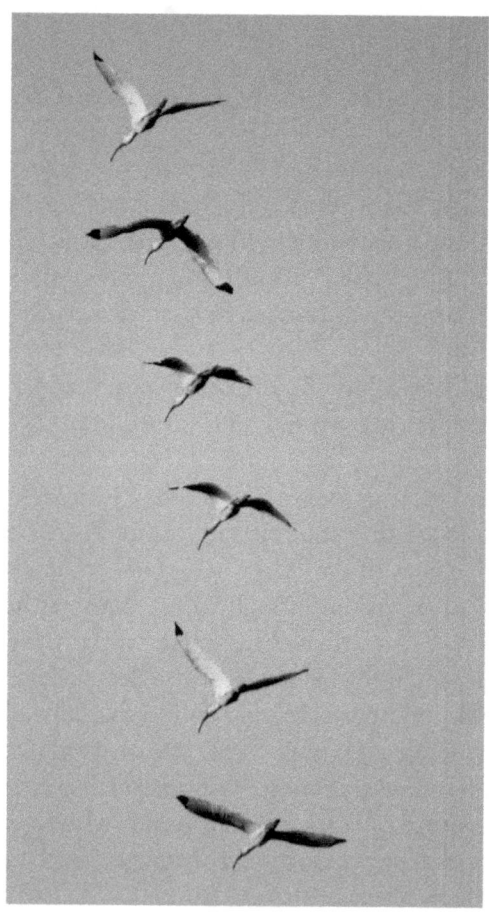

THE OTHER WOMAN

Young Latimer stood on one of the lower steps of the hall stairs, leaning with one hand on the broad railing and smiling down at her. She had followed him from the drawing-room and had stopped at the entrance, drawing the curtains behind her, and making, unconsciously, a dark background for her head and figure. He thought he had never seen her look more beautiful, nor that cold, fine air of thorough breeding about her which was her greatest beauty to him, more strongly in evidence.

"Well, sir," she said, "why don't you go?"

He shifted his position slightly and leaned more comfortably upon the railing, as though he intended to discuss it with her at some length.

"How can I go," he said, argumentatively, "with you standing there—looking like that?"

"I really believe," the girl said, slowly, "that he is afraid; yes, he is afraid. And you always said," she added, turning to him, "you were so brave."

"Oh, I am sure I never said that," exclaimed the young man, calmly. "I may be brave, in fact, I am quite brave, but I never said I was. Some one must have told you."

"Yes, he is afraid," she said, nodding her head to the tall clock across the hall, "he is temporizing and trying to save time. And afraid of a man, too, and such a good man who would not hurt any one."

"You know a bishop is always a very difficult sort of a person," he said, "and when he happens to be your father, the combination is just a bit awful. Isn't it now? And especially when one means to ask him for his daughter. You know it isn't like asking him to let one smoke in his study."

"If I loved a girl," she said, shaking her head and smiling up at him, "I wouldn't be afraid of the whole world; that's what they say in books, isn't it? I would be so bold and happy."

"Oh, well, I'm bold enough," said the young man, easily; "if I had not been, I never would have asked you to marry me; and I'm happy enough—that's because I did ask you. But what if he says no," continued the youth; "what if he says he has greater ambitions for you, just as they say in books, too. What will you do? Will you run away with me? I can borrow a coach just as they used to do, and we can drive off through the Park and be married, and come back and ask his blessing on our knees—unless he should overtake us on the elevated."

"That," said the girl, decidedly, "is flippant, and I'm going to leave you. I never thought to marry a man who would be frightened at the very first. I am greatly disappointed."

She stepped back into the drawing-room and pulled the curtains to behind her, and then opened them again and whispered, "Please don't be long," and disappeared. He waited, smiling, to see if she would make another appearance, but she did not, and he heard her touch the keys of the piano at the other end of the drawing-room. And so, still smiling and with her last words sounding in his ears, he walked slowly up the stairs and knocked at the door of the bishop's study. The bishop's room was not ecclesiastic in its character. It looked much like the room of any man of any calling who cared for his books and to have pictures about him, and copies of the beautiful things he had seen on his travels. There were pictures of the Virgin and the Child, but they were those that are seen in almost any house, and there were etchings and plaster casts, and there were hundreds of books, and dark red curtains, and an open fire that lit up the pots of brass with ferns in them, and the blue and white plaques on the top of the bookcase. The bishop sat before his writing-table, with one hand shading his eyes from the light of a red-covered lamp, and looked up and smiled pleasantly and nodded as the young man entered. He had a very strong face, with white hair hanging at the side, but was still a young man for one in such a high office. He was a man interested in many things, who could talk to men of any profession or to the mere man of pleasure, and could interest them in what he said, and force their respect and liking. And he was very good, and had, they said, seen much trouble.

"I am afraid I interrupted you," said the young man, tentatively.

"No, I have interrupted myself," replied the bishop. "I don't seem to make this clear to myself," he said, touching the paper in front of him, "and so I very much doubt if I am going to make it clear to any one else. However," he added, smiling, as he pushed the manuscript to one side, "we are not going to talk about that now. What have you to tell me that is new?"

The younger man glanced up quickly at this, but the bishop's face showed that his words had had no ulterior meaning, and that he suspected nothing more serious to come than the gossip of the clubs or a report of the local political fight in which he was keenly interested, or on their mission on the East Side. But it seemed an opportunity to Latimer.

"I *have* something new to tell you," he said, gravely, and with his eyes turned toward the open fire, "and I don't know how to do it exactly. I mean I don't just know how it is generally done or how to tell it best." He hesitated and leaned forward, with his hands locked in front of him, and his elbows resting on his knees. He was not in the least frightened. The bishop had listened to many strange stories, to many confessions, in this same study, and had learned to take them as a matter of course; but to-night something in the manner of the young man before him made him stir uneasily, and he waited for him to disclose the object of his visit with some impatience.

"I will suppose, sir," said young Latimer, finally, "that you know me rather well—I mean you know who my people are, and what I am doing here in New York, and who my friends are, and what my work amounts to. You have let me see a great deal of you, and I have appreciated your doing so very much; to so young a man as myself it has been a great compliment, and it has been of great benefit to me. I know that better than any one else. I say this because unless you had shown me this confidence it would have been almost impossible for me to say to you what I am going to say now. But you have allowed me to come here frequently, and to see you and talk with you here in your study, and to see even more of your daughter. Of course, sir, you did not suppose that I came here only to see you. I came here because I found that if I did not see Miss Ellen for a day, that that day was wasted, and that I spent it uneasily and discontentedly, and the necessity of seeing her even more frequently has grown so great that I cannot come here as often as I seem to want to come unless I am engaged to her, unless I come as her husband that is to be." The young man had been speaking very slowly and picking his words, but now he raised his head and ran on quickly.

"I have spoken to her and told her how I love her, and she has told me that she loves me, and that if you will not oppose us, will marry me. That is the news I have to tell you, sir. I don't know but that I might have told it differently, but that is it. I need not urge on you my position and all that, because I do not think that weighs with you; but I do tell you that I love Ellen so dearly that, though I am not worthy of her, of course, I have no other pleasure than to give her pleasure and to try to make her happy. I have the power to do it; but what is much more, I have the wish to do it; it is all I think of now, and all that I can ever think of. What she thinks of me you must ask her; but what she is to me neither she can tell you nor do I believe that I myself could make you understand." The young man's face was flushed and eager, and as he finished speaking he raised his head and watched the bishop's countenance anxiously. But the older man's face was hidden by his hand as he leaned with his elbow on his writing-table. His other hand was playing with a pen, and when he began to speak, which he did after a long pause, he still turned it between his fingers and looked down at it.

"I suppose," he said, as softly as though he were speaking to himself, "that I should have known this; I suppose that I should have been better prepared to hear it. But it is one of those things which men put off—I mean those men who have children, put off—as they do making their wills, as something that is in the future and that may be shirked until it comes. We seem to think that our daughters will live with us always, just as we expect to live on ourselves until death comes one day and startles us and finds us unprepared." He took down his hand and smiled gravely at the younger man with an evident effort, and said, "I did not mean to speak so gloomily, but you see my point of view must be different from yours. And she says she loves you, does she?" he added, gently.

Young Latimer bowed his head and murmured something inarticulately in reply, and then held his head erect again and waited, still watching the bishop's face.

"I think she might have told me," said the older man; "but then I suppose this is the better way. I am young enough to understand that the old order changes, that the customs of my father's time differ from those of to-day. And there is no alternative, I suppose," he said, shaking his head. "I am stopped and told to deliver, and have no choice. I will get used to it in time," he went on, "but it seems very hard now. Fathers are selfish, I imagine, but she is all I have."

Young Latimer looked gravely into the fire and wondered how long it would last. He could just hear the piano from below, and he was anxious to return to her. And at the same time he was drawn toward the older man before him, and felt rather guilty, as though he really were robbing him. But at the bishop's next words he gave up any thought of a speedy release, and settled himself in his chair.

"We are still to have a long talk," said the bishop. "There are many things I must know, and of which I am sure you will inform me freely. I believe there are some who consider me hard, and even narrow on different points, but I do not think you will find me so, at least let us hope not. I must confess that for a moment I almost hoped that you might not be able to answer the questions I must ask you, but it was only for a moment. I am only too sure you will not be found wanting, and that the conclusion of our talk will satisfy us both. Yes, I am confident of that."

His manner changed, nevertheless, and Latimer saw that he was now facing a judge and not a plaintiff who had been robbed, and that he was in turn the defendant. And still he was in no way frightened.

"I like you," the bishop said, "I like you very much. As you say yourself, I have seen a great deal of you, because I have enjoyed your society, and your views and talk were good and young and fresh, and did me good. You have served to keep me in touch with the outside world, a world of which I used to know at one time a great deal. I know your people and I know you, I think, and many people have spoken to me of you. I see why now. They, no doubt, understood what was coming better than myself, and were meaning to reassure me concerning you. And they said nothing but what was good of you. But there are certain things of which no one can know but yourself, and concerning which no other person, save myself, has a right to question you. You have promised very fairly for my daughter's future; you have suggested more than you have said, but I understood. You can give her many pleasures which I have not been able to afford; she can get from you the means of seeing more of this world in which she lives, of meeting more people, and of indulging in her charities, or in her extravagances, for that matter, as she wishes. I have no fear of her bodily comfort; her life, as far as that is concerned, will be easier and broader, and with more power for good. Her future, as I say, as you say also, is assured; but I want to ask you this," the bishop leaned forward and watched the young man anxiously, "you can protect her in the future, but can you assure me that you can protect her from the past?"

Young Latimer raised his eyes calmly and said, "I don't think I quite understand."

"I have perfect confidence, I say," returned the bishop, "in you as far as your treatment of Ellen is concerned in the future. You love her and you would do everything to make the life of the woman you love a happy one; but this is it, Can you assure me that there is nothing in the past that may reach forward later and touch my daughter through you—no ugly story, no oats that have been sowed, and no boomerang that you have thrown wantonly and that has not returned—but which may return?"

"I think I understand you now, sir," said the young man, quietly. "I have lived," he began, "as other men of my sort have lived. You know what that is, for you must have seen it about you at college, and after that before you entered the Church. I judge so from your friends, who were your friends then, I understand. You know how they lived. I never went in for dissipation, if you mean that, because it never attracted me. I am afraid I kept out of it not so much out of respect for others as for respect for myself. I found my self-respect was a very good thing to keep, and I rather preferred keeping it and losing several pleasures that other men managed to enjoy, apparently with free consciences. I confess I used to rather envy them. It is no particular virtue on my part; the thing struck me as rather more vulgar than wicked, and so I have had no wild oats to speak of; and no woman, if that is what you mean, can write an anonymous letter, and no man can tell you a story about me that he could not tell in my presence."

There was something in the way the young man spoke which would have amply satisfied the outsider, had he been present; but the bishop's eyes were still unrelaxed and anxious. He made an impatient motion with his hand.

"I know you too well, I hope," he said, "to think of doubting your attitude in that particular. I know you are a gentleman, that is enough for that; but there is something beyond these more common evils. You see, I am terribly in earnest over this—you may think unjustly so, considering how well I know you, but this child is my only child. If her mother had lived, my responsibility would have been less great; but, as it is, God has left her here alone to me in my hands. I do not think He intended my duty should end when I had fed and clothed her, and taught her to read and write. I do not think He meant that I should only act as her guardian until the first man she fancied, fancied her. I must look to her happiness not only now when she is with me, but I must assure myself of it when she leaves my roof. These common sins of youth I acquit you of. Such things are beneath you, I believe, and I did not even consider them. But there are other toils in which men become involved, other evils or misfortunes which exist, and which threaten all men who are young and free and attractive in many ways to women, as well as men. You have lived the life of the young man of this day. You have reached a place in your profession when you can afford to rest and marry and assume the responsibilities of marriage. You look forward to a life of content and peace and honorable ambition—a life, with your wife at your side, which is to last forty or fifty years. You consider where you will be twenty years from now, at what point of your career you may become a judge or give up practice; your perspective is unlimited; you even think of the college to which you may send your son. It is a long, quiet future that you are looking forward to, and you choose my daughter as the companion for that future, as the one woman with whom you could live content for that length of time. And it is in that spirit that you come to me to-night and that you ask me for my daughter. Now I am going to ask you one question, and as you answer that I will tell you whether or not you can have Ellen for your wife. You look forward, as I say, to many years of life, and you have chosen her as best suited to live that period with you; but I ask you this, and I demand that you answer me truthfully, and that you remember that you are speaking to her father. Imagine that I had the power to tell you, or rather that some superhuman agent could convince you, that you had but a month to live, and that for what you did in that month you would not be held responsible either by any moral law or any law made by man, and that your life hereafter would not be influenced by your conduct in that month, would you spend it, I ask you—and on your answer depends mine—would you spend those thirty days, with death at the end, with my daughter, or with some other woman of whom I know nothing?"

Latimer sat for some time silent, until indeed, his silence assumed such a significance that he raised his head impatiently and said with a motion of the hand, "I mean to answer you in a minute; I want to be sure that I understand."

The bishop bowed his head in assent, and for a still longer period the men sat motionless. The clock in the corner seemed to tick more loudly, and the dead coals dropping in the grate had a sharp, aggressive sound. The notes of the piano that had risen from the room below had ceased.

"If I understand you," said Latimer, finally, and his voice and his face as he raised it were hard and aggressive, "you are stating a purely hypothetical case. You wish to try me by conditions which do not exist, which cannot exist. What justice is there, what right is there, in asking me to say how I would act under circumstances which are impossible, which lie beyond the limit of human experience? You cannot judge a man by what he would do if he were suddenly robbed of all his mental and moral training and of the habit of years. I am not admitting, understand me, that if the conditions which you suggest did exist that I would do one whit differently from what I will do if they remain as they are. I am merely denying your right to put such a question to me at all. You might just as well judge the shipwrecked sailors on a raft who eat each other's flesh as you would judge a sane, healthy man who did such a thing in his own home. Are you going to condemn men who are ice-locked at the North Pole, or buried in the heart of Africa, and who have given up all thought of return and are half mad and wholly without hope, as you would judge ourselves? Are they to be weighed and balanced as you and I are, sitting here within the sound of the cabs outside and with a bake-shop around the corner? What you propose could not exist, could never happen. I could never be placed where I should have to make such a choice, and you have no right to ask me what I would do or how I would act under conditions that are super-human—you used the word yourself—where all that I have held to be good and just and true would be obliterated. I would be unworthy of myself, I would be unworthy of your daughter, if I considered such a state of things for a moment, or if I placed my hopes of marrying her on the outcome of such a test, and so, sir," said the young man, throwing back his head, "I must refuse to answer you."

The bishop lowered his hand from before his eyes and sank back wearily into his chair. "You have answered me," he said.

"You have no right to say that," cried the young man, springing to his feet. "You have no right to suppose anything or to draw any conclusions. I have not answered you." He stood with his head and shoulders thrown back, and with his hands resting on his hips and with the fingers working nervously at his waist.

"What you have said," replied the bishop, in a voice that had changed strangely, and which was inexpressibly sad and gentle, "is merely a curtain of words to cover up your true feeling. It would have been so easy to have said, 'For thirty days or for life Ellen is the only woman who has the power to make me happy.' You see that would have answered me and satisfied me. But you did not say that," he added, quickly, as the young man made a movement as if to speak.

"Well, and suppose this other woman did exist, what then?" demanded Latimer. "The conditions you suggest are impossible; you must, you will surely, sir, admit that."

"I do not know," replied the bishop, sadly; "I do not know. It may happen that whatever obstacle there has been which has kept you from her may be removed. It may be that she has married, it may be that she has fallen so low that you cannot marry her. But if you have loved her once, you may love her again; whatever it was that separated you in the past, that separates you now, that makes you prefer my daughter to her, may come to an end when you are married, when it will be too late, and when only trouble can come of it, and Ellen would bear that trouble. Can I risk that?"

"But I tell you it is impossible," cried the young man. "The woman is beyond the love of any man, at least such a man as I am, or try to be."

"Do you mean," asked the bishop, gently, and with an eager look of hope, "that she is dead?"

Latimer faced the father for some seconds in silence. Then he raised his head slowly. "No," he said, "I do not mean she is dead. No, she is not dead."

Again the bishop moved back wearily into his chair. "You mean then," he said, "perhaps, that she is a married woman?" Latimer pressed his lips together at first as though he would not answer, and then raised his eyes coldly. "Perhaps," he said.

The older man had held up his hand as if to signify that what he was about to say should be listened to without interruption, when a sharp turning of the lock of the door caused both father and the suitor to start. Then they turned and looked at each other with anxious inquiry and with much concern, for they recognized for the first time that their voices had been loud. The older man stepped quickly across the floor, but before he reached the middle of the room the door opened from the outside, and his daughter stood in the door-way, with her head held down and her eyes looking at the floor.

"Ellen!" exclaimed the father, in a voice of pain and the deepest pity.

The girl moved toward the place from where his voice came, without raising her eyes, and when she reached him put her arms about him and hid her face on his shoulder. She moved as though she were tired, as though she were exhausted by some heavy work.

"My child," said the bishop, gently, "were you listening?" There was no reproach in his voice; it was simply full of pity and concern.

"I thought," whispered the girl, brokenly, "that he would be frightened; I wanted to hear what he would say. I thought I could laugh at him for it afterward. I did it for a joke. I thought—" she stopped with a little gasping sob that she tried to hide, and for a moment held herself erect and then sank back again into her father's arms with her head upon his breast.

Latimer started forward, holding out his arms to her. "Ellen," he said, "surely, Ellen, you are not against me. You see how preposterous it is, how unjust it is to me. You cannot mean—"

The girl raised her head and shrugged her shoulders slightly as though she were cold. "Father," she said, wearily, "ask him to go away, Why does he stay? Ask him to go away."

Latimer stopped and took a step back as though some one had struck him, and then stood silent with his face flushed and his eyes flashing. It was not in answer to anything that they said that he spoke, but to their attitude and what it suggested. "You stand there," he began, "you two stand there as though I were something unclean, as though I had committed some crime. You look at me as though I were on trial for murder or worse. Both of you together against me. What have I done? What difference is there? You loved me a half-hour ago, Ellen; you said you did. I know you loved me; and you, sir," he added, more quietly, "treated me like a friend. Has anything come since then to change me or you? Be fair to me, be sensible. What is the use of this? It is a silly, needless, horrible mistake. You know I love you, Ellen; love you better than all the world. I don't have to tell you that; you know it, you can see and feel it. It does not need to be said; words can't make it any truer. You have confused yourselves and stultified yourselves with this trick, this test by hypothetical conditions, by considering what is not real or possible. It is simple enough; it is plain enough. You know I love you, Ellen, and you only, and that is all there is to it, and all that there is of any consequence in the world to me. The matter stops there; that is all there is for you to consider. Answer me, Ellen, speak to me. Tell me that you believe me."

He stopped and moved a step toward her, but as he did so, the girl, still without looking up, drew herself nearer to her father and shrank more closely into his arms; but the father's face was troubled and doubtful, and he regarded the younger man with a look of the most anxious scrutiny. Latimer did not regard this. Their hands were raised against him as far as he could understand, and he broke forth again proudly, and with a defiant indignation:

"What right have you to judge me?" he began; "what do you know of what I have suffered, and endured, and overcome? How can you know what I have had to give up and put away from me? It's easy enough for you to draw your skirts around you, but what can a woman bred as you have been bred know of what I've had to fight against and keep under and cut away? It was an easy, beautiful idyl to you; your love came to you only when it should have come, and for a man who was good and worthy, and distinctly eligible—I don't mean that; forgive me, Ellen, but you drive me beside myself. But he is good and he believes himself worthy, and I say that myself before you both. But I am only worthy and only good because of that other love that I put away when it became a crime, when it became impossible. Do you know what it cost me? Do you know what it meant to me, and what I went through, and how I suffered? Do you know who this other woman is whom you are insulting with your doubts and guesses in the dark? Can't you spare her? Am I not enough? Perhaps it was easy for her, too; perhaps her silence cost her nothing; perhaps she did not suffer and has nothing but happiness and content to look forward to for the rest of her life; and I tell you that it is because we did put it away, and kill it, and not give way to it that I am whatever I am to-day; whatever good there is in me is due to that temptation and to the fact that I beat it and overcame it and kept myself honest and clean. And when I met you and learned to know you I believed in my heart that God had sent you to me that I might know what it was to love a woman whom I could marry and who could be my wife; that you were the reward for my having overcome temptation and the sign that I had done well. And now you throw me over and put me aside as though I were something low and unworthy, because of this temptation, because of this very thing that has made me know myself and my own strength and that has kept me up for you."

As the young man had been speaking, the bishop's eyes had never left his face, and as he finished, the face of the priest grew clearer and decided, and calmly exultant. And as Latimer ceased he bent his head above his daughter's, and said in a voice that seemed to speak with more than human inspiration. "My child," he said, "if God had given me a son I should have been proud if he could have spoken as this young man has done."

But the woman only said, "Let him go to her."

"Ellen, oh, Ellen!" cried the father.

He drew back from the girl in his arms and looked anxiously and feelingly at her lover. "How could you, Ellen," he said, "how could you?" He was watching the young man's face with eyes full of sympathy and concern. "How little you know him," he said, "how little you understand. He will not do that," he added quickly, but looking questioningly at Latimer and speaking in a tone almost of command. "He will not undo all that he has done; I know him better than that." But Latimer made no answer, and for a moment the two men stood watching each other and questioning each other with their eyes. Then Latimer turned, and without again so much as glancing at the girl walked steadily to the door and left the room. He passed on slowly down the stairs and out into the night, and paused upon the top of the steps leading to the street. Below him lay the avenue with its double line of lights stretching off in two long perspectives. The lamps of hundreds of cabs and carriages flashed as they advanced toward him and shone for a moment at the turnings of the cross-streets, and from either side came the ceaseless rush and murmur, and over all hung the strange mystery that covers a great city at night. Latimer's rooms lay to the south, but he stood looking toward a spot to the north with a reckless, harassed look in his face that had not been there for many months. He stood so for a minute, and then gave a short shrug of disgust at his momentary doubt and ran quickly down the steps. "No," he said, "if it were for a month, yes; but it is to be for many years, many more long years." And turning his back resolutely to the north he went slowly home.

VAN BIBBER AND THE SWAN-BOATS

It was very hot in the Park, and young Van Bibber, who has a good heart and a great deal more money than good-hearted people generally get, was cross and somnolent. He had told his groom to bring a horse he wanted to try to the Fifty-ninth Street entrance at ten o'clock, and the groom had not appeared. Hence Van Bibber's crossness.

He waited as long as his dignity would allow, and then turned off into a by-lane end dropped on a bench and looked gloomily at the Lohengrin swans with the paddle-wheel attachment that circle around the lake. They struck him as the most idiotic inventions he had ever seen, and he pitied, with the pity of a man who contemplates crossing the ocean to be measured for his fall clothes, the people who could find delight in having some one paddle them around an artificial lake.

Two little girls from the East Side, with a lunch basket, and an older girl with her hair down her back, sat down on a bench beside him and gazed at the swans.

The place was becoming too popular, and Van Bibber decided to move on. But the bench on which he sat was in the shade, and the asphalt walk leading to the street was in the sun, and his cigarette was soothing, so he ignored the near presence of the three little girls, and remained where he was.

"I s'pose," said one of the two little girls, in a high, public school voice, "there's lots to see from those swan-boats that youse can't see from the banks."

"Oh, lots," assented the girl with long hair.

"If you walked all round the lake, clear all the way round, you could see all there is to see," said the third, "except what there's in the middle where the island is."

"I guess it's mighty wild on that island," suggested the youngest.

"Eddie Case he took a trip around the lake on a swan-boat the other day. He said that it was grand. He said youse could see fishes and ducks, and that it looked just as if there were snakes and things on the island."

"What sort of things?" asked the other one, in a hushed voice.

"Well, wild things," explained the elder, vaguely; "bears and animals like that, that grow in wild places."

Van Bibber lit a fresh cigarette, and settled himself comfortably and unreservedly to listen.

"My, but I'd like to take a trip just once," said the youngest, under her breath. Then she clasped her fingers together and looked up anxiously at the elder girl, who glanced at her with severe reproach.

"Why, Mame!" she said; "ain't you ashamed! Ain't you having a good time 'nuff without wishing for everything you set your eyes on?"

Van Bibber wondered at this—why humans should want to ride around on the swans in the first place, and why, if they had such a wild desire, they should not gratify it.

"Why, it costs more'n it costs to come all the way up town in an open car," added the elder girl, as if in answer to his unspoken question.

The younger girl sighed at this, and nodded her head in submission, but blinked longingly at the big swans and the parti-colored awning and the red seats.

"I beg your pardon," said Van Bibber, addressing himself uneasily to the eldest girl with long hair, "but if the little girl would like to go around in one of those things, and—and hasn't brought the change with her, you know, I'm sure I should be very glad if she'd allow me to send her around."

"Oh! will you?" exclaimed the little girl, with a jump, and so sharply and in such a shrill voice that Van Bibber shuddered. But the elder girl objected.

"I'm afraid maw wouldn't like our taking money from any one we didn't know," she said with dignity; "but if you're going anyway and want company—"

"Oh! my, no," said Van Bibber, hurriedly. He tried to picture himself riding around the lake behind a tin swan with three little girls from the East Side, and a lunch basket.

"Then," said the head of the trio, "we can't go."

There was such a look of uncomplaining acceptance of this verdict on the part of the two little girls, that Van Bibber felt uncomfortable. He looked to the right and to the left, and then said desperately, "Well, come along." The young man in a blue flannel shirt, who did the paddling, smiled at Van Bibber's riding-breeches, which were so very loose at one end and so very tight at the other, and at his gloves and crop. But Van Bibber pretended not to care. The three little girls placed the awful lunch basket on the front seat and sat on the middle one, and Van Bibber cowered in the back. They were hushed in silent ecstasy when it started, and gave little gasps of pleasure when it careened slightly in turning. It was shady under the awning, and the motion was pleasant enough, but Van Bibber was so afraid some one would see him that he failed to enjoy it.

But as soon as they passed into the narrow straits and were shut in by the bushes and were out of sight of the people, he relaxed, and began to play the host. He pointed out the fishes among the rocks at the edges of the pool, and the sparrows and robins bathing and ruffling their feathers in the shallow water, and agreed with them about the possibility of bears, and even tigers, in the wild part of the island, although the glimpse of the gray helmet of a Park policeman made such a supposition doubtful.

And it really seemed as though they were enjoying it more than he ever enjoyed a trip up the Sound on a yacht or across the ocean on a record-breaking steamship. It seemed long enough before they got back to Van Bibber, but his guests were evidently but barely satisfied. Still, all the goodness in his nature would not allow him to go through that ordeal again.

He stepped out of the boat eagerly and helped out the girl with long hair as though she had been a princess and tipped the rude young man who had laughed at him, but who was perspiring now with the work he had done; and then as he turned to leave the dock he came face to face with A Girl He Knew and Her brother.

Her brother said, "How're you, Van Bibber? Been taking a trip around the world in eighty minutes?" And added in a low voice, "Introduce me to your young lady friends from Hester Street."

"Ah, how're you—quite a surprise!" gasped Van Bibber, while his late guests stared admiringly at the pretty young lady in the riding-habit, and utterly refused to move on. "Been taking ride on the lake," stammered Van Bibber; "most exhilarating. Young friends of mine— these young ladies never rode on lake, so I took 'em. Did you see me?"

"Oh, yes, we saw you," said Her brother, dryly, while she only smiled at him, but so kindly and with such perfect understanding that Van Bibber grew red with pleasure and bought three long strings of tickets for the swans at some absurd discount, and gave each little girl a string.

"There," said Her brother to the little ladies from Hester Street, "now you can take trips for a week without stopping. Don't try to smuggle in any laces, and don't forget to fee the smoking-room steward."

The Girl He Knew said they were walking over to the stables, and that he had better go get his other horse and join her, which was to be his reward for taking care of the young ladies. And the three little girls proceeded to use up the yards of tickets so industriously that they were sunburned when they reached the tenement, and went to bed dreaming of a big white swan, and a beautiful young gentleman in patent-leather riding-boots and baggy breeches.

THE CYNICAL MISS CATHERWAIGHT

Miss Catherwaight's collection of orders and decorations and medals was her chief offence in the eyes of those of her dear friends who thought her clever but cynical.

All of them were willing to admit that she was clever, but some of them said she was clever only to be unkind.

Young Van Bibber had said that if Miss Catherwaight did not like dances and days and teas, she had only to stop going to them instead of making unpleasant remarks about those who did. So many people repeated this that young Van Bibber believed finally that he had said something good, and was somewhat pleased in consequence, as he was not much given to that sort of thing.

Mrs. Catherwaight, while she was alive, lived solely for society, and, so some people said, not only lived but died for it. She certainly did go about a great deal, and she used to carry her husband away from his library every night of every season and left him standing in the doorways of drawing-rooms, outwardly courteous and distinguished looking, but inwardly somnolent and unhappy. She was a born and trained social leader, and her daughter's coming out was to have been the greatest effort of her life. She regarded it as an event in the dear child's lifetime second only in importance to her birth; equally important with her probable marriage and of much more poignant interest than her possible death. But the great effort proved too much for the mother, and she died, fondly remembered by her peers and tenderly referred to by a great many people who could not even show a card for her Thursdays. Her husband and her daughter were not going out, of necessity, for more than a year after her death, and then felt no inclination to begin over again, but lived very much together and showed themselves only occasionally.

They entertained, though, a great deal, in the way of dinners, and an invitation to one of these dinners soon became a diploma for intellectual as well as social qualifications of a very high order.

One was always sure of meeting some one of consideration there, which was pleasant in itself, and also rendered it easy to let one's friends know where one had been dining. It sounded so flat to boast abruptly, "I dined at the Catherwaights' last night"; while it seemed only natural to remark, "That reminds me of a story that novelist, what's his name, told at Mr. Catherwaight's," or "That English chap, who's been in Africa, was at the Catherwaights' the other night, and told me—"

After one of these dinners people always asked to be allowed to look over Miss Catherwaight's collection, of which almost everybody had heard. It consisted of over a hundred medals and decorations which Miss Catherwaight had purchased while on the long tours she made with her father in all parts of the world. Each of them had been given as a reward for some public service, as a recognition of some virtue of the highest order—for personal bravery, for statesmanship, for great genius in the arts; and each had been pawned by the recipient or sold outright. Miss Catherwaight referred to them as her collection of dishonored honors, and called them variously her Orders of the Knights of the Almighty Dollar, pledges to patriotism and the pawnshops, and honors at second-hand.

It was her particular fad to get as many of these together as she could and to know the story of each. The less creditable the story, the more highly she valued the medal. People might think it was not a pretty hobby for a young girl, but they could not help smiling at the stories and at the scorn with which she told them.

"These," she would say, "are crosses of the Legion of Honor; they are of the lowest degree, that of chevalier. I keep them in this cigar box to show how cheaply I got them and how cheaply I hold them. I think you can get them here in New York for ten dollars;

they cost more than that—about a hundred francs—in Paris. At second-hand, of course. The French government can imprison you, you know, for ten years, if you wear one without the right to do so, but they have no punishment for those who choose to part with them for a mess of pottage.

"All these," she would run on, "are English war medals. See, on this one is 'Alma,' 'Balaclava,' and 'Sebastopol.' He was quite a veteran, was he not? Well, he sold this to a dealer on Wardour Street, London, for five and six. You can get any number of them on the Bowery for their weight in silver. I tried very hard to get a Victoria Cross when I was in England, and I only succeeded in getting this one after a great deal of trouble. They value the cross so highly; you know that it is the only other decoration in the case which holds the Order of the Garter in the Jewel Room at the Tower. It is made of copper, so that its intrinsic value won't have any weight with the man who gets it, but I bought this nevertheless for five pounds. The soldier to whom it belonged had loaded and fired cannon all alone when the rest of the men about the battery had run away. He was captured by the enemy, but retaken immediately afterward by re-enforcements from his own side, and the general in command recommended him to the Queen for decoration. He sold his cross to the proprietor of a curiosity shop and drank himself to death. I felt rather meanly about keeping it and hunted up his widow to return it to her, but she said I could have it for a consideration.

"This gold medal was given, as you see, to 'Hiram J. Stillman, of the sloop *Annie Barker*, for saving the crew of the steamship *Olivia*, June 18, 1888,' by the President of the United States and both houses of Congress. I found it on Baxter Street in a pawnshop. The gallant Hiram J. had pawned it for sixteen dollars and never came back to claim it."

"But, Miss Catherwaight," some optimist would object, "these men undoubtedly did do something brave and noble once. You can't get back of that; and they didn't do it for a medal, either, but because it was their duty. And so the medal meant nothing to them: their conscience told them they had done the right thing; they didn't need

234

a stamped coin to remind them of it, or of their wounds, either, perhaps."

"Quite right; that's quite true," Miss Catherwaight would say. "But how about this? Look at this gold medal with the diamonds: 'Presented to Colonel James F. Placer by the men of his regiment, in camp before Richmond.' Every soldier in the regiment gave something toward that, and yet the brave gentleman put it up at a game of poker one night, and the officer who won it sold it to the man who gave it to me. Can you defend that?"

Miss Catherwaight was well known to the proprietors of the pawnshops and loan offices on the Bowery and Park Row. They learned to look for her once a month, and saved what medals they received for her and tried to learn their stories from the people who pawned them, or else invented some story which they hoped would answer just as well.

Though her brougham produced a sensation in the unfashionable streets into which she directed it, she was never annoyed. Her maid went with her into the shops, and one of the grooms always stood at the door within call, to the intense delight of the neighborhood. And one day she found what, from her point of view, was a perfect gem. It was a poor, cheap-looking, tarnished silver medal, a half-dollar once, undoubtedly, beaten out roughly into the shape of a heart and engraved in script by the jeweler of some country town. On one side were two clasped hands with a wreath around them, and on the reverse was this inscription: "From Henry Burgoyne to his beloved friend Lewis L. Lockwood"; and below, "Through prosperity and adversity." That was all. And here it was among razors and pistols and family Bibles in a pawnbroker's window. What a story there was in that! These two boy friends and their boyish friendship that was to withstand adversity and prosperity, and all that remained of it was this inscription to its memory like the wording on a tomb!

"He couldn't have got so much on it any way," said the pawnbroker, entering into her humor. "I didn't lend him more'n a quarter of a dollar at the most."

Miss Catherwaight stood wondering if the Lewis L. Lockwood could be Lewis Lockwood, the lawyer one read so much about. Then she remembered his middle name was Lyman, and said quickly, "I'll take it, please."

She stepped into the carriage, and told the man to go find a directory and look for Lewis Lyman Lockwood. The groom returned in a few minutes and said there was such a name down in the book as a lawyer, and that his office was such a number on Broadway; it must be near Liberty. "Go there," said Miss Catherwaight.

Her determination was made so quickly that they had stopped in front of a huge pile of offices, sandwiched in, one above the other, until they towered mountains high, before she had quite settled in her mind what she wanted to know, or had appreciated how strange her errand might appear. Mr. Lockwood was out, one of the young men in the outer office said, but the junior partner, Mr. Latimer, was in and would see her. She had only time to remember that the junior partner was a dancing acquaintance of hers, before young Mr. Latimer stood before her smiling and with her card in his hand.

"Mr. Lockwood is out just at present, Miss Catherwaight," he said, "but he will be back in a moment. Won't you come into the other room and wait? I'm sure he won't be away over five minutes. Or is it something I could do?"

She saw that he was surprised to see her and a little ill at ease as to just how to take her visit. He tried to make it appear that he considered it the most natural thing in the world, but he overdid it, and she saw that her presence was something quite out of the common. This did not tend to set her any more at her ease. She already regretted the step she had taken. What if it should prove to be the same Lockwood, she thought, and what would they think of her?

"Perhaps you will do better than Mr. Lockwood," she said, as she followed him into the inner office. "I fear I have come upon a very foolish errand, and one that has nothing at all to do with the law."

"Not a breach of promise suit, then?" said young Latimer, with a smile. "Perhaps it is only an innocent subscription to a most worthy charity. I was afraid at first," he went on lightly, "that it was legal redress you wanted, and I was hoping that the way I led the Courdert's cotillion had made you think I could conduct you through the mazes of the law as well."

"No," returned Miss Catherwaight, with a nervous laugh; "it has to do with my unfortunate collection. This is what brought me here," she said, holding out the silver medal. "I came across it just now in the Bowery. The name was the same, and I thought it just possible Mr. Lockwood would like to have it; or, to tell you the truth, that he might tell me what had become of the Henry Burgoyne who gave it to him."

Young Latimer had the medal in his hand before she had finished speaking, and was examining it carefully. He looked up with just a touch of color in his cheeks and straightened himself visibly.

"Please don't be offended," said the fair collector. "I know what you think. You've heard of my stupid collection, and I know you think I meant to add this to it. But, indeed, now that I have had time to think—you see I came here immediately from the pawnshop, and I was so interested, like all collectors, you know, that I didn't stop to consider. That's the worst of a hobby; it carries one rough-shod over other people's feelings, and runs away with one. I beg of you, if you do know anything about the coin, just to keep it and don't tell me, and I assure you what little I know I will keep quite to myself."

Young Latimer bowed, and stood looking at her curiously, with the medal in his hand.

"I hardly know what to say," he began slowly. "It really has a story. You say you found this on the Bowery, in a pawnshop. Indeed! Well, of course, you know Mr. Lockwood could not have left it there."

Miss Catherwaight shook her head vehemently and smiled in deprecation.

"This medal was in his safe when he lived on Thirty-Fifth Street at the time he was robbed, and the burglars took this with the rest of the silver and pawned it, I suppose. Mr. Lockwood would have given more for it than any one else could have afforded to pay." He paused a moment, and then continued more rapidly: "Henry Burgoyne is Judge Burgoyne. Ah! You didn't guess that? Yes, Mr. Lockwood and he were friends when they were boys. They went to school in Westchester County. They were Damon and Pythias and that sort of thing. They roomed together at the State college and started to practice law in Tuckahoe as a firm, but they made nothing of it, and came on to New York and began reading law again with Fuller & Mowbray. It was while they were at school that they had these medals made. There was a mate to this, you know; Judge Burgoyne had it. Well, they continued to live and work together. They were both orphans and dependent on themselves. I suppose that was one of the strongest bonds between them; and they knew no one in New York, and always spent their spare time together. They were pretty poor, I fancy, from all Mr. Lockwood has told me, but they were very ambitious. They were—I'm telling you this, you understand, because it concerns you somewhat: well, more or less. They were great sportsmen, and whenever they could get away from the law office they would go off shooting. I think they were fonder of each other than brothers even. I've heard Mr. Lockwood tell of the days they lay in the rushes along the Chesapeake Bay waiting for duck. He has said often that they were the happiest hours of his life. That was their greatest pleasure, going off together after duck or snipe along the Maryland waters. Well, they grew rich and began to know people; and then they met a girl. It seems they both thought a great deal of her, as half the New York men did, I am told; and she was the reigning belle and toast, and had other admirers, and neither met with that favor she showed—well, the man she married, for instance. But for a while each thought, for some reason or other, that he was especially favored. I don't know anything about it. Mr. Lockwood never spoke of it to me. But they both fell very deeply in love with her, and each thought the other disloyal, and so they quarreled; and—and then, though the woman married, the two men kept apart. It was the one great passion of their lives, and both were proud, and each thought the other in the wrong, and so they have kept apart ever since. And—well, I believe that is all."

Miss Catherwaight had listened in silence and with one little gloved hand tightly clasping the other.

"Indeed, Mr. Latimer, indeed," she began, tremulously, "I am terribly ashamed of myself. I seemed to have rushed in where angels fear to tread. I wouldn't meet Mr. Lockwood *now* for worlds. Of course I might have known there was a woman in the case, it adds so much to the story. But I suppose I must give up my medal. I never could tell that story, could I?"

"No," said young Latimer, dryly; "I wouldn't if I were you."

Something in his tone, and something in the fact that he seemed to avoid her eyes, made her drop the lighter vein in which she had been speaking, and rise to go. There was much that he had not told her, she suspected, and when she bade him good-by it was with a reserve which she had not shown at any other time during their interview.

"I wonder who that woman was?" she murmured, as young Latimer turned from the brougham door and said "Home," to the groom. She thought about it a great deal that afternoon; at times she repented that she had given up the medal, and at times she blushed that she should have been carried in her zeal into such an unwarranted intimacy with another's story.

She determined finally to ask her father about it. He would be sure to know, she thought, as he and Mr. Lockwood were contemporaries. Then she decided finally not to say anything about it at all, for Mr. Catherwaight did not approve of the collection of dishonored honors as it was, and she had no desire to prejudice him still further by a recital of her afternoon's adventure, of which she had no doubt but he would also disapprove. So she was more than usually silent during the dinner, which was a tête-à-tête family dinner that night, and she allowed her father to doze after it in the library in his great chair without disturbing him with either questions or confessions.

They had been sitting there some time, he with his hands folded on the evening paper and with his eyes closed, when the servant brought in a card and offered it to Mr. Catherwaight. Mr. Catherwaight fumbled over his glasses, and read the name on the card aloud: "'Mr. Lewis L. Lockwood.' Dear me!" he said; "what can Mr. Lockwood be calling upon me about?"

Miss Catherwaight sat upright, and reached out for the card with a nervous, gasping little laugh.

"Oh, I think it must be for me," she said; "I'm quite sure it is intended for me. I was at his office to-day, you see, to return him some keepsake of his that I found in an old curiosity shop. Something with his name on it that had been stolen from him and pawned. It was just a trifle. You needn't go down, dear; I'll see him. It was I he asked for, I'm sure; was it not, Morris?"

Morris was not quite sure; being such an old gentleman, he thought it must be for Mr. Catherwaight he'd come.

Mr. Catherwaight was not greatly interested. He did not like to disturb his after-dinner nap, and he settled back in his chair again and refolded his hands.

"I hardly thought he could have come to see me," he murmured, drowsily; "though I used to see enough and more than enough of Lewis Lockwood once, my dear," he added with a smile, as he opened his eyes and nodded before he shut them again. "That was before your mother and I were engaged, and people did say that young Lockwood's chances at that time were as good as mine. But they weren't, it seems. He was very attentive, though; *very* attentive."

Miss Catherwaight stood startled and motionless at the door from which she had turned.

"Attentive—to whom?" she asked quickly, and in a very low voice. "To my mother?"

Mr. Catherwaight did not deign to open his eyes this time, but moved his head uneasily as if he wished to be let alone.

"To your mother, of course, my child," he answered; "of whom else was I speaking?"

Miss Catherwaight went down the stairs to the drawing-room slowly, and paused half-way to allow this new suggestion to settle in her mind. There was something distasteful to her, something that seemed not altogether unblamable, in a woman's having two men quarrel about her, neither of whom was the woman's husband. And yet this girl of whom Latimer had spoken must be her mother, and she, of course, could do no wrong. It was very disquieting, and she went on down the rest of the way with one hand resting heavily on the railing and with the other pressed against her cheeks. She was greatly troubled. It now seemed to her very sad indeed that these two one-time friends should live in the same city and meet, as they must meet, and not recognize each other. She argued that her mother must have been very young when it happened, or she would have brought two such men together again. Her mother could not have known, she told herself; she was not to blame. For she felt sure that had she herself known of such an accident she would have done something, said something, to make it right. And she was not half the woman her mother had been, she was sure of that.

There was something very likable in the old gentleman who came forward to greet her as she entered the drawing-room; something courtly and of the old school, of which she was so tired of hearing, but of which she wished she could have seen more in the men she met. Young Mr. Latimer had accompanied his guardian, exactly why she did not see, but she recognized his presence slightly. He seemed quite content to remain in the background. Mr. Lockwood, as she had expected, explained that he had called to thank her for the return of the medal. He had it in his hand as he spoke, and touched it gently with the tips of his fingers as though caressing it.

"I knew your father very well," said the lawyer, "and I at one time had the honor of being one of your mother's younger friends.

That was before she was married, many years ago." He stopped and regarded the girl gravely and with a touch of tenderness. "You will pardon an old man, old enough to be your father, if he says," he went on, "that you are greatly like your mother, my dear young lady— greatly like. Your mother was very kind to me, and I fear I abused her kindness; abused it by misunderstanding it. There was a great deal of misunderstanding; and I was proud, and my friend was proud, and so the misunderstanding continued, until now it has become irretrievable."

He had forgotten her presence apparently, and was speaking more to himself than to her as he stood looking down at the medal in his hand.

"You were very thoughtful to give me this," he continued; "it was very good of you. I don't know why I should keep it though, now, although I was distressed enough when I lost it. But now it is only a reminder of a time that is past and put away, but which was very, very dear to me. Perhaps I should tell you that I had a misunderstanding with the friend who gave it to me, and since then we have never met; have ceased to know each other. But I have always followed his life as a judge and as a lawyer, and respected him for his own sake as a man. I cannot tell—I do not know how he feels toward me."

The old lawyer turned the medal over in his hand and stood looking down at it wistfully.

The cynical Miss Catherwaight could not stand it any longer.

"Mr. Lockwood," she said, impulsively, "Mr. Latimer has told me why you and your friend separated, and I cannot bear to think that it was she—my mother—should have been the cause. She could not have understood; she must have been innocent of any knowledge of the trouble she had brought to men who were such good friends of hers and to each other. It seems to me as though my finding that coin is more than a coincidence. I somehow think that the daughter is to help undo the harm that her mother has caused—unwittingly caused. Keep the medal and don't give it back to me, for I am sure your friend has kept his, and I am sure he is still your friend at heart. Don't think I am speaking hastily or that I am thoughtless in what I am saying, but it seems to me as if friends—good, true friends—were so few that one cannot let them go without a word to bring them back. But though I am only a girl, and a very light and unfeeling girl, some people think, I feel this very much, and I do wish I could bring your old friend back to you again as I brought back his pledge."

"It has been many years since Henry Burgoyne and I have met," said the old man, slowly, "and it would be quite absurd to think that he still holds any trace of that foolish, boyish feeling of loyalty that we once had for each other. Yet I will keep this, if you will let me, and I thank you, my dear young lady, for what you have said. I thank you from the bottom of my heart. You are as good and as kind as your mother was, and—I can say nothing, believe me, in higher praise."

He rose slowly and made a movement as if to leave the room, and then, as if the excitement of this sudden return into the past could not be shaken off so readily, he started forward with a move of sudden determination.

"I think," he said, "I will go to Henry Burgoyne's house at once, to-night. I will act on what you have suggested. I will see if this has or has not been one long, unprofitable mistake. If my visit should be fruitless, I will send you this coin to add to your collection of dishonored honors, but if it should result as I hope it may, it will be your doing, Miss Catherwaight, and two old men will have much to thank you for. Good-night," he said as he bowed above her hand, "and—God bless you!"

Miss Catherwaight flushed slightly at what he had said, and sat looking down at the floor for a moment after the door had closed behind him.

Young Mr. Latimer moved uneasily in his chair. The routine of the office had been strangely disturbed that day, and he now failed to recognize in the girl before him with reddened cheeks and trembling eyelashes the cold, self-possessed young woman of society whom he had formerly known.

"You have done very well, if you will let me say so," he began, gently. "I hope you are right in what you said, and that Mr. Lockwood will not meet with a rebuff or an ungracious answer. Why," he went on quickly, "I have seen him take out his gun now every spring and every fall for the last ten years and clean and polish it and tell what great shots he and Henry, as he calls him, used to be. And then he would say he would take a holiday and get off for a little shooting. But he never went. He would put the gun back into its case again and mope in his library for days afterward. You see, he never married, and though he adopted me, in a manner, and is fond of me in a certain way, no one ever took the place in his heart his old friend had held."

"You will let me know, will you not, at once,—to-night, even,— whether he succeeds or not?" said the cynical Miss Catherwaight. "You can understand why I am so deeply interested. I see now why you said I would not tell the story of that medal. But, after all, it may be the prettiest story, the only pretty story I have to tell."

Mr. Lockwood had not returned, the man said, when young Latimer reached the home the lawyer had made for them both. He did not know what to argue from this, but determined to sit up and wait, and so sat smoking before the fire and listening with his sense of hearing on a strain for the first movement at the door.

He had not long to wait. The front door shut with a clash, and he heard Mr. Lockwood crossing the hall quickly to the library, in which he waited. Then the inner door was swung back, and Mr. Lockwood came in with his head high and his eyes smiling brightly.

There was something in his step that had not been there before, something light and vigorous, and he looked ten years younger. He crossed the room to his writing-table without speaking and began tossing the papers about on his desk. Then he closed the rolling-top lid with a snap and looked up smiling.

"I shall have to ask you to look after things at the office for a little while," he said. "Judge Burgoyne and I are going to Maryland for a few weeks' shooting."

ELEANORE CUYLER

Miss Eleanore Cuyler had dined alone with her mother that night, and she was now sitting in the drawing-room, near the open fire, with her gloves and fan on the divan beside her, for she was going out later to a dance.

She was reading a somewhat weighty German review, and the contrast which the smartness of her gown presented to the seriousness of her occupation made her smile slightly as she paused for a moment to cut the leaves.

And when the bell sounded in the hall she put the book away from her altogether, and wondered who it might be.

It might be young Wainwright, with the proof-sheets of the new story he had promised to let her see, or flowers for the dance from Bruce-Brice, of the English Legation at Washington, who for the time being was practising diplomatic moves in New York, or some of her working-girls with a new perplexity for her to unravel, or only one of the men from the stable to tell her how her hunter was getting on after his fall. It might be any of these and more. The possibilities were diverse and all of interest, and she acknowledged this to herself, with a little sigh of content that it was so. For she found her pleasure in doing many things, and in the fact that there were so many. She rejoiced daily that she was free, and her own mistress in everything; free to do these many things denied to other young women, and that she had the health and position and cleverness to carry them on and through to success. She did them all, and equally well and gracefully, whether it was the rejection of a too ambitious devotee who dared to want to have her all to himself, or the planning of a woman's luncheon, or the pushing of a bill to provide kindergartens in the public schools. But it was rather a relief when the man opened the curtains and said, "Mr. Wainwright," and Wainwright walked quickly towards her, tugging at his glove.

"You are very good to see me so late," he said, speaking as he entered, "but I had to see you to-night, and I wasn't asked to that dance. I'm going away," he went on, taking his place by the fire, with his arm resting on the mantel. He had a trick of standing there when he had something of interest to say, and he was tall and well-looking enough to appear best in that position, and she was used to it. He was the most frequent of her visitors.

"Going away," she repeated, smiling up at him; "not for long, I hope. Where are you going now?"

"I'm going to London," he said. "They cabled me this morning. It seems they've taken the play, and are going to put it on at once." He smiled, and blushed slightly at her exclamation of pleasure. "Yes, it is rather nice. It seems 'Jilted' was a failure, and they've taken it off, and are going to put on 'School,' with the old cast, until they can get my play rehearsed, and they want me to come over and suggest things."

She stopped him with another little cry of delight that was very sweet to him, and full of moment.

"Oh, how glad I am!" she said. "How proud you must be! Now, why do you pretend you are not? And I suppose Tree and the rest of them will be in the cast, and all that dreadful American colony in the stalls, and you will make a speech—and I won't be there to hear it." She rose suddenly with a quick, graceful movement, and held out her hand to him, which he took, laughing and conscious-looking with pleasure.

She sank back on the divan, and shook her head doubtfully at him. "When will you stop?" she said. "Don't tell me you mean to be an Admirable Crichton. You are too fine for that."

He looked down at the fire, and said, slowly, "It is not as if I were trying my hand at an entirely different kind of work. No, I don't think I did wrong in dramatizing it. The papers all said, when the book first came out, that it would make a good play; and then so many men wrote to me for permission to dramatize it that I thought I might as well try to do it myself. No, I think it is in line with my other work. I don't think I am straying after strange gods."

"You should not," she said, softly. "The old ones have been so kind to you. But you took me too seriously," she added.

"I am afraid sometimes," he answered, "that you do not know how seriously I do take you."

"Yes, I do," she said, quickly. "And when I am serious, that is all very well; but to-night I only want to laugh. I am very happy, it is such good news. And after the New York managers refusing it, too. They will *have* to take it *now*, now that it is a London success."

"Well, it isn't a London success yet," he said, dryly. "The books went well over there because the kind of Western things I wrote about met their ideas of this country—cowboys and prairies and Indian maidens and all that. And so I rather hope the play will suit them for the same reason."

"And you will go out a great deal, I hope," she said. "Oh, you will have to! You will find so many people to like, almost friends already. They were talking about you even when I was there, and I used to shine in reflected glory because I knew you."

"Yes, I can fancy it," he said. "But I should like to see something of them if I have time. Lowes wants me to stay with them, and I suppose I will. He would feel hurt if I didn't. He has a most absurd idea of what I did for him on the ranch when he had the fever that time, and ever since he went back to enjoy his ill-gotten gains and his title and all that, he has kept writing to me to come out. Yes, I suppose I will stay with them. They are in town now."

Miss Cuyler's face was still lit with pleasure at his good fortune, but her smile was less spontaneous than it had been. "That will be very nice. I quite envy you," she said. "I suppose you know about his sister?"

"The Honorable Evelyn?" he asked. "Yes; he used to have a photograph of her, and I saw some others the other day in a shop-window on Broadway."

"She is a very nice girl," Miss Cuyler said, thoughtfully. "I wonder how you two will get along?" and then she added, as if with sudden compunction, "but I am sure you will like her very much. She is very clever, besides."

"I don't know how a professional beauty will wear if one sees her every day at breakfast," he said. "One always associates them with functions and varnishing days and lawn-parties. You will write to me, will you not?" he added.

"That sounds," she said, "as though you meant to be gone such a very long time."

He turned one of the ornaments on the mantel with his fingers, and looked at it curiously. "It depends," he said, slowly—"it depends on so many things. No," he went on, looking at her; "it does not depend on many things; just on one."

Miss Cuyler looked up at him questioningly, and then down again very quickly, and reached meaninglessly for the book beside her. She saw something in his face and in the rigidity of his position that made her breathe more rapidly. She had not been afraid of this from him, because she had always taken the attitude towards him of a very dear friend and of one who was older, not in years, but in experience of the world, for she had lived abroad while he had gone from the university to the West, which he had made his own, in books. They were both very young.

She did not want him to say anything. She could only answer him in one way, and in a way that would hurt and give pain to them both. She had hoped he could remain just as he was, a very dear friend, with a suggestion sometimes in the background of his becoming something more. She was, of course, too experienced to believe in a long platonic friendship.

Uppermost in her mind was the thought that, no matter what he urged, she must remember that she wanted to be free, to live her own life, to fill her own sphere of usefulness, and she must not let him tempt her to forget this. She had next to consider him, and that she must be hard and keep him from speaking at all; and this was very difficult, for she cared for him very dearly. She strengthened her determination by thinking of his going away, and of how glad she would be when he had gone that she had committed herself to nothing. This absence would be a test for both of them; it could not have been better had it been arranged on purpose. She had ideas of what she could best do for those around her, and she must not be controlled and curbed, no matter how strongly she might think she wished it. She must not give way to the temptation of the moment, or to a passing mood. And then there were other men. She had their photographs on her dressing-table, and liked each for some qualities the others did not possess in such a degree; but she liked them all because no one of them had the right to say "must" or even "you might" to her, and she fancied that the moment she gave one of them this right she would hate him cordially, and would fly to the others for sympathy; and she was not a young woman who thought that matrimony meant freedom to fly to any one but her husband for that. But this one of the men was a little the worst; he made it harder for her to be quite herself. She noticed that when she was with him she talked more about her feelings than with the other men, with whom she was satisfied to discuss the play, or what girl they wanted to take into dinner. She had touches of remorse after these confidences to Wainwright, and wrote him brisk, friendly notes the next morning, in which the words "your friend" were always sure to appear, either markedly at the beginning or at the end, or tucked away in the middle. She thought by this to unravel the web she might have woven the day before. But she had apparently failed. She stood up suddenly from pure nervousness, and crossed the room as though she meant to go to the piano, which was a very unfortunate move, as she seldom played, and never for him. She sat down before it, nevertheless, rather hopelessly, and crossed her hands in front of her. He had turned, and followed her with his eyes; they were very bright and eager, and her own faltered as she looked at them.

"You do not show much interest in the one thing that will bring me back," he said. He spoke reproachfully and yet a little haughtily, as though he had already half suspected she had guessed what he meant to say.

"Ah, you cannot tell how long you will be there," she said, lightly. "You will like it much more than you think. I—" she stopped hopelessly, and glanced, without meaning to do so, at the clock-face on the mantel beside him.

"Oh," he said, with quick misunderstanding, "I beg your pardon, I am keeping you, I forgot how late it was, and you are going out." He came towards her as though he meant to go. She stood up and made a quick, impatient gesture with her hands. He was making it very hard for her.

"Fancy!" she said. "You know I want to talk to you; what does the dance matter? Why are you so unlike yourself?" she went on, gently. "And it is our last night, too."

The tone of her words seemed to reassure him, for he came nearer and rested his elbow beside her on the piano and said, "Then you are sorry that I am going?"

It was very hard to be unyielding to him when he spoke and looked as he did then; but she repeated to herself, "He will be gone to-morrow, and then I shall be so thankful that I did not bind myself—that I am still free. He will be gone, and I shall be so glad. It will only be a minute now before he goes, and if I am strong I will rejoice at leisure." So she looked up at him without a sign of the effort it cost her, frankly and openly, and said, "Sorry? Of course I am sorry. One does not have so many friends that one can spare them for long, even to have them grow famous. I think it is very selfish of you to go, for you are famous enough already."

As he looked at her and heard her words running on smoothly and meaninglessly, he knew that it was quite useless to speak, and he grew suddenly colder, and sick, and furious at once with a confused anger and bitterness. And then, for he was quite young, so young that he thought it was the manly thing to do to carry his grief off lightly instead of rather being proud of his love, however she might hold it,—he drew himself up and began pulling carefully at his glove.

"Yes," he said, slowly, "I fancy the change will be very pleasant." He was not thinking of his words or of how thoughtless they must sound. He was only anxious to get away without showing how deeply he was hurt. If he had not done this; if he had let her see how miserable he was, and that plays and books and such things were nothing to him now, and that she was just all there was in the whole world to him, it might have ended differently. But he was untried, and young. So he buttoned the left glove with careful scrutiny and said, "They always start those boats at such absurd hours; the tides never seem to suit one; you have to go on board without breakfast, or else stay on board the night before, and that's so unpleasant. Well, I hope you will enjoy the dance, and tell them I was very much hurt that I wasn't asked."

He held out his hand quite steadily. "I will write you if you will let me," he went on, "and send you word where I am as soon as I know." She took his hand and said, "Good-by, and I hope it will be a grand success: I know it will. And come back soon; and, yes, do write to me. I hope you will have a very pleasant voyage."

He had reached the door and stopped uncertainly at the curtains. "Thank you," he said; and "Oh," he added, politely, "will you say good-by to your mother for me, please?"

She nodded her head and smiled and said, "Yes; I will not forget. Good-by."

She did not move until she heard the door close upon him, and then she turned towards the window as though she could still follow him through the closed blinds, and then she walked over to the divan and picked up her fan and gloves and remained looking down at them in her hand. The room seemed very empty. She glanced at the place where he had stood and at the darkened windows again, and sank down very slowly against the cushions of the divan, and pressed her hands against her cheeks.

She did not hear the rustle of her mother's dress as she came down the stairs and parted the curtains.

"Are you ready, Eleanore?" she said, briskly. "Tell me, how does this lace look? I think there is entirely too much of it."

It was a month after this, simultaneously with the announcements by cable of the instant success in London of "A Western Idyl," that Miss Cuyler retired from the world she knew, and disappeared into darkest New York by the way of Rivington Street. She had discovered one morning that she was not ill nor run down nor overtaxed, but just mentally tired of all things, and that what she needed was change of air and environment, and unselfish work for the good of others, and less thought of herself. Her mother's physician suggested to her, after a secret and hasty interview with Mrs. Cuyler, that change of air was good, but that the air of Rivington Street was not of the best; and her friends, both men and women, assured her that they appreciated her much more than the people of the east side possibly could do, and that they were much more worthy of her consideration, and in a fair way of improvement yet if she would only continue to shine upon and before them. But she was determined in her purpose, and regarded the College Settlement as the one opening and refuge for the energies which had too long been given to the arrangement of paper chases across country, and the routine of society, and dilettante interest in kindergartens. Life had become for her real and earnest, and she rejected Bruce-Brice of the British Legation with the sad and hopeless kindness of one who almost contemplates taking the veil, and to whom the things of this world outside of tenements are hollow and unprofitable. She found a cruel disappointment at first, for the women of the College Settlement had rules and ideas of their own, and had seen enthusiasts like herself come into Rivington Street before, and depart again. She had thought she would nurse the sick and visit the prisoners on the Island, and bring cleanliness and hope into miserable lives, but she found that this was the work of women tried in the service, who understood it, and who made her first serve her apprenticeship by reading the German Bible to old women whose eyes were dim, but who were as hopelessly clean and quite as self-respecting in their way as herself. The heroism and the self-sacrifice of a Father Damien or a

Florence Nightingale were not for her; older and wiser young women saw to that work with a quiet matter-of-fact cheerfulness and a common-sense that bewildered her. And they treated her kindly, but indulgently, as an outsider. It took her some time to understand this, and she did not confess to herself without a struggle that she was disappointed in her own usefulness; but she brought herself to confess it to her friends "uptown," when she visited that delightful country from which she was self-exiled. She went there occasionally for an afternoon's rest or to a luncheon or a particularly attractive dinner, but she always returned to the Settlement at night, and this threw an additional interest about her to her friends—an interest of which she was ashamed, for she knew how little she was really doing, and that her sacrifice was one of discomfort merely. The good she did now, it was humiliating to acknowledge, was in no way proportionate to that which her influence had wrought among people of her own class.

And what made it very hard was that wherever she went they seemed to talk of him. Now it would be a girl just from the other side who had met him on the terrace of the Lower House, "where he seemed to know every one," and another had driven with him to Ascot, where he had held the reins, and had shown them what a man who had guided a mail-coach one whole winter over the mountains for a living could do with a coach for pleasure. And many of the men had met him at the clubs and at house parties in the country, and they declared with enthusiastic envy that he was no end of a success. Her English friends all wrote of him, and wanted to know all manner of little things concerning him, and hinted that they understood they were very great friends. The papers seemed to be always having him doing something, and there was apparently no one else in London who could so properly respond to the toasts of America at all the public dinners. She had had letters from him herself—of course bright, clever ones—that suggested what a wonderfully full and happy life his was, but with no reference to his return. He was living with his young friend Lord Lowes, and went everywhere with him and his people; and then as a final touch, which she had already anticipated, people began to speak of him and the Honorable Evelyn. What could be more natural? they said. He had saved her brother's life while out West half a dozen times at least, from all accounts; and he was rich, and well-looking, and well-born, and rapidly becoming famous.

A young married woman announced it at a girls' luncheon. She had it from her friend the Marchioness of Pelby, who was Evelyn's first-cousin. So far, only the family had been told; but all London knew it, and it was said that Lord Lowes was very much pleased. One of the girls at the table said you never could tell about those things; she had no doubt the Marchioness of Pelby was an authority, but she would wait until she got their wedding-cards before she believed it. For some reason this girl did not look at Miss Cuyler, and Miss Cuyler felt grateful to her, and thought she was a nice, bright little thing; and then another girl said it was only turn about. The Englishmen had taken all the attractive American girls, and it was only fair that the English girls should get some of the nice American men. This girl was an old friend of Eleanore's; but she was surprised at her making such a speech, and wondered why she had not noticed in her before similar exhibitions of bad taste. She walked back to Rivington Street from the luncheon; composing the letter she would write to him, congratulating him on his engagement. She composed several. Some of them were very short and cheery, and others rather longer and full of reminiscences. She wondered with sudden fierce bitterness how he could so soon forget certain walks and afternoons they had spent together; and the last note, which she composed in bed, was a very sad and scornful one, and so pathetic as a work of composition that she cried a little over it, and went to sleep full of indignation that she had cried.

She told herself the next morning that she had cried because she was frankly sorry to lose the companionship of so old and good a friend, and because now that she had been given much more important work to do, she was naturally saddened by the life she saw around her, and weakened by the foul air of the courts and streets, and the dreary environments of the tenements. As for him, she was happy in his happiness; and she pictured how some day, when he proudly brought his young bride to this country to show her to his friends, he would ask after her. And they would say: "Who! Eleanore Cuyler? Why, don't you know? While you were on your honeymoon she was in the slums, where she took typhoid fever nursing a child, and died!" Or else some day, when she had grown into a beautiful sweet-faced old lady, with white hair, his wife would die, and he would return to her, never having been very happy with his first wife, but having nobly hidden from her and from the world his true feelings. He would find her working among the poor, and would ask her forgiveness, and she could not quite determine whether she would forgive him or not. These pictures comforted her even while they saddened her, and she went about her work, feeling that it was now her life's work, and that she was in reality an old, old woman. The rest, she was sure, was but a weary waiting for the end.

It was about six months after this, in the early spring, while Miss Cuyler was still in Rivington Street, that young Van Bibber invited his friend Travers to dine with him, and go on later to the People's Theatre, on the Bowery, where Irving Willis, the Boy Actor, was playing "Nick of the Woods." Travers dispatched a hasty and joyous note in reply to this to the effect that he would be on hand. He then went off with a man to try a horse at a riding academy, and easily and promptly forgot all about it. He did remember, as he was dressing for dinner, that he had an appointment somewhere, and took some consolation out of this fact, for he considered it a decided step in advance when he could remember that he had an engagement, even if he could not recall what it was. The stern mental discipline necessary to do this latter would, he hoped, come in time. So he dined unwarily at home, and was, in consequence, seized upon by his father, who sent him to the opera, as a substitute for himself, with his mother and sisters, while he went off delightedly to his club to play whist.

Travers did not care for the opera, and sat in the back of the box and dozed, and wondered moodily what so many nice men saw in his sisters to make them want to talk to them. It was midnight, and just as he had tumbled into bed, when the nature of his original engagement came back to him, and his anger and disappointment were so intense that he kicked the clothes over the foot of his bedstead.

As for Van Bibber, he knew his friend too well to wait for him, and occupied a box at the People's Theatre in solitary state, and from its depths gurgled with delight whenever the Boy Actor escaped being run over by a real locomotive, or in turn rescued the stout heroine from six red shirted cowboys. There were quite as many sudden deaths and lofty sentiments as he had expected, and he left the theatre with the pleased satisfaction of an evening well spent and with a pitying sympathy for Travers who had missed it. The night was pleasant and filled with the softness of early spring, and Van Bibber turned down the Bowery with a cigar between his teeth and no determined purpose except the one that he did not intend to go to bed. The streets were still crowded, and the lights showed the many types of this "Thieves' Highway" with which Van Bibber, in his many excursions in search of mild adventure, had become familiar. They were so familiar that the unfamiliarity of the hurrying figure of a girl of his own class who passed in front of him down Grand Street brought him, abruptly wondering, to a halt. She had passed directly under an electric light, and her dress, and walk, and bearing he seemed to recognize, but as belonging to another place. What a girl, well-born and well-dressed, could be doing at such an hour in such a neighborhood aroused his curiosity; but it was rather with a feeling of *noblesse oblige*, and a hope of being of use to one of his own people, that he crossed to the opposite side of the street and followed her. She was evidently going somewhere; that was written in every movement of her regular quick walk and her steadfast look ahead. Her veil hid the upper part of her face, and the passing crowd shut her sometimes entirely from view; but Van Bibber, himself unnoticed, succeeded in keeping her in sight, while he speculated as to the nature of her errand and her personality. At Eldridge Street she turned sharply to the north, and, without a change in her hurrying gait, passed on quickly, and turned again at Rivington. "Oh," said Van Bibber, with relieved curiosity, "one of the College Settlement," and stopped satisfied. But the street had now become deserted, and though he disliked the idea of following a woman, even though she might not be aware of his doing so, he disliked even more the idea of leaving her to make her way in such a place alone. And so he started on again, and as there was now more likelihood of her seeing him in the empty street, he dropped farther to the rear and kept in the shadow; and as he did so, he saw a man, whom he had before noticed on the opposite side of the street, quicken his pace and draw nearer to the girl. It seemed impossible to Van Bibber that any man could mistake the standing of this woman and the evident purpose of her haste; but the man was apparently settling his pace to match hers, as if only waiting an opportunity to approach her. Van Bibber tucked his stick under his arm and moved forward more quickly. It was midnight, and the street was utterly strange to him. From the light of the lamps he could see signs in Hebrew and the double eagle of Russia painted on the windows of the saloons. Long rows of trucks and drays stood ranged along the pavements for the night, and on some of the stoops and fire-escapes of the tenements a few dwarfish specimens of the Polish Jew sat squabbling in their native tongue.

But it was not until they had reached Orchard Street, and when Rivington Street was quite empty, that the man drew up uncertainly beside the girl, and, bending over, stared up in her face, and then, walking on at her side, surveyed her deliberately from head to foot. For a few steps the girl moved on as apparently unmindful of his near presence as though he were a stray dog running at her side; but when he stepped directly in front of her, she stopped and backed away from him fearfully. The man hesitated for an instant, and then came on after her, laughing.

Van Bibber had been some distance in the rear. He reached the curb beside them just as the girl turned back, with the man still following her, and stepped in between them. He had come so suddenly from out of the darkness that they both started. Van Bibber did not look at the man. He turned to the girl, and raised his hat slightly, and recognized Eleanore Cuyler instantly as he did so; but as she did not seem to remember him he did not call her by name, but simply said, with a jerk of his head, "Is this man annoying you?"

Miss Cuyler seemed to wish before everything else to avoid a scene.

"He—he just spoke to me, that is all," she said. "I live only a block below here; if you will please let me go on alone, I would be very much obliged."

"Certainly, do go on," said Van Bibber, "but I shall have to follow you until you get in-doors. You needn't be alarmed, no one will speak to you." Then he turned to the man, and said, in a lower tone, "You wait here till I get back, will you? I want to talk to you."

The man paid no attention to him whatsoever. He was so far misled by Van Bibber's appearance as to misunderstand the situation entirely. "Oh, come now," he said, smiling knowingly at the girl, "you can't shake me for no dude."

He put out his hand as he spoke as though he meant to touch her. Van Bibber pulled his stick from under his arm and tossed it out of his way, and struck the man twice heavily in the face. He was very cool and determined about it, and punished him, in consequence, much more effectively than if his indignation had made him excited. The man gave a howl of pain, and stumbled backwards over one of the stoops, where he dropped moaning and swearing, with his fingers pressed against his face.

"*Please*, now," begged Van Bibber, quickly turning to Miss Cuyler, "I am very sorry, but if you had *only* gone when I asked you to." He motioned impatiently with his hand. "Will you please go?"

But the girl, to his surprise, stood still and looked past him over his shoulder. Van Bibber motioned again for her to pass on, and then, as she still hesitated, turned and glanced behind him. The street had the blue-black look of a New York street at night. There was not a lighted window in the block. It seemed to have grown suddenly more silent and dirty and desolate-looking. He could see the glow of the elevated station at Allen Street, and it seemed fully a half-mile away. Save for the girl and the groaning fool on the stoop, and the three figures closing in on him, he was quite alone. The foremost of the three men stopped running, and came up briskly with his finger held interrogatively in front of him. He stopped when it was within a foot of Van Bibber's face.

"Are you looking for a fight?" he asked.

There was enough of the element of the sport in Van Bibber to enable him to recognize the same element in the young man before him. He knew that this was no whimpering blackguard who followed women into side streets to insult them; this was one of the purest specimens of the tough of the East-Side water-front, and he and his companions would fight as readily as Van Bibber would smoke—and they would not fight fair. The adventure had taken on a grim and serious turn, and Van Bibber gave an imperceptible shrug and a barely audible exclamation of disgust as he accepted it.

"Because," continued his new opponent with business-like briskness, "if you're looking for a fight, you can set right to me. You needn't think you can come down here and run things—you—" He followed this with an easy roll of oaths, intended to goad his victim into action.

A reformed prize-fighter had once told Van Bibber that there were six rules to observe in a street fight. He said he had forgotten the first five, but the sixth one was to strike first. Van Bibber turned his head towards Miss Cuyler. "You had better run," he said, over his shoulder; and then, turning quickly, he brought his left fist, with all the strength and weight of his arm and body back of it, against the end of the new-comer's chin.

This is a most effective blow. This is so because the lower jaw is anatomically loose; and when it is struck heavily, it turns and jars the brain, and the man who is struck feels as though the man who struck him had opened the top of his skull and taken his brains in his hand and wrenched them as a brakeman wrenches a brake. If you shut your teeth hard, and rap the tip of your chin sharply with your knuckles, you can get an idea of how effective this is when multiplied by an arm and all the muscles of a shoulder.

The man threw up his arms and went over backwards, groping blindly with his hands.

Van Bibber heard a sharp rapping behind him frequently repeated; he could not turn to see what it was, for one of the remaining men was engaging him in front, and the other was kicking at his knee-cap, and striking at his head from behind. He was no longer cool; he was grandly and viciously excited; and, rushing past his opponent, he caught him over his hip with his left arm across his breast, and so tossed him, using his hip for a lever.

A man in this position can be thrown so that he will either fall as lightly as a baby falls from his pillow to the bed, or with sufficient force to break his ribs. Van Bibber, being excited, threw him the latter way. Seeing this, the second man, who had so far failed to find Van Bibber's knee-cap, backed rapidly away, with his hands in front of him.

"Here," he cried, "lem'me alone; I'm not in this."

"Oh yes, you are," cried Van Bibber, gasping, but with fierce politeness. "Excuse me, but you are. Put up your hands; I'm going to kill *you*."

He had a throbbing feeling in the back of his head, and his breathing was difficult. He could still hear the heavy, irregular rapping behind him, but it had become confused with the throbbing in his head. "Put up your hands," he panted.

The third man, still backing away, placed his arms in a position of defense, and Van Bibber beat them down savagely, and caught him by the throat and pounded him until his arm was tired, and he had to drop him at his feet.

As he turned dizzily, he heard a sharp answering rap down the street, and saw coming towards him the burly figure of a policeman running heavily and throwing his night-stick in front of him by its leather thong, so that it struck reverberating echoes out of the pavement.

And then he saw to his amazement that Miss Cuyler was still with him, standing by the curb and beating it with his heavy walking-stick as calmly as though she were playing golf, and looking keenly up and down the street for possible aid. Van Bibber gazed at her with breathless admiration.

"Good heavens!" he panted, "didn't I ask you *please* to go home?"

The policeman passed them and dived uncertainly down a dark area-way as one departing figure disappeared into the open doorway of a tenement, on his way to the roof, and the legs of another dodged between the line of drays.

"Where'd them fellows go?" gasped the officer, instantly reappearing up the steps of the basement.

"How should I know?" answered Van Bibber, and added, with ill-timed lightness, "they didn't leave any address." The officer stared at him with severe suspicion, and then disappeared again under one of the trucks.

"I am very, very much obliged to you, Miss Cuyler," Van Bibber said. He tried to raise his hat, but the efforts of the gentleman who had struck him from behind had been successful and the hat came off only after a wrench that made him wince.

"You were very brave," he went on. "And it was very good of you to stand by me. You won't mind my saying so, now, will you? But you gave the wrong rap. I hadn't time to tell you to change it." He mopped the back of his head tenderly with his handkerchief, and tried to smile cheerfully. "You see, you were giving the rap," he explained politely, "for a fire-engine; but it's of no consequence." Miss Cuyler came closer to him, and he saw that her face showed sudden anxiety.

"Mr. Van Bibber!" she exclaimed. "Oh, I didn't know it was you! I didn't know it was any one who knew me. What will you think?"

"I beg your pardon," said Van Bibber, blankly.

"You must not believe," she went on, quickly, "that I am subject to this sort of thing. Please do not imagine I am annoyed down here like this. It has never happened before. I was nursing a woman, and her son, who generally goes home with me, was kept at the works, and I thought I could risk getting back alone. You see," she explained, as Van Bibber's face showed he was still puzzled, "my people do not fancy my living down here; and if they should hear of this they would never consent to my remaining another day, and it means so much to me now."

"They need not hear of it," Van Bibber answered, sympathetically. "They certainly won't from me, if that's what you mean."

The officer had returned, and interrupted them brusquely. It seemed to him that he was not receiving proper attention.

"Say, what's wrong here?" he demanded. "Did that gang take anything off'n you."

"They did not," said Van Bibber. "They held me up, but they didn't take nothin' off'n of me."

The officer flushed uncomfortably, and was certain now that he was being undervalued. He surveyed the blood running down over Van Bibber's collar with a smile of malicious satisfaction.

"They done you up, any way," he suggested.

"Yes, they done me up," assented Van Bibber, cheerfully, "and if you'd come a little sooner they'd done you up too."

He stepped to Miss Cuyler's side, and they walked on down the street to the College Settlement in silence, the policeman following uncertainly in the rear.

"I haven't thanked you, Mr. Van Bibber," said Miss Cuyler. "It was really fine of you, and most exciting. You must be very strong. I can't imagine how you happened to be there, but it was most fortunate for me that you were. If you had not, I—"

"Oh, that's all right," said Van Bibber, hurriedly. "I haven't had so much fun without paying for it for a long time. Fun," he added, meditatively, "costs so much."

"And you will be so good, then, as not to speak of it," she said, as she gave him her hand at the door.

"Of course not. Why should I?" said Van Bibber, and then his face beamed and clouded again instantly. "But, oh," he begged, "I'm afraid I'll have to tell Travers! Oh, please let me tell Travers! I'll make him promise not to mention it, but it's too good a joke on him, when you think what he missed. You see," he added, hastily, "we were to have gone out together, and he forgot, as usual, and missed the whole thing, and he wasn't *in it*, and it will just about break his heart. He's always getting grinds on me," he went on, persuasively, "and now I've got this on him. You will really have to let me tell Travers."

Miss Cuyler looked puzzled and said "Certainly," though she failed to see why Mr. Travers should want his head broken, and then she thanked Van Bibber again and nodded to the officer and went indoors.

The policeman, who had listened to the closing speeches, looked at Van Bibber with dawning admiration.

"Now then, officer," said Van Bibber, briskly, "which of the saloons around here break the law by keeping open after one? You probably know, and if you don't I'll have to take your number." And peace being in this way restored, the two disappeared together into the darkness to break the law.

Van Bibber told Travers about it the next morning, and Travers forgot he was not to mention it, and told the next man he met. By one o'clock the story had grown in his telling, and Van Bibber's reputation had grown with it.

Travers found three men breakfasting together at the club, and drew up a chair. "Have you heard the joke Van Bibber's got on me?" he asked, sadly, by way of introduction.

Wainwright was sitting at the next table with his back to them. He had just left the customs officers, and his wonder at the dirtiness of the streets and height of the buildings had given way to the pleasure of being home again, and before the knowledge that "old friends are best." He had meant to return again immediately as soon as he had arranged for the production of his play in New York; his second play was to be brought out in London in a month. But the heartiness of his friends' greetings, and the anxiety of men to be recognized who had been mere acquaintances hitherto, had touched and amused him. He was too young to be cynical over it, and he was glad, on the whole, that he had come back.

His mind was wide awake, and shifting from one pleasant thought to another, when he heard Travers's voice behind him raised impressively. "And they both went at Van hammer and tongs," he heard Travers say, "one in front and the other behind, kicking and striking all over the shop. And," continued Travers, interrupting himself suddenly with a shrill and anxious tone of interrogation, "where was I while this was going on? That's the pathetic part of it— where was I?" His voice rose to almost a shriek of disappointment. "*I* was sitting in a red-silk box listening to a red-silk opera with a lot of *girls*—that's what *I* was doing. I wasn't in it; I wasn't. I—"

"Well, never mind what you were doing," said one of the men, soothingly; "you weren't in it, as you say. Return to the libretto."

"Well," continued Travers, meekly, "let me see; where was I?"

"You were in a red-silk box," suggested one of the men, reaching for the coffee.

"Go on, Travers," said the first man. "The two men were kicking Van Bibber."

"Oh, yes," cried Travers. "Well, Van just threw the first fellow over his head, and threw him *hard*. He must have broken his ribs, for the second fellow tried to get away, and begged off, but Van wouldn't have it, and rushed him. He got the tough's head under his arm, and pummelled it till his arm ached, and then he threw him into the street, and asked if any other gentleman would like to try his luck. That's what Van did, and he told me not to tell any one, so I hope you will not mention it. But I had to tell you, because I want to know if you have ever met a harder case of hard luck than that. Think of it, will you? Think of me sitting there in a red-silk box listening to a—"

"What did the girl do?" interrupted one of the men.

"Oh, yes," said Travers, hastily; "that's the best part of it; that's the plot—the girl. Now, who do you think the girl was?" He looked around the table proudly, with the air of a man who is sure of his climax.

"How should I know?" one man said. "Some actress going home from the theatre, maybe—"

"No," said Travers. "It's a girl you all know." He paused impressively. "What would you say now," he went on, dropping his voice, "if I was to tell you it was Eleanore Cuyler?"

The three men looked up suddenly and at each other with serious concern. There was a moment's silence. "Well," said one of them, softly, "that *is* rather nasty."

"Now, what I want to know is," Travers ran on, elated at the sensation his narrative had made—"what I want to know is, where is that girl's mother, or sister, or brother? Have they anything to say? Has any one anything to say? Why, one of Eleanore Cuyler's little fingers is worth more than all the East and West Side put together; and she is to be allowed to run risks like—"

Wainwright pushed his chair back, and walked out of the room.

"See that fellow, quick," said Travers; "that's Wainwright who writes plays and things. He's a thoroughbred sport, too, and he just got back from London. It's in the afternoon papers."

Miss Cuyler was reading to Mrs. Lockmuller, who was old and bedridden and cross. Under the influence of Eleanore's low voice she

266

frequently went to sleep, only to wake and demand ungratefully why the reading had stopped.

Miss Cuyler was very tired. It was close and hot, and her head ached a little, and the prospect across the roofs of the other tenements was not cheerful. Neither was the thought that she was to spend her summer making working-girls happy on a farm on Long Island.

She had grown sceptical as to working-girls, and of the good she did them—or any one else. It was all terribly dreary and forlorn, and she wished she could end it by putting her head on some broad shoulder and by being told that it didn't matter, and that she was not to blame if the world would be wicked and its people unrepentant and ungrateful. Corrigan, on the third floor, was drunk again and promised trouble. His voice ascended to the room in which she sat, and made her nervous, for she was feeling the reaction from the excitement of the night before. There were heavy footsteps on the stairs, and a child's shrill voice cried, "She's in there," and, suspecting it might be Corrigan, she looked up fearfully, and then the door opened and she saw the most magnificent and the handsomest being in the world. His magnificence was due to a Bond Street tailor, who had shown how very small a waist will go with very broad shoulders, and if he was handsome, that was the tan of a week at sea. But it was not the tan, nor the unusual length of his coat, that Eleanore saw, but the eager, confident look in his face—and all she could say was, "Oh, Mr. Wainwright," feebly.

Wainwright waved away all such trifling barriers as "Mister" and "Miss." He came towards her with his face stern and determined. "Eleanore," he said, "I have a hansom at the door, and I want you to come down and get into it."

Was this the young man she had been used to scold and advise and criticize? She looked at him wondering and happy. It seemed to rest her eyes just to see him, and she loved his ordering her so, until a flash of miserable doubt came over her that if he was confident, it was because he was not only sure of himself, but of some one else on the other side of the sea.

And all her pride came to her, and thankfulness that she had not shown him what his coming meant, and she said, "Did my mother send you? How did you come? Is anything wrong?"

He took her hand in one of his and put his other on top of it firmly. "Yes," he said. "Everything is wrong. But we'll fix all that."

He did not seem able to go on immediately, but just looked at her. "Eleanore," he said, "I have been a fool, all sorts of a fool. I came over here to go back again at once, and I am going back, but not alone. I have been alone too long. I had begun to fancy there was only one woman in the world until I came back, and then—something some man said proved to me there was another one, and that she was the only one, and that I—had come near losing her. I had tried to forget about her. I had tried to harden myself to her by thinking she had been hard to me. I said—she does not care for you as the woman you love must care for you, but it doesn't matter now whether she cares or not, for I love *her* so. I want her to come to me and scold me again, and tell me how unworthy I am, and make me good and true like herself, and happy. The rest doesn't count without her, it means nothing to me unless she takes it and keeps it in trust for me, and shares it with me." He had both her hands now, and was pressing them against the flowers in the breast of the long coat.

"Eleanore," he said, "I tried to tell you once of the one thing that would bring me back and you stopped me. Will you stop me now?"

She tried to look up at him, but she would not let him see the happiness in her face just then, and lowered it and gently said, "No, no."

It must have taken him a long time to tell it, for after he had driven them twice around the Park the driver of the hansom decided that he could ask eight dollars at the regular rates, and might even venture on ten, and the result showed that as a judge of human nature he was a success.

They were married in May, and Lord Lowes acted as best man, and his sister sent her warmest congratulations and a pair of silver candlesticks for the dinner-table, which Wainwright thought were very handsome indeed, but which Miss Cuyler considered a little showy. Van Bibber and Travers were ushers, and, indeed, it was Van Bibber himself who closed the door of the carriage upon them as they were starting forth after the wedding. Mrs. Wainwright said something to her husband, and he laughed and said, "Van, Mrs. Wainwright says she's much obliged."

"Yes?" said Van Bibber, pleased and eager, putting his head through the window of the carriage. "What for, Mrs. Wainwright— the chafing-dish? Travers gave half, you know."

And then Mrs. Wainwright said, "No; not for the chafing-dish."

And they drove off, laughing.

"Look at 'em," said Travers, morosely. "*They* don't think the wheels are going around, do they? *They* think it is just the earth revolving with them on top of it, and nobody else. We don't have to say 'please' to no one, not much! We can do just what we jolly well please, and dine when we please and wherever we please. You say to me, Travers, let's go to Pastor's to-night, and I say, I won't, and you say I won't go to the Casino, because I don't want to, and there you are, and all we have to do is to agree to go somewhere else."

"I wonder," said Van Bibber, dreamily, as he watched the carriage disappear down the avenue, "what brings a man to the proposing point?"

"Some other man," said Travers, promptly. "Some man he thinks has more to do for the girl than he likes."

"Who," persisted Van Bibber, innocently, "do you think was the man in that case?"

"How should I know?" exclaimed Travers, impatiently, waving away such unprofitable discussion with a sweep of his stick, and coming down to the serious affairs of life. "What I want to know is to what theatre we are going—that's what I want to know."

The Hungry Man was Fed

Young Van Bibber broke one of his rules of life one day and came down-town. This unusual journey into the marts of trade and finance was in response to a call from his lawyer, who wanted his signature to some papers. It was five years since Van Bibber had been south of the north side of Washington Square, except as a transient traveler to the ferries on the elevated road. And as he walked through the City Hall Square he looked about him at the new buildings in the air, and the bustle and confusion of the streets, with as much interest as a lately arrived immigrant.

He rather enjoyed the novelty of the situation, and after he had completed his business at the lawyer's office he tried to stroll along lower Broadway as he did on the Avenue.

But people bumped against him, and carts and drays tried to run him down when he crossed the side streets, and those young men whom he knew seemed to be in a great hurry, and expressed such amused surprise at seeing him that he felt very much out of place indeed. And so he decided to get back to his club window and it's quiet as soon as possible.

"Hello, Van Bibber," said one of the young men who were speeding by, "what brings you here? Have you lost your way?"

"I think I have," said Van Bibber. "If you'll kindly tell me how I can get back to civilization again, be obliged to you."

"Take the elevated from Park Place," said his friend from over his shoulder, as he nodded and dived into the crowd.

The visitor from up-town had not a very distinct idea as to where Park Place was, but he struck off Broadway and followed the line of the elevated road along Church Street. It was at the corner of Vesey Street that a miserable-looking, dirty, and red-eyed object stood still in his tracks and begged Van Bibber for a few cents to buy food. "I've come all the way from Chicago," said the Object, "and I haven't tasted food for twenty-four hours."

Van Bibber drew away as though the Object had a contagious disease in his rags, and handed him a quarter without waiting to receive the man's blessing.

"Poor devil!" said Van Bibber. "Fancy going without dinner all day!" He could not fancy this, though he tried, and the impossibility of it impressed him so much that he amiably determined to go back and hunt up the Object and give him more money. Van Bibber's ideas of a dinner were rather exalted. He did not know of places where a quarter was good for a "square meal," including "one roast, three vegetables, and pie." He hardly considered a quarter a sufficiently large tip for the waiter who served the dinner, and decidedly not enough for the dinner itself. He did not see his man at first, and when he did the man did not see him. Van Bibber watched him stop three gentlemen, two of whom gave him some money, and then the Object approached Van Bibber and repeated his sad tale in a monotone. He evidently did not recognize Van Bibber, and the clubman gave him a half-dollar and walked away, feeling that the man must surely have enough by this time with which to get something to eat, if only a luncheon.

This retracing of his footsteps had confused Van Bibber, and he made a complete circuit of the block before he discovered that he had lost his bearings. He was standing just where he had started, and gazing along the line of the elevated road, looking for a station, when the familiar accents of the Object again saluted him.

When Van Bibber faced him the beggar looked uneasy. He was not sure whether or not he had approached this particular gentleman before, but Van Bibber conceived an idea of much subtlety, and deceived the Object by again putting his hand in his pocket.

"Nothing to eat for twenty-four hours! Dear me!" drawled the clubman, sympathetically. "Haven't you any money, either?"

"Not a cent," groaned the Object, "an' I'm just faint for food, sir. S' help me. I hate to beg, sir. It isn't the money I want, its jest food. I'm starvin', sir."

"Well," said Van Bibber, suddenly, "if it is just something to eat you want, come in here with me and I'll give you your breakfast." But the man held back and began to whine and complain that they wouldn't let the likes of him in such a fine place.

"Oh, yes, they will," said Van Bibber, glancing at the bill of fare in front of the place. "It seems to be extremely cheap. Beefsteak fifteen cents, for instance. Go in," he added, and there was something in his tone which made the Object move ungraciously into the eating-house.

It was a very queer place, Van Bibber thought, and the people stared very hard at him and his gloves and the gardenia in his coat and at the tramp accompanying him.

"You ain't going to eat two breakfasts, are yer?" asked one of the very tough-looking waiters of the Object. The Object looked uneasy, and Van Bibber, who stood beside his chair, smiled in triumph.

"You're mistaken," he said to the waiter. "This gentleman is starving; he has not tasted food for twenty-four hours. Give him whatever he asks for!"

The Object scowled and the waiter grinned behind his tin tray, and had the impudence to wink at Van Bibber, who recovered from this in time to give the man a half-dollar and so to make of him a friend for life. The Object ordered milk, but Van Bibber protested and ordered two beefsteaks and fried potatoes, hot rolls and two omelet's, coffee, and ham with bacon.

"Holy smoke! watcher think I am?" yelled the Object, in desperation.

"Hungry," said Van Bibber, very gently. "Or else an impostor. And, you know, if you should happen to be the latter, I should have to hand you over to the police."

Van Bibber leaned easily against the wall and read the signs about him, and kept one eye on a policeman across the street. The Object was choking and cursing through his breakfast. It did not seem to agree with him. Whenever he stopped Van Bibber would point with his stick to a still unfinished dish, and the Object, after a husky protest, would attack it as though it were poison. The people sitting about were laughing, and the proprietor behind the desk smiling grimly.

"There, darn ye!" said the Object at last. "I've eat all I can eat for a year. You think you're mighty smart, don't ye? But if you choose to pay that high for your fun, I s'pose you can afford it. Only don't let me catch you around these streets after dark, that's all."

And the Object started off, shaking his fist.

"Wait a minute," said Van Bibber. "You haven't paid them for your breakfast."

"Haven't what?" shouted the Object. "Paid 'em! How could I pay him? Youse asked me to come in here and eat. I didn't want no breakfast, did I? Youse'll have to pay for your fun yerself, or they'll throw yer out. Don't try to be too smart."

"I gave you," said Van Bibber, slowly, "seventy-five cents with which to buy a breakfast. This check calls for eighty-five cents, and extremely cheap it is," he added, with a bow to the fat proprietor. "Several other gentlemen, on your representation that you were starving, gave you other sums to be expended on a breakfast. You have the money with you now. So pay what you owe at once or I'll call that officer across the street and tell him what I know, and have you put where you belong."

"I'll see you blowed first!" gasped the Object.

Van Bibber turned to the waiter.

"Kindly beckon to that officer," said he.

The waiter ran to the door and the Object ran too, but the tough waiter grabbed him by the back of his neck and held him.

"Lemme go!" yelled the Object. "Lemme go an' I'll pay you."

Everybody in the place came up now and formed a circle around the group and watched the Object count out eighty-five cents into the waiter's hand, which left him just one dime to himself.

"You have forgotten the waiter who served you," said Van Bibber, severely pointing with his stick at the dime.

"No, you don't," groaned the Object.

"Oh, yes," said Van Bibber, "do the decent thing now, or I'll—"

The Object dropped the dime in the waiter's hand, and Van Bibber, smiling and easy, made his way through the admiring crowd and out into the street.

"I suspect," said Mr. Van Bibber later in the day, when recounting his adventure to a fellow-clubman, "that, after I left, fellow tried to get tip back from waiter, for I saw him come out of place very suddenly, you see, and without touching pavement till he lit on back of his head in gutter. He was most remarkable waiter."

A WALK UP THE AVENUE

He came down the steps slowly, and pulling mechanically at his gloves.

He remembered afterwards that some woman's face had nodded brightly to him from a passing brougham, and that he had lifted his hat through force of habit, and without knowing who she was.

He stopped at the bottom of the steps, and stood for a moment uncertainly, and then turned toward the north, not because he had any definite goal in his mind, but because the other way led toward his rooms, and he did not want to go there yet.

He was conscious of a strange feeling of elation, which he attributed to his being free, and to the fact that he was his own master again in everything. And with this he confessed to a distinct feeling of littleness, of having acted meanly or unworthily of himself or of her.

And yet he had behaved well, even quixotically. He had tried to leave the impression with her that it was her wish, and that she had broken with him, not he with her.

He held a man who threw a girl over as something contemptible, and he certainly did not want to appear to himself in that light; or, for her sake, that people should think he had tired of her, or found her wanting in any one particular. He knew only too well how people would talk. How they would say he had never really cared for her; that he didn't know his own mind when he had proposed to her; and that it was a great deal better for her as it is than if he had grown out of humor with her later. As to their saying she had jilted him, he didn't mind that. He much preferred they should take that view of it, and he was chivalrous enough to hope she would think so too.

He was walking slowly, and had reached Thirtieth Street. A great many young girls and women had bowed to him or nodded from the passing carriages, but it did not tend to disturb the measure of his thoughts. He was used to having people put themselves out to speak to him; everybody made a point of knowing him, not because he was so very handsome and well-looking, and an over-popular youth, but because he was as yet unspoiled by it.

But, in any event, he concluded, it was a miserable business. Still, he had only done what was right. He had seen it coming on for a month now, and how much better it was that they should separate now than later, or that they should have had to live separated in all but location for the rest of their lives! Yes, he had done the right thing—decidedly the only thing to do.

He was still walking up the Avenue, and had reached Thirty-second Street, at which point his thoughts received a sudden turn. A half-dozen men in a club window nodded to him, and brought to him sharply what he was going back to. He had dropped out of their lives as entirely of late as though he had been living in a distant city. When he had met them he had found their company uninteresting and unprofitable. He had wondered how he had ever cared for that sort of thing, and where had been the pleasure of it. Was he going back now to the gossip of that window, to the heavy discussions of traps and horses, to late breakfasts and early suppers? Must he listen to their congratulations on his being one of them again, and must he guess at their whispered conjectures as to how soon it would be before he again took up the chains and harness of their fashion? He struck the pavement sharply with his stick. No, he was not going back.

She had taught him to find amusement and occupation in many things that were better and higher than any pleasures or pursuits he had known before, and he could not give them up. He had her to thank for that at least. And he would give her credit for it too, and gratefully. He would always remember it, and he would show in his way of living the influence and the good effects of these three months in which they had been continually together.

He had reached Forty-second Street now. Well, it was over with, and he would get to work at something or other. This experience had shown him that he was not meant for marriage; that he was intended to live alone. Because, if he found that a girl as lovely as she undeniably was palled on him after three months, it was evident that he would never live through life with any other one. Yes, he would always be a bachelor. He had lived his life, had told his story at the age of twenty-five, and would wait patiently for the end, a marked and gloomy man. He would travel now and see the world. He would go to that hotel in Cairo she was always talking about, where they were to have gone on their honeymoon; or he might strike further into Africa, and come back bronzed and worn with long marches and jungle fever, and with his hair prematurely white. He even considered himself, with great self-pity, returning and finding her married and happy, of course. And he enjoyed, in anticipation, the secret doubts she would have of her later choice when she heard on all sides' praise of this distinguished traveler.

And he pictured himself meeting her reproachful glances with fatherly friendliness, and presenting her husband with tiger-skins, and buying her children extravagant presents.

This was at Forty-fifth Street.

Yes, that was decidedly the best thing to do. To go away and improve himself, and study up all those painters and cathedrals with which she was so hopelessly conversant.

He remembered how out of it she had once made him feel, and how secretly he had admired her when she had referred to a modern painting as looking like those in the long gallery of the Louvre. He thought he knew all about the Louvre, but he would go over again and locate that long gallery, and become able to talk to her understandingly about it.

And then it came over him like a blast of icy air that he could never talk over things with her again. He had reached Fifty-fifth Street now, and the shock brought him to a standstill on the corner, where he stood gazing blankly before him. He felt rather weak physically, and decided to go back to his rooms, and then he pictured how cheerless they would look, and how little of comfort they contained. He had used them only to dress and sleep in of late, and the distaste with which he regarded the idea that he must go back to them to read and sit and live in them, showed him how utterly his life had become bound up with the house on Twenty-seventh Street.

"Where was he to go in the evening?" he asked himself, with pathetic hopelessness, "or in the morning or afternoon for that matter?" Were there to be no more of those journeys to picture-galleries and to the big publishing houses, where they used to hover over the new book counter and pull the books about, and make each other innumerable presents of daintily bound volumes, until the clerks grew to know them so well that they never went through the form of asking where the books were to be sent? And those tete-a-tete luncheons at her house when her mother was upstairs with a headache or a dressmaker, and the long rides and walks in the Park in the afternoon, and the rush down town to dress, only to return to dine with them, ten minutes late always, and always with some new excuse, which was allowed if it was clever, and frowned at if it was common-place—was all this really over?

Why, the town had only run on because she was in it, and as he walked the streets the very shop windows had suggested her to him—florists only existed that he might send her flowers, and gowns and bonnets in the milliners' windows were only pretty as they would become her; and as for the theatres and the newspapers, they were only worth while as they gave her pleasure. And he had given all this up, and for what, he asked himself, and why?

He could not answer that now. It was simply because he had been surfeited with too much content, he replied, passionately. He had not appreciated how happy he had been. She had been too kind, too gracious. He had never known until he had quarrelled with her and lost her how precious and dear she had been to him.

He was at the entrance to the Park now, and he strode on along the walk, bitterly upbraiding himself for being worse than a criminal—a fool, a common blind mortal to whom a goddess had stooped.

He remembered with bitter regret a turn off the drive into which they had wandered one day, a secluded, pretty spot with a circle of box around it, and into the turf of which he had driven his stick, and claimed it for them both by the right of discovery. And he recalled how they had used to go there, just out of sight of their friends in the ride, and sit and chatter on a green bench beneath a bush of box, like any nursery maid and her young man, while her groom stood at the brougham door in the bridle-path beyond. He had broken off a sprig of the box one day and given it to her, and she had kissed it foolishly, and laughed, and hidden it in the folds of her riding-skirt, in burlesque fear lest the guards should arrest them for breaking the much-advertised ordinance.

And he remembered with a miserable smile how she had delighted him with her account of her adventure to her mother, and described them as fleeing down the Avenue with their treasure, pursued by a squadron of mounted policemen.

This and a hundred other of the foolish, happy fancies they had shared in common came back to him, and he remembered how she had stopped one cold afternoon just outside of this favorite spot, beside an open iron grating sunk in the path, into which the rain had washed the autumn leaves, and pretended it was a steam radiator, and held her slim gloved hands out over it as if to warm them.

How absurdly happy she used to make him, and how light-hearted she had been! He determined suddenly and sentimentally to go to that secret place now, and bury the engagement ring she had handed back to him under that bush as he had buried his hopes of happiness, and he pictured how some day when he was dead she would read of this in his will, and go and dig up the ring, and remember and forgive him. He struck off from the walk across the turf straight toward this dell, taking the ring from his waistcoat pocket and clinching it in his hand. He was walking quickly with rapt interest in this idea of abnegation when he noticed, unconsciously at first and then with a start, the familiar outlines and colors of her brougham drawn up in the drive not twenty yards from their old meeting-place. He could not be mistaken; he knew the horses well enough, and there was old Wallis on the box and young Wallis on the path.

He stopped breathlessly, and then tipped on cautiously, keeping the encircling line of bushes between him and the carriage. And then he saw through the leaves that there was some one in the place, and that it was she. He stopped, confused and amazed. He could not comprehend it. She must have driven to the place immediately on his departure. But why? And why to that place of all others?

He parted the bushes with his hands, and saw her lovely and sweet-looking as she had always been, standing under the box bush beside the bench, and breaking off one of the green branches. The branch parted and the stem flew back to its place again, leaving a green sprig in her hand. She turned at that moment directly toward him, and he could see from his hiding-place how she lifted the leaves to her lips, and that a tear was creeping down her cheek.

Then he dashed the bushes aside with both arms, and with a cry that no one but she heard sprang toward her.

Young Van Bibber stopped his mail phaeton in front of the club, and went inside to recuperate, and told how he had seen them driving home through the Park in her brougham and unchaperoned.

"Which I call very bad form," said the punctilious Van Bibber, "even though they are engaged

MR. TRAVERS'S FIRST HUNT

Young Travers, who had been engaged to a girl down on Long Island for the last three months, only met her father and brother a few weeks before the day set for the wedding. The brother is a master of hounds near Southampton, and shared the expense of importing a pack from England with Van Bibber. The father and son talked horse all day and until one in the morning; for they owned fast thoroughbreds, and entered them at the Sheepshead Bay and other race-tracks. Old Mr. Paddock, the father of the girl to whom Travers was engaged, had often said that when a young man asked him for his daughter's hand he would ask him in return, not if he had lived straight, but if he could ride straight. And on his answering this question in the affirmative depended his gaining her parent's consent. Travers had met Miss Paddock and her mother in Europe, while the men of the family were at home. He was invited to their place in the fall when the hunting season opened, and spent the evening most pleasantly and satisfactorily with his *fiancée* in a corner of the drawing-room. But as soon as the women had gone, young Paddock joined him and said, "You ride, of course?" Travers had never ridden; but he had been prompted how to answer by Miss Paddock, and so said there was nothing he liked better. As he expressed it, he would rather ride than sleep.

"That's good," said Paddock. "I'll give you a mount on Satan to-morrow morning at the meet. He is a bit nasty at the start of the season; and ever since he killed Wallis, the second groom, last year, none of us care much to ride him. But you can manage him, no doubt. He'll just carry your weight."

Mr. Travers dreamed that night of taking large, desperate leaps into space on a wild horse that snorted forth flames, and that rose at solid stone walls as though they were hayricks.

He was tempted to say he was ill in the morning—which was, considering his state of mind, more or less true—but concluded that, as he would have to ride sooner or later during his visit, and that if he did break his neck it would be in a good cause, he determined to do his best. He did not want to ride at all, for two excellent reasons—first, because he wanted to live for Miss Paddock's sake, and, second, because he wanted to live for his own.

The next morning was a most forbidding and doleful-looking morning, and young Travers had great hopes that the meet would be declared off; but, just as he lay in doubt, the servant knocked at his door with his riding things and his hot water.

He came down-stairs looking very miserable indeed. Satan had been taken to the place where they were to meet, and Travers viewed him on his arrival there with a sickening sense of fear as he saw him pulling three grooms off their feet.

Travers decided that he would stay with his feet on solid earth just as long as he could, and when the hounds were thrown off and the rest had started at a gallop he waited, under the pretence of adjusting his gaiters, until they were all well away. Then he clenched his teeth, crammed his hat down over his ears, and scrambled up on to the saddle. His feet fell quite by accident into the stirrups, and the next instant he was off after the others, with an indistinct feeling that he was on a locomotive that was jumping the ties. Satan was in among and had passed the other horses in less than five minutes, and was so close on the hounds that the whippers-in gave a cry of warning. But Travers could as soon have pulled a boat back from going over the Niagara Falls as Satan, and it was only because the hounds were well ahead that saved them from having Satan ride them down. Travers had taken hold of the saddle with his left hand to keep himself down, and sawed and swayed on the reins with his right. He shut his eyes whenever Satan jumped, and never knew how he happened to stick on; but he did stick on, and was so far ahead that no one could see in the misty morning just how badly he rode. As it was, for daring and speed he led the field, and not even young Paddock was near him from the start. There was a broad stream in front of him, and a hill just on its other side. No one had ever tried to take this at a jump. It was considered more of a swim than anything else, and the hunters always crossed it by the bridge, towards the left.

Travers saw the bridge and tried to jerk Satan's head in that direction; but Satan kept right on as straight as an express train over the prairie. Fences and trees and furrows passed by and under Travers like a panorama run by electricity, and he only breathed by accident. They went on at the stream and the hill beyond as though they were riding at a stretch of turf, and, though the whole field set up a shout of warning and dismay, Travers could only gasp and shut his eyes. He remembered the fate of the second groom and shivered. Then the horse rose like a rocket, lifting Travers so high in the air that he thought Satan would never come down again; but he did come down, with his feet bunched, on the opposite side of the stream. The next instant he was up and over the hill, and had stopped panting in the very centre of the pack that were snarling and snapping around the fox. And then Travers showed that he was a thoroughbred, even though he could not ride, for he hastily fumbled for his cigar-case, and when the field came pounding up over the bridge and around the hill, they saw him seated nonchalantly on his saddle, puffing critically at a cigar and giving Satan patronizing pats on the head.

"My dear girl," said old Mr. Paddock to his daughter as they rode back, "if you love that young man of yours and want to keep him, make him promise to give up riding. A more reckless and more brilliant horseman I have never seen. He took that double jump at the gate and that stream like a centaur. But he will break his neck sooner or later, and he ought to be stopped." Young Paddock was so delighted with his prospective brother-in-law's great riding that that night in the smoking-room he made him a present of Satan before all the men.

"No," said Travers, gloomily, "I can't take him. Your sister has asked me to give up what is dearer to me than anything next to herself, and that is my riding. You see, she is absurdly anxious for my safety, and she has asked me to promise never to ride again, and I have given my word."

A chorus of sympathetic remonstrance rose from the men.

"Yes, I know," said Travers to her brother, "it is rough, but it just shows what sacrifices a man will make for the woman he loves."

Love Me, Love My Dog

Young Van Bibber had been staying with some people at Southampton, L. I., where, the fall before, his friend Travers made his reputation as a cross-country rider. He did this, it may be remembered, by shutting his eyes and holding on by the horse's mane and letting the horse go as it pleased. His recklessness and courage are still spoken of with awe; and the place where he cleared the water jump that every one else avoided is pointed out as Travers's Leap to visiting horsemen, who look at it gloomily and shake their heads. Miss Arnett, whose mother was giving the house-party, was an attractive young woman, with an admiring retinue of youths who gave attention without intention, and for none of whom Miss Arnett showed particular preference. Her whole interest, indeed, was centered in a dog, a Scotch collie called Duncan. She allowed this dog every liberty, and made a decided nuisance of him for every one, around her. He always went with her when she walked, or trotted beside her horse when she rode. He stretched himself before the fire in the dining-room, and startled people at table by placing his cold nose against their hands or putting his paws on their gowns. He was generally voted a most annoying adjunct to the Arnett household; but no one, dared hint so to Miss Arnett, as she only loved those who loved the dog or pretended to do it. On the morning of the afternoon on which Van Bibber and his bag arrived, the dog disappeared and could not be recovered. Van Bibber found the household in a state of much excitement in consequence, and his welcome was necessarily brief. The arriving guest was not to be considered at all with the departed dog. The men told Van Bibber, in confidence, that the general relief among the guests was something ecstatic, but this was marred later by the gloom of Miss Arnett and her inability to think of anything else but the finding of the lost collie. Things became so feverish that for the sake of rest and peace the house-party proposed to contribute to a joint purse for the return of the dog, as even, nuisance as it was, it was not so bad as having their visit spoiled by Miss Arnett's abandonment to grief and crossness.

"I think," said the young woman, after luncheon, "that some of you men might be civil enough to offer to look for him. I'm sure he can't have gone far, or, if he has been stolen, the men who took him couldn't have gone very far away either. Now which of you will volunteer? I'm sure you'll do it to please me. Mr. Van Bibber, now: you say you're so clever. We're all the time hearing of your adventures. Why don't you show how full of expedients you are and rise to the occasion?" The suggestion of scorn in this speech nettled Van Bibber.

"I'm sure I never posed as being clever," he said, "and finding a lost dog with all Long Island to pick and choose from isn't a particularly easy thing to pull off successfully, I should think."

"I didn't suppose you'd take a dare like that, Van Bibber," said one of the men. "Why, it's just the sort of thing you do so well."

"Yes," said another, "I'll back you to find him if you try."

"Thanks," said Van Bibber, dryly. "There seems to be a disposition on the part of the young men present to turn me into a dog-catcher. I doubt whether this is altogether unselfish. I do not say that they would rather remain indoors and teach the girls how to play billiards, but I quite appreciate their reasons for not wishing to roam about in the snow and whistle for a dog. However, to oblige the despondent mistress of this valuable member of the household, I will risk pneumonia, and I will, at the same time, in order to make the event interesting to all concerned, back myself to bring that dog back by eight o'clock. Now, then, if any of you unselfish youths have any

286

sporting blood, you will just name the sum."

They named one hundred dollars, and arranged that Van Bibber was to have the dog back by eight o'clock or just in time for dinner; for Van Bibber said he wouldn't miss his dinner for all the dogs in the two hemispheres, unless the dogs happened to be his own.

Van Bibber put on his great-coat and told the man to bring around the dog-cart; then he filled his pockets with cigars and placed a flask of brandy under the seat, and wrapped the robes around his knees.

"I feel just like a relief expedition to the North Pole. I think I ought to have some lieutenants," he suggested.

"Well," cried one of the men, "suppose we make a pool and each chip in fifty dollars, and the man who brings the dog back in time gets the whole of it?"

"That bet of mine stands doesn't it?" asked Van Bibber.

The men said it did, and went off to put on their riding things, and four horses were saddled and brought around from the stable. Each of the four explorers was furnished with a long rope to tie to Duncan's collar, and with which he was to be led back if they found him. They were cheered ironically by the maidens they had deserted on compulsion, and were smiled upon severally by Miss Arnett. Then they separated and took different roads. It was snowing gently, and was very cold. Van Bibber drove aimlessly ahead, looking to the right and left and scanning each back yard and side street. Every now and then he hailed some passing farm wagon and asked the driver if he had seen a stray collie dog, but the answer was invariably in the negative. He soon left the village in the rear, and plunged out over the downs. The wind was bitter cold, and swept from the water with a chill that cut through his clothes.

"Oh, this is great," said Van Bibber to the patient horse in front of him; "this IS sport, this is. The next time I come to this part of the world I'll be dragged here with a rope. Nice, hospitable people those Arnetts, aren't they? Ask you to make yourself at home chasing dogs over an ice fjord. Don't know when I've enjoyed myself so much." Every now and then he stood up and looked all over the hills and valleys to see if he could not distinguish a black object running over the white surface of the snow, but he saw nothing like a dog, not even the track of one.

Twice he came across one of the other men, shivering and swearing from his saddle, and with teeth chattering. "Well," said one of them, shuddering, "you haven't found that dog yet, I see."

"No," said Van Bibber. "Oh, no. I've given up looking for the dog. I'm just driving around enjoying myself. The air's so invigorating, and I like to feel the snow settling between my collar and the back of my neck."

At four o'clock Van Bibber was about as nearly frozen as a man could be after he had swallowed half a bottle of brandy. It was so cold that the ice formed on his cigar when he took it from his lips, and his feet and the dashboard seemed to have become stuck together.

"I think I'll give it up," he said, finally, as he turned the horse's head towards Southampton. "I hate to lose three hundred and fifty dollars as much as any man; but I love my fair young life, and I'm not going to turn into an equestrian statue in ice for anybody's collie dog."

He drove the cart to the stable and unharnessed the horse himself, as all the grooms were out scouring the country, and then went upstairs unobserved and locked himself in his room, for he did not care to have the others know that he had given out so early in the chase. There was a big open fire in his room, and he put on his warm things and stretched out before it in a great easy-chair, and smoked and sipped the brandy and chuckled with delight as he thought of the four other men racing around in the snow.

"They may have more nerve than I," he soliloquized, "and I don't say they have not; but they can have all the credit and rewards they want, and I'll be satisfied to stay just where I am."

At seven he saw the four riders coming back dejectedly, and without the dog. As they passed his room he heard one of the men ask if Van Bibber had got back yet, and another say yes, he had, as he had left the cart in the stable, but that one of the servants had said that he had started out again on foot.

"He has, has he?" said the voice. "Well, he's got sporting blood, and he'll need to keep it at fever heat if he expects to live. I'm frozen so that I can't bend my fingers."

Van Bibber smiled, and moved comfortably in the big chair; he had dozed a little, and was feeling very contented. At half-past seven he began to dress, and at five minutes to eight he was ready for dinner and stood looking out of the window at the moonlight on the white lawn below. The snow had stopped falling, and everything lay quiet and still as though it were cut in marble. And then suddenly across the lawn, came a black, bedraggled object on four legs, limping painfully, and lifting its feet as though there were lead on them.

"Great heavens!" cried Van Bibber, "it's the dog!" He was out of the room in a moment and down into the hall. He heard the murmur of voices in the drawing-room, and the sympathetic tones of the women who were pitying the men. Van Bibber pulled on his overshoes and a great-coat that covered him from his ears to his ankles, and dashed out into the snow. The dog had just enough spirit left to try and dodge him, and with a leap to one side went off again across the lawn. It was, as Van Bibber knew, but three minutes to eight o'clock, and have the dog he must and would. The collie sprang first to one side and then to the other, and snarled and snapped; but Van Bibber was keen with the excitement of the chase, so he plunged forward recklessly and tackled the dog around the body, and they both rolled over and over together. Then Van Bibber scrambled to his feet and dashed up the steps and into the drawing-room just as the people were in line for dinner, and while the minute-hand stood at a minute to eight o'clock.

"How is this?" shouted Van Bibber, holding up one hand and clasping the dog under his other arm.

Miss Arnett flew at the collie and embraced it, wet as it was, and ruined her gown, and all the men glanced instinctively at the clock and said:

"You've won, Van."

"But you must be frozen to death," said Miss Arnett, looking up at him with gratitude in her eyes.

"Yes, yes," said Van Bibber, beginning to shiver. "I've had a terrible long walk, and I had to carry him all the way. If you'll excuse me, I'll go change my things."

He reappeared again in a suspiciously short time for one who had to change outright, and the men admired his endurance and paid up the bet.

"Where did you find him, Van?" one of them asked.

"Oh, yes," they all chorused. "Where was he?"

"That," said Mr. Van Bibber "is a thing known to only two beings, Duncan and myself. Duncan can't tell, and I won't. If I did, you'd say I was trying to make myself out clever, and I never boast about the things I do."

VAN BIBBER AS BEST MAN

Young Van Bibber came up to town in June from Newport to see his lawyer about the preparation of some papers that needed his signature. He found the city very hot and close, and as dreary and as empty as a house that has been shut up for some time while its usual occupants are away in the country.

As he had to wait over for an afternoon train, and as he was down town, he decided to lunch at a French restaurant near Washington Square, where some one had told him you could get particular things particularly well cooked. The tables were set on a terrace with plants and flowers about them, and covered with a tricolored awning. There were no jangling horse-car bells nor dust to disturb him, and almost all the other tables were unoccupied. The waiters leaned against these tables and chatted in a French argot; and a cool breeze blew through the plants and billowed the awning, so that, on the whole, Van Bibber was glad he had come.

There was, beside himself, an old Frenchman scolding over his late breakfast; two young artists with Van Dyke beards, who ordered the most remarkable things in the same French argot that the waiters spoke; and a young lady and a young gentleman at the table next to his own. The young man's back was toward him, and he could only see the girl when the youth moved to one side. She was very young and very pretty, and she seemed in a most excited state of mind from the tip of her wide-brimmed, pointed French hat to the points of her patent- leather ties. She was strikingly well-bred in appearance, and Van Bibber wondered why she should be dining alone with so young a man.

"It wasn't my fault," he heard the youth say earnestly. "How could I know he would be out of town? and anyway it really doesn't matter. Your cousin is not the only clergyman in the city."

"Of course not," said the girl, almost tearfully, "but they're not my cousins and he is, and that would have made it so much, oh, so very much different. I'm awfully frightened!"

"Runaway couple," commented Van Bibber. "Most interesting. Read about 'em often; never seen 'em. Most interesting."

He bent his head over an entree, but he could not help hearing what followed, for the young runaways were indifferent to all around them, and though he rattled his knife and fork in a most vulgar manner, they did not heed him nor lower their voices.

"Well, what are you going to do?" said the girl, severely but not unkindly. "It doesn't seem to me that you are exactly rising to the occasion."

"Well, I don't know," answered the youth, easily. "We're safe here anyway. Nobody we know ever comes here, and if they did they are out of town now. You go on and eat something, and I'll get a directory and look up a lot of clergymen's addresses, and then we can make out a list and drive around in a cab until we find one who has not gone off on his vacation. We ought to be able to catch the Fall River boat back at five this afternoon; then we can go right on to Boston from Fall River to-morrow morning and run down to Narragansett during the day."

"They'll never forgive us," said the girl.

"Oh, well, that's all right," exclaimed the young man, cheerfully. "Really, you're the most uncomfortable young person I ever ran away with. One might think you were going to a funeral. You were willing enough two days ago, and now you don't help me at all. Are you sorry?" he asked, and then added, "but please don't say so, even if you are."

"No, not sorry, exactly," said the girl; "but, indeed, Ted, it is going to make so much talk. If we only had a girl with us, or if you had a best man, or if we had witnesses, as they do in England, and a parish registry, or something of that sort; or if Cousin Harold had only been at home to do the marrying."

The young gentleman called Ted did not look, judging from the expression of his shoulders, as if he were having a very good time.

He picked at the food on his plate gloomily, and the girl took out her handkerchief and then put it resolutely back again and smiled at him. The youth called the waiter and told him to bring a directory, and as he turned to give the order Van Bibber recognized him and he recognized Van Bibber. Van Bibber knew him for a very nice boy, of a very good Boston family named Standish, and the younger of two sons. It was the elder who was Van Bibber's particular friend. The girl saw nothing of this mutual recognition, for she was looking with startled eyes at a hansom that had dashed up the side street and was turning the corner.

"Ted, O Ted!" she gasped. "It's your brother. There! In that hansom. I saw him perfectly plainly. Oh, how did he find us? What shall we do?"

Ted grew very red and then very white.

"Standish," said Van Bibber, jumping up and reaching for his hat, "pay this chap for these things, will you, and I'll get rid of your brother."

Van Bibber descended the steps lighting a cigar as the elder Standish came up them on a jump.

"Hello, Standish!" shouted the New Yorker. "Wait a minute; where are you going? Why, it seems to rain Standishes to-day! First see your brother; then I see you. What's on?"

"You've seen him?" cried the Boston man, eagerly. "Yes, and where is he? Was she with him? Are they married? Am I in time?"

Van Bibber answered these different questions to the effect that he had seen young Standish and Mrs. Standish not a half an hour before, and that they were just then taking a cab for Jersey City, whence they were to depart for Chicago.

"The driver who brought them here, and who told me where they were, said they could not have left this place by the time I would reach it," said the elder brother, doubtfully.

"That's so," said the driver of the cab, who had listened curiously. "I brought 'em here not more'n half an hour ago. Just had time to get back to the depot. They can't have gone long."

"Yes, but they have," said Van Bibber. "However, if you get over to Jersey City in time for the 2.30, you can reach Chicago almost as soon as they do. They are going to the Palmer House, they said."

"Thank you, old fellow," shouted Standish, jumping back into his hansom. "It's a terrible business. Pair of young fools. Nobody objected to the marriage, only too young, you know. Ever so much obliged."

"Don't mention it," said Van Bibber, politely.

"Now, then," said that young man, as he approached the frightened couple trembling on the terrace, "I've sent your brother off to Chicago. I do not know why I selected Chicago as a place where one would go on a honeymoon. But I'm not used to lying and I'm not very good at it. Now, if you will introduce me, I'll see what can be done toward getting you two babes out of the woods."

Standish said, "Miss Cambridge, this is Mr. Cortlandt Van Bibber, of whom you have heard my brother speak," and Miss Cambridge said she was very glad to meet Mr. Van Bibber even under such peculiarly trying circumstances.

"Now what you two want to do," said Van Bibber, addressing them as though they were just about fifteen years old and he were at least forty, "is to give this thing all the publicity you can."

"What?" chorused the two runaways, in violent protest.

"Certainly," said Van Bibber. "You were about to make a fatal mistake. You were about to go to some unknown clergyman of an unknown parish, who would have married you in a back room, without a certificate or a witness, just like any eloping farmer's daughter and lightning-rod agent. Now it's different with you two. Why you were not married respectably in church I don't know, and I do not intend to ask, but a kind Providence has sent me to you to see that there is no talk nor scandal, which is such bad form, and which would have got your names into all the papers. I am going to arrange this wedding properly, and you will kindly remain here until I send a carriage for you. Now just rely on me entirely and eat your luncheon in peace. It's all going to come out right—and allow me to recommend the salad, which is especially good."

Van Bibber first drove madly to the Little Church Around the Corner, where he told the kind old rector all about it, and arranged to have the church open and the assistant organist in her place, and a district-messenger boy to blow the bellows, punctually at three o'clock. "And now," he soliloquized, "I must get some names. It doesn't matter much whether they happen to know the high contracting parties or not, but they must be names that everybody knows. Whoever is in town will be lunching at Delmonico's, and the men will be at the clubs." So he first went to the big restaurant, where, as good luck would have it, he found Mrs. "Regy" Van Arnt and Mrs. "Jack" Peabody, and the Misses Brookline, who had run up the Sound for the day on the yacht *Minerva* of the Boston Yacht Club, and he told them how things were and swore them to secrecy, and told them to bring what men they could pick up.

At the club he pressed four men into service who knew everybody and whom everybody knew, and when they protested that they had not been properly invited and that they only knew the bride and groom by sight, he told them that made no difference, as it was only their names he wanted. Then he sent a messenger boy to get the biggest suit of rooms on the Fall River boat and another one for flowers, and then he put Mrs. "Regy" Van Arnt into a cab and sent her after the bride, and, as best man, he got into another cab and carried off the groom.

"I have acted either as best man or usher forty-two times now," said Van Bibber, as they drove to the church, "and this is the first time I ever appeared in either capacity in russia-leather shoes and a blue serge yachting suit. But then," he added, contentedly, "you ought to see the other fellows. One of them is in a striped flannel."

Mrs. "Regy" and Miss Cambridge wept a great deal on the way up town, but the bride was smiling and happy when she walked up the aisle to meet her prospective husband, who looked exceedingly conscious before the eyes of the men, all of whom he knew by sight or by name, and not one of whom he had ever met before. But they all shook hands after it was over, and the assistant organist played the Wedding March, and one of the club men insisted in pulling a cheerful and jerky peal on the church bell in the absence of the janitor, and then Van Bibber hurled an old shoe and a handful of rice—which he had thoughtfully collected from the chef at the club—after them as they drove off to the boat.

"Now," said Van Bibber, with a proud sigh of relief and satisfaction, "I will send that to the papers, and when it is printed to-morrow it will read like one of the most orthodox and one of the smartest weddings of the season. And yet I can't help thinking—"

"Well?" said Mrs. "Regy," as he paused doubtfully.

"Well, I can't help thinking," continued Van Bibber, "of Standish's older brother racing around Chicago with the thermometer at 102 in the shade. I wish I had only sent him to Jersey City. It just shows," he added, mournfully, "that when a man is not practiced in lying, he should leave it alone."

VAN BIBBER'S BURGLAR

There had been a dance up town, but as Van Bibber could not find Her there, he accepted young Travers's suggestion to go over to Jersey City and see a "go" between "Dutchy" Mack and a colored person professionally known as the Black Diamond. They covered up all signs of their evening dress with their great-coats, and filled their pockets with cigars, for the smoke which surrounds a "go" is trying to sensitive nostrils, and they also fastened their watches to both key-chains. Alf Alpin, who was acting as master of ceremonies, was greatly pleased and flattered at their coming, and boisterously insisted on their sitting on the platform. The fact was generally circulated among the spectators that the "two gents in high hats" had come in a carriage, and this and their patent-leather boots made them objects of keen interest. It was even whispered that they were the "parties" who were putting up the money to back the Black Diamond against the "Hester Street Jackson." This in itself entitled them to respect. Van Bibber was asked to hold the watch, but he wisely declined the honor, which was given to Andy Spielman, the sporting reporter of the *Track and Ring*, whose watch-case was covered with diamonds, and was just the sort of a watch a timekeeper should hold.

It was two o'clock before "Dutchy" Mack's backer threw the sponge into the air, and three before they reached the city. They had another reporter in the cab with them besides the gentleman who had bravely held the watch in the face of several offers to "do for" him; and as Van Bibber was ravenously hungry, and as he doubted that he could get anything at that hour at the club, they accepted Spielman's invitation and went for a porterhouse steak and onions at the Owl's Nest, Gus McGowan's all-night restaurant on Third Avenue.

It was a very dingy, dirty place, but it was as warm as the engine-room of a steamboat, and the steak was perfectly done and tender. It was too late to go to bed, so they sat around the table, with their chairs tipped back and their knees against its edge. The two club men had thrown off their great-coats, and their wide shirt fronts and silk facings shone grandly in the smoky light of the oil lamps and the red glow from the grill in the corner. They talked about the life the reporters led, and the Philistines asked foolish questions, which the gentleman of the press answered without showing them how foolish they were.

"And I suppose you have all sorts of curious adventures," said Van Bibber, tentatively.

"Well, no, not what I would call adventures," said one of the reporters. "I have never seen anything that could not be explained or attributed directly to some known cause, such as crime or poverty or drink. You may think at first that you have stumbled on something strange and romantic, but it comes to nothing. You would suppose that in a great city like this one would come across something that could not be explained away something mysterious or out of the common, like Stevenson's Suicide Club. But I have not found it so. Dickens once told James Payn that the most curious thing he ever saw In his rambles around London was a ragged man who stood crouching under the window of a great house where the owner was giving a ball. While the man hid beneath a window on the ground floor, a woman wonderfully dressed and very beautiful raised the sash from the inside and dropped her bouquet down into the man's hand, and he nodded and stuck it under his coat and ran off with it.

"I call that, now, a really curious thing to see. But I have never come across anything like it, and I have been in every part of this big city, and at every hour of the night and morning, and I am not lacking in imagination either, but no captured maidens have ever beckoned to me from barred windows nor 'white hands waved from a passing hansom.' Balzac and De Musset and Stevenson suggest that they have had such adventures, but they never come to me. It is all commonplace and vulgar, and always ends in a police court or with a 'found drowned' in the North River."

McGowan, who had fallen into a doze behind the bar, woke suddenly and shivered and rubbed his shirt-sleeves briskly. A woman knocked at the side door and begged for a drink "for the love of heaven," and the man who tended the grill told her to be off. They could hear her feeling her way against the wall and cursing as she staggered out of the alley. Three men came in with a hack driver and wanted everybody to drink with them, and became insolent when the gentlemen declined, and were in consequence hustled out one at a time by McGowan, who went to sleep again immediately, with his head resting among the cigar boxes and pyramids of glasses at the back of the bar, and snored.

"You see," said the reporter, "it is all like this. Night in a great city is not picturesque and it is not theatrical. It is sodden, sometimes brutal, exciting enough until you get used to it, but it runs in a groove. It is dramatic, but the plot is old and the motives and characters always the same."

The rumble of heavy market wagons and the rattle of milk carts told them that it was morning, and as they opened the door the cold fresh air swept into the place and made them wrap their collars around their throats and stamp their feet. The morning wind swept down the cross- street from the East River and the lights of the street lamps and of the saloon looked old and tawdry. Travers and the reporter went off to a Turkish bath, and the gentleman who held the watch, and who had been asleep for the last hour, dropped into a nighthawk and told the man to drive home. It was almost clear now and very cold, and Van Bibber determined to walk. He had the strange feeling one gets when one stays up until the sun rises, of having lost a day somewhere, and the dance he had attended a few hours before seemed to have come off long ago, and the fight in Jersey City was far back in the past.

The houses along the cross-street through which he walked were as dead as so many blank walls, and only here and there a lace curtain waved out of the open window where some honest citizen was sleeping. The street was quite deserted; not even a cat or a policeman moved on it and Van Bibber's footsteps sounded brisk on the sidewalk. There was a great house at the corner of the avenue and the cross-street on which he was walking. The house faced the avenue and a stone wall ran back to the brown stone stable which opened on the side street. There was a door in this wall, and as Van Bibber approached it on his solitary walk it opened cautiously, and a man's head appeared in it for an instant and was withdrawn again like a flash, and the door snapped to. Van Bibber stopped and looked at the door and at the house and up and down the street. The house was tightly closed, as though some one was lying inside dead, and the streets were still empty.

Van Bibber could think of nothing in his appearance so dreadful as to frighten an honest man, so he decided the face he had had a glimpse of must belong to a dishonest one. It was none of his business, he assured himself, but it was curious, and he liked adventure, and he would have liked to prove his friend the reporter, who did not believe in adventure, in the wrong. So he approached the door silently, and jumped and caught at the top of the wall and stuck one foot on the handle of the door, and, with the other on the knocker, drew himself up and looked cautiously down on the other side. He had done this so lightly that the only noise he made was the rattle of the door-knob on which his foot had rested, and the man inside thought that the one outside was trying to open the door, and placed his shoulder to it and pressed against it heavily. Van Bibber, from his perch on the top of the wall, looked down directly on the other's head and shoulders. He could see the top of the man's head only two feet below, and he also saw that in one hand he held a revolver and that two bags filled with projecting articles of different sizes lay at his feet.

It did not need explanatory notes to tell Van Bibber that the man below had robbed the big house on the corner, and that if it had not been for his having passed when he did the burglar would have escaped with his treasure. His first thought was that he was not a policeman, and that a fight with a burglar was not in his line of life; and this was followed by the thought that though the gentleman who owned the property in the two bags was of no interest to him, he was, as a respectable member of society, more entitled to consideration than the man with the revolver.

The fact that he was now, whether he liked it or not, perched on the top of the wall like Humpty Dumpty, and that the burglar might see him and shoot him the next minute, had also an immediate influence on his movements. So he balanced himself cautiously and noiselessly and dropped upon the man's head and shoulders, bringing him down to the flagged walk with him and under him. The revolver went off once in the struggle, but before the burglar could know how or from where his assailant had come, Van Bibber was standing up over him and had driven his heel down on his hand and kicked the pistol out of his fingers. Then he stepped quickly to where it lay and picked it up and said, "Now, if you try to get up I'll shoot at you." He felt an unwarranted and ill-timedly humorous inclination to add, "and I'll probably miss you," but subdued it. The burglar, much to Van Bibber's astonishment, did not attempt to rise, but sat up with his hands locked across his knees and said: "Shoot ahead. I'd a damned sight rather you would."

His teeth were set and his face desperate and bitter, and hopeless to a degree of utter hopelessness that Van Bibber had never imagined.

"Go ahead," reiterated the man, doggedly, "I won't move. Shoot me."

It was a most unpleasant situation. Van Bibber felt the pistol loosening in his hand, and he was conscious of a strong inclination to lay it down and ask the burglar to tell him all about it.

"You haven't got much heart," said Van Bibber, finally. "You're a pretty poor sort of a burglar, I should say."

"What's the use?" said the man, fiercely. "I won't go back—I won't go back there alive. I've served my time forever in that hole. If I have to go back again—s'help me if I don't do for a keeper and die for it. But I won't serve there no more."

"Go back where?" asked Van Bibber, gently, and greatly interested; "to prison?"

"To prison, yes!" cried the man, hoarsely: "to a grave. That's where. Look at my face," he said, "and look at my hair. That ought to tell you where I've been. With all the color gone out of my skin, and all the life out of my legs. You needn't be afraid of me. I couldn't hurt you if I wanted to. I'm a skeleton and a baby, I am. I couldn't kill a cat. And now you're going to send me back again for another lifetime. For twenty years, this time, into that cold, forsaken hole, and after I done my time so well and worked so hard." Van Bibber shifted the pistol from one hand to the other and eyed his prisoner doubtfully.

"How long have you been out?" he asked, seating himself on the steps of the kitchen and holding the revolver between his knees. The sun was driving the morning mist away, and he had forgotten the cold.

"I got out yesterday," said the man.

Van Bibber glanced at the bags and lifted the revolver. "You didn't waste much time," he said.

"No," answered the man, sullenly, "no, I didn't. I knew this place and I wanted money to get West to my folks, and the Society said I'd have to wait until I earned it, and I couldn't wait. I haven't seen my wife for seven years, nor my daughter. Seven years, young man; think of that—seven years. Do you know how long that is? Seven years without seeing your wife or your child! And they're straight people, they are," he added, hastily. "My wife moved West after I was put away and took another name, and my girl never knew nothing about me. She thinks I'm away at sea. I was to join 'em. That was the plan. I was to join 'em, and I thought I could lift enough here to get the fare, and now," he added, dropping his face in his hands, "I've got to go back. And I had meant to live straight after I got West,—God help me, but I did! Not that it makes much difference now. An' I don't care whether you believe it or not neither," he added, fiercely.

"I didn't say whether I believed it or not," answered Van Bibber, with grave consideration.

He eyed the man for a brief space without speaking, and the burglar looked back at him, doggedly and defiantly, and with not the faintest suggestion of hope in his eyes, or of appeal for mercy. Perhaps it was because of this fact, or perhaps it was the wife and child that moved Van Bibber, but whatever his motives were, he acted on them promptly. "I suppose, though," he said, as though speaking to himself, "that I ought to give you up."

"I'll never go back alive," said the burglar, quietly.

"Well, that's bad, too," said Van Bibber. "Of course I don't know whether you're lying or not, and as to your meaning to live honestly, I very much doubt it; but I'll give you a ticket to wherever your wife is, and I'll see you on the train. And you can get off at the next station and rob my house to-morrow night, if you feel that way about it. Throw those bags inside that door where the servant will see them before the milkman does, and walk on out ahead of me, and keep your hands in your pockets, and don't try to run. I have your pistol, you know."

The man placed the bags inside the kitchen door; and, with a doubtful look at his custodian, stepped out into the street, and walked, as he was directed to do, toward the Grand Central station. Van Bibber kept just behind him, and kept turning the question over in his mind as to what he ought to do. He felt very guilty as he passed each policeman, but he recovered himself when he thought of the wife and child who lived in the West, and who were "straight."

"Where to?" asked Van Bibber, as he stood at the ticket-office window. "Helena, Montana," answered the man with, for the first time, a look of relief. Van Bibber bought the ticket and handed it to the burglar. "I suppose you know," he said, "that you can sell that at a place down town for half the money." "Yes, I know that," said the burglar. There was a half-hour before the train left, and Van Bibber took his charge into the restaurant and watched him eat everything placed before him, with his eyes glancing all the while to the right or left. Then Van Bibber gave him some money and told him to write to him, and shook hands with him. The man nodded eagerly and pulled off his hat as the car drew out of the station; and Van Bibber came down town again with the shop girls and clerks going to work, still wondering if he had done the right thing.

He went to his rooms and changed his clothes, took a cold bath, and crossed over to Delmonico's for his breakfast, and, while the waiter laid the cloth in the cafe, glanced at the headings in one of the papers. He scanned first with polite interest the account of the dance on the night previous and noticed his name among those present. With greater interest he read of the fight between "Dutchy" Mack and the "Black Diamond," and then he read carefully how "Abe" Hubbard, alias "Jimmie the Gent," a burglar, had broken jail in New Jersey, and had been traced to New York. There was a description of the man, and Van Bibber breathed quickly as he read it. "The detectives have a clew of his whereabouts," the account said; "if he is still in the city they are confident of recapturing him. But they fear that the same friends who helped him to break jail will probably assist him from the country or to get out West."

"They may do that," murmured Van Bibber to himself, with a smile of grim contentment; "they probably will."

Then he said to the waiter, "Oh, I don't know. Some bacon and eggs and green things and coffee.

Van Bibber's Man Servant

Van Bibber's man Walters was the envy and admiration of his friends. He was English, of course, and he had been trained in the household of the Marquis Bendinot, and had travelled, in his younger days, as the valet of young Lord Upton. He was now rather well on in years, although it would have been impossible to say just how old he was. Walters had a dignified and repellent air about him, and he brushed his hair in such a way as to conceal his baldness.

And when a smirking, slavish youth with red checks and awkward gestures turned up in Van Bibber's livery, his friends were naturally surprised, and asked how he had come to lose Walters. Van Bibber could not say exactly, at least he could not rightly tell whether he had dismissed Walters or Walters had dismissed himself. The facts of the unfortunate separation were like this:

Van Bibber gave a great many dinners during the course of the season at Delmonico's, dinners hardly formal enough to require a private room, and yet too important to allow of his running the risk of keeping his guests standing in the hall waiting for a vacant table. So he conceived the idea of sending Walters over about half-past six to keep a table for him. As everybody knows, you can hold a table yourself at Delmonico's for any length of time until the other guests arrive, but the rule is very strict about servants. Because, as the head waiter will tell you, if servants were allowed to reserve a table during the big rush at seven o'clock, why not messenger boys? And it would certainly never do to have half a dozen large tables securely held by minute messengers while the hungry and impatient waited their turn at the door.

But Walters looked as much like a gentleman as did many of the diners; and when he seated himself at the largest table and told the waiter to serve for a party of eight or ten, he did it with such an air that the head waiter came over himself and took the orders. Walters knew quite as much about ordering a dinner as did his master; and when Van Bibber was too tired to make out the menu, Walters would look over the card himself and order the proper wines and side dishes; and with such a carelessly severe air and in such a masterly manner did he discharge this high function that the waiters looked upon him with much respect.

But respect even from your equals and the satisfaction of having your fellow-servants mistake you for a member of the Few Hundred are not enough. Walters wanted more. He wanted the further satisfaction of enjoying the delicious dishes he had ordered; of sitting as a coequal with the people for whom he had kept a place; of completing the deception he practiced only up to the point where it became most interesting.

It certainly was trying to have to rise with a subservient and unobtrusive bow and glide out unnoticed by the real guests when they arrived; to have to relinquish the feast just when the feast should begin. It would not be pleasant, certainly, to sit for an hour at a big empty table, ordering dishes fit only for epicures, and then, just as the waiters bore down with the Little Neck clams, so nicely iced and so cool and bitter-looking, to have to rise and go out into the street to a table d'hote around the corner.

This was Walters's state of mind when Mr. Van Bibber told him for the hundredth time to keep a table for him for three at Delmonico's. Walters wrapped his severe figure in a frock-coat and brushed his hair, and allowed himself the dignity of a walking-stick. He would have liked to act as a substitute in an evening dress-suit, but Van Bibber would not have allowed it. So Walters walked over to Delmonico's and took a table near a window, and said that the other gentlemen would arrive later. Then he looked at his watch and ordered the dinner. It was just the sort of dinner he would have ordered had he ordered it for himself at some one else's expense. He suggested Little Neck clams first, with Chablis, and pea-soup, and caviare on toast, before the oyster crabs, with Johannisberger Cabinet; then an entree of calves' brains and rice; then no roast, but a bird, cold asparagus with French dressing, Camembert cheese, and Turkish coffee. As there were to be no women, he omitted the sweets and added three other wines to follow the white wine. It struck him as a particularly well-chosen dinner, and the longer he sat and thought about it the more he wished he were to test its excellence. And then the people all around him were so bright and happy, and seemed to be enjoying what they had ordered with such a refinement of zest that he felt he would give a great deal could he just sit there as one of them for a brief hour.

At that moment the servant deferentially handed him a note which a messenger boy had brought. It said:

> "Dinner off called out town send clothes and things after me to Young's Boston."

> "VAN BIBBER."

Walters rose involuntarily, and then sat still to think about it. He would have to countermand the dinner which he had ordered over half an hour before, and he would have to explain who he was to those other servants who had always regarded him as such a great gentleman. It was very hard.

And then Walters was tempted. He was a very good servant, and he knew his place as only an English servant can, and he had always accepted it, but to-night he was tempted—and he fell. He met the waiter's anxious look with a grave smile.

"The other gentlemen will not be with me to-night," he said, glancing at the note. "But I will dine here as I intended. You can serve for one."

That was perhaps the proudest night in the history of Walters. He had always felt that he was born out of his proper sphere, and to-night he was assured of it. He was a little nervous at first, lest some of Van Bibber's friends should come in and recognize him; but as the dinner progressed and the warm odor of the dishes touched his sense, and the rich wines ran through his veins, and the women around him smiled and bent and moved like beautiful birds of beautiful plumage, he became content, grandly content; and he half closed his eyes and imagined he was giving a dinner to everybody in the place. Vain and idle thoughts came to him and went again, and he eyed the others about him calmly and with polite courtesy, as they did him, and he felt that if he must later pay for this moment it was worth the paying.

Then he gave the waiter a couple of dollars out of his own pocket and wrote Van Bibber's name on the check, and walked in state into the cafe, where he ordered a green mint and a heavy, black, and expensive cigar, and seated himself at the window, where he felt that he should always have sat if the fates had been just. The smoke hung in light clouds about him, and the lights shone and glistened on the white cloths and the broad shirt-fronts of the smart young men and distinguished foreign-looking older men at the surrounding tables.

And then, in the midst of his dreamings, he heard the soft, careless drawl of his master, which sounded at that time and in that place like the awful voice of a condemning judge. Van Bibber pulled out a chair and dropped into it. His side was towards Walters, so that he did not see him. He had some men with him, and he was explaining how he had missed his train and had come back to find that one of the party had eaten the dinner without him, and he wondered who it could be; and then turning easily in his seat he saw Walters with the green mint and the cigar, trembling behind a copy of the London Graphic.

"Walters!" said Van Bibber, "what are you doing here?"

Walters looked his guilt and rose stiffly. He began with a feeble "If you please, sir—"

"Go back to my rooms and wait for me there," said Van Bibber, who was too decent a fellow to scold a servant in public.

Walters rose and left the half-finished cigar and the mint with the ice melting in it on the table. His one evening of sublimity was over, and he walked away, bending before the glance of his young master and the smiles of his master's friends.

When Van Bibber came back he found on his dressing-table a note from Walters stating that he could not, of course, expect to remain longer in his service, and that he left behind him the twenty-eight dollars which the dinner had cost.

"If he had only gone off with all my waistcoats and scarf-pins, I'd have liked it better," said Van Bibber, "than his leaving me cash for infernal dinner. Why, a servant like Walters is worth twenty-eight-dollar dinners—twice a day."

THE BOY SCOUT

A rule of the Boy Scouts is every day to do some one a good turn. Not because the copy-books tell you it deserves another, but in spite of that pleasing possibility. If you are a true scout, until you have performed your act of kindness your day is dark. You are as unhappy as is the grown-up who has begun his day without shaving or reading the New York *Sun*. But as soon as you have proved yourself you may, with a dear conscience, look the world in the face and untie the knot in your kerchief.

Jimmie Reeder untied the accusing knot in his scarf at just ten minutes past eight on a hot August morning after he had given one dime to his sister Sadie. With that she could either witness the first-run films at the Palace, or by dividing her fortune patronize two of the nickel shows on Lenox Avenue. The choice Jimmie left to her. He was setting out for the annual encampment of the Boy Scouts at Hunter's Island, and in the excitement of that adventure even the movies ceased to thrill. But Sadie also could be unselfish. With a heroism of a camp-fire maiden she made a gesture which might have been interpreted to mean she was returning the money.

"I can't, Jimmie!" she gasped. "I can't take it off you. You saved it, and you ought to get the fun of it."

"I haven't saved it yet," said Jimmie. "I'm going to cut it out of the railroad fare. I'm going to get off at City Island instead of at Pelham Manor and walk the difference. That's ten cents cheaper."

Sadie exclaimed with admiration:

"An' you carryin' that heavy grip!"

"Aw, that's nothin'," said the man of the family.

"Good-by, mother. So long, Sadie."

To ward off further expressions of gratitude he hurriedly advised Sadie to take in "The Curse of Cain" rather than "The Mohawk's Last Stand," and fled down the front steps.

He wore his khaki uniform. On his shoulders was his knapsack, from his hands swung his suitcase, and between his heavy stockings and his "shorts" his kneecaps, unkissed by the sun, as yet unscathed by blackberry vines, showed as white and fragile as the wrists of a girl. As he moved toward the "L" station at the corner, Sadie and his mother waved to him; in the street, boys too small to be Scouts hailed him enviously; even the policeman glancing over the newspapers on the news-stand nodded approval.

"You a Scout, Jimmie?" he asked.

"No," retorted Jimmie, for was not he also in uniform? "I'm Santa Claus out filling Christmas stockings."

The patrolman also possessed a ready wit.

"Then get yourself a pair," he advised. "If a dog was to see your legs—"

Jimmie escaped the insult by fleeing up the steps of the Elevated.

An hour later, with his valise in one hand and staff in the other, he was tramping up the Boston Post Road and breathing heavily. The day was cruelly hot. Before his eyes, over an interminable stretch of asphalt, the heat waves danced and flickered. Already the knapsack on his shoulders pressed upon him like an Old Man of the Sea; the linen in the valise had turned to pig iron, his pipe-stem legs were wabbling, his eyes smarted with salt sweat, and the fingers supporting the valise belonged to some other boy, and were giving that boy much pain. But as the motor-cars flashed past with raucous warnings, or, that those who rode might better see the boy with bare knees, passed at "half speed," Jimmie stiffened his shoulders and stepped jauntily forward. Even when the joy-riders mocked with "Oh, you Scout!" he smiled at them. He was willing to admit to those who rode that the laugh was on the one who walked. And he regretted—oh, so bitterly—having left the train. He was indignant that for his "one good turn a day" he had not selected one less strenuous—that, for instance, he had not assisted a frightened old lady through the traffic. To refuse the dime she might have offered, as all true scouts refuse all tips, would have been easier than to earn it by walking five miles, with the sun at ninety-nine degrees, and carrying excess baggage. Twenty times James shifted the valise to the other hand, twenty times he let it drop and sat upon it.

And then, as again he took up his burden, the good Samaritan drew near. He drew near in a low gray racing-car at the rate of forty miles an hour, and within a hundred feet of Jimmie suddenly stopped and backed toward him. The good Samaritan was a young man with white hair. He wore a suit of blue, a golf cap; the hands that held the wheel were disguised in large yellow gloves. He brought the car to a halt and surveyed the dripping figure in the road with tired and uncurious eyes.

"You a Boy Scout?" he asked.

With alacrity for the twenty-first time Jimmie dropped the valise, forced his cramped fingers into straight lines, and saluted.

The young man in the car nodded toward the seat beside him.

"Get in," he commanded.

When James sat panting happily at his elbow the old young man, to Jimmie's disappointment, did not continue to shatter the speed limit. Instead, he seemed inclined for conversation, and the car, growling indignantly, crawled.

"I never saw a Boy Scout before," announced the old young man. "Tell me about it. First, tell me what you do when you're not scouting."

Jimmie explained volubly. When not in uniform he was an office boy, and from peddlers and beggars guarded the gates of Carroll and Hastings, stock-brokers. He spoke the names of his employers with awe. It was a firm distinguished, conservative, and long established. The white-haired young man seemed to nod in assent.

"Do you know them?" demanded Jimmie suspiciously. "Are you a customer of ours?"

"I know them," said the young man. "They are customers of mine."

Jimmie wondered in what way Carroll and Hastings were customers of the white-haired young man. Judging him by his outer garments, Jimmie guessed he was a Fifth Avenue tailor; he might be even a haberdasher. Jimmie continued. He lived, he explained, with his mother at One Hundred and Forty-sixth Street; Sadie, his sister, attended the public school; he helped support them both, and he now was about to enjoy a well-earned vacation camping out on Hunter's Island, where he would cook his own meals, and, if the mosquitoes permitted, sleep in a tent.

"And you like that?" demanded the young man. "You call that fun?"

"Sure!" protested Jimmie. "Don't *you* go camping out?"

"I go camping out," said the good Samaritan, "whenever I leave New York."

Jimmie had not for three years lived in Wall Street not to understand that the young man spoke in metaphor.

"You don't look," objected the young man critically, "as though you were built for the strenuous life."

Jimmie glanced guiltily at his white knees.

"You ought ter see me two weeks from now," he protested. "I get all sunburnt and hard—hard as anything!"

The young man was incredulous.

"You were near getting sunstruck when I picked you up," he laughed. "If you're going to Hunter's Island, why didn't you go to Pelham Manor?"

"That's right!" assented Jimmie eagerly. "But I wanted to save the ten cents so's to send Sadie to the movies. So I walked."

The young man looked his embarrassment.

"I beg your pardon," he murmured.

But Jimmie did not hear him. From the back of the car he was dragging excitedly at the hated suitcase.

"Stop!" he commanded. "I got ter get out. I got ter *walk*."

The young man showed his surprise.

"Walk!" he exclaimed. "What is it—a bet?"

Jimmie dropped the valise and followed it into the roadway. It took some time to explain to the young man. First, he had to be told about the Scout law and the one good turn a day, and that it must involve some personal sacrifice. And, as Jimmie pointed out, changing from a slow suburban train to a racing-car could not be listed as a sacrifice. He had not earned the money, Jimmie argued; he had only avoided paying it to the railroad. If he did not walk he would be obtaining the gratitude of Sadie by a falsehood. Therefore, he must walk.

"Not at all," protested the young man. "You've got it wrong. What good will it do your sister to have you sunstruck? I think you *are* sunstruck. You're crazy with the heat. You get in here, and we'll talk it over as we go along."

Hastily Jimmie backed away. "I'd rather walk," he said.

The young man shifted his legs irritably.

"Then how'll this suit you?" he called. "We'll declare that first 'one good turn' a failure and start afresh. Do *me* a good turn."

Jimmie halted in his tracks and looked back suspiciously.

"I'm going to Hunter's Island Inn," called the young man, "and I've lost my way. You get in here and guide me. That'll be doing me a good turn."

On either side of the road, blotting out the landscape, giant hands picked out in electric-light bulbs pointed the way to Hunter's Island Inn. Jimmie grinned and nodded toward them.

"Much obliged," he called. "I got ter walk." Turning his back upon temptation, he waddled forward into the flickering heat waves.

315

The young man did not attempt to pursue. At the side of the road, under the shade of a giant elm, he had brought the car to a halt and with his arms crossed upon the wheel sat motionless, following with frowning eyes the retreating figure of Jimmie. But the narrow-chested and knock-kneed boy staggering over the sun-baked asphalt no longer concerned him. It was not Jimmie, but the code preached by Jimmie, and not only preached but before his eyes put into practice, that interested him. The young man with white hair had been running away from temptation. At forty miles an hour he had been running away from the temptation to do a fellow mortal "a good turn." That morning, to the appeal of a drowning Caesar to "Help me, Cassius, or I sink," he had answered: "Sink!" That answer he had no wish to reconsider. That he might not reconsider he had sought to escape. It was his experience that a sixty-horse-power racing-machine is a jealous mistress. For retrospective, sentimental, or philanthropic thoughts she grants no leave of absence. But he had not escaped. Jimmie had halted him, tripped him by the heels, and set him again to thinking. Within the half-hour that followed those who rolled past saw at the side of the road a car with her engine running, and leaning upon the wheel, as unconscious of his surroundings as though he sat at his own fireplace, a young man who frowned and stared at nothing. The half-hour passed and the young man swung his car back toward the city. But at the first road-house that showed a blue-and-white telephone sign he left it, and into the iron box at the end of the bar dropped a nickel. He wished to communicate with Mr. Carroll, of Carroll and Hastings; and when he learned Mr. Carroll had just issued orders that he must not be disturbed, the young man gave his name.

The effect upon the barkeeper was instantaneous. With the aggrieved air of one who feels he is the victim of a jest he laughed scornfully.

"What are you putting over?" he demanded.

The young man smiled reassuringly. He had begun to speak and, though apparently engaged with the beer-glass he was polishing, the barkeeper listened.

Down in Wall Street the senior member of Carroll and Hastings also listened. He was alone in the most private of all his private offices, and when interrupted had been engaged in what, of all undertakings, is the most momentous. On the desk before him lay letters to his lawyer, to the coroner, to his wife; and hidden by a mass of papers, but within reach of his hand, was an automatic pistol. The promise it offered of swift release had made the writing of the letters simple, had given him a feeling of complete detachment, had released him, at least in thought, from all responsibilities. And when at his elbow the telephone coughed discreetly, it was as though some one had called him from a world from which already he had made his exit.

Mechanically, through mere habit, he lifted the receiver.

The voice over the telephone came in brisk, staccato sentences.

"That letter I sent this morning? Forget it. Tear it up. I've been thinking and I'm going to take a chance. I've decided to back you boys, and I know you'll make good. I'm speaking from a road-house in the Bronx; going straight from here to the bank. So you can begin to draw against us within an hour. And—hello!—will three millions see you through?"

From Wall Street there came no answer, but from the hands of the barkeeper a glass crashed to the floor.

The young man regarded the barkeeper with puzzled eyes.

"He doesn't answer," he exclaimed. "He must have hung up."

"He must have fainted!" said the barkeeper.

The white-haired one pushed a bill across the counter. "To pay for breakage," he said, and disappeared down Pelham Parkway.

Throughout the day, with the bill, for evidence, pasted against the mirror, the barkeeper told and retold the wondrous tale.

"He stood just where you're standing now," he related, "blowing in million-dollar bills like you'd blow suds off a beer. If I'd knowed it was *him*, I'd have hit him once and hid him in the cellar for the reward. Who'd I think he was? I thought he was a wire-tapper, working a con game!"

Mr. Carroll had not "hung up," but when in the Bronx the beer-glass crashed, in Wall Street the receiver had slipped from the hand of the man who held it, and the man himself had fallen forward. His desk hit him in the face and woke him—woke him to the wonderful fact that he still lived; that at forty he had been born again; that before him stretched many more years in which, as the young man with the white hair had pointed out, he still could make good.

The afternoon was far advanced when the staff of Carroll and Hastings were allowed to depart, and, even late as was the hour, two of them were asked to remain. Into the most private of the private offices Carroll invited Gaskell, the head clerk; in the main office Hastings had asked young Thorne, the bond clerk, to be seated.

Until the senior partner has finished with Gaskell young Thorne must remain seated.

"Gaskell," said Mr. Carroll, "if we had listened to you, if we'd run this place as it was when father was alive, this never would have happened. It *hasn't* happened, but we've had our lesson. And after this we're going slow and going straight. And we don't need you to tell us how to do that. We want you to go away—on a month's vacation. When I thought we were going under I planned to send the children on a sea voyage with the governess—so they wouldn't see the newspapers. But now that I can look them in the eye again, I need them, I can't let them go. So, if you'd like to take your wife on an ocean trip to Nova Scotia and Quebec, here are the cabins I reserved for the kids. They call it the royal suite—whatever that is— and the trip lasts a month. The boat sails to-morrow morning. Don't sleep too late or you may miss her."

The head clerk was secreting the tickets in the inside pocket of his waistcoat. His fingers trembled, and when he laughed his voice trembled.

"Miss the boat!" the head clerk exclaimed. "If she gets away from Millie and me she's got to start now. We'll go on board to-night!"

A half-hour later Millie was on her knees packing a trunk, and her husband was telephoning to the drug-store for a sponge-bag and a cure for seasickness.

Owing to the joy in her heart and to the fact that she was on her knees, Millie was alternately weeping into the trunk-tray and offering up incoherent prayers of thanksgiving. Suddenly she sank back upon the floor.

"John!" she cried, "doesn't it seem sinful to sail away in a 'royal suite' and leave this beautiful flat empty?"

Over the telephone John was having trouble with the drug clerk.

"No!" he explained, "I'm not seasick *now*. The medicine I want is to be taken later. I *know* I'm speaking from the Pavonia; but the Pavonia isn't a ship; it's an apartment-house."

He turned to Millie. "We can't be in two places at the same time," he suggested.

"But, think," insisted Millie, "of all the poor people stifling to-night in this heat, trying to sleep on the roofs and fire-escapes; and our flat so cool and big and pretty—and no one in it."

John nodded his head proudly.

"I know it's big," he said, "but it isn't big enough to hold all the people who are sleeping to-night on the roofs and in the parks."

"I was thinking of your brother—and Grace," said Millie. "They've been married only two weeks now, and they're in a stuffy hall bedroom and eating with all the other boarders. Think what our flat would mean to them; to be by themselves, with eight rooms and their own kitchen and bath, and our new refrigerator and the gramophone! It would be heaven! It would be a real honeymoon!"

Abandoning the drug clerk, John lifted Millie in his arms and kissed her, for, next to his wife, nearest his heart was the younger brother.

The younger brother and Grace were sitting on the stoop of the boarding-house. On the upper steps, in their shirt-sleeves, were the other boarders; so the bride and bridegroom spoke in whispers. The air of the cross street was stale and stagnant; from it rose exhalations of rotting fruit, the gases of an open subway, the smoke of passing taxicabs. But between the street and the hall bedroom, with its odors of a gas-stove and a kitchen, the choice was difficult.

"We've got to cool off somehow," the young husband was saying, "or you won't sleep. Shall we treat ourselves to ice-cream sodas or a trip on the Weehawken ferry-boat?"

"The ferry-boat!" begged the girl, "where we can get away from all these people."

A taxicab with a trunk in front whirled into the street, kicked itself to a stop, and the head clerk and Millie spilled out upon the pavement. They talked so fast, and the younger brother and Grace talked so fast, that the boarders, although they listened intently, could make nothing of it.

They distinguished only the concluding sentences:

"Why don't you drive down to the wharf with us," they heard the elder brother ask, "and see our royal suite?"

But the younger brother laughed him to scorn.

"What's your royal suite," he mocked, "to our royal palace?"

An hour later, had the boarders listened outside the flat of the head clerk, they would have heard issuing from his bathroom the cooling murmur of running water and from his gramophone the jubilant notes of "Alexander's Ragtime Band."

When in his private office Carroll was making a present of the royal suite to the head clerk, in the main office Hastings, the junior partner, was addressing "Champ" Thorne, the bond clerk. He addressed him familiarly and affectionately as "Champ." This was due partly to the fact that twenty-six years before Thorne had been christened Champneys and to the coincidence that he had captained the football eleven of one of the Big Three to the championship.

"Champ," said Mr. Hastings, "last month, when you asked me to raise your salary, the reason I didn't do it was not because you didn't deserve it, but because I believed if we gave you a raise you'd immediately get married."

The shoulders of the ex-football captain rose aggressively; he snorted with indignation.

"And why should I *not* get married?" he demanded. "You're a fine one to talk! You're the most offensively happy married man I ever met."

"Perhaps I know I am happy better than you do," reproved the junior partner; "but I know also that it takes money to support a wife."

"You raise me to a hundred a week," urged Champ, "and I'll make it support a wife whether it supports me or not."

"A month ago," continued Hastings, "we could have *promised* you a hundred, but we didn't know how long we could pay it. We didn't want you to rush off and marry some fine girl—"

"Some fine girl!" muttered Mr. Thorne. "The finest girl!"

322

"The finer the girl," Hastings pointed out, "the harder it would have been for you if we had failed and you had lost your job."

The eyes of the young man opened with sympathy and concern.

"Is it as bad as that?" he murmured.

Hastings sighed happily.

"It *was*," he said, "but this morning the Young Man of Wall Street did us a good turn—saved us—saved our creditors, saved our homes, saved our honor. We're going to start fresh and pay our debts, and we agreed the first debt we paid would be the small one we owe you. You've brought us more than we've given, and if you'll stay with us we're going to 'see' your fifty and raise it a hundred. What do you say?"

Young Mr. Thorne leaped to his feet. What he said was: "Where'n hell's my hat?"

But by the time he had found the hat and the door he mended his manners.

"I say, 'Thank you a thousand times,'" he shouted over his shoulder. "Excuse me, but I've got to go. I've got to break the news to—"

He did not explain to whom he was going to break the news; but Hastings must have guessed, for again he sighed happily and then, a little hysterically laughed aloud. Several months had passed since he had laughed aloud.

In his anxiety to break the news Champ Thorne almost broke his neck. In his excitement he could not remember whether the red flash meant the elevator was going down or coming up, and sooner than wait to find out he started to race down eighteen flights of stairs when fortunately the elevator-door swung open.

"You get five dollars," he announced to the elevator man, "if you drop to the street without a stop. Beat the speed limit! Act like the building is on fire and you're trying to save me before the roof falls."

Senator Barnes and his entire family, which was his daughter Barbara, were at the Ritz-Carlton. They were in town in August because there was a meeting of the directors of the Brazil and Cuyaba Rubber Company, of which company Senator Barnes was president. It was a secret meeting. Those directors who were keeping cool at the edge of the ocean had been summoned by telegraph; those who were steaming across the ocean, by wireless.

Up from the equator had drifted the threat of a scandal, sickening, grim, terrible. As yet it burned beneath the surface, giving out only an odor, but an odor as rank as burning rubber itself. At any moment it might break into flame. For the directors, was it the better wisdom to let the scandal smoulder, and take a chance, or to be the first to give the alarm, the first to lead the way to the horror and stamp it out?

It was to decide this that, in the heat of August, the directors and the president had forgathered.

Champ Thorne knew nothing of this; he knew only that by a miracle Barbara Barnes was in town; that at last he was in a position to ask her to marry him; that she would certainly say she would. That was all he cared to know.

A year before he had issued his declaration of independence. Before he could marry, he told her, he must be able to support a wife on what he earned, without her having to accept money from her father, and until he received "a minimum wage" of five thousand dollars they must wait.

"What is the matter with my father's money?" Barbara had demanded.

Thorne had evaded the direct question.

"There is too much of it," he said.

"Do you object to the way he makes it?" insisted Barbara. "Because rubber is most useful. You put it in golf balls and auto tires and galoshes. There is nothing so perfectly respectable as galoshes. And what is there 'tainted' about a raincoat?"

Thorne shook his head unhappily.

"It's not the finished product to which I refer," he stammered; "it's the way they get the raw material."

"They get it out of trees," said Barbara. Then she exclaimed with enlightenment—"Oh!" she cried, "you are thinking of the Congo. There it is terrible! *That* is slavery. But there are no slaves on the Amazon. The natives are free and the work is easy. They just tap the trees the way the farmers gather sugar in Vermont. Father has told me about it often."

Thorne had made no comment. He could abuse a friend, if the friend were among those present, but denouncing any one he disliked as heartily as he disliked Senator Barnes was a public service he preferred to leave to others. And he knew besides that if the father she loved and the man she loved distrusted each other, Barbara would not rest until she learned the reason why.

One day, in a newspaper, Barbara read of the Puju Mayo atrocities, of the Indian slaves in the jungles and backwaters of the Amazon, who are offered up as sacrifices to "red rubber." She carried the paper to her father. What it said, her father told her, was untrue, and if it were true it was the first he had heard of it.

Senator Barnes loved the good things of life, but the thing he loved most was his daughter; the thing he valued the highest was her good opinion. So when for the first time she looked at him in doubt, he assured her he at once would order an investigation.

"But, of course," he added, "it will be many months before our agents can report. On the Amazon news travels very slowly."

In the eyes of his daughter the doubt still lingered.

"I am afraid," she said, "that that is true."

That was six months before the directors of the Brazil and Cuyaba Rubber Company were summoned to meet their president at his rooms in the Ritz-Carlton. They were due to arrive in half an hour, and while Senator Barnes awaited their coming Barbara came to him. In her eyes was a light that helped to tell the great news. It gave him a sharp, jealous pang. He wanted at once to play a part in her happiness, to make her grateful to him, not alone to this stranger who was taking her away. So fearful was he that she would shut him out of her life that had she asked for half his kingdom he would have parted with it.

"And besides giving my consent," said the rubber king, "for which no one seems to have asked, what can I give my little girl to make her remember her old father? Some diamonds to put on her head, or pearls to hang around her neck, or does she want a vacant lot on Fifth Avenue?"

The lovely hands of Barbara rested upon his shoulders; her lovely face was raised to his; her lovely eyes were appealing, and a little frightened.

"What would one of those things cost?" asked Barbara.

The question was eminently practical. It came within the scope of the senator's understanding. After all, he was not to be cast into outer darkness. His smile was complacent. He answered airily:

"Anything you like," he said; "a million dollars?"

The fingers closed upon his shoulders. The eyes, still frightened, still searched his in appeal.

"Then, for my wedding-present," said the girl, "I want you to take that million dollars and send an expedition to the Amazon. And I will choose the men. Men unafraid; men not afraid of fever or sudden death; not afraid to tell the truth—even to *you*. And all the world will know. And they—I mean *you*—will set those people free!"

Senator Barnes received the directors with an embarrassment which he concealed under a manner of just indignation.

"My mind is made up," he told them. "Existing conditions cannot continue. And to that end, at my own expense, I am sending an expedition across South America. It will investigate, punish, and establish reforms. I suggest, on account of this damned heat, we do now adjourn."

That night, over on Long Island, Carroll told his wife all, or nearly all. He did not tell her about the automatic pistol. And together on tiptoe they crept to the nursery and looked down at their sleeping children. When she rose from her knees the mother said: "But how can I thank him?"

By "him" she meant the Young Man of Wall Street.

"You never can thank him," said Carroll; "that's the worst of it."

But after a long silence the mother said: "I will send him a photograph of the children. Do you think he will understand?"

Down at Seabright, Hastings and his wife walked in the sunken garden. The moon was so bright that the roses still held their color.

"I would like to thank him," said the young wife. She meant the Young Man of Wall Street. "But for him we would have lost *this*."

Her eyes caressed the garden, the fruit-trees, the house with wide, hospitable verandas. "To-morrow I will send him some of these roses," said the young wife. "Will he understand that they mean our home?"

At a scandalously late hour, in a scandalous spirit of independence, Champ Thorne and Barbara were driving around Central Park in a taxicab.

"How strangely the Lord moves, his wonders to perform," misquoted Barbara. "Had not the Young Man of Wall Street saved Mr. Hastings, Mr. Hastings could not have raised your salary; you would not have asked me to marry you, and had you not asked me to marry you, father would not have given me a wedding-present, and—"

"And," said Champ, taking up the tale, "thousands of slaves would still be buried in the jungles, hidden away from their wives and children and the light of the sun and their fellow men. They still would be dying of fever, starvation, tortures."

He took her hand in both of his and held her finger-tips against his lips.

"And they will never know," he whispered, "when their freedom comes, that they owe it all to *you*."

On Hunter's Island, Jimmie Reeder and his bunkie, Sam Sturges, each on his canvas cot, tossed and twisted. The heat, the moonlight, and the mosquitoes would not let them even think of sleep.

"That was bully," said Jimmie, "what you did to-day about saving that dog. If it hadn't been for you he'd ha' drownded."

"He would *not!*" said Sammy with punctilious regard for the truth; "it wasn't deep enough."

"Well, the scout-master ought to know," argued Jimmie; "he said it was the best 'one good turn' of the day!"

328

Modestly Sam shifted the lime-light so that it fell upon his bunkie.

"I'll bet," he declared loyally, "*your* 'one good turn' was a better one!"

Jimmie yawned, and then laughed scornfully.

"Me!" he scoffed. "I didn't do nothing. I sent my sister to the movies."

"Fine Books for Great Readers"

ABOUT THE EDITOR

Thomas Saunders is an editor and publisher of niche books in Michigan. Writing for many years, he is a winner in the Robert Benchley Society Writing Contest and writes for journals and magazines in addition to the duties as Editor at Glendower Media. An alum of Wayne State University he is also involved in radio and television in Ann Arbor, Michigan. He writes a series of books about Peter Strand, an unlikely and indifferent hero. His latest Strand book will be published in 2013.